COLD EARTH

In the dark days of a Shetland winter, torrential rain triggers a landslide that crosses the main Lerwick-Sumburgh road and sweeps down to the sea. At the burial of his old friend Magnus Tait, Jimmy Perez watches the flood of mud and peaty water smash through a croft house in its path. Everyone thinks the croft is uninhabited, but in the wreckage he finds the body of a dark-haired woman wearing a red silk dress. In his mind she shares his Mediterranean ancestry, and soon he becomes obsessed with tracing her identity. Then it emerges that she was already dead before the landslide hit the house. Perez knows he must find out who she was, and how she died.

ANN CLEEVES

COLD EARTH

Complete and Unabridged

PUBLISHER SELECTION
Leicester

First published in Great Britain in 2016 by
Macmillan
an imprint of Pan Macmillan
London

First Ulverscroft Edition
published 2019
by arrangement with
Pan Macmillan
London

A catalogue record for this book is available
from the British Library.

ISBN 978–1–4448–4323–1

Published by
F. A. Thorpe (Publishing)
Anstey, Leicestershire

Set by Words & Graphics Ltd.
Anstey, Leicestershire
Printed and bound in Great Britain by
T. J. International Ltd., Padstow, Cornwall

This book is printed on acid-free paper

For Sara, my friend
and the agent who's been with me
almost since the beginning.

Acknowledgements

Thanks to the whole team at Pan Macmillan — you're a great bunch to work with.

Thanks to Maura who has quickly become indispensable.

And thanks as ever to all the people in Shetland who provide help and inspiration and forgive my mistakes with grace.

1

The land slipped while Jimmy Perez was standing beside the grave. The dead man's family had come from Foula originally and they'd carried the coffin on two oars, the way bodies were always brought for burial on that island. The pall-bearers were distant relatives whose forebears had moved south to England, but they must have thought the tradition worth reviving. They'd had time to plan the occasion; Magnus had suffered a stroke and had been in hospital for six weeks before he died. Perez had visited him every Sunday, sat by his bed and talked about the old times. Not the bad old times, when Magnus had been accused of murder, but the more recent good times, when Ravenswick had included him in all their community events. Magnus had come to love the parties and the dances and the Sunday teas. He'd never responded to Perez's chat in the hospital, and his death had come as no surprise.

The coffin was lowered into the grave before the landslide started. Perez looked away from the hole in the ground, as the first earth was scattered on the coffin, and saw the community of Ravenswick stretching away from him. He could see Hillhead, Magnus's croft, right at the top of the bank next to the converted chapel where Perez lived with his stepdaughter Cassie. Nearer to the coast was the kirk and the manse that had been turned into a private home, much grander than the kirk itself. There were the polytunnels at Gilsetter farm and a tiny croft house hidden from the road. He didn't know who stayed there now. The school where Cassie was a pupil was further north, not visible from the cemetery; and hidden by the headland was the Ravenswick Hotel and a smart holiday complex of Scandinavian chalets. This was his home and he couldn't imagine living anywhere else.

The view was filtered by the rain. It seemed it had been raining for months. There'd been talk of cancelling Up Helly Aa two weeks earlier because of the weather, but the fire festival had never been stopped in peacetime and had gone ahead, despite the storm-force winds and the downpour. Now Perez turned his attention back to the minister's words, but at the same time he was remembering Fran, Cassie's mother and the love of his life, who was buried here too.

The landslide made no noise at first. The hill had been heavily grazed all year; sheep had tugged at the grass, disturbing the roots, exposing the black peat beneath. Now, after months of deluge, water had seeped under the surface, loosening the earth, and it was as if the whole hillside was starting to move. The contour of the landscape changed, exposing the rock below. But at this point Perez had turned back to look at the grave where Magnus Tait had just been laid to rest, and he had no warning of what was to come.

The rumbling started when the landslide

picked up speed and gathered boulders and the stones from field dykes. When it crossed the main road it missed a car but ploughed into the small croft. Relentless as a river in flood, the mountain of earth moved with a power that flattened the outhouses of the tiny croft house and forced its way through the main building, smashing windows and breaking down the door. Perez heard the noise when it hit the house as a roar, and felt it as a vibration under his feet. He turned at the same time as the other mourners. In Shetland, cemeteries are located by water. Before roads were built, bodies were carried to their graves by boat. The Ravenswick graveyard lay on flat land at the bottom of a valley next to the sea, in the shelter of a headland. Now the steep valley was filling with mud and debris and the landslide was gathering speed as it rolled towards them. The sound was so thunderous that the mourners had warning of its approach. They paused for a second and then scattered, clambering for higher ground. Perez put his arm round an elderly neighbour and almost carried him to safety. The minister, a middle-aged woman, was helped by one of the younger men. They were just in time. They watched as headstones were tipped over like dominoes and the landslide rolled across the pebble beach beyond and into the water. Fran's headstone was simple and had been carved by a friend of hers, a sculptor. It was engraved with the image of a curlew, her favourite bird. Perez watched the tide of mud sweep it away.

Perez recovered his composure very quickly. There was nothing of Fran left in the grave and he didn't need a stone to remember her by. He turned to check that everyone was well. He wondered what Magnus Tait, who had been a recluse for much of his life, would have made of the drama at his funeral. He thought Magnus would have given a shy grin and chuckled. He'd suggest that they all go back to the community hall for a dram. *No point standing out here in the wild, boys. No point at all.* Because, except for the minister, the mourners *were* all men. This was an old-fashioned funeral and women didn't go to the grave. They were a small group. While people had made more of an effort to get to know Magnus towards the end of his life, he had few contacts outside Ravenswick. Now they stood, shaken by the power of the landslide. From a distance they would have looked like giant sheep scattered over the hillside, aimless and lost.

Perez stared back up the bank. He was thinking that if the landslide had started a mile further north, the Ravenswick school would be as devastated as the croft house, which looked as if it had been smashed by a bomb. The slide had missed the farm at Gilsetter and the old manse by less than that distance. He looked at the ruin.

'Who lives in there?' He couldn't believe that anyone inside would still be alive. They'd be smothered by mud or crushed by the debris caught up in the slide. But he couldn't

4

remember anyone living in the croft since Minnie Laurenson had died.

'I think it's empty, Jimmy. Stuart Henderson's son stayed there for a while, but he moved out months ago.' The speaker was Kevin Hay, a big, middle-aged man who lived at Gilsetter and farmed most of the Ravenswick land. Perez couldn't remember the last time he'd seen Hay in a shirt and tie. Probably at the last Ravenswick funeral. His black hair was so wet with the rain that it was plastered to his forehead. It looked as if it had been painted on.

'It hasn't been let out?' Accommodation was still so tight that at this time of year even holiday homes were rented to oil or gas workers. There were few empty houses in Shetland.

'Not as far as I know.' Hay seemed less sure now. 'I haven't noticed anyone in there. No cars parked outside. But the sycamores and our polytunnels mean we can't see it from the house.'

'Unlikely that it's occupied then,' Perez said. It would be hard to manage so far from town without a vehicle. The other mourners were now gathering together around the minister. She was calm and composed and seemed to be taking charge. He supposed they were making plans for getting home. The cemetery car park was on higher ground and their vehicles were undamaged, but some lived on the other side of the slip. 'I'd like to check it out, though.'

There were sheep tracks running up the valley slopes and Perez and Hay followed one of these. They looked down on the ruined house from

5

above. Now the landslide had passed through, there was no sound but the rain. A strange eerie silence after the reverberating noise caused by the slip. People had already called the emergency services and soon there would be fire engines and police cars, but not yet.

The main walls of the croft house were almost intact, but the surge of the slide had weakened the inside walls and the roof had collapsed over half of the house, giving glimpses of the interior. Everything was black, the colour of the peaty earth. Perez slid further down the bank so that he could get a better view of the exposed rooms.

Hay followed, but put a hand on Perez's shoulder. 'Don't get too close, Jimmy. The hill's not too stable. There could be another slide. And I don't think there's anyone to save in there. No point putting your life at risk.'

Perez nodded. He saw that the mourners had reached the car park and people were driving away north, carrying with them friends who lived to the south of the slide. He supposed they'd be moving on to the community hall. The women would have a spread laid out. No point wasting that, and they'd all be ready for a hot drink.

'We should join them, Jimmy,' Kevin Hay said. 'Nothing we can do here.' In the distance they heard the sound of sirens. He looked back at the hill, worried about another landslide.

'You go. I need to stay anyway.' Perez looked beyond the house. There'd been a lean-to shed on the back of the kitchen and that had been completely destroyed: glass and the corrugated iron roof would have been swept into the mud.

6

Beyond it, though, a stone wall that separated the small garden from the open grazing beyond was almost undamaged; it seemed to have funnelled the landslip through a gap where a wooden gate had once been. Nearest the space, the edges of the wall were ragged, eaten away like unravelled knitting, but beyond the gap on each side they were quite solid. The tide of earth had deposited debris there, thrown it up on its way through. Perez saw a bedhead, a couple of plastic garden chairs that must have been stored in the lean-to. And something else, bright against the grey wall and the black soil. A splash of red. Brighter than blood.

He scrambled down the bank towards it. A woman's body had been left behind by the ebbing tide of earth. She wore a red silk dress, exotic, glamorous. Not the thing for a February day in Shetland, even if she'd been indoors when the landslide swept her away. Her hair and her eyes were black and Perez felt a strange atavistic connection. She could be Spanish, like his ancestors of centuries ago. Kevin Hay was already walking back to the cars and Perez stood alone with her until the emergency services arrived.

2

The landslide caused chaos. The main road from Lerwick to Sumburgh Airport would be closed for at least the next day, and just where the slip had been there were no roads to set up a diversion. Flights into Sumburgh had been diverted to Scatsta Airport in North Mainland, which was normally only used for oil- and gas-related traffic, but was now stretched to capacity. Business people fired off emails of complaint to the council, as if *they* could influence the elements, and then booked themselves onto the ferry. Power lines were down — the slide had snapped poles and dragged them from their foundations. In the south of the island, people lucky enough still to have them reverted to the little generators they had used before mains electricity, and which they kept for emergencies. Others made do with candles and paraffin lamps.

The day after the incident Jimmy Perez was busy. He was the boss, so it was mostly meetings: with the council, to work on getting the road open as soon as possible; with social services, to check that the vulnerable and elderly had food delivered to them, and that their houses were warm. Not exactly police work, but in the islands it was important to be flexible. He disliked being trapped in the police station and in endless discussions. And still it rained, so he looked out

8

at a grey town, the horizon between the sea and the sky blurred with cloud. Today it hardly seemed to get light.

The main focus of his colleagues was to identify the woman who'd been killed in the landslide. As far as they could tell, she'd been the only casualty. There were no pockets in the silk dress and no handbag had been found. So there was nothing to identify her, no credit card or passport. The fire service said it was too dangerous yet to get into the ruined house to search for belongings. The bottom of her face, her jaw and her nose had been damaged beyond recognition and there were wounds to the back of her head; Perez thought she'd been gathered up by the moving hillside, tumbled and battered until she'd been left adrift at the stone dyke. Yet her forehead and her eyes had seemed oddly untouched. There were scratches and tears in the skin, but the structure of that part of the face had been left intact. Her dark eyes had stared out at him. Perez hoped that the first impact had killed her, knocked her out at least, so she'd had no knowledge of what was happening to her. He still felt the weird and irrational attachment that he'd experienced at the scene.

They assumed she must have been staying in the croft house that had been half-flattened and filled with black earth. On holiday perhaps. Yesterday had been the eve of St Valentine's, and in Perez's head she'd been trying on the red dress for her lover. Making sure that she would look good for the following evening. Perhaps she'd planned to cook him dinner. Something spicy and Mediterranean, made with peppers and tomatoes as red as the dress. Perez knew all these were fantasies, but he couldn't help himself. He wanted a name for her.

They still hadn't tracked down the owner of the house, though they did have a name for *it*: Tain. Apparently it had been inherited by a woman who lived in America, from an elderly aunt. Word in the community was that she rented it out on an ad hoc basis. She had plans to do it up and didn't want to let it out long-term. Robert Henderson, whose brother had been the last tenant, was enjoying a Caribbean cruise, and the brother himself was working in the Middle East. It was all frustrating and unsatisfactory. Perez knew there would be a logical explanation and that soon somebody would come forward to identify her, but at present the dead woman remained mysterious, fuelling his imagination and making him feel ridiculous.

Her body would be sent by ferry to Aberdeen for the post-mortem and Perez hoped they could get a name from dental records, once the pathologist James Grieve had started his work, but that could take days. And they needed some idea who she was before they could find her dentist. Perez didn't think there was any point checking in the islands. She wasn't local. He would have seen her in town or heard about the dark lady who lived on the edge of his community.

Now he was between meetings. He'd made coffee and stared out of his window towards the

10

town hall. Its bulk was a shadow against the grey sky. Sandy Wilson knocked and came in.

'I've spoken to most of the estate agents in Lerwick. None of them managed the Ravenswick house or rented it out.'

'We need to track down the owner then.' Perez continued looking out of the window at the rain. 'The dead woman might have been their friend or relative. Do we still have no idea who it belongs to?'

Sandy shook his head. 'The person who might have had an idea is dead.'

'What do you mean?'

'Magnus Tait. He would have grown up with Minnie Laurenson, the old lady who used to live there. He might have been able to point us in the direction of the niece who inherited it.'

But Magnus had died after a stroke at the age of eighty-five and Perez suddenly realized that he still needed to grieve for the man. Magnus had been a part of his life for the past few years. The landslide cutting short the funeral had disturbed the natural process of mourning. At least Magnus had been laid to rest with some dignity, lowered into the ground before the cemetery had been inundated with mud.

Perez had first met Fran, his fiancée, because she'd been Magnus's neighbour, and the crofter had arrived at Perez's door soon after *Fran*'s funeral. Looking as awkward as a shy child. Clutching in his hand a bag of the sweets he knew Cassie loved. *For the bairn. Yon wife was a good woman.* Then he'd turned and walked down the bank to his croft, making no other demands, not expecting Perez to chat or to invite him in.

'The woman in the red dress couldn't have been the owner?' After all, why not? Perez thought. He'd imagined the dead woman as exotic and Spanish, but perhaps an American woman would wear red silk too.

Sandy shrugged. He didn't like to speculate in case he got things wrong.

'And you're sure that nobody has been reported missing?' Perez thought the woman couldn't have been staying in the house alone. Or if she was there alone, she had known people in the islands. February wasn't the time for a walking holiday or sightseeing. And if she was that sort of tourist, she wouldn't be dressed the way they'd found her. She'd be wearing jeans and a sweater, woollen socks — even indoors. 'When will they go in?'

'Soon,' Sandy said. 'Before it gets dark. They've got a generator set up, but they'd rather start during daylight.'

Perez nodded. 'You be there, Sandy. But before you go, talk to Radio Shetland about putting out a request for information on this evening's show. A phone number for the owner, or a contact. She'd have somebody to clean the place between visitors and to hold the keys. And a description of our mysterious woman.'

'We weren't in time to get the dead woman onto yesterday evening's ferry,' Sandy said, as if he'd just remembered and this was something Perez should know. 'She'll be going south to Aberdeen tonight. James Grieve is ready for her.'

12

'It would be good to have a name before James starts the post-mortem,' Perez said. 'I'd like to tell the relatives what's happening, before he begins his work.' His phone rang. He was expecting a summons to another meeting, but it was Kathryn Rogerson, the young woman who'd recently taken over as the teacher at Ravenswick school.

'I'm afraid we're closing the school today, Mr Perez. The engineers' department wants to survey the hill all the way along to Gailsgarth. It might need shoring up from the road. If there was another landslide there, the school would be right in its path, and we've been advised we have to get all the children away.' She still sounded like a child herself, rather earnest and desperate to do the right thing. Perez knew her father, who was a lawyer with an office just off Commercial Street. 'I know Maggie Thomson sometimes cares for Cassie when you're at work, but she's away at her sister's and her flight's been cancelled.'

So now he'd have to start ringing round to sort out childcare. The last thing he needed. Duncan Hunter, Cassie's natural father, was in Spain, apparently making out a deal with a company supplying holiday villas for the rental market. In practice, avoiding the most miserable of Shetland's weather. This was the time of year for islanders who could afford it to take their holidays.

'I wondered if you'd like me to bring Cassie back to Lerwick and she can spend the afternoon with me.' The teacher sounded hesitant, as if the

13

offer might be considered impertinent. 'She'd be no bother, and at least you'd know she'd be safe in town. We're nowhere near the danger zone.'

'Are you sure? It sounds above and beyond the call of duty to act as childminder to your pupils when the school's closed.'

'Not at all!' Perez could picture the teacher in the little office in the school. She was small and tidy and had a pleasant manner with the bairns, but she stood no nonsense. Cassie adored her. 'We'll probably be shut at least until after the weekend, so if you need me to have Cassie on any other day, just let me know.'

'That's very kind. I'll try to sort out something else for later in the week, though.' Perez felt uncomfortable. Partly because he thought he couldn't take advantage of the woman's good nature. Partly because he hated being in emotional debt. He'd never been very good at accepting help. 'I'm not sure what time I'll be able to pick Cassie up this evening.'

'Have supper with us,' Kathryn said. 'My mother always cooks enough for an army.'

Perez was still trying to think of an excuse that didn't sound rude when the teacher ended the call.

3

It was 14 February. Sandy had a new girlfriend who filled his mind and dulled his concentration. Louisa was a teacher in Yell, a north isle that was a ferry ride away; he'd known her since they were at school together, but they'd only been going out for a few months and he was still feeling his way. It was midweek, so they hadn't planned to meet to celebrate Valentine's Day, but had decided to get together on Saturday night. Sandy had asked Louisa what she'd like to do, but she hadn't been much help: 'Why don't you surprise me, Sandy?' Which seemed like a sort of challenge. He was anxious and had even begun to hope that the road would still be closed and the dead woman still unidentified, so that he could claim he needed to be at work.

Now he wondered if he should phone her, to show that he'd remembered the date. Or would she think that was soppy? Louisa was the least sentimental woman he'd ever met. He knew she would hate the pink cards he'd seen in the shops, the shiny hearts and the teddy bears, the balloons. He hadn't bought her anything. In the end he sent her a text: *Thinking of you today. Speak later.* Surely she couldn't object to that?

On the way to his car he bumped into Reg Gilbert, who must have been lurking there for most of the day. Reg was the senior reporter on

The Shetland Times. He'd previously worked on a big regional daily in the Midlands and had been lured north by a woman who'd immediately dumped him. Now Reg was stranded in the islands, a strange alien creature, a newshound with virtually nothing of interest to the outside world to report.

Except now, when the landslide had become national news. There were dramatic pictures after all, and Jimmy Perez always said the press loved images more than words. Sandy suspected that Reg had been the writer of some of the more lurid headlines, the ones about the primary school being missed by inches and an island economy devastated by the weather.

'Well, Sandy.' The journalist had a nasal voice and a thin, rodent face. His incisors protruded over his bottom lip. 'Any closer to finding out who was killed in the mud?'

In the past an innate politeness would have caused Sandy to answer, but he'd been had by Reg once too often — quoted out of context and made to look foolish. He walked past the journalist in silence.

It was only mid-afternoon, but Sandy needed his headlights for the drive south. He took the dark winter days in his stride but he was looking forward to the spring now. He could understand how the long nights turned some incomers a bit mad. He rounded a bend in the road and suddenly the site of the landslip was ahead of him, all white lights and black silhouettes. The firefighters had rigged up a generator at Tain, so the ruined house was illuminated. From the

16

road, the scene didn't look like Shetland at all, not the Shetland of hill sheep and peat banks that Sandy had grown up with. This was almost industrial: heavy machinery outlined against the artificial lights. Another generator and more lights showed a team of men starting to clear the debris from the road. The bank would have to be shored up before it could be opened again, but they wouldn't be able to see what was needed until the road was cleared.

A lay-by normally used by sightseers looking out to the isle of Mousa had been turned into a car park and Sandy pulled in there. He put on the wellingtons and an anorak that he'd stuck in the boot before setting off, and went out to meet the team working on the house. They'd already cleared the track that had led to the croft. Sandy had passed by here on hundreds of occasions — every time he'd gone to pick up a relative from the airport, or gone to show visitors the puffins on the cliffs at Sumburgh — but he struggled to remember the layout of the land before the slide. He thought a short track had curved down the valley from the main road and that it had led only to Tain. There'd been a good new road built for the cemetery, when it had been extended a few years before, but the entrance to that was further north. And it also led to the Hays' land at Gilsetter, with its bigger house and polytunnels. Where the track ended at Tain there'd been parking for a couple of cars, and a small garden at the front with a fence around it. It had been possible to see that from the main road. Then, at the back, more land separated by a wall from the rest of the hill, and on each side of the house a shelter-belt of wind-blown sycamores, which seemed to have survived the slide.

Sandy shut his eyes for a moment and tried to picture the building. Low, whitewashed and single-storey. A traditional croft house, from the outside at least. There was no sign of that now. The team had cut a track straight down the hill to where the front door had been. They were dressed in high-vis coats and heavy steel-capped boots, so at first they all looked the same. Sandy stood for a moment, knowing that if he went any closer he'd be in the way. He was often in the way.

One of the men caught sight of him and waved him over. 'Hello, Sandy! You can come on down. Stay in the middle of the path and you'll be safe enough.' He had to shout to make himself heard above the background noise of the generator and a small digger.

Tim Barton, a man from the English West Country who'd come to the islands to join the firefighters in Lerwick. Now he was going with a local girl; they'd set up home together at Gulberwick. Sandy thought he'd heard rumours that there was a child on the way. He wondered what that must be like. Since he'd taken up with Louisa, fatherhood had crossed his mind at times. It seemed that he should have been concentrating on where he put his feet, not daydreaming about making a baby with Louisa, because the path was slippery and he slid and fell awkwardly on his back. His coat would be filthy.

Barton laughed, but came over and pulled him to his feet.

'How's it going?' Sandy nodded towards the house.

'No access yet, but it shouldn't be long.'

'We need to know if there's anyone else inside.'

'That's what we all want to know. No chance of finding anyone alive, though. We've been working on this for nearly twenty-four hours, and from the time we arrived it was clear there couldn't be any survivors.' Tim turned and stretched. Sandy saw that his face and his hands were streaked black.

'You haven't had a break?' Sandy thought that must be some kind of nightmare. Working in this mud, with the rain still pouring.

'A couple of hours to get a shower and thaw out. Some hot food. But we want to get it done. See what we'll find. If you stay here, I'll let you know when it's clear to get in. Or you can wait in your car. At least you'll be dry there.'

'Nah, I can't get any dirtier.' Sandy thought it wouldn't be fair to sit in the warm car while these boys were digging their way into the house.

★   ★   ★

It was only half an hour before Barton came back to where Sandy was standing. 'We've made the roof safe and cleared most of the shite out of the rooms. You can come down if you like, though there's not much to see.'

'Anyone there?'

19

Barton shook his head. 'Nothing human. There's the corpse of a cat in what must have been the kitchen.'

Sandy followed Barton towards the house. The cat seemed odd to him. Visitors to Shetland might bring a dog with them, but he'd never heard of anyone bringing their cat. Did that mean the dead woman had been living here more permanently? He shook his head and thought he was making problems where none existed. Cats sought out food and warmth. It probably belonged to Kevin Hay's farm and had found its way inside.

They stood where the front door had once been. The weight of the landslide had ripped the door from its hinges and smashed it to pieces, so it looked like kindling. Half of the roof had been removed by the firefighters and there was the same persistent drizzle soaking into the body of the building. The floor was still covered in inches of black mud. Not smooth, but littered with rocks as big as a man's fist, mixed with roots and grit. The smell was of damp and decay - organic. Everything looked strange because of the light on the tower outside throwing odd shadows. Sandy followed Barton inside. The house was very small: a kitchen that had acted as living room too, a bedroom and a shower room made out of what had probably once been a small second bedroom. There were pieces of furniture that had survived the landslide. A sofa, upturned, had been thrown against one wall; and in the bedroom, swimming in the mud, a gilt-framed mirror was miraculously intact.

'We need something to identify the dead woman.' Sandy knew that was what Jimmy Perez wanted from him. 'The boss needs a name for her.'

'We'll be finishing here for the day soon,' Barton said. 'The boys are dead on their feet. We just had to check that there was nobody inside. I'll get them to leave the big light until last, so you can see what you're doing.'

Sandy thanked him and watched him leave. He wished he had another police officer with him. Someone he could share a joke with or a complaint about the conditions. He had never enjoyed being on his own.

He started the search by the front door and quartered the floor, as he'd seen Vicki Hewitt, the CSI from Inverness, do. Some of the kitchen units had been ripped off the wall and there was shattered crockery among the other muck. One cupboard was still standing. He opened it, to find baking trays and pans. Two expensive pans, solid, cast-iron. Fran had bought some just the same and Perez had said they'd cost an arm and a leg. So the owner, or the woman in the red dress, had enjoyed cooking. Minnie Laurenson wouldn't have used pans like that. The shower cubicle had been smashed into small shards of plastic, and water was running from where the shower head had once been. The toilet bowl was covered in mud, but otherwise seemed undamaged.

Sandy moved through to the bedroom. There was a bed, but no bedhead. The mattress was filthy, as muddy water had soaked into it as if it was a sponge. This must have been a pleasant room, with a window looking down towards the sea and a tiled grate. The roof was still on here, but the glass had been pushed out and the rain came in that way. Outside it was completely dark now and the room was lit by a big arc-light shining through the gap in the outside wall. His shadow looked weird: long and very sharp, like a cutout in black paper. Each side of the fireplace there were fitted cupboards. In one there were clothes still on their hangers and surprisingly clean. A woman's coat. Sandy wiped the dirt from his fingers before touching it. It was deep blue and very soft. He thought it was expensive, like the pans. Two pairs of trousers, well tailored, and some blouses, crisply ironed. In the other cupboard there were shelves. Jerseys neatly folded. A hardback book, of the sort that showed you how to live your life: *Think Yourself to a Better Future*. And a wooden box inlaid with mother-of-pearl. His grandmother, Mima, had had a very similar box and had kept her treasures in it. Sandy pulled on blue latex gloves and slid the book into an evidence bag. There might be fingerprints. He took the box from the cupboard, held his breath and opened it.

He'd been hoping for a passport, even a birth certificate. From the box came a faint smell of sandalwood. Inside there were two photos, one of two small children and one of an elderly couple. And a handwritten letter. He thought it might be a love letter because it began: *My dearest Alis*. Sandy put the letter back in the box without reading on. He'd never been a curious

22

man and he was cold and uncomfortable. The damp had seeped through his clothes. He wanted to be dry and warm, before investigating further, and he thought Jimmy Perez should be the man to read the letter first. But he was already planning the call he'd make to Perez, once he'd dried out and was feeling more human. *At least we have a first name for her. Part of a first name.*

4

Perez knocked on the Rogersons' door and waited. If he'd known the people better, he might just have gone in, but perhaps he would have waited all the same; this was the town and they did things differently here. The house was solid and stone, and could have been in Aberdeen or Edinburgh. It looked out over the play park where the galley had recently been set alight for Up Helly Aa. The curtains were drawn, so he couldn't see inside. He heard footsteps on the other side of the door and it opened. The young teacher stood there. She'd changed out of her work clothes and looked even younger in jeans and a sweatshirt. She wore no shoes and her socks were striped pink and blue.

'Mr Perez.' She stood aside to let him in.

'Jimmy, please.'

She gave him a little shy smile. 'Cassie's in the kitchen. She's been helping Mum with the cooking.'

The house seemed very warm to him, coming in out of the chill drizzle. There was a smell of meat and vegetables. Plain and no-nonsense, but comforting. Mince and tatties. Kathryn led him to the back of the house. A plump middle-aged woman was stirring a pan at the stove, and Cassie was on a high stool cutting circles out of pastry. She looked up and saw him. 'I'm making jam tarts,' she said. Then she added, 'Do you remember? I used to do this with Mum?'

He had a flashback so vivid that he could smell the slightly burnt sugar and Fran's perfume, the pervasive background scent of turpentine and paint, because the Ravenswick kitchen had been Fran's studio too. In his mind that's where they were: in the house overlooking the water, where he still lived with Cassie. On impulse he'd come to call, one of his first social visits to Fran's home. It had been early spring. Fran had looked over to him and smiled towards a younger Cassie, who'd been spooning jam into pastry cases. 'They'll taste disgusting, but you'll have to eat one.' Her voice too low for Cassie to hear. 'Otherwise she'll never forgive you.'

Now, in the Rogerson house in Lerwick, Cassie was looking at him, waiting for an answer. 'Of course I remember.'

'You'll have to eat one of those very special tarts,' Kathryn said and there was another jolt of memory, because the words were almost the ones Fran had used. 'We'll have them instead of pudding after our supper.'

Perez had his excuse already prepared for making a quick exit before supper, but he heard Fran's voice in his head again and just nodded. 'That would be splendid.'

There were just the four of them for the meal. Tom Rogerson was at an emergency council meeting; the lawyer was a councillor for Shetland Islands Council, and a popular politician. The conversation at the table was of the landslide and the inconvenience it had caused.

'Such a shame for those folk who live in the south and can't get to town for their work.' Mavis Rogerson was an Orcadian and her voice rose and fell with an accent that sounded more Welsh than Shetland. 'Do you know when the road will be clear, Jimmy?'

'They're hoping to get one lane open by late tomorrow morning.' Perez had hardly slept the night before, and the warm kitchen and starchy food were making him drowsy. 'It'll mean traffic lights and delays for a couple of months while they work on shoring up the bank, but at least we'll have access to the airport.'

'I've been told the school will stay shut until after the weekend.' Kathryn was clearing the plates and stacking them on the draining board. 'Would you like us to have Cassie tomorrow, Jimmy? Really, it'll be no bother. You can just drop her in on your way to work.'

If he'd been less tired, Perez would have thought of an alternative. He could see how eager the teacher was to help, and it crossed his mind even then that it might not be kind to encourage her. Then he thought he was probably fifteen years older than her, and a bonny lass like Kathryn would surely have a boyfriend. He was flattering himself if he believed she had romantic feelings for him. And besides, Cassie was looking at him with eyes as big as a seal pup's and he still found it hard to refuse her anything she really wanted.

'Well,' he said. 'If you're sure.'

* * *

26

When they arrived back at the house in Ravenswick it was Cassie's bedtime. Further south, the men were still working to clear the road and there was a background rumble of heavy machinery, but Cassie slept much better these days. There were fewer nightmares.

Jimmy had made tea and a fire, when Sandy phoned. 'What have you got for me, Sandy?'

'I wondered if I could come round. There's something I'd like you to see.'

'Why not?' It no longer felt like an intrusion to have colleagues in the house that he'd shared very briefly with Fran. 'But tell me, have we got a name for our woman in the red dress?' He wanted a name — a little dignity for her.

'One name,' Sandy said. 'Or maybe part of a name.'

He arrived more quickly than Perez had expected. He must have been ready to leave home just before phoning. There was a gentle tap on the door and then he came in, carrying a small wooden box and a couple of bottles of Unst beer. Sandy preferred lager himself, but he knew Perez liked White Wife.

'We're lucky to live north of the landslide,' Perez said, 'or we'd be stranded too, with no chance to get into town.' He knew Sandy didn't like to be rushed into giving information. It took Sandy a little time to get his thoughts in order, so the small talk was about giving him some breathing space.

'I went down to Tain earlier,' Sandy said. 'The boys had cleared it just enough to make it safe to get in.'

27

'Did they find anyone inside?' But Perez thought even Sandy would have passed on a fact like that straight away.

'Nothing human. The body of a cat.' Sandy paused. 'And that seemed kind of weird. I mean, if it had been a holiday let?'

Perez thought that was a sensible query. 'We need to find out who's in charge of letting the place. A priority for tomorrow. Maybe they advertise privately through the Promote Shetland or Visit Scotland website. Someone must have a phone number for the owner in the US.' A pause. 'But you're right. A cat actually inside the house does seem a bit strange.'

'I think the woman's name was Alis,' Sandy said. 'Spelled with an s. If it is a proper name. I didn't find anything useful like a passport, but there was this.' He set the box very carefully on the table, as if it was a valuable gift. 'It was inside a cupboard and it wasn't damaged at all by the landslide.'

Alis. Surely that was an abbreviation. Perez lifted the lid and took out two photographs. The first was of an elderly couple sitting on a white wooden bench in a garden. The bench seemed to stand on sandy soil. The woman wore a flowery summer dress and the man had a brown face, creased like old leather. She looked rather stern, even hostile, with her feet flat on the ground. His legs were slightly splayed and he had a wide, gappy smile. Both squinted slightly because they were looking into bright sunshine.

'Where do you think that was taken? Somewhere hot, I'd say. Greece? Spain?' Perez hoped it was Spain. He wanted to believe that Alis came from the country of his ancestors. He imagined a landscape that smelled of thyme and olive oil.

Sandy shook his head. He didn't know anything about hot countries. How could he, when he'd never lived away from Shetland?

'I don't know. It could have been taken in a sunny garden anywhere in the world. The background's all blurry. It could even have been taken in Shetland on a fine day in midsummer.'

But Perez's imagination had taken him to Spain. 'Are they her parents, do you think?' They'd be the right sort of age.'

'Aye, maybe.' Sandy drank his beer slowly and watched Perez take the other photo from the box.

Two children aged about five and seven, not on the bench, but on swings in a play park. There was the same sandy soil beneath the swing. The girl was the older. She was wearing shorts and a jumper and stared defiantly at the camera. She'd lost almost as many teeth as the old man, but Perez supposed that she'd get new ones. The boy had curly hair and a smile that must have charmed old ladies. 'And are these Alis's children?'

Now it was clear that Perez was talking to himself, and Sandy made no attempt to answer. Perez turned both pictures so that he could look at the back, hoping for a name or a date, but there was nothing. 'So how did you get a name for her, Sandy?'

'From the letter.' Sandy nodded back to the box. 'I haven't read it all. I thought I'd wait for you.'

Perez laid the letter on the table in front of him. There was no address from the sender at the top. The writing was precise and rather formal. He thought it must have been written some time ago. Even older people now used email and texting. Everyone had forgotten the art of writing, and any handwritten notes he received these days were sprawling and untidy.

My dearest Alis
What a joy to know that you'll be back
in the islands again, after so many years!
I've so enjoyed our rare encounters on my
visits south and I know you're the same
beautiful woman who first attracted me
when we first met. I'm sure we can make a
go of things and that we'll have a wonder-
ful future together.

There was no signature at the bottom, just a row of kisses, and Perez wondered what that suggested. Perhaps this was a married man who didn't want to leave any evidence of his adultery. Someone cautious, keeping his options open, despite his promise of a future with the now-dead woman. Or perhaps the writer felt that a name was superfluous. Of course Alis would know the identity of the writer.

'And this was all you could find?' Perez tried to keep his voice free of irritation, but he found these brief glimpses into the woman's life frustrating. He could make up a story about the dark woman, about her parents and her children and the island man who'd fallen for her, but that

30

would be a fiction. He needed something more concrete to help identify her.

'There's this book. I thought we might get fingerprints.'

'Which will only help if she's on our system.'

'I was very thorough, Jimmy.' Sandy had taken the words as criticism, despite Perez's efforts. 'Tain is a small house and there was very little left inside. If we search through the debris left in the garden, we might have more success.'

Perez didn't answer immediately. 'Was there any response to the Radio Shetland appeal for information?

'Jane Hay called in,' Sandy said. 'She thought she might have seen someone of that description in the Co-op in Brae a week ago. I was thinking I'd go and see her tomorrow.' He paused. 'She seems like a sensible woman. I can't see that she'd make up something like that.'

'No, I'll talk to her.' Perez wanted to be the person to breathe life into the dead woman. It was ridiculous but he couldn't help himself. 'I can call in on my way to work. She's a neighbour. The Hay place is right next to Tain. Kevin said he hadn't seen anyone in the house, but Jane might have done.'

Sandy stood up and Perez led him out. Usually it would have been quiet and dark. There were no street lights here, and Magnus's house was still empty. But further south the men were working to get the road clear for the following day, and the powerful arc-lights threw strange shadows across the hill.

31

5

Jane Hay settled on the wooden chair and nodded to the other people in the circle. There were fewer than usual this evening. There must be friends who couldn't get to the meeting because of the landslide. She sipped tea, waited for the latecomers and was aware of the calm and gratitude that always accompanied her here on meeting nights. The community hall was heated by a Calor gas heater and the fumes caught in her nostrils and at the back of her throat, but she was so used to them that they had become a part of the experience.

Alf Walters spoke a couple of words of welcome and they started. Jane cleared her throat and there was a brief moment of tension as she waited for her turn. She'd been coming to meetings for more than eleven years, but she was still a little nervous.

'My name's Jane and I'm an alcoholic.'

She stayed behind for half an hour afterwards because she was sponsoring a young woman, an emergency doctor based at the Gilbert Bain Hospital, and wanted to see how she was doing. Rachel had been coming to meetings for three months, but she was still struggling. After a stressful day at work, her colleagues all turned to a glass of wine to help them relax. For Rachel one glass, or one bottle, would never be enough. She still occasionally phoned Jane in the early hours of the morning, either very drunk or needing support and reassurance: 'I'm sorry. I'm such a failure.' Jane could tell she was sobbing.

Jane understood what she was going through and was always patient. 'You're not a failure at all. This is a disease and the treatment is brutal. If you were going through chemo for cancer, you wouldn't be so hard on yourself.'

Kevin was less tolerant of the late-night calls. 'Is that one of your alkie pals, pissed again?'

He thought Jane's attendance at meetings was a form of masochistic indulgence. Tonight he'd had a go at her as she left the house. 'You've been sober for years. Since just after the kids started school. Why do you still need all that nonsense? It's not so convenient, you disappearing up to town two nights a week. And I'll be worried about you being out on a night like this.'

Usually she let it go. She couldn't change him, just as he couldn't change her. But she'd been tense all day. The rain and the background noise of the machinery at the landslide had stretched her nerves. The boys had been moody too, sniping at each other over the supper table, answering their parents in monosyllabic grunts. They were such different characters that usually they got on fine, but that evening she'd sensed an underlying animosity between them, something bitter and brooding. She'd felt the stress as a tightness in her arms and spine, in the twitch of a nerve in her face.

'Would you rather I was drinking?' They'd been on their own in the kitchen. The boys had disappeared to their rooms, to relieve their own

33

tension by killing people on separate computer screens. Or so she supposed. She'd felt herself trembling, could hear the shrill voice that was almost out of control. 'You'd rather I was disappearing off into the night and coming back bladdered in a taxi in the early hours of the morning? Not knowing where I'd been, not being able to care for the bairns and a total mess.'

He'd stared at her without speaking for a moment. 'You know what?' He'd turned away to look out of the window into the dark, so she couldn't see his face. 'You were a lot more fun in those days. At least we could have a bit of a laugh.'

He'd turned back to the room quickly to hug her and apologize, but she'd heard the wistfulness in his voice. She'd told herself then that the outburst was to do with Kevin feeling middle-aged; he was looking back to his youth with nostalgia. Now, driving back towards the farm, she wasn't so sure. For the first time in years she felt the compulsion to drink. Tesco's was still open. She could buy a bottle of wine and sit in the furthest corner of the car park, where nobody would see her. If it had a screw top, she'd have no problem opening it. She imagined the sensation of the alcohol in her bloodstream. It would relax her. The tension in her back would disappear. The jangling nerves would quieten. She wouldn't need to drink it all — just enough to make her forget the anxieties of the day. She would drive home, be more pleasant to Kevin and the boys, and she would sleep more easily than she had for weeks. Nobody need ever know.

At the roundabout on the edge of Lerwick she signalled to turn into the supermarket car park and then at the last minute changed her mind, causing the taxi driver behind her to hit his horn and mouth obscenities about women drivers. She took no notice and continued on the road south towards Gilsetter.

Kevin was waiting for her. He'd lit the wood-burner and some candles. There was the smell of real coffee, beeswax and peat.

'What's all this about?' She was shaking off her coat, pulling off her boots at the living-room door. This was her favourite room in the house, but they spent most of their time in the kitchen. He'd been sitting in front of the television, but zapped it off when he stood up to greet her. She thought he'd been dozing. He had that tousled little-boy look that he had when he first woke up.

'It's Valentine's Day. I thought I'd remember it, for once.'

She walked towards him and was aware of the contrast of polished floorboards and sheepskin rugs on her bare feet.

'And I'm sorry about earlier,' he said. 'That was just crass. I don't know why I said it. Frustrated about the weather maybe, and needing someone to blame.' He was going to say more. Jane knew what it would be: how he couldn't manage without her. The sort of things you might say to a housekeeper or a mother, though with a little less emotion. She put a finger to his lips to stop him talking and took him into her arms.

* * *

Jane had just got the boys out to the bus the next day when Jimmy Perez arrived. She'd waved her sons out of the house just as she had done when they were tiny. Andy had left school the year before, but he still went into town each day. He'd started at university in Glasgow on an English course. She'd thought he'd adore it; he was the sparky one, always full of adventure, telling her about his reading, the films that he watched. But when he'd arrived back at Christmas he'd announced that he wouldn't be going back. No reason given, and not open to persuasion. He'd found a job in the bar in the Mareel arts centre in Lerwick and it seemed to suit him; he was working with other arty young people and he didn't mind doing the late shift, if there was music.

Michael, the younger son, had never had ambitions to leave the island. He was doing his Highers, but they all thought he'd join the family business when school was over. They'd always known he was more practical than academic and, besides, he had Gemma to hold him here. They'd been seeing each other since they were fifteen and they already seemed like a settled married couple. Jane thought it might not be too long before she became a grandmother.

So when Jimmy Perez arrived, the house was quiet. Kevin had been out for a while, contracted

36

by the council to work on clearing the road. He was happy. He'd felt he'd put things right between them and he hated an atmosphere. Watching through the kitchen window, Jane saw that the inspector had his small daughter with him.

'Sorry about this.' Perez nodded towards the child. 'The school's closed until after the weekend. Kathyn Rogerson's offered to mind her, but I thought I'd come here before heading off to Lerwick.'

'Have you got time for a coffee?' She was pleased that she'd already loaded the dishwasher with the breakfast plates. Jane hated mess. She was proud of this house. When she'd first moved here with Kevin, soon after their marriage, his parents had only recently moved out to a modern bungalow in town. The farmhouse had been modernized by Kevin's father in the early Seventies and not touched again until Kevin and Jane moved in; it had had loud orange wallpaper and clashing carpets, both mostly hidden by mounds of clutter. She and Kevin had extended it, and Jane had designed it to her taste.

'Why not?' Perez smiled at her, and she thought how handsome he was, dark like a storybook pirate.

She found crayons and paper for Cassie and sat her at the table. 'What can I do for you, Jimmy?'

'We're trying to identify the woman who was living at Tain, the one who was killed in the landslide. You phoned in, to say you might have seen her.'

'Yes.' Jane had called the police station on impulse when she'd heard the description on Radio Shetland, before going out to her meeting. Kevin had come into the kitchen while she was making the call and, when she'd described the woman she'd seen, he'd frowned.

'I was with Jimmy at Tain yesterday,' he'd said.

'You didn't say!' It had seemed such a huge thing, to have seen a dead woman thrown up by the tide of mud, like flotsam on a beach. She couldn't believe that Kevin hadn't told her.

'I walked away before he found her,' he'd continued. 'I didn't know anything about it, until the ambulance turned up. I helped clear a way for them. Besides, it's not something you'd want to remember.' Looking back, it seemed that their argument of the night before had started there, with Kevin brooding about the imagined picture of a dead woman, holding it to himself as if it was something he couldn't bear to share.

Now she saw that Jimmy Perez was waiting for her to describe her meeting with the strange woman and she tried to remember the encounter in detail. 'I was in Brae,' she said. 'I was up there chatting to Ingirid Eunson. I'm hoping she'll help me out with the business this year. They have a couple of polytunnels too. She might grow some stuff for me. I'm running out of space.'

Jimmy nodded. 'How's the business doing?'

'Really well!' Once the boys were at school, Jane had developed her own enterprise on the croft. She grew herbs, fruit and salads under polythene and, after a slow start, things were

38

going well. She supplied most of the hotels and restaurants in the islands and had been approached about exporting her products to mainland Scotland and beyond. Now she had three giant polycrubs on the land closest to the house. She'd chosen a sheltered position for them but, even so, at this time of year Kevin helped her to cover them with fishing nets, pegged into the earth to stop the tunnels from blowing away.

Jane returned to her story. 'I stopped off at the Co-op just to pick up a couple of things for my lunch, and I saw the dead woman there. I'm sure it was her. She was buying champagne.' She still noticed what people bought to drink. That never left her. She paused, distracted by a sudden thought. 'If she lived in Tain, why would she be all the way north in Brae doing her shopping? There'd be more choice in Lerwick, and it'd be much closer to go there.'

'Can you describe her?' Perez's voice was quiet. At the other end of the table Cassie didn't seem to have heard him speaking.

'She was very dark and exotic,' Jane said, 'with beautiful black hair.'

'Age?' He looked up from his coffee.

'Not young. Late thirties maybe. Forties and well preserved? No grey in the hair, but that doesn't mean anything these days, when we can get it in a bottle.'

'Did you hear her speak? It would be helpful if we had some idea of her accent.'

Again Jane tried to imagine herself back in the shop in Brae. It had been busy, two tills open.

She'd been standing next to the woman in a different queue, squinting across because she was curious about her. 'Not Shetland,' she said now to Perez. The woman hadn't said much to the guy on the till, but there'd been an exchange about the champagne. He'd asked if she was celebrating.

'English?'

'Maybe. She didn't have a strong accent, but I'd say she was from the south.' Jane paused. 'I couldn't swear to anything, though. She only said a few words and there was a lot of background noise. She could have come from anywhere in the world.' *Almost repeating Sandy's comment about the photo, the night before.*

'Did she pay by cash or credit card?' Perez's voice was measured, but she could tell this mattered.

Jane shook her head. 'I'm sorry. I was paying then myself. I didn't notice.'

'Did you see where she went when she left the shop?'

Jane replayed the events in her head again. There'd been a sudden downpour, the rain dramatic after a morning of persistent drizzle. She had stood in the entrance of the shop hoping it would pass. She'd only walked from the shop's car park, but she would be drenched in the time it would take to run back to her vehicle. Had the dark woman been there too?

'There was a car waiting for her.' She saw it very clearly: a car driving up almost to the door of the shop and the dark woman, politely pushing her way through the other waiting customers, then running through the downpour to climb into the vehicle.

'Someone else was driving?' Perez had started making notes. He looked up.

'Oh yes, she got in the passenger door. The rest of us were jealous. We knew we'd get wet, even running to the car park.'

'Did you see the driver at all?'

Jane shook her head. 'He was furthest away from us. He'd driven, so the passenger door was closest to the shop.'

'But you think it was a *he*?'

'I'm not sure,' she said. 'Perhaps I just made that assumption. Because of the champagne. Because it was running up to Valentine's Day.'

Jimmy Perez smiled to show he understood the way her mind had been working. 'Can you tell me anything about the car?' He set down his pen and gave her his full attention.

She shut her eyes for a moment in the hope of fixing the image. 'Dark,' she said. 'A medium-sized family saloon. But the rain was so fierce, Jimmy, and the light was so bad that any colour seemed washed away. And I couldn't tell you the make. I'm not interested in cars. I couldn't even start to think about a registration number.'

'I didn't expect that for a minute.' He grinned, but she could tell he was disappointed.

'It had a Shetland flag stuck on the back bumper!' The memory shot into her mind. 'The white cross against the blue was caught in the light from the store and seemed bright in the gloom. And I thought it was odd, because I'd

41

decided the woman wasn't local.'

She was rewarded by a sudden smile that lit up his face. She remembered Jimmy smiling a lot like that when Fran was alive. It was as if the artist had given him permission to be silly. More recently he'd become grave and responsible again.

'Had you seen her round here?' Perez looked up from his coffee. 'You'd have been her nearest neighbour. Perhaps you noticed the same car at the house?'

'No,' she said. 'Not a car. And you can't quite see Tain from here. It's hidden in that dip in the hill and by the trees.' She paused and tried to remember. 'I saw lights in there one day. I'd been out for a walk to the shore and took a shortcut back to the house.'

'When was that?'

'About a month ago. Between Hogmanay and Up Helly Aa.' She pictured the scene. It had been about four o'clock and already dark. She'd been hurrying back because it was a meeting night and she'd wanted to start cooking tea, so that she could get into Lerwick on time. Then she'd seen the lights spilling out from the croft. She'd been grateful to have the path lit up, but embarrassed too, because she'd been in effect walking through someone else's garden.

'Did you see anyone inside?'

'Yes.' She'd hurried past the window, hoping the person inside wouldn't turn round. 'A woman.'

'Could it have been the woman you saw in Brae?'

Jane nodded. 'She had dark hair, certainly. Long dark hair. I only saw her back, not her face.' She was about to continue, but really, what else was there to say?

'That's very helpful,' he said. 'Really. Thanks. And for the only decent cup of coffee I'll get all day.'

She walked with him and Cassie out into the yard. She was brooding about the woman in Tain, then her mind switched direction and she thought Jimmy Perez would make a fine husband for someone one day.

6

Back in his office, Jimmy Perez phoned the Co-op in Brae and asked to talk to the manager.

'I'm interested in a purchase made a couple of days ago. February the twelfth. A bottle of champagne.'

'Moët and Chandon was on special offer.' A pause. 'Along with our own-brand chocolates. It was the run-up to Valentine's Day.'

'Yes, I know.' Perez was thinking back to his first Valentine's Day with Fran. He'd invited her to his house on the water in Lerwick and cooked for her. Nothing special, but he could remember every mouthful. He'd used some of the Fair Isle shoulder of lamb he had left in the freezer and made a Moroccan dish with dried apricots. He'd found the recipe online and followed it slavishly. They'd talked about how they might go to North Africa one day, had daydreamed about spice markets and deserts, as the Bressay ferry criss-crossed the Sound outside the window. Flashes of memory like that weren't as painful as they'd once been, but they still unnerved him, threw him off-track.

'We sold a fair few bottles.' The manager's voice was English and broke into the daydream. 'I'm not sure my staff would remember every purchase.'

'Would you be able to check a credit-card sale, if I gave you an approximate time? I'd like the name of the card-holder.'

'That should be possible. It might take a while, though.' The manager sounded less than enthusiastic about the effort it would take to trace the sale. 'Can I call you back?'

'I'll send someone up to talk to your staff,' Perez said. 'They'll be there in an hour. It would be good if you could have the information ready by then.' He couldn't help being sharp. James Grieve would have started the post-mortem by now. He'd promised to do it as soon as the body arrived in Aberdeen from the boat. Perez hated the idea of his dark-eyed lady being cut open as an anonymous corpse.

Sandy stuck his head round the door. 'I'm still trying to track down a contact for the owner of Tain. The landslide's been all over the national news and you'd think they'd get in touch, just to start things moving with their insurers.'

'No joy?'

'I've talked to Stuart Henderson. His son Craig leased it for six months last year. Craig's in the oil business and he's on contract in the UAE, but his time is up. He's travelling back just now and he'll be home at the weekend. At least we'll have a contact then. The lettings all seem to have been done on a private basis. I haven't seen the house advertised anywhere, either through the estate agents or as a holiday let. Promote Shetland didn't know anything about it.' Sandy moved into the room and landed on the other side of Perez's desk. 'Was Jane Hay any help?'

'Jane saw a woman in Brae Co-op the day before the landslide. Lunchtime. Her description

45

matches our Alis. Go up and chat to the staff, Sandy. See if she's a regular. That might mean she was working in North Mainland: at Sullom Voe maybe or one of the hotels there. She wasn't on her own. A guy picked her up in a car. A local car with a Shetland flag on the bumper. Jane saw her buying a bottle of champagne. I've asked the manager to check credit-card sales for the day, to see if we can confirm a name.'

Sandy had just left the office when the phone rang again.

'Jimmy.' James Grieve had worked in Aberdeen for years but hadn't lost his west-coast accent. 'We might have a bit of a problem.'

'What sort of a problem.' Perez was still worrying over identification; he was thinking of the children in the photo, who might be older now but had probably lost a mother and needed to be told. And of elderly parents who'd lost a child without knowing.

'Your woman didn't die by accident. The knocks to the head and the contusions on the face happened post-mortem.'

'If she didn't die in the landslide, what killed her?' Perez wondered why he wasn't more surprised. The strangeness of her dress, perhaps. The exotic look that was so out of place in Shetland. It seemed fitting that her death should be dramatic too. He was imagining a grand, almost operatic suicide.

'She was strangled. The ligature mark was hidden by the damage caused by the slide.'

'She didn't hang herself?' The melodramatic gesture of suicide had remained with him.

'No!' The retort was furious and explosive.

'I didn't see any petichiae.' Perez remembered the dark, staring eyes. He hadn't noticed any burst blood vessels.

'No? Well, maybe the light wasn't so great when you saw her and there was a lot of muck over her face. You're not questioning my judgement, I hope, Inspector.' His voice was faintly mocking, but the tone was firm enough for Perez to realize he was on dangerous ground. James Grieve was good at his job and knew it. He was accustomed to having his opinions accepted immediately.

Perez tried to think back to his first sight of the dead woman, thrown up against the wall at Tain. The professor was right. It had been raining so hard that visibility had been atrocious. Was the image he carried round in his head a fiction, idealized? Had he become obsessed by the victim, just because he hadn't seen her clearly? 'What else can you tell me?'

'The ligature was narrow and hard. A leather belt perhaps. That sort of width, though no sign of a buckle mark. There were some indentations; maybe the belt was embossed. You might find a match.' The pathologist paused. 'Her clothes have gone for analysis. It'll be pretty near-impossible to separate the filth from the landslip from anything that might have been there previously. The same for under her fingernails, I'd have thought, though there might be scraps of skin beneath the mud. Possibly her own skin, if she was trying to pull the ligature away from her neck.'

'Any idea what time she was killed? It'd be useful to know how long she had been dead before the landslide hit the house.'

'You *are* joking, I hope.' James Grieve was always scathing about colleagues who claimed any sort of accuracy around time of death. 'It was almost two days before I saw her, Jimmy, and it would have been impossible, even if I'd been called straight to the scene.'

Jane Hay claimed to have seen the woman in Brae at lunchtime on the 12th. If that information was right, she must have been killed between then and the landslide on the afternoon of the 13th. Not such a long gap. 'We still don't have a definitive ID,' Perez said. 'Anything you can give me to help with that?'

'She's had some dental work, but nothing recent. If she's just moved to Shetland or she's a visitor, that's not a lot of use to you. She's never had a child.'

So who were the children in the photo? The boy and the girl. The girl older, with a mind of her own. The boy a charmer. Perez looked at the image he'd pinned to the board in his office.

At the other end of the line the pathologist was still talking. 'Her last meal was lamb, stewed with spices. Couscous.'

With a jolt, Perez remembered again the meal he'd cooked for Fran on Valentine's Day. The odd synergy between him and the murdered woman was unsettling him. He tried to push her image from his mind, to concentrate on the matter in hand and stay detached.

'Alcohol?'

'Not enough to be significant.'

So why had she been buying champagne? If the woman in Brae was indeed the murder victim.

'I'll get a full report to you this afternoon,' the professor said. 'You'll want to get started on the investigation, I expect. Let Inverness know, so they can get their finest onto a plane.'

'There's not much of the crime scene left for the CSI to work on. The firefighters had to clear it, to check there hadn't been other fatalities.' But Perez was already thinking of another woman. Chief Inspector Willow Reeves, who was as different from the victim as it was possible to be. Strong as a Viking with wild, tangled hair. A vegetarian who'd never eat lamb, even with cumin and couscous. Brought up in a commune in the Western Isles, she'd seen joining the police as a form of rebellion, but she still practised yoga every morning. Like the dark-eyed victim at Tain, Willow troubled and distracted him.

All the same she was the first person he phoned when he ended his call to James Grieve. She sounded distant and a little bored when she answered.

'Reeves. Serious Crime Squad.'

'Willow, it's Jimmy Perez.'

There was a pause. He didn't know what to make of that. Was she pleased to hear from him? Irritated?

'Jimmy, how can I help you?' Colleague-to-colleague friendly, but very professional.

He explained the situation. 'We assumed it was an accidental death. Nothing to suggest otherwise at the time, though maybe I should have picked up the petichiae.'

'You're a detective, not a scientist, and in those conditions I doubt the professor would have done any better.'

He found himself smiling. Willow always managed to make him feel better about himself. 'You know the patch now. I was hoping you might take it on as SIO. If you're not tied up with anything important.'

Another pause. He wondered if he'd said the wrong thing, if he should have made a more formal request, or made it clear that he valued her competence as well as her experience of the islands. He hated to think he might have offended her. He held his breath and realized how much he wanted Willow Reeves to be in Shetland with him. He couldn't imagine running the investigation with any other officer.

'Just you try and stop me, Jimmy Perez.' Suddenly she sounded like a child offered a day off from school. 'I'll be on the first plane north.'

'No!' He had to speak quickly before she replaced the receiver. 'Wait until tomorrow. At least one lane of the road north from Sumburgh should be clear by then. Just now all the flights are coming into Scatsta and there are terrible delays. If you want to get started on the case, we still haven't identified the victim. There was a letter in the house addressed to an Alis. A. L. I. S. An unusual name. Obviously an abbreviation. Maybe you could get your people onto the ferry company and the airline, see if that fits with any of their passengers. It would be terrific if we

50

could find a surname for her. I'm assuming she's an outsider and travelled up relatively recently. All my officers are tied up here in the aftermath of the disaster. There are still people cut off. No electricity. And that sort of enquiry takes time.'

He realized that sounded like an excuse for his own inaction. Again he wondered if he'd overstepped the mark. It wasn't his place to tell a superior officer from the mainland what to do.

'Of course, Jimmy. I'll get a couple of my team onto it. Anything else you'd like me to do, while I'm idling my time here at HQ?'

He knew she was teasing him.

'Could you see if Vicki Hewitt is free to come up with you? It's a nightmare of a scene. The landslide went straight through the house and then they had to bring in heavy machinery to clear a path and dig out a lot of the interior. And it's still raining. But I'd like her to look at it. At the interior of the house and at the debris trapped behind the wall where we found the body.'

'Can you email me the photos, Jimmy?' She was in work mode now. Efficient. Buzzing with energy. 'And anything else that you have.'

'Book yourself onto the first plane into Sumburgh tomorrow,' he said. 'I'll be at the airport to meet you.'

'I'll pack a bottle of that island malt you like.' She paused for a moment. 'Anything else I can fetch you from the civilized world?'

He almost said something soppy. *Just you — that'll be enough for me.* But he caught himself just in time. 'Aye,' he said, 'a change in the weather. Before the whole island washes away.'

7

Perez phoned just as Sandy was pulling into the car park to the side of the Brae Co-op. The children in the school across the road were on their mid-morning break and although there was still a bit of a drizzle, they were out in the yard, chasing and shouting. The worst of the rain had stopped, and Sandy thought they were like cows, let out after being in all winter, frisky and a bit mad.

'The woman's death wasn't an accident,' Perez said. 'She was already dead before the landslide happened. James Grieve has it down as murder.'

Sandy took a while to make sense of that. 'But the killer couldn't have known about the landslip.'

'Of course not.' Sandy could tell that Perez was using his patient voice. People in authority, those who knew him well, had been using the same tone to Sandy since he was a boy. It wasn't that he was stupid, but they realized he needed to think things through in his own time. 'Perhaps the killer planned to dispose of the body and the landslide got in the way. Or perhaps the woman was left at Tain — it seems as if there were no regular visitors, and the murderer could have been away from the islands before she was discovered. We don't even know for certain that she was killed at the house.' Perez paused. 'But this is a murder investigation now, Sandy. It's even more urgent that we identify the victim. So be thorough and don't take any crap from the manager. Come back with a name for me.'

No pressure then.

The school bell rang as Sandy got out of the car and the pupils ran inside. The shop was large and well stocked. It served the whole of North Mainland. A big new hotel had been built for oilies just down the road and Sandy assumed that would be good for business too. A couple of women were walking down the aisles and a young man stood behind the till, with the bottles of more expensive wine and spirits on a shelf behind him. He was reading a magazine that he was hiding under the counter and had the look of someone who was counting the minutes until a colleague took over at lunchtime. Sandy didn't recognize him.

'Where's the manager?'

The boy looked up. The shape of his nose was hidden by an explosion of acne. He seemed suddenly more interested in the world around him. 'Are you the police? Colin said you'd be coming.'

'Colin?'

'The manager. Colin Sandford.'

Sandy *did* recognize that name. He'd played five-aside football with Colin for a few seasons, until work had got in the way or it had seemed too much effort to go out in the evening.

'Can I speak to him?'

The boy pressed a button and spoke into a microphone. 'This is a staff announcement. Mr

54

Sandford to the tills, please.' The message echoed through the store and the assistant beamed. Hearing his own voice was the most excitement he got in his working day.

Sandy was led to a glorified cupboard that Colin called his office. It had his name on the door and piles of toilet rolls under the desk.

'Have you tracked down a credit-card purchase for the twelfth? We think it would have been about midday, but my boss wanted you to check an hour either side, just to be sure.' Sandy had never taken to Colin. He was one of those English men who considered himself superior to the islanders and talked at length about what he was missing out on, by being there. His partner had come to work at Sullom Voe and Colin had followed. In the south he'd worked in a flashy car showroom, and he usually managed to squeeze into the conversation the fact that he'd been salesman-of-the-year three times running. And that he'd had a company Beamer.

'I have checked.' Colin smirked. He'd had the same expression every time he'd scored a goal in the Clickimin Leisure Centre, turning round as if he expected applause from a non-existent crowd. 'The only credit-card use within those two hours was for multiple purchases.' He paused and as Sandy was about to ask another question, he added: 'None of the customers bought any champagne. It must have been a cash purchase.'

'Were you on duty that day?'

'Yes, but I wasn't on the shop floor all the time.'

Hiding out in here, while your minions did all the work.

'Did you see this woman?'

Perez had got an artist friend of Fran's to do a drawing from the photograph they'd taken of the dead woman's face. No gashes or broken skin. The original drawing had sat on Perez's desk after they'd scanned and printed out copies. Sandy had caught the inspector brooding over it.

Colin stared at the picture. 'Is she foreign?'

'We don't know! We haven't got an identification for her yet.'

'We get some foreign workers in here. They work at the new hotel as chambermaids or waitresses.' He sniffed. 'It's hard to tell them apart.'

'We think she lived in Ravenswick,' Sandy said. 'She was swept out of her house by the landslide.'

'I don't recognize her.' Colin was prepared to be definite now.

'Was that lad on the till here on Tuesday?'

'Peter. Yes, but you won't get much sense out of him. He's thick as mince.'

'Can you take over from him, so I can chat properly?' Sandy hoped there'd be a sudden rush of demanding customers as soon as Colin got behind the counter.

'I don't do the tills unless there's an emergency. Carolynn's stocking up. I'll get her out front. You can talk to Peter in the staffroom.'

The staffroom was a slightly bigger cupboard, with a Formica table, a kettle, an ancient and very grubby microwave and a small fridge. They were still surrounded by towers of toilet rolls and tins of soup. Peter had become a cocktail of anxiety and excitement. Sandy thought he'd probably watched too many US crime shows.

'What am I supposed to have done?'

'Nothing at all.' Sandy nodded towards the kettle. 'Any chance of a coffee? I bet you could do with one too.'

'My break isn't for another forty minutes. The boss'll be expecting me back.'

'Well, this is police business and it might take a while. I won't tell him about the coffee, if you don't.'

Peter switched on the kettle and pulled a jar of instant coffee from a cupboard. He spooned it into stained mugs. He seemed happier moving. Sandy wiped the table with a tea towel, before putting the drawing of the dead woman in front of the man.

'We think she was in here on Tuesday. Do you recognize her?'

'What's she done?' Peter's eyes flicked around the room. He seemed very twitchy. It occurred to Sandy that he might be into drugs. Or perhaps he was just desperate for a cigarette.

'She's dead,' Sandy said. 'We found her body after the landslide on Wednesday night, but we don't know who she is. We need to track down her relatives.'

Peter stared at her. 'Aye, she was in. She bought a bottle of champagne.'

'Anything else?'

The boy screwed up his eyes, a pantomime of

thinking. 'A packet of couscous.'

'You can remember that? After all the customers you serve?' Sandy was all admiration. He knew how little praise it took for an insecure person to feel grateful.

'Aye well, I've always had a good memory. Besides, she was striking, you ken, with that long black hair.' He blushed. 'I mean she was old enough to be my mother, but it still made me feel good just looking at her.'

'Did you chat at all?'

'Not really. There was a queue behind her. Just while I was ringing up the items. I asked her if the champagne was for Valentine's Day, and I said her man should be buying it for *her*.' He blushed again. 'Soppy, huh? But the boss says we should engage with the customers.'

'What did *she* say?' Sandy thought how lucky he was that he didn't have a boss like Colin.

'She said she didn't need a special occasion to drink champagne.'

'Accent?'

'Not local, but I didn't notice. Not really.'

'I can tell you're more a visual person.' Sandy turned on the flattery again. 'Can you tell me what she was wearing?'

Peter screwed up his face again, but it seemed he did have a visual memory. 'A coat. Long and dark blue, and reaching almost to her ankles. Kind of stylish, like you might wear in the city. Not waterproof, like most of the women here would wear. Black boots with a narrow heel. A blue silk scarf.'

'So office clothes?'

'Smart, yeah. I couldn't see what she was wearing underneath the coat.' He blushed again.

Sandy was thinking that he'd seen a coat like that in the cupboard at Tain. Another confirmation that they had found the right woman.

'Had you seen her before? I mean, is she a regular customer?'

'No, not a regular. I've seen her before, though.' Peter had reached into a drawer for a packet of biscuits and dunked one into his coffee. It fell apart before he could get it into his mouth, and soggy crumbs fell back into the mug. He swore under his breath.

'In the shop?'

'Nah, in Lerwick. In the bar in Mareel. Upstairs. I was waiting to see a film.'

'When was this?' Sandy sipped the coffee as if he had all the time in the world.

'A week ago. The Friday night. I was going to meet some friends, got there a bit early. Perhaps that's why I noticed her when she came into the shop the other day; I knew I'd seen her before.'

'Was she on her own?'

'No, she was with a bloke,' Peter said. 'Smart. Jacket and tie. Not a suit, but he'd made an effort.'

'You didn't know him?' Because Sandy thought the boy would have blurted out a name if he'd had one. He'd want to show off.

Peter shook his head. 'He was older, you know. He wasn't someone I'd have gone to school with.'

'Anything else that might help us trace him?'

'Sorry.'

Outside the rain had stopped and a faint, milky sunlight filtered through the gloom. Instead of turning back towards Lerwick, Sandy headed towards Sullom Voe and stopped at the new hotel that had been built just outside the village of Brae. Its accommodation was used solely for oil, gas and construction workers and had been full since it had been slotted together like a giant bit of Lego several years before. Sandy had been inside once for the Sunday-lunch carvery. It had felt a bit like going abroad and wandering into another world. There were foreign voices, loud and confident, and even those who spoke English were sharing jokes he couldn't understand.

Now reception was crowded with men waiting to check out. They stood with their holdalls at their feet, impatient. Sandy supposed they'd been stranded because of the restricted flights and were anxious to get home. He waited until the queue had cleared and then went up to the desk.

'Do you know this woman?'

Sandy thought he saw a spark of recognition, but the receptionist shook his head. 'Sorry.'

'She doesn't work here?'

'No, I'm certain about that.' The man had an accent too. Sandy thought it was probably Eastern European, but his English was just as good as Sandy's.

'You know all the staff?'

The receptionist nodded. 'Most of us live in.

60

Those who aren't Shetlanders — and she doesn't look like a local. So if she worked here I would recognize her.'

'You've never seen her as a guest in the bar or the restaurant?'

This time there was a brief hesitation. 'I don't think so. She's not a regular. But lots of people wander through, and I'm stuck on the desk.'

'She's kind of striking,' Sandy said. 'I think you'd notice.'

Another pause. 'Sorry, I really don't think I can help.'

The queue had built up behind Sandy again. He could hear muttered comments and felt intimidated by the oil men's bulk and hostility. He nodded to the receptionist and walked outside. The cloud had lifted even further, so now he could see down the voe towards the terminal. He thought he'd achieved very little. He had one snippet of fresh information from Peter — that the woman had been in the bar in Mareel a week ago with a smartly dressed man — but they still had no clue what she was doing in Shetland. And they still had no name for her. Sandy knew that Jimmy Perez would be disappointed in him.

8

Jane Hay let herself into the largest of the polytunnels and the familiar smell of compost and vegetation made her feel she was coming home. She'd met Kevin at college in Aberdeen; he'd been doing agriculture, but her subject was horticulture. On their first date he'd taken her hands in his and laughed at the ingrained soil under her thumbnail. Later he'd told her he knew then that she was the girl for him.

Her parents had grown soft fruit, and the plan had always been that she would join the family business once she'd graduated. Her father had been more addicted to drinking than horticulture, even before Jane started at college, and she'd seen herself in the role of saviour. She'd dreamed of returning home with the knowledge and the passion to take on the company and make it profitable again. But her father had died suddenly, when his liver gave up its unequal struggle with the booze, and her mother had sold up immediately without consulting Jane about her plans. That had been the start of Jane's strange relationship with alcohol. It had covered up her sadness and made her fun to be with. Later it became her secret consolation.

Now she prepared the soil in the polytunnel and thought her father had at least given her this: the ability to work magic with seeds and earth, an understanding of what made things grow. She was planting early potatoes and carrots, for family use. When the rest of Shetland was still dark and grey, in her polythene world spring would have arrived. The boys had preferred frozen chips and baked beans when they were young, but she'd always felt a thrill when she put the first new potatoes on the table. It was warm in the strange plastic bubble and she took off her sweater. Outside, drizzle ran in streaks down the tunnel, clouding the polythene so that she had no sense of the outside world. And all the time she was thinking about the dark-haired woman who'd stayed in Tain.

She hadn't been entirely honest when she'd spoken to Jimmy Perez that morning. It wasn't that she'd lied. Lies had come easily to her when she'd been drinking. That was something all alcoholics had in common. They lied to their friends and their families and themselves. They lived in a strange fantasy world of obsession and escape. She tried to be honest these days, though sometimes it was hard with Kevin, who needed more reassurance than her sons did.

Of course I love you. I couldn't live without you. Of course I'm happy with what we have.

Now she wondered if that was the truth. When the hill had slipped, fracturing their land and cutting it in two, it seemed that her image of herself as wife and mother had shattered too. She began to consider a parallel life away from the islands. How would she have ended up if she hadn't met Kevin, if he hadn't fallen wildly in love with a lass from Perth with soil under her thumbnail? She'd known from the beginning

63

that there was no question of him staying in the Scottish mainland with *her*. He might love her, but not enough to give up the family croft. Would she have become an alcoholic if things had been different? She pushed that thought away quickly. There was nobody to blame for her drinking, not even her father, who'd been as much a victim of the illness as she had been. As she frequently told Rachel, alcoholism was a disease and not a lifestyle choice.

But although she hadn't lied to Jimmy Perez, she hadn't told him the whole story. That afternoon, when she'd hurried back from the shore in the dark and seen the woman in Tain, her silhouette against the light, there had been somebody else in the house with the stranger. Jane had seen a shadow on the wall behind the woman. Impossible to make out who was there and, besides, it had only been a glimpse. She could have been mistaken. But later, from her own kitchen window, she'd seen a torch light moving up the path between Tain and their house through the sycamores; and soon afterwards Kevin had come in, his hair damp from the drizzle, looking a little confused and strange.

'Where have you been?'

'Just to the shed,' he'd said. 'To check on the cows.'

But Tain was in quite the other direction from the cowshed, and who else would be walking up the path with a torch in his hand? The boys had been around, but they weren't given to wandering about outside in the rain.

Now, straightening to fetch water from the

butt outside, she couldn't believe that she hadn't demanded an explanation. *But you've just walked up from Tain. I saw your torch. What were you doing with the dark-haired woman?* She'd developed the habit of being passive and apologetic, she decided. Once she'd been passionate about all kind of things — not just her work. About books and music. She still talked about those with her friend Simon. Once she'd been passionate about Kevin. Now perhaps she just didn't care enough to make a fuss.

When she finished planting she left the polycrub reluctantly. She'd arranged to meet Simon for lunch, and went into the house to shower and change. She had books to return to the library, so she went into town early. Standing at the counter in the converted church that was Lerwick library, she was aware that the talk all around her was of the results of the landslide. She learned that the road to the airport had opened, but there was still chaos because only one lane was clear and a big section was controlled by traffic lights. Flights were coming into Sumburgh again. She waved to people she knew, but didn't stop to chat.

There was a new cafe right on the shore near the supermarket where she'd been tempted to stop for wine the night before. Simon Agnew was already sitting at a table near the window and she felt happier just seeing him; he could always make her laugh, and somehow he understood her in a way that her Shetland pals didn't. They were unlikely friends. He was old enough to be her father, white-haired, lanky. Jane had worked out, from the things he'd let drop, that he must be in his late sixties at least, but he didn't seem at all elderly. A life of sport, adventure and exploration had left him with no spare flesh at all. She thought he was all muscle and sinew and movement.

Even now, reading a book at the table, Simon couldn't keep still. He stretched his legs into the aisle, ready to trip up any unsuspecting waitress. He didn't wear specs and she wondered occasionally if his eyes were so blue because he wore contacts. He was vain enough. He looked up, saw Jane, waved and jumped to his feet. He had more energy than anyone else she knew. He'd moved to Shetland and into the old manse in Ravenswick when he'd retired from his work at a university in the south. Looking for peace, he'd said, though from the beginning there had been nothing peaceful about him. He was restless, still looking for excitement and new projects.

He'd blown into Ravenswick like a storm and stirred the settlement into action, bringing them together for meals at the manse, a book group, a community choir. He was into wild swimming and had them all out on the beach early one midsummer's morning skinny-dipping for charity. Even Jimmy Perez's Fran. They had found out more about him over time. He'd trained as a psychologist and worked in a busy hospital, before becoming an academic. His holidays were spent trekking to little known corners of the world. He still wrote books and his house was full of them. There'd been a wife, but he'd divorced years ago. 'Can't blame her, poor woman, I wasn't at all what she needed.' No kids, which was a shame because he was great with Andy and Michael. Even Kevin liked him and didn't see Simon as any sort of threat. Because although Jane enjoyed Simon's company immensely, she didn't fancy him in the slightest and Kevin knew her well enough to see that.

Now Jane waved back and approached him, her face thrust forward and tilted up for the mandatory kiss on the cheek.

When did we all start kissing each other? She tried to remember when this form of greeting had become common. When she'd been young she'd only kissed her grandparents and her father, and him only when he'd been drunk and maudlin and had demanded a show of affection.

'How's it going?' she asked. They had both sat down and were studying the menu. Jane suddenly felt very hungry. 'The landslide must be a bit of a nightmare, with the manse so close to the slip. Were you OK the day it happened?'

'I was at Magnus Tait's funeral.'

'Of course, Kevin said you were there when the landslide happened. Poor Magnus.' Jane had never got to know Magnus, who'd always seemed strange and a little scary, but Simon had been a regular visitor and had been the person to call the ambulance the day Magnus had a stroke.

'I think he would have rather enjoyed it,' Simon said. 'He had an odd sense of humour. The sight of us scrambling out of the way of the mud, falling over, would have appealed to him.

He was never one to stand on his dignity.' There was a moment of silence. 'I need to ask your advice.'

Jane looked up, shocked. Simon sometimes *gave* advice, even if it hadn't been asked for. He'd been trained for it, after all. She couldn't remember him asking for it, though. 'I'm not sure if I'll be able to help. What is it?'

'Did you hear that a woman was killed in the landslide?'

'Of course,' Jane said. 'She was a kind of neighbour, I suppose.'

'Did you know her?' He looked at her sideways, waiting for an answer.

'Not at all. I don't think she can have been staying in the house for very long.'

'I met her once,' Simon said.

'Where? Have you told the police?' Jane thought that the dark woman from Tain was taking over her life. She felt almost as if she were being stalked. How ridiculous was that? It was impossible to be stalked by a dead woman.

'No.'

'You should,' Jane said. 'They haven't got a name for her yet. I spoke to Jimmy Perez this morning.' She paused. 'How did you know her?'

There was another silence, which stretched. The young waiter came with their bill.

'I didn't know her. Not really.' Simon looked out over the water. 'But it was a very bizarre encounter.'

She could tell he was about to launch into one of his stories. 'What do you mean? Did you visit her at Tain?'

'No, nothing like that. I met her in Lerwick. And I'm not even sure that I should be talking about it.'

'But of course you should!' And Jane knew he *wanted* to talk about it. Simon loved gossip of all kinds. He said that he'd become a psychologist because it gave him a way of prying into other people's lives.

'You know we set up a counselling service for Shetlanders? A small charitable trust. Something outside the health service, which doesn't always have the time or experience to do intensive work. Most of our focus is on families, but we do see individuals too, if that's needed. Individuals in trouble.'

Jane nodded. 'Befriending Shetland' was one of Simon's projects. A good cause, but sometimes she thought he'd only set it up out of boredom — that restlessness that always needed a challenge. He was still involved, though, still made the trek into Lerwick three times a week to run sessions.

'We run a drop-in service one evening a week,' Simon went on. 'It's usually me and a volunteer. Often nobody turns up and we just have a good gossip and drink tea.' Another pause. 'But that night I was on my own.'

'And the dead woman came along?'

Simon nodded.

'When was it?' Jane was fascinated now.

'Ten days ago.'

'What did she want?'

'I'm not sure I can tell you.' He suddenly seemed serious. 'It's confidential. That's the big promise we make to everyone who comes to us.'

'But she's dead!' Jane must have spoken more loudly than she intended, because a woman at a far table stared at her. She lowered her voice. 'Even if you don't talk to me, you'll have to tell the police.'

'That's why I wanted your advice. I suppose I knew what you'd say.' Simon was staring out of the window. For the first time since she'd joined him in the cafe he was sitting quite still.

'You need to talk to Jimmy Perez. He lives in Ravenswick with Fran Hunter's daughter. You must know him.'

'I've seen him outside the house, but I've never really talked to him. I called once after Fran died, but he made it clear he didn't want my company or my help. Perhaps it was just too soon, but I didn't want to go back after that.'

'I'll come with you, if you like,' Jane said. 'I know him and I haven't got anything special on this afternoon.' She looked at Simon, waiting for his response, and realized that she was holding her breath. She was desperate to go with him to the police station. She wanted to find out everything she could about the dark woman. If Kevin had been visiting her at Tain, this was more than simple curiosity about a dead stranger. She stood up. 'Well, are you coming?'

Simon hesitated for just a moment longer and then stood up too. 'I suppose,' he said, 'I haven't really got any choice.'

★ ★ ★

70

Jane hadn't expected to see Jimmy Perez, even though she'd mentioned his name to Simon. She'd thought there would be a junior officer to take statements. But when she explained to the constable on the desk why they were there, Jimmy himself came down to greet them and took them up to his office. He offered them coffee.

'It was good to see you at Magnus's funeral, Simon. I know he enjoyed your visits.'

'A pity the burial itself was quite so dramatic.'

'Magnus was always saying that folk were keeping too many sheep on the hill these days,' Perez said. 'I can imagine him chuckling and saying: *You see, boys, I told you so.*'

Simon smiled. 'I was telling Jane that he had an odd sense of humour.'

Jane had wondered if she might be excluded from the conversation, asked to wait in a different room perhaps, but both Simon and Perez seemed to take it for granted that she would be there. Outside the sky was brightening a little and the gulls seemed very white against the grey sky.

'So,' Perez said, 'tell me about your contact with the woman.' He leaned back in his chair.

'It was by phone first. The organization has an emergency number. We can't man the line twenty-four hours — we're not the Samaritans and we don't have enough volunteers. If no one's around there's a recorded message, giving our opening hours, but if I'm there I answer the phone.'

'What impression did you get from that first

call?' Perez paused. 'I'm guessing you learn to assess people quickly in your business.'

'She sounded quite calm,' Simon said. 'Not inebriated at all. Not manic. But there was a kind of quiet desperation in her voice. I suppose I felt that if she talked about taking her life, she might mean it.'

'And did she talk about taking her life?'

'I think her words were: *I've come to the end. I can't take any more.*'

Jane remembered the woman she'd seen in the shop in Brae. She'd seemed calm, cheerful even. What had happened to change her life in the week since her contact with Simon? Had it been the man who'd collected her in the car? Had he made the difference to her? A voice in her head was screaming: *At least it wasn't Kevin. If it had been Kevin, you'd have recognized the car even in that weather.*

'And did she give you her name during that initial phone call?' It was Perez again, as quiet and probing as a psychologist himself. 'You said you told her yours.'

Simon didn't answer at once. 'She said her name was Alissandra. But I can't remember when she told me. It could have been over the phone or when she came in later that evening.'

'Alissandra? You're sure.' Perez seemed especially interested in that.

'It was an unusual name,' Simon said. 'I thought it might be Greek. Of course it stuck in my memory.'

Perez gave a little nod. 'So she asked if she

could come in and talk to you. What did you say?'

'That she was welcome to do that, but that I'd only be there until nine-thirty.'

'What was the time of the first call?' Perez looked up from his coffee.

'Eight-fifteen. I don't know why, but I always make a note. I told her where to find us, but I had the impression that she'd already checked out our address. It's on the website.'

'And what time did she arrive?'

'Twenty minutes later.' Simon shut his eyes briefly as if he was remembering the encounter. 'We have a waiting area where we can meet people. A couple of easy chairs and a coffee table. On the drop-in evenings we take in a kettle to make tea and coffee. It's less formal than using the offices, where we see people during the day.

Perez broke in with a question. 'Is that usual? Someone phoning first on a drop-in night?'

'It's not unusual.'

'I'm trying to picture it.' Now it was Perez's turn to close his eyes for a moment. 'Do clients walk straight in from the pavement?'

'There's a buzzer on the door, after hours. I wasn't expecting Alissandra to arrive so quickly and it made me jump rather. I hurried to let her in. Of course it was dark and raining and I didn't want her to stand outside getting wetter than she already was.'

'Once again, first impressions, please. If you wouldn't mind.'

'Honestly?' Simon said. 'That she was a very

73

beautiful woman. When I let her in she was wearing a long coat. She took the coat off and shook it, and I saw her long dark hair and almost black eyes. When I saw the drawing you've been circulating I recognized her immediately. There was no doubt in my mind.' There was a pause and he resumed his story of that night. 'At first I didn't think the person who walked in was the same woman who'd phoned. She seemed too confident and too controlled. Not in need of our help. But as she came further into the room she began to cry. Almost silently, you know, and then she gave a sob and held a handkerchief to her mouth as if the sound had been obscene and she needed to stop it happening again.'

'What age would you say?' Perez's voice was very quiet and Jane, furthest away from him, struggled to make out the words.

'Early forties. It was hard to tell.'

'What did you do?'

'Nothing at first. We both sat down and I waited for her to compose herself. There was a box of tissues on the table and I pushed it towards her. Eventually she started to speak.' There was a silence in Jimmy Perez's room. Jane supposed it was similar to the silence in the charity's office as Simon waited for the woman to explain why she was so desperate. She thought Simon in work mode must be very different from the man she knew. *That* Simon was impatient and never waited for anyone. Now the psychologist continued, 'First she apologized for being so emotional. She said she'd got into a mess and she could see no way

74

out, apart from killing herself.'

'What sort of mess?'

Simon shook his head. 'I'm sorry, Jimmy, but she wasn't very specific. There seemed to be a lot of guilt. She talked about being trapped and about being worried about her family. She kept saying it was all her fault. Then suddenly she was quite calm again, as she'd appeared to be on the phone and when I'd first opened the door to her. She stood up and put on her coat. She'd put it over a chair close to the radiator, and I remember seeing it steaming while we were talking. She said of course she wouldn't kill herself. There were people who depended on her, people who loved her. She'd panicked for a while, that was all. Now she felt rather foolish for taking up my time. She shook my hand as if we'd been having a professional meeting and she left. I called after her that she should ring back if ever she wanted to talk again, if ever she felt that she couldn't cope on her own, but she didn't reply.'

There was silence and once more Jane could picture the scene in the charity's office, the rain on the windowpane, the steam rising from the stylish coat, the box of tissues on the low table. Then the woman suddenly becoming quite controlled, almost dignified, and walking away into the night.

'Is that how the woman appeared to you?' Perez asked. 'Like a professional woman? If you were to guess what work she did, what would you say?'

'I suppose I assumed she was in the oil or gas business.' Simon seemed surprised by the question. 'Because of the way she spoke — her confidence once the tears were over. I imagined her heading up a team, having a certain responsibility.'

'Alissandra's a foreign name, as you say. Southern Mediterranean. Did she have an accent?'

Simon paused for a moment. *His* voice was upper-class English. Sometimes Jane teased him about it.

'Perhaps there was a trace of an accent, but if she came from overseas, her English was very good.'

'Did you arrange to meet again?'

There was a moment of silence.

'No,' Simon said. 'I never expected to see her again.'

9

Perez walked to collect Cassie on Friday night — the Rogerson house was close to the police station — and glimpsed domestic scenes through uncurtained windows along the street. Happy families. Maybe. The door was opened by Kathryn's father, Tom. Perez knew him by sight and had bumped into him at a couple of meetings. Tom was a solicitor, senior partner in a firm of lawyers who dealt with everything from divorce to crime, but much of his work seemed to involve one of the contractors at Sullom Voe. Perez served on a council working group that planned for disaster, if a tanker should hit the rocks or there was a major oil spill at the terminal, and Tom Rogerson was often present, either representing the contractor or in his role as councillor. It seemed ironic now that nobody had planned for the disaster of a landslide triggered by natural causes.

Tom had worked in the south straight after university and only came home when his daughter was born.

'Where better to bring up a child?' he'd said when he first met Perez and found out that he had a stepdaughter. 'I loved the freedom of being a kid here and my wife's an Orcadian, so she felt just the same. It meant a drop in salary, but money's not everything. Isn't that right, Jimmy?'

Now he stepped back to let Perez into the

house. Perez remembered that they'd met on social occasions too, at a couple of weddings. One a marathon affair in Whalsay. Tom Rogerson was a great dancer, very light on his feet, and even just stepping away from the door he moved as if he had music in his head.

'That Cassie's a fine young lassie. The women have enjoyed every minute of having her here.'

'I'm very grateful,' Perez said. 'But I hope the school will re-open on Monday and I won't have to impose on you again.' He realized that he sounded a little stuffy. Willow Reeves would have pulled a face and laughed at him, if she were there.

'Aye well, Kathryn will know more about that. I've not long got in from work. You'll stay for a cup of tea, Jimmy?' And before Perez could answer, he was shouting through to the kitchen, 'Put the kettle on, Mavis, the inspector has arrived for the bairn.'

This time Cassie was in the living room, with a big box of dressing-up clothes. Kathryn had propped a long mirror against the wall so that the child could look at herself. As he walked past, Perez stuck his head in the room to say hello, but Cassie was engrossed in fastening a silk princess dress with a wide blue ribbon and only waved. Kathryn was in the kitchen drinking tea with her mother.

'Cassie looks as if she's having fun.' Was he a failure as a father because he'd never thought Cassie might like dressing up?

'I work with the Youth Theatre — the little ones — and there are always lots of costumes in

78

the house.' A pause. 'She hasn't been in *all* day, though. It cleared up a bit this afternoon, so we went for a walk.'

'I'm sure she's had a great time.'

The kettle squealed and Mavis refilled a big china pot standing on the Rayburn. 'Help yourself to a scone, Jimmy. They're just out of the oven.'

He wanted to collect Cassie and take her home. In the quiet of his own house he could reflect on the information provided by Simon Agnew. But Perez knew it would be rude to insist on leaving without taking the tea and at least one scone. This family had provided free childcare for two days and the least he could do was accept their hospitality.

'They're saying that the woman swept away from Tain by the landslide was murdered,' Tom said. 'Is that right, Jimmy?'

Perez didn't ask who'd passed on that information. In Shetland news spread like a virus. 'The death's being treated as suspicious.' He realized he sounded pompous again. 'You don't know anything about her? We think she was staying at Tain.' Then there was a sudden thought and he turned to Kathryn. This was something he should have checked before, even though James Grieve had said the dead woman had never given birth. 'You didn't have any kids in the school from there, did you?'

Kathryn shook her head. 'We haven't had any new children since I started, and none of our pupils live in Tain.'

'What about you, Tom? Did you ever meet the

woman? Dark hair, exotic-looking. Not local.'
Because Tom Rogerson seemed to know
everyone. He provided a bridge between
islanders and soothmoothers, the oil industry
and environmentalists. With his easy manner and
charm, he would invite confidences and gossip.

'I don't remember meeting her, Jimmy, and
from the sound of her, I *would* remember, eh?'
He gave a roguish smile and what was almost a
wink.

Perez glanced at Mavis Rogerson, but there
was no response. He'd heard rumours that Tom
was a bit of a lady's man, but perhaps he just
enjoyed the reputation and played up to it. Perez
thought Mavis Rogerson would know better than
to take a daft middle-aged man's showing-off too
seriously. 'You haven't heard anything about the
woman?' he asked. 'We still don't have a name
for her, but we think she might be called
Alissandra. Maybe Alis for short.'

The woman only shook her head. 'I'm sorry,
Jimmy, I only work a couple of stints in the Red
Cross shop these days. I'm sure I haven't had a
customer like your woman.' Perez wondered
what it must be like to have a husband like Tom
Rogerson, who was out at meetings most nights,
while Mavis herself had little reason to leave this
dark and rather claustrophobic house in the
winter.

'We've been told the school can open as usual
on Monday,' Kathryn said.

Perez was pleased he wouldn't have to make
the visit to the Rogerson home a regular event.
The news made him feel suddenly gracious. He

took another mug of tea and congratulated Mavis on her baking, but when he left soon afterwards with Cassie, it was with a sense of freedom. Life was slowly coming back to normal; the following day Cassie had been invited to spend the weekend with some friends. And Willow Reeves would arrive.

★   ★   ★

Willow phoned soon after he'd put Cassie to bed. He'd lit the fire and the house was warm.

'I've been working all day on your behalf, Inspector.'

'We think we have a first name for her,' he said. 'Alissandra. I'm wondering if she could be American — the owner of the cottage that was destroyed in the landslide.' Perez wondered why he was so resistant to that idea. Because he'd had a romantic notion about a Spanish beauty who was a stranger to the islands, not a middle-aged American with an aunt who was a Shetlander? Not someone northern, restrained and buttoned up, checking out that her inheritance was safe.

'Ha! Well, that checks out with what we have!' Willow sounded triumphant. 'An Alissandra Sechrest was booked on the ferry at the beginning of January. I assume that she's your victim. Boat passengers don't have to show any ID, but it'd be too much of a coincidence if it was a different woman.'

So now they had a name for her. They'd be able to check with Craig Henderson, the last tenant of Tain, if she was the owner of the croft.

81

But again Perez felt slightly disappointed. Sechrest wasn't a southern European name. He felt his dream of the dead woman slipping away from him; instead she was taking on a completely new identity.

'She called Befriending Shetland, a counselling charity, the week before she died,' he said. 'It seems she was contemplating suicide.'

'But her death *was* murder?'

'According to James Grieve, there's no doubt about that.' Perez stretched out his legs towards the fire. 'And when she was last seen, the day before the landslide, she seemed almost cheerful.'

'Ah, we can all put on a show when we need to. It doesn't stop us being desperate inside.'

Perez didn't know how to answer that. He couldn't imagine Willow Reeves ever feeling desperate. She was the strongest and most resilient person he'd ever met. 'I'll be at the airport to meet you tomorrow,' he said. 'We can stop and look at the scene on the way back to Lerwick.'

There was a brief silence at the end of the phone. 'I'll look forward to it, Jimmy.' It was lightly said, but he could tell that she meant it. He was about to answer but the line had already gone dead.

★　★　★

Craig Henderson, Tain's previous tenant, arrived at Sumburgh from Aberdeen an hour before Willow was scheduled to come in from

82

Inverness. It was a brighter day and the planes were all on time, flying from the east and landing into the wind. Sandy was with Perez, though they'd driven separately to the airport. Sandy had been at school with Craig and gave a wave of recognition as the man sauntered up to the baggage belt. He was brown and fit and his hand-luggage was a smart leather holdall. He'd have looked more at home in Dubai than Sumburgh. Perez watched the encounter between the younger men from a distance. It was civil enough, but he could tell they weren't bosom pals. Sandy led Craig towards an office they'd borrowed from the airport staff. That was when Perez joined them and introduced himself.

'So I get the big boss too, do I?' Craig said. 'Do they not trust you to do the job yourself, Sandy? Do you need a minder these days? Well, that figures.' He took a seat by the desk.

The office was near the departure lounge and looked out over the runway. An Eastern Airways charter had just brought in a group of workers for Sullom Voe and they were walking from the plane towards the airport building.

There was a moment of silence, broken by Craig. 'What's this about, Sandy? What am I supposed to have done? I've been away for six months, so I don't think you can pin anything on me this time.' His voice still had a Shetland accent, the tone amused, a little arrogant.

Perez had looked up Henderson's record. He'd been charged for fighting in a bar in Lerwick, and Sandy had been the arresting officer, so that explained the needle.

'We're after a bit of information,' Sandy said. 'That's all.'

'And it couldn't have waited for a few hours until I got home, had a shower and a beer.' Craig looked up suddenly and his voice changed. 'Has anything happened to one of the family? Has my father taken ill again? He had a heart attack a year ago, but he seems to have been fine since then.'

'Nothing like that.' Sandy shook his head. 'Have you heard about the landslide that blocked the Sumburgh road for a couple of days?'

'My mother texted me about it, but I only picked up the message when I got to Aberdeen.'

'The slide went straight through Tain, completely wrecked the house, and we found the body of a woman in the garden. You were the last person to rent the house. We're still trying to identify the woman and we thought you might be able to help. How did you come to be living there?'

Perez was sitting away from the table and he found his mind wandering. By now Willow should be aboard the plane in Inverness. It should even have taken off. He had to force his attention back into the room.

Craig was speaking. 'I work away on contract in the Middle East. Six months on and three months off. It suits me just fine. By the end of my leave in Shetland I'm desperate to get back to work. And the money's good. My folks would be happy for me to spend all my leave with them, but they make me feel like a bairn again. They want to know when I'll be in for my tea and if

84

I'm going to be back for the night, and there's always pressure to have me back working for the family business. It kind of cramps my style. So last time I was home I rented the house at Tain. Close enough to get to my mother's for her to do the laundry, but my own space. You know what I mean?' A grin to show that he was only being half-serious.

Sandy nodded. 'How did you come to rent that place in particular? I can't find any record of it being advertised as being up for let.'

'Old Magnus Tait told me about it.'

The room fell quiet until Sandy spoke. His voice was soft. 'Did you hear that Magnus died?'

There was another moment of silence before the man replied. 'Nah, but he had a stroke right at the end of my last leave, and my mother told me he never really got over it. I'm not surprised. I'll miss our chats, though.'

'They were burying Magnus when the landslide hit,' Sandy said. 'You know that Tain is just up the hill from the cemetery.'

'Poor old bugger.'

'Were you friends?' Perez asked.

'I suppose we were, in a way. When I was home last, I saw him struggling to clip his sheep and offered to help. He was an old man. Still strong, but the arthritis had got into his fingers and his wrists and he found it hard to manage. I used to give my grandfather a hand when I was a boy. He had a croft out at Nibon.' There was a moment of hesitation while Craig seemed to be remembering happy times. 'Magnus didn't say much while we were working, but he took me

85

into the house for a dram afterwards. It was just as it must have been a hundred years ago. I felt as if I was stepping back in time. And then he started telling his stories about the old days. Fascinating. It was just like talking to my granddad, when he was alive. My folks aren't interested in any of that. They just want the new kitchen every couple of years and their holiday to Spain in the summer. Money for a flash, showy car.' Craig paused again. 'I'd go round to see Magnus some evenings. Take a bottle with me. He'd ask about my work abroad and then, after a couple of drams, he'd start with his stories.'

'And he suggested Tain might be available for rent?' Perez turned his back on the runway and leaned towards the desk where Sandy and Craig were sitting.

'He was the same generation as Minnie Laurenson, who used to live there. I remember her. Always dressed in black, with a hooked nose, so she looked like a raven. She seemed ancient even when I was a peerie boy. She died a peerie while ago. She didn't have any relatives left in Shetland. She'd never married. Tain was empty after she died. Magnus told me it had gone to a niece. Some kind of niece. The daughter of a cousin, maybe. You know what it's like with Shetlanders, Jimmy. We're all related, if you dig back far enough. Anyway this woman lived in America and Magnus said she might let me stay there. He could tell I was restless at home and needed my own space. 'I lived with my mother for too long,' he said to me. 'A man needs a house of his own.''

'Did Magnus give you the address of the owner?'

'Yes, Minnie had written it down for him. She never trusted lawyers, apparently. She asked Magnus to write to the woman in America when she died, to tell her that Tain was hers. He did that and they'd been in touch ever since.'

Was that why she was in Shetland? Perez wondered. *Because she knew that Magnus was dying and she wanted to meet him before it was too late. And then perhaps she intended to go to his funeral. But she never made it to the kirk because she was killed.*

'What was her name?'

'She called herself Sandy. I'm not sure what that was short for. Sandy Sechrest, her name was. I phoned her and asked if I could stay in the place. I told her I'd do it up for her a bit, so at least it would be fit for her to stay in, if she came over. She said if I was prepared to do that, I could have it rent-free. Just pay for any fuel I used. I hadn't offered the work for any return. But I get bored easily. And when I'm bored, I get into bother.' He shot another quick grin in Sandy's direction.

'Did you ever meet her?'

Craig shook his head. She talked about coming over, but in the end something got in the way. Work, I think.'

'What did she do for work?'

'She was a publisher. Based in New York.'

'Did you ever see a photo?' Because Perez was struggling to reconcile the dark-eyed woman he'd imagined with a publisher from New York.

'No! Why would I?'

'I don't suppose you know if she was planning to visit Shetland this winter?'

Again Craig shook his head. 'We only spoke a couple of times on the phone. Once before I moved in, and again just before I left for the Middle East. I did email her a couple of photos, to show her how the work on the house was going.'

'We'll need her email address.'

'No problem.' Craig took his iPhone out of his shirt pocket and pressed a few buttons, before handing it to Perez. The address was on the screen: A.Sechrest@mullion.com. 'I think Mullion is the name of the publishing company, so that's probably a work email. She didn't give me a personal one.'

The publisher's name seemed familiar, but Perez couldn't quite remember how he knew it. He thought they had the woman pinned down now. Her employer would know whether she'd taken holiday to visit Shetland. But if she'd only been in the islands for a few weeks, how had she managed to become so friendly with local people? There was the man who'd picked her up from the Co-op in Brae, in the car with the Shetland bumper sticker, and the smart man in the suit who'd been drinking with her in the bar in Mareel. These could be the same person, but if so, why hadn't he come forward to say that he'd known her? There had been publicity all over the islands. It occurred to Perez that if they could identify the man, perhaps they would have found their murderer. The case might not be so complicated after all.

Sandy and Craig had already stood up to go. Perez went with them into the busy terminal and watched them walk outside. For an awkward moment they were crushed together in the revolving door and then they disappeared from view.

★ ★ ★

Willow's plane was early. Perez hung back from the scattering of people waiting for relatives to emerge through the narrow door into the arrivals area. She was one of the last passengers to appear and walked out with Vicki Hewitt, the CSI; the two of them were sharing a joke. He couldn't hear Willow's laugh from where he was standing, but he saw her throw back her head and turn to her colleague. Her wild hair was loose. She wore blue cord trousers, frayed a little at the bottoms, big boots and an anorak. Perez had taken in all these details within seconds. He couldn't have described Vicki at all.

Willow caught a glimpse of him and waved and he went to join her at the luggage belt.

'We should stop meeting like this, Inspector.' Her accent was mongrel, a mix between gentle Western Isles — she'd grown up in a commune in North Uist — and posh English, inherited from her educated, dropout parents.

He was never sure what to say to her. He couldn't quite match her lightness of tone and her banter. 'Welcome back to Shetland.' He paused. 'You've brought some better weather with you, at least.'

'I always aim to please, Jimmy. You know that.'

In the car, Willow sat next to him. Vicki was small and slight and used her short legs as an excuse to go in the back. Perez drove away in silence, passing the Sumburgh Hotel and the Jarlshof archaeological site, before pausing at the crossing at the airport perimeter because the lights were flashing.

'So what have we got so far, Jimmy? Tell me about your mysterious dark woman.'

The approaching plane landed, the lights stopped flashing and Perez drove carefully across the edge of the runway. 'I'm not sure she's so mysterious any more. We think she was probably the owner of Tain, the croft where we found her body.' He described the conversation they'd had with Craig Henderson. 'I'm assuming the Sandy Sechrest he emailed is the same as the Alis of the letter. One name with two diminutive forms. Her email address is 'A dot Sechrest'. It must be the same woman who booked onto the ferry.'

He thought Willow might congratulate him on making a probable identification, but she only nodded in agreement.

'It's still very early in the US, even on the East Coast,' Perez said. 'I'll call her employer's office as soon as we get back to the station. If I email them the drawing of our victim, we should have a confirmed ID by the end of the day.'

There was another silence. Vicki asked a question about the scene.

'It's a total mess,' Perez said. 'When we first found the body we put her death down as accidental, caused by the landslide, and the fire

90

officer's first thought was to check that there wasn't another body in the house. It didn't occur to any of us that we should be preserving a crime scene. The local farmer was called in to help too, so there are tractor tracks and footprints everywhere. Because the landslip picked up debris on its way through, it'll be hard to tell which of the objects actually originated at the site.'

'A challenge then.' He saw Vicki grinning at him in the driver's mirror.

'It's certainly that.' He'd come to a queue of traffic ahead of them and slowed down. 'Only one lane is open from here to beyond the croft. They're still working to make the hill secure.'

The cloud had rolled back in from the sea, dense, grey and straggly like a carded fleece. He thought Willow had been lucky that her flight managed to land. An hour later and it might have been forced to turn back. The cars inched forward. At last they came to the track cut by the fire service down to Tain and he pulled out of the queue of traffic and parked by the ruined house. Everything was still covered in mud, and below them they could see the path of the landslide right down to the coast, a black scar in the brown winter hillside.

Now there was a persistent drizzle and Willow pulled up her hood. 'It would have been a lonely place for a woman on her own, even before the damage,' she said.

'There's a farm just round the hill beyond those trees. Kevin and Jane Hay live there and they're friendly-enough people, but they don't

91

seem to have made any contact with the victim. Jane knew someone was staying there, but assumed it was a holidaymaker. Kevin says he thought it was empty. They never saw a car parked outside, but they wouldn't, unless they walked right past.'

'How on earth could she manage here without a car?'

'She had a friend. A male friend. He picked her up from the Co-op in Brae and was seen drinking wine with her in the bar at Mareel.'

If it was the same man. But surely it was too much of a coincidence to believe that she had two men in tow, after such a short time in the islands. And was this the man who'd written the letter in the box?

'All the same . . . ' Willow's face was hidden by the deep hood, but he could tell she found the situation difficult to fathom. 'If she'd inherited the house, surely there would have been relatives to visit. Otherwise why would she be here? It's not the best time of year for a holiday. I don't understand why she wasn't recognized when you first asked for information. None of it quite makes sense.'

Vicki Hewitt was pulling a scene-suit over her jeans and jacket. She held onto Willow's shoulder to keep her balance.

'Do you need that? The scene's so contaminated anyway?'

'Old habits die hard. Besides, if we come to court, you might be grateful.' Vicki straightened. 'Do you want to leave me here and come back for me later? You'd be two more people to have tramped around, contaminating the place, and I can focus better on my own.'

'You mean we'd just be in the way!' Perez found it much easier to be natural with Vicki than with Willow. 'I'll get Sandy to come back and work with you, as soon as he's finished with Craig Henderson's folks. He's been through the house already.'

'Tell him to bring some cans of Coke with him,' Vicki said. 'I think better when I'm rattling with caffeine. I can picture the scenario more clearly.'

'Will do.' But Perez thought Vicki hadn't heard him. Her attention was already on the ruin below her. She started to slide down the bank towards it, leaving him alone with Willow Reeves.

10

Craig Henderson's parents lived in a modern bungalow in a settlement north of Ravenswick, right on the coast. The Hendersons ran a complex of holiday chalets on the same site. The chalets were very smart, upmarket, of Scandinavian design and, according to rumour, cost a fortune to rent. The crazy tourists must be mad enough to pay, because in the season they always seemed to be fully booked. Sandy had been shown round them once by a girlfriend who cleaned there and he had marvelled at the granite worktops and individual saunas, the hot tubs and polished wooden floors.

The bungalow was more traditional, with pebbledash render and decking at the top of the garden, though there was a hot tub there too. Sandy thought it would make a fine place to sit on a summer's day. He imagined a barbecue, wine straight from the fridge and expensive foreign lager. Stuart and Angie Henderson struck him as the sort of people who'd enjoy a party. Now the decking was slippery and rain dripped from the eaves.

The parents were looking out for Craig and came into the porch to greet him as soon as they saw the car. There were screams of delight from Angie about how brown the man was, and then she started on about it being time he found himself a nice Shetland girl and stayed at home.

She'd missed him so much. Her hair was too black to be natural and she wore thick mascara and big earrings. Stuart had thrust a can of beer into his son's hand before they'd had a chance to get into the kitchen. Sandy could understand why Craig had felt he needed a place of his own.

They sat in the open-plan downstairs room. Angie had offered coffee and was fidgeting with a fancy machine. Sandy felt he was in the way, but Jimmy Perez had asked him to talk to Craig's parents: *If they're as protective as he makes out, they might have found out more about the owner of Tain.*

Sandy found it hard to squeeze into the conversation at first, but once he brought up the subject of the dead woman at Tain, the Hendersons were eager to talk about her.

'I was just glad that Craig had moved out.' Angie brought Sandy a cappuccino and set it on a coaster on the glass coffee table. 'Imagine if he'd still been living there; it could have been him in the mortuary in Aberdeen, not some strange woman.' The implication was that the only safe place for Craig to be was at home with her.

'Did you know Minnie Laurenson?'

'We all knew Minnie. She taught us in Sunday school and terrified the life out of us, didn't she, Stuart?'

Stuart nodded and took another swig from his can.

'So you'd have heard that she'd left the house to a relative in America when she died?'

'We all wondered what would happen to the

house when she passed away,' Angie said. 'As far as we knew, there were no living relatives. Then nothing happened and I suppose we forgot all about it. The house was hidden from the road, and really it was none of our business. It was only when Magnus put Craig in touch with Minnie's niece that we found out about the woman in America.'

'You didn't get in touch with her yourselves? With Craig travelling so much, it might have made sense if you were the first point of contact.'

There was no immediate reply and then Angie looked at her son. 'I did try and get in touch once. Just a few weeks ago. I thought I'd go in and tidy the place up a bit, before Craig moved back in, and I wanted to find out who had the keys. I couldn't find them in Craig's room.'

'That had been arranged, had it?' Sandy directed his question to Craig. 'You were going to rent Tain again?'

'The plan was that I'd spend the first couple of weeks here at home and then move into Tain. No chance of that now.' Craig turned to his mother. 'You had no right to contact the American woman. How did you find her number anyway?'

'I must have made a note of it when you first decided to leave us.' The words were defiant. Sandy thought Angie had taken the number from her son's phone when he wasn't looking.

Craig shrugged. He'd obviously decided there was no point pursuing the argument. She would always win.

'Did you get hold of the keys?' Sandy asked.

96

'I didn't speak to the woman. All I got was her voicemail message.' Angie paused. 'I did go up to the house, though. If it had been empty for a few months, it would be damp and I couldn't bear the thought of Craig coming back to a place like that. I thought I might be able to get in, air it for him and push the Hoover over it. It might not even have been locked.'

'When exactly was this?' Sandy thought Perez had been right about chatting to the parents. There were no boundaries for Angie — no idea of privacy. But then, Jimmy Perez was usually right.

'About a fortnight ago.'

'Could you be more precise, Mrs Henderson? I'd be very grateful.'

'It was the same day as we went up to town for the country-music night at Mareel. When was that, Stuart? It should still be marked on the calendar. Go and have a look.'

Stuart did as he was told. 'It was February the first.'

Sandy made a note of the date. 'So you went to Tain. You drove up?'

'Of course I drove.' There was a big 4x4 and a new VW Golf parked outside the bungalow. It was hard to imagine Angie walking anywhere.

'What time of day did you go up to Tain?' Sandy knew that Jimmy liked detail.

'Mid-morning. Stuart was doing a bit of maintenance on a couple of the chalets and I thought I'd just go on spec. I stuck the Hoover in the back of the car, just in case I could get in.'

'And what did you find?'

'The door was locked. The front door and the door at the back of the house that led into the lean-to.'

Sandy had a sudden thought and turned to Craig. 'What had you done with your set of keys at the end of your stay?'

'I gave them in to a solicitors' office in Lerwick. Rogerson and Taylor. They dealt with Minnie Laurenson's estate.'

'You never said!' Angie sounded hurt. 'That would have saved me a lot of bother. I could have got the keys from them.'

'You don't need to know everything about my life!' There was a sudden flash of anger and Sandy was reminded of the young man who'd started a fight in the bar in Lerwick, about something so trivial that he couldn't remember the next day what had set him off. But the man probably had jetlag, and Angie Henderson would try the patience of a saint.

'What did you do when you couldn't get into Tain? Did you drive straight home?' But Sandy thought that wasn't Angie's style at all.

'I had a quick look through the windows,' she said. 'I had given the place a good clean the day before Craig left it. I wanted to see what sort of state it was in. I thought I'd have heard if there'd been another tenant in, but you can never tell.'

'And what state was it in?'

'Someone was staying there!' She seemed as affronted as if the place had been taken over by squatters.

'You saw somebody inside the house?'

'No.' Angie was obviously disappointed. 'I

98

knocked at the door, but there was no reply. There were signs that the place was lived in, though. I walked round the house while I was trying the doors and I looked through the windows.'

'Could you tell me what you saw?'

'It was tidy enough.' There was a pause and she shut her eyes as if she was trying to picture the rooms she'd seen through the small windows. 'The bed had been made up. We took bedding down from here for Craig when he first moved in, and brought it all home the day before he flew out. He spent his last night here with us. We had a bit of a party to see him off. The new stuff looked expensive. I'm not sure where you'd get it locally. It must have been bought online. Some of Minnie Laurenson's furniture was still there — it had been there when Craig had the place too. He wanted to keep it. I'd have got in new.' Another pause. 'I suppose there's not much left of it now.'

Sandy thought of the house, wrecked by the landslide and flooded with mud. He shook his head. 'Not much. What did you do then?'

'I came home,' she said. 'What else could I do?'

★ ★ ★

Sandy phoned Jimmy Perez from his car. He'd stopped at a community shop on the way through to buy Coke and chocolate for Vicki and made the call before setting off again. He was eager to tell Jimmy that Tom Rogerson's firm had managed Minnie Laurenson's estate, but there was no answer and he had to leave a message. Back at Tain, he found Vicki Hewitt in the garden, sifting through the debris close to the wall. It was midday, but there was hardly any light and in her scene-suit she looked like a small, white ghost in the gloom. He pulled on a scene-suit of his own. Vicki heard his footsteps and turned.

'There's enough stuff here to take a whole team a month to sort through properly.' But she sounded cheerful enough and he could tell that she wasn't daunted. She wasn't the sort to complain.

'You'll have to make do with me,' Sandy said. 'Sorry.'

She grinned. 'I thought it was best to start out here. The material still inside the house is relatively stable — it survived the landslide, after all. A bad gale and all this could disappear. I'm bagging as much as I can and pegging the plot, taking lots of photos. If you follow behind me and mark up the bags, that would speed us up.'

So Sandy squatted beside her and followed her instructions. He was always happiest when he had clear instructions to follow, and the crime-scene investigator was very precise about what she wanted him to do. Vicki seemed not to notice the drizzle or cold. Occasionally she stood up to stretch or take a drink, but her focus was always on the small patch of ground just in front of her. Close to the ruins of the house, tucked out of the worst of the weather, a pile of plastic bags showed how much progress she'd already made.

Now she was sorting through a small pile of kitchen implements: a corkscrew, a cheese grater and a sieve; they were all intact, and all had been trapped by the wall. The tide of mud must have swept them out through the kitchen door. The random nature of the items reminded Sandy of the bric-a-brac stalls that appeared occasionally at the fund-raising Sunday teas run in community halls throughout the summer. Vicki was like one of the elderly women who scrabbled through the junk hoping to find treasure. He couldn't see how the objects might be of interest, but each item was bagged and he scribbled on the labels. There was a single woman's shoe, size five, suede, with leather trimmings, an ankle strap and small heel.

'Was she wearing shoes when they found the body?' Vicki sat on her heels and stretched her back and arms.

'No.' Sandy wondered if that was significant, but Vicki didn't say anything and he couldn't work out how it might be.

She turned her attention back to some sodden scraps of paper, sliding them carefully into a bag.

'This isn't newsprint. It could provide corroboration of identity, if the techies can dry it out.'

Or it could be some junk mail, trying to sell the occupant a credit card or double glazing. Sandy was starving. He'd missed out on lunch, but he knew Vikki hadn't eaten, either. She seemed to keep going with the bottle of Coke,

101

which she drained in one go and then returned carefully to her rucksack. He wasn't going to be the one to call it a day, but he was thinking ahead to his night out with Louisa. He'd told Jimmy Perez that he was happy to work if he was needed, but Jimmy had only laughed and told him that nobody was indispensable. So Sandy had booked a table for dinner in the Scalloway Hotel. And a room for afterwards. He'd blinked when he'd heard the price of the overnight stay, but Louisa was worth every penny. Anyway, it would save him the bother of tidying his flat, if they weren't going back there for the night.

The light was fading now and the cars crawling along the road above them were already using their headlights. Soon it would be too dark to continue working and then even Vikki would have to give up. The firefighters had taken away their generator and lights and there was no colour left in the landscape.

'Ten more minutes.' She stood upright. 'Then it's back to civilization for a bath and a meal.'

He nodded. *And Louisa.*

Vicki crouched again, began sifting through another square foot of debris and then froze.

'Didn't Prof. Grieve say the ligature that killed the woman could be a belt?'

'I think so.' Sandy never liked to be too definite. 'Narrow. No sign of the buckle piercing the skin, but some marks, which might have come from indentations in the leather.'

'Best get a photo of this, then.' There was a flash that blinded him for a moment. Vikki shifted position and took another photograph, then she pulled out a thin leather belt embossed with flowers.

'A woman's.' Sandy was disappointed. 'It could have belonged to the victim and been swept out of the house with all the other junk.'

'Maybe. If it matches the marks on the neck, it could tell us something about the crime, though.' She curled the belt so that it looked like a snake and dropped it into a bag.

'Yeah?' Sandy thought for a moment. 'I suppose it would make this the crime scene. Tain, I mean. Unlikely that she was killed elsewhere, if the murder weapon is here.'

'And it would suggest that the murder was opportunistic. If the killer was a man, that is. He didn't bring the murder weapon with him. It belonged to the victim, and the killer picked up what was to hand.' Hours on her hands and knees in the damp soil didn't seem to have dulled Vicki's enthusiasm.

'It's all kind of negative, though, isn't it? And uncertain.' He felt almost disloyal, as if he was questioning her expertise.

'It's a start,' she said. 'It's more than we had this morning.'

11

Willow Reeves thought *this* Shetland — the Shetland of winter gloom and dark shadows — was quite different from the midsummer Shetland of her memory. That had been all pink and silver, sparkling light on water, flowers on the headlands. This was her third time in the islands, but it was as if she was making her first visit, seeing the place as a stranger. Perhaps she needed a reality check, she thought. She couldn't go through life like a teenager, dreaming for the tall, dark man who brooded about the perfect woman who'd died. Her parents had been dreamers. They'd thrown away their comfortable life as academics to set up a commune on the Hebridean island of North Uist. In the end, the other settlers had lost enthusiasm and drifted away, but Willow's parents were still there, scraping a living from the sandy soil, unwilling to admit that the experiment had been a huge mistake.

She sat in Jimmy Perez's office and listened while he made the phone call to New York. They'd decided that Americans probably started work early, and first thing in the working day might be a good time to reach Ms Sechrest's employer. Perez spoke slowly and moderated his voice so that the accent almost disappeared.

What do I know about him, after all? Who is this man, who can be whatever is needed to get his work done?

'I'm a police officer from the UK,' Perez was saying.

Willow couldn't hear what was said on the other end of the line, but she could guess when Perez said, without a trace of impatience, 'Well, no, not English, but Scottish. Yes, almost the same thing. I'm based in the Shetland Islands.' He gave a little laugh and pulled a face at Willow. 'I need information about someone who I believe works for your company. Her name is Alissandra Sechrest. Yes, of course I'll hold.'

There was a click on the other end of the line and Perez pressed a button so that the phone was on speaker, and suddenly the room was filled with an American voice: 'Yes, Sandy Sechrest speaking. How may I help you?'

For a moment Willow was tempted to laugh, because Perez seemed so incredulous. They'd been convinced they'd tracked down the identity of the dead woman, and now it seemed she was alive and well and working in New York. It took him a little while to answer.

'Excuse me for disturbing you, but I'd be grateful if you could answer a few questions, before I explain. Did you have relatives from Shetland?'

'One distant relative. An aunt.' She sounded older than the dead woman. Willow guessed she must be close to retirement. But she was sharp and fiercely intelligent.

'And she left you property in her will?'

'She did. A small house in the village of Ravenswick. And I still intend to visit it one day, when things aren't quite so busy here.' A pause.

'What is this about, Officer?'

'I'm afraid your house was damaged in a landslide this week.'

'Well, it's very good of you to notify me. I'll inform my insurers. If you could email me the details, I won't need to trouble you further.' She was about to replace the receiver.

'Someone died,' Perez said. 'A woman. We think she was staying in your house. Do you know anything about that?'

'No!' The response was immediate. 'I gave permission for a man to stay there. He was the friend of an elderly guy who knew my aunt. But he left six months ago. He'd asked if he might use the house again, in return for general maintenance and repairs, and I agreed. He'd have been moving in again in a couple of weeks.'

'The dead woman was calling herself Alissandra Sechrest,' Perez said. 'At least she travelled into the islands using your name and made at least one appointment under it.'

'And you thought I was dead?' Sandy Sechrest gave a sharp, barking laugh.

'It was rather a shock when you came on the phone.'

'Are you thinking fraud? Identity theft? Just so she had somewhere to stay.'

'Honestly, I'm not quite sure what I think just now. If I email you a likeness of the dead woman, perhaps you could let me know if you recognize her.' Perez paused for a moment. 'Are you aware of any fraud? Money missing from your bank account? Your credit card used without your knowledge? She might even have

106

been using a false passport in your name.'

'I haven't noticed anything, but I'll certainly go back and check.'

Perez looked at Willow and raised his eyebrows to see if she had any questions.

She mouthed: 'Ask her about the solicitor.'

'Who looks after your affairs in Shetland, Ms Sechrest?'

'A firm of lawyers: Rogerson and Taylor. They contacted me about my aunt's will and asked what my plans were for the property. They arranged to have it cleared of all but big items of furniture; there was nothing of value. A few items of cheap jewellery, which they mailed to me. Apparently there were pictures and photos, but I asked for them to be kept in the house. That was where I felt they belonged. Then they used a contract cleaner to go through the place. My aunt had been elderly and hadn't been able to look after herself, or her home, so well recently.'

'Do you remember the name of the cleaning company?'

Perez's interruption seemed to throw her for a moment, but she answered after a beat. 'No, but the lawyers should have a record. I was sent an invoice.'

'And then?'

'Then I asked them to make sure it was secure and to hang onto the keys until I could get there myself, or make some decision about the place. I'd almost forgotten about it, when I got the phone call from the guy asking if he could rent it. I checked him out with the lawyers' office and they said he was legit. It made more sense to have someone in the house than have it stand empty.'

'Can you remember who you talked to at Rogerson and Taylor about allowing a tenant into Tain?' Willow noticed that Perez had let a trace of Shetland back into his voice.

'I'm sorry, Officer. I don't think it was one of the partners. It was a woman. She could even have been someone working on reception. But she said she knew Craig Henderson and that he came from a good family. That was good enough for me. Crazy for the place to stay empty when somebody local needed it.'

Willow thought Sandy Sechrest was a woman who would make decisions easily and then stick to them.

'And who at the office did you instruct to clean and secure the house?' Perez said. 'Was that the same woman?'

'No, that was definitely one of the lawyers. His name was Paul Taylor.' She paused, as if waiting for a further question, and when none came immediately she said, 'If that's all, Officer, I should be in a meeting.'

'The woman who died,' Perez said. 'She wasn't killed in the landslide. It wasn't an accident. She was murdered.'

For the first time Sandy Sechrest seemed to lose her composure. 'I don't understand.'

'She was strangled,' Perez said. 'We assume that her body had been left in the house and was swept out when the landslide hit. Otherwise she wouldn't have been discovered until Craig moved back in.'

'And she was using my name and pretending to be me.'

'I have to ask if there's any reason why someone might want to kill you.' Perez's voice was calm and even.

She gave the same barking laugh as when she'd first started talking. It was a smoker's laugh. Smoking would be her secret vice. 'Well, I've made a few enemies in my career: authors I've rejected or dropped, other editors who dislike the fact that I've poached their stars. But nobody who hates me enough to want me dead. And nobody who'd cross the Atlantic to do it. Besides, as soon as they saw the woman, they'd realize they'd got the wrong person.'

'What kind of books do you publish?'

'We're a general publisher, but my specialism is non-fiction. Mostly self-help books.'

'Is *Think Yourself to a Better Future* one of your titles?'

'Well, yes, Inspector. One of our big sellers.' She seemed flattered rather than curious.

'Would you have sent a copy to your aunt?'

She gave another throaty laugh. 'I hardly knew she existed and, besides, I don't think she'd have been interested.'

So what was the Mullion title doing among the dead woman's possessions?

'Are you in contact with anyone else in the islands?'

'There was an old man called Magnus Tait. He was a friend of my aunt and he used to phone occasionally after she died. I think he'd recently had the phone installed in his house, and it was

109

like a toy. Maybe he didn't have anyone else to call. He rang to tell me the cleaning firm had been into Tain and that they'd done a pretty good job. And then to ask if Craig could rent the place from me. I could hardly understand a word he said, but it was kind of sweet. It made me feel a part of a place I'd never even visited. But I haven't heard from him in several months.'

'I knew Magnus,' Perez said. 'He's been very ill for a while and he died quite recently.'

'Oh!' She sounded genuinely upset. 'I'm sorry.'

'Did Magnus have a set of keys to Tain?'

'I think he must have done,' Sandy Sechrest said. 'I think he found my aunt's body, and he phoned me before the solicitor did to tell me that she was dead.'

Perez looked at Willow again and this time she shook her head. She had no more questions for Sandy Sechrest at this point. Perez had covered everything. Now she was already trying to process the information he'd gained. If Sandy had no friends in Shetland, if she'd never visited, if her only contact was by email to her lawyer, it seemed unlikely that she'd been the intended victim of the Tain murder. The most important task now was to track down the man, or men, with whom the impostor had been seen.

Perez was ending the call. He replaced the receiver. Willow grinned at him. 'Well,' she said. 'Now the fun starts.'

★　★　★

They went for lunch in Mareel, walking down the bank from the police station and past the new council offices. The arts centre stood right on the water. Willow thought it was a concrete-and-glass statement of confidence in Shetland's artistic future. Nothing like this would be considered in the island where she'd been brought up. Since the oil, Shetland seemed to think it was capable of anything. She said as much to Perez.

'I'm not sure,' he said. 'This probably wouldn't be built here now.' He seemed lost in thought and didn't give any further explanation.

In the small downstairs bar they had to wait to be served and, aware that they might be overheard, they waited in silence in the queue. There seemed to be lots of mothers with kids. Jolly young women wearing hand-knitted sweaters, talking about breast-feeding and toddler groups. Willow wondered idly if she would ever be a mother.

She reconsidered the question and this time the possibility hit her with a physical sensation like an electric shock. She was almost surprised Perez hadn't noticed a change in her, because he had his hand on her elbow, helping her through the crowd, and in her heightened state she thought he must have experienced the jolt too. Perhaps the idea of motherhood had been bubbling just under her consciousness for some time, but now the possibility that *she* might become a mother struck her with such force that she reeled under the enormity of it. How inconvenient that the notion should surface here, when she was with Perez and in the middle of an investigation! She needed more time to think about it. She couldn't decide now if the idea would pass or if it would become a compulsion; she only knew that time was sliding by and a decision would have to be made.

They took their drinks upstairs. The space there was almost empty.

'This is where she was seen in the days before her death,' Perez said. 'According to a witness, our mystery woman sat just here sharing a drink with a smartly dressed man.'

'The same man who picked her up from the Co-op in Brae?' Willow tried to ignore her hormones and focus on the investigation.

'That's my guess. Too much of a coincidence otherwise.' Perez set his tray on the table. There was a view down to the bar below them. The mothers were gathering up babies and toddlers and making their way outside. Now the talk was of a language class for under-fives, started in the community centre.

I could never do that. I could never make a profession of bringing up my babies. All those websites and discussion groups about education and childcare. They're surely just for women who miss being at work. Maybe my parents had it right, and all kids need is love, fresh air and a bit of healthy neglect.

'How did she know to use Alissandra Sechrest's name?' Willow watched the women trail away, laden with kids and bags and buggies. The lunchtime rush was over and even the bar downstairs was quiet now. 'I can see how she could con the house keys out of the lawyers — if she gave her name and a bit of the background, they probably wouldn't ask to see any formal ID — but very few people here knew who that house belonged to, and she'd have needed that information to start the process.'

'Perhaps there was something in *The Shetland Times*.'

'Would she have had access to that, if she came from the south?' Willow unscrewed the top from her bottle of mineral water. 'And why the elaborate charade? Why not just come to the islands and book into a B&B, if she wanted to visit the place?'

The food arrived before Perez had time to answer. It was carried by a young man in a black uniform T-shirt and black jeans. His hair flopped over his forehead and he had a string of studs over an eyebrow. One of the arty kids who'd found a spiritual home in Mareel. Willow thought there had been nowhere like this when she'd been growing up. Her social life had consisted of underage drinking in the only bar in the island, illicit encounters behind the community hall while the old folk danced to fiddles and accordions inside. Perez waited until the young man had slid the tray onto the table and then he spoke.

'It's Andy, isn't it? Jane and Kevin's lad? I heard you'd come home for a while.' Perez held out the drawing of the dead woman. 'Do you recognize her? She had a drink in here. It would have been about a week ago in the evening. She would have been with a middle-aged man.'

Willow watched the young man's face. It was impassive. No interest and no curiosity. That seemed odd, but perhaps he'd practised being cool and it had become a habit. Andy Hay shook his head. 'Sorry.'

She expected Perez to push the point, but he only handed over the drawing. 'Take it with you. Show it to your colleagues. Anyone recognize her, ask them to come and let us know.'

'Sure. Bye, Jimmy.'

After the meal their plates were cleared by a large young man, wearing the same uniform of black jeans and Mareel shirt as Andy Hay. His face had a slightly grubby look, caused by an incipient beard and adolescent bad skin. His badge gave his name as Ryan.

'Did Andy show you the drawing?' Willow pushed her soup bowl towards him. He seemed incapable of energetic movement.

'What drawing? Andy's just gone off-shift. I usually work on the ticket desk, but they're short-staffed so they asked me to help.' A sniff of resentment. Clearing tables seemed to be beneath him.

'This drawing.' Perez pulled out another copy and laid it on the table.

Ryan pulled up a chair and sat with them. Willow thought the Shetland kids displayed the same confidence as the building itself. They'd grown up in a time of plenty, when anything seemed possible.

'Do you know this woman?' Perez shifted his chair to make more room. 'She was having a drink here with a middle-aged guy.'

'I don't work in the bar — still at school. I'm on the desk in the lobby at weekends, selling tickets. I'm pretty sure I've seen her, though.'

'Have you not seen her face in the paper, heard the news on Radio Shetland?'

'I don't really bother with the paper.' The boy was unrepentant. 'Too busy working for Highers.' A quick grin to show that was only an excuse. *The Shetland Times* was for his parents. He had his phone and tablet for information.

'Tell me about the time you saw her.'

'Well, it would have been a Saturday night. Saturday's the only evening I do, and it was definitely an evening.' He leaned back in his chair.

'She came to the desk downstairs to buy tickets?'

'For the movie, yeah.'

'Did she pay?'

'Yes, but it was just one ticket. She was on her own.'

'Are you sure? Another witness saw her in here with a middle-aged man. Perhaps she was with him, but he paid for himself?'

The boy screwed up his face into a grimace to show he was thinking. Willow supposed most of the kids working in Mareel had artistic ambitions. It seemed this witness had a theatrical bent too.

'No,' he said. 'She was definitely on her own.'

Willow sensed Perez's frustration. He'd hoped for more from this encounter: a description of the dead woman's companion, even if they couldn't get a name. He'd been battling to

115

identify her for two days. Willow smiled at the boy. 'What time did you serve her?'

'I'm not sure.' No histrionics this time.

'Was she in a hurry? Was it almost time for the film to start?' Another smile of encouragement. Perez was usually very good at this, at putting a witness at ease, but he'd become too close to the case already. It had become a personal challenge to put a name to the victim.

'No, there was no rush,' Ryan said. 'There was still about half an hour to go, I think. She went straight from the counter into the bar.'

'It was busy there?'

'Yes, that time of night it's usually busy. Not just with folk coming to the cinema or a gig, but people stopping for a drink or a coffee on their way home. We're close to the business park.' He nodded vaguely in the direction of the sea.

'So she could have met the guy later? He could have bought his own ticket and joined her in the bar.' *Or they could have met up by chance. Perhaps he was one of the businessmen on his way home from work. If the place was busy, they could have been forced to share a table. But in that case he would have got in touch with the police by now. Middle-aged people would read* The Shetland Times.

'Yeah, I guess so.'

'Were you still on duty when the film finished?' Willow had taken over the conversation. Perez was staring into his coffee. But he was listening. The thing about Jimmy Perez was that he was always listening. Willow wondered if he listened in his sleep.

'Saturday night I'm always on the late shift.'

'Did you notice the woman leaving?'

'No,' the boy said. 'But that didn't mean she wasn't there. It's always a crush when the film ends. And we just want them away.'

'That Saturday, what else was going on here? Was anything happening in the small hall?'

He shook his head. 'It's usually quite quiet at this time of year. Folk are still recovering from Up Helly Aa.'

'Thank you, Ryan.' Willow dismissed him with a smile.

Perez gave the boy a brief wave as he walked away, but said nothing.

*   *   *

Perez had booked her into a new B&B. It was run by a friend of his, some lad he'd been to school with, someone who had gone south to make his way in the world. Another person who had come home when there was a child on the way. It was the old sheriffs house, on one of the lanes leading up from Commercial Street, an easy walk away from the police station, but quiet. It had a garden with mature trees, unusual in this part of the town. Perez shouted, walked in and led Willow down to the basement kitchen. It was warm. A large Aga took up the whole of one wall. A very pregnant woman sat at the table peeling carrots and potatoes. Willow couldn't help staring and had the same odd sensation as when she'd seen the women drinking coffee in Mareel. This time she identified it: envy. *I want*

*to carry a child in my body. I want to look like
that.*

The woman lifted herself to her feet and
moved the kettle onto the hot plate.

'My God, Rosie,' Perez said. 'How much
longer is it now? That thing can't get any bigger
or you'll burst.'

Rosie smiled. 'There's a week or so yet, Jimmy.
You'll need to get the case wrapped up before
then, or John will be on breakfast duty.' She
turned to Willow. 'And trust me, you wouldn't
want that.'

Willow's room was at the top of the house
under sloping eaves. Perez took her up, carrying
one of the bags, to save Rosie the stairs. It was
freshly decorated in seaside blues and greens,
with a view of Bressay Sound.

'What does John do?'

'He's an accountant, managed to get a job
with the council. Might give it up, if the B&B
takes off. The water's his first love. Plan is to get
a small boat and do tours round the islands, take
visitors out for a day's fishing.'

She nodded. 'It must be hard to spend your
day doing one thing, all the time dreaming of
doing something else.'

'Ah,' Perez said. 'John's happy enough.'

There was a slightly awkward silence. Neither
of them was very good at talking about personal
stuff. It was a relief when Perez's phone rang.

'That was Sandy,' he said when the call had
ended. 'He and Vicki are on their way back to
the station. They've run out of light. He says
there's something we should see.'

118

'Give me two minutes to wash my hands. I'll see you downstairs.'

She heard his feet disappear down two flights of polished wooden stairs, but she was thinking of Rosie, wondering what it would feel like to hold in her belly a child that was pushing and straining to get out.

12

When Sandy and Vicki reached the police station it was quite dark. On the way north the rain had become heavier and there was standing water in dips in the road. Sandy couldn't wait until spring, for some light and warm breezes to blow away the gloom. Perez and Willow were waiting for them. Perez sat at his desk and seemed to be brooding. Sometimes depression caught up with the inspector and seemed to swamp him. Then Sandy knew better than to try to cheer him up. Best to let Perez pull himself out of the black mood in his own time.

'So what have you got for us, Sandy?' Willow never sounded gloomy.

'Vicki found it.' He turned to Vicki, who put the belt in its evidence bag on the desk in front of them. 'We were wondering, possible murder weapon. If the marks in the leather match the marks on the dead woman's neck.'

'I wish we had a name for her.' Perez was almost shouting. He was angrier than Sandy had known him for months. He was like a teenager having a tantrum about something he couldn't control. 'I hate calling her 'the woman' or 'the victim'.'

'I thought she was Alissandra Sechrest.'

'Apparently not,' Willow said. 'Alissandra Sechrest is a publisher in New York City and she's very much alive.'

120

Sandy wanted to ask questions about that, about the letter they'd found and the fact that a woman of that name had travelled into Shetland. But he could see that Jimmy Perez wasn't in the frame of mind when he would welcome questions, so he kept quiet.

'I wondered if there might still be fingerprints on the belt.' Vicki had perched on the edge of the desk because they'd run out of chairs. 'They'll be degraded after being out in the weather, but I found the belt in the shelter of the wall and some might still be intact. We might find prints that don't belong to the woman in Tain. Her prints will be in the house, of course. I assume you've tried to identify her from those?'

'Of course.' Perez hardly looked up. 'And James Grieve took prints from the body. They match most of those in the house, but they're not on record.'

'Were there other prints in the house?'

'Some, but the damp and the silt had turned everything in the place to sludge. I'm not convinced we'll get anything we can use.'

There was a silence. A sudden gust blew rain against the windowpane. Outside a driver hit his horn.

'So what do we do next?' This was Willow, cheerful, practical. 'We'll get the belt down to Aberdeen, of course. But what can we do here to trace our dark-haired woman?'

Sandy thought Perez would like that. The fact that Willow was trying to make the victim sound more human. And for the first time the inspector seemed to engage with the conversation.

'It's hard to tell of course, but according to Jane Hay and Angie Henderson, there was no evidence of a break-in to Tain. So how did our impostor get keys?' Perez leaned forward across the desk. 'We need to go to the solicitors' and see if she went there, pretending to be the real Alissandra.'

'Magnus Tait had a set,' Willow said. She gave a quick look at Sandy and gave him what might have been a wink. *See how I can handle him!*

'Magnus was in hospital when the woman arrived into Shetland.'

'But I'm guessing his house was hardly Fort Knox,' Willow said. 'I'm assuming that Tain was properly locked, because the lawyers had responsibility for it. An old man in a croft with little to steal suddenly disappears to hospital, I assume it wouldn't be hard to find a way into his house.'

'Hillhead is just up the bank from me.' Perez almost sounded enthusiastic. 'I'll take a look this evening.'

'I'd like to go back to the scene tomorrow.' Vicki slid off the desk. 'There's still masses of stuff in the garden, and I haven't moved inside the house yet.'

'Do you want me to do the solicitors', Jimmy? Play the senior officer card?' Willow was standing up too.

Sandy looked at his watch and thought he'd have plenty of time to change, before he needed to meet Louisa in Scalloway. For a moment, here in Jimmy Perez's office, he'd forgotten about her, but now thoughts of her were filling his mind again. He heard Perez arranging to take Vicki to check into the B&B, and Willow asking if she might go with the inspector to Magnus Tait's old house in Ravenswick, but he didn't take any of it in. He was anxious. He seldom got things right first time, but he couldn't afford to make a mistake with Louisa.

★ ★ ★

Sandy got to the Scalloway Hotel before her. She'd planned to spend the afternoon in Lerwick and then visit an old school friend on the island of Burra. Her mother was getting some respite care these days and would spend the weekend in the care home in Yell. Burra was linked by bridge to the mainland at Scalloway, so it had made sense for them to meet in the hotel, but now, as he waited, Sandy wished he'd arranged something different. He didn't want to drink too much; Louisa wasn't a woman for boozing and getting wild and silly. Sipping his pint at the bar while the Saturday-night crowd swirled around him, he felt quite separate from them. It was as if he was waiting for an interview, when a party was going on in the same building.

Then he saw her in the hall that led from the street. It must have started to rain more heavily, because she took off her coat and shook it and there were drops of water on her hair. He walked towards her and stumbled over the foot of an elderly woman sitting close to the door. The woman gave a little scream of pain and it seemed as if the whole room was staring at him. As he was apologizing, Louisa seemed to disappear and he had a moment of panic. Was he so clumsy and stupid that she'd given up on him completely? Then she appeared again at the door of the bar and he saw that she was carrying the coat, folded now, so that the lining faced outside.

'I wondered if there was anywhere I could put this to dry.'

'I've booked a room,' he said. 'You could hang it up there.'

He saw the surprise in her face and realized he hadn't told her about the room. Was that a mistake? They'd spent the night together before, but perhaps he shouldn't have assumed that it was a good plan. He should have asked her first.

She frowned. 'Oh, Sandy!' She stood on her toes and kissed him lightly on the lips. 'What a splendid idea. What a treat!'

He could feel himself blushing. The people who'd watched him step on the old woman's toes were still staring.

'I have the key,' he said. 'I'll take you up.'

★　★　★

They ate late, when the restaurant was quiet. They had a table in the window. Perhaps because of the rain, the street outside was empty and there was no traffic. The lights of the accommodation ships were muted by the downpour and the vessels blurred into the background, so they seemed less oppressive. Sandy let his mind empty. They were sharing a bottle of wine and he felt relaxed, that he could say whatever came into his head without seeming stupid. Louisa was wearing a dress he hadn't seen before. It came to him that she'd bought it just for the occasion and that made him smile.

'What are you thinking about?' She must have seen the smile.

Usually he hated that question. Women liked deep and intense conversations, and his thoughts were usually about his next meal or not screwing up at work. He didn't have the imagination to dream up a response that would satisfy them. Today the reply was easy. 'I'm just thinking how happy you make me.'

'You're a flatterer, Sandy Wilson.' But he could tell she was pleased.

The waiter brought them coffee and little pieces of Shetland tablet. Even the bar was emptying now. Perhaps the rain had eased a little, because people were gathering on the pavement to say goodbye to their friends or for a last cigarette. It was impossible to make out the conversations through the glass but they could hear car doors slamming. The door from the restaurant to the bar was open and Sandy could see that only two couples were left inside. One couple was elderly: the white-haired woman whose foot he'd trodden on and a weather-beaten man, who reminded Sandy a little of the man in the photo he'd found in the box in Tain. Sandy thought if they'd been drinking since first arrived in the hotel, they'd both be unste on their feet, and he hoped they had someb to make sure they got home safely.

The other couple had been tucked into

corner, but now they stood up and began to make their way towards the corridor that led outside. They had to wait for a moment, because the older couple had decided to move too and had blocked the doorway. Sandy got a good look at the man and he was immediately familiar: squat and muscular, with the build of a boxer. His photo was often in *The Shetland Times*, taken at civic occasions. Councillor Tom Rogerson, the solicitor whose firm had managed Minnie Laurenson's will and had taken possession of the keys to Tain.

Sandy didn't recognize the woman with Tom, but he knew she wasn't his wife. Mavis sometimes volunteered in the Red Cross shop in the street. She was comfortable and well padded and she wore hand-knitted yoked cardigans with slacks or tweed skirts. This woman was in her thirties, as tall as Tom, and tonight she seemed even taller because she was wearing heels that must make walking tricky. She wore a tight black dress that clung to her body like polythene around fresh meat in Tesco's. Her hair was blonde and very straight.

Louisa must have noticed him staring because she gave Sandy a playful thump on the shoulder. He wanted to tell her that he wasn't interested, not in that way at all. That *she* was the only woman he wanted to stare at. But he knew Jimmy Perez would be interested in the blonde, who was now following the councillor out of the bar. For a moment he was torn. He could pretend he hadn't noticed Tom Rogerson. He could turn back to Louisa and not spoil her

126

evening by worrying about work.

'What is it?' Louisa didn't sound angry, only intrigued.

'It's work. I should see where they go.'

'Well, hurry away then. Just leave me your tablet. I could use another coffee.'

He looked at her. He wondered if she was angry or being sarcastic, but she seemed very easy, sitting with her coffee, staring out at the street and the water beyond.

He stood in the entrance to the hotel. The elderly couple were walking away from him, arm-in-arm, apparently quite sure-footed on the narrow pavement. Rogerson was standing in the small car park on the other side of the street from Sandy, still in conversation with the younger woman. They were speaking quietly, and Sandy couldn't make out what was being said. He didn't want to get any closer. It didn't seem to him that this was a romantic farewell. From the body language, it looked more as if a deal was being closed — some business wrapped up after an evening of negotiation. Eventually the woman got into a small hire car. Sandy made a mental note of the company and scrabbled in his pocket for a pencil to write down the registration number. But he'd changed into his smart suit and had nothing with him to write with. Before she drove off, Rogerson approached the woman and she wound down her window. Now he did raise his voice, so Sandy could hear the words. 'So you're clear then. You'll do as we agreed?'

Her response was to put her foot on the pedal and to drive away as quickly as the little Fiat would let her. Rogerson stood for a moment staring after her and then got into his own car and drove back towards Lerwick.

13

Perez and Willow walked from Fran's house, the house where Perez now lived with her daughter, to Magnus Tait's old croft at Hillhead. It wasn't far and despite the weather they both felt the need for fresh air and exercise. The landslide had started close to the Hillhead boundary, and Magnus's croft was undamaged. There was traffic below them, headlights sweeping occasionally across the hill like spotlights, but the cars moved slowly through the single-lane stretch of the road and there was little noise. A stony track led up towards Magnus's house. Perez shone his torch down at the path so that Willow could follow it, but occasionally she missed her footing and he could hear her swearing under her breath.

The house had been whitewashed only a couple of months before Magnus had suffered the stroke, and it gleamed as they approached it, a beacon to aim for through the darkness. Perez had joined the small group of local people who had volunteered to help paint it. Guilt at their previous hostility towards the old man had led to the formation of the work party. Perez thought *he* would have resented the sudden shift in relationship; he'd have found the visits, the delivery of home-bakes, the offers of help patronizing, but Magnus had enjoyed every minute of the day that the house had been whitewashed. He'd flirted gently with the women and joked with the men. It had been a fine evening and, when the work was done, someone had suggested an impromptu barbecue. Perez hadn't stayed long. He'd found himself swamped with self-pity; he'd thought suddenly how much Fran would have enjoyed the event. He'd carried Cassie back to their house on his shoulders, and even when he'd got her to bed and sat alone in the late-evening sunshine, he'd fancied he could hear the laughter outside and he felt sorry for himself all over again.

Now the drizzle seeped through his jeans and Perez forced himself back to the present. The last few years he'd lived too much in the past. They'd reached the house. There was the bench made from driftwood where Magnus had sat watching the painters at work, and again in his head Perez was back on that sunny afternoon. Magnus had wanted to help but they'd told him to relax, and he'd done as he was told, just grateful for the company. He'd turned to Perez at one point: 'It's as though the old place has woken up after years asleep.' No bitterness at the years of isolation, only joy for the present.

Now it felt as if the old place was sleeping again. There were no sheep on the in-bye land and the grass was brown and overgrown. No smell of peat smoke or tobacco coming from the house. Willow joined Perez on the flagstone doorstep. 'Well, is it open?'

He tried the door. There was a simple latch and it opened immediately. The wood was a little warped and it stuck for a moment against the stone floor, but another push and they were inside. Perez felt on the rough wall for a light switch and suddenly the room was illuminated by a bare bulb hanging from the ceiling. The place was much as he remembered. The scrubbed table under the window, the Shetland chair with its uneven drawer under the seat, the sheepskin rugs on the stone floor. It felt cold — Magnus had lit a fire every evening, even in the summer — and there was a layer of dust on the furniture.

'Did you know him well?' Willow moved to the ledge over the fire. The round-faced clock had stopped. Perez remembered its ticking as a background to the uncomfortable conversations he'd had with the man. The two of them sitting, face-to-face, discussing the disappearance of a child. That had been winter too, but the weather had been unusually still and there'd been snow on the ground.

'I arrested him once.'

Perhaps something in his voice told her that the idea still disturbed him, or perhaps she knew all about that case, because she didn't follow it up with a further question.

'So we're assuming that Magnus must have had the keys to Tain and we want to know if they're still here.' Her voice was brisk and cheerful. He wondered if she'd ever been sad — so sad that nothing in the world outside her head mattered. Then he thought he was being self-indulgent; what his first wife Sarah had called emotionally incontinent. Perhaps Willow was just better at handling grief. She was a stronger and more balanced individual.

'I think so. He was a very trusting soul. He'd have given up the keys to anyone with a reasonable explanation for wanting them. And of course he'd never met Alissandra Sechrest, so it'd be easy enough for someone to take him in.' Perez began opening the painted wooden cupboards. Magnus had very few possessions: some pans and pots, a couple of cups, saucers and plates, sufficient cutlery for two people in a handmade wooden box. Perez thought there'd been more clutter when he'd first visited, remnants of the old man's childhood, his mother's belongings. Perez remembered that Magnus had donated some items to the jumble stall at the Ravenswick Sunday teas. Perhaps that had been his way of coming to terms with the past. Or maybe he'd just thought they were ugly and gathering dust and he'd wanted shot of them.

'He'd heard Alissandra Sechrest speak, though,' Willow said. 'Anyone coming to see him, to collect the keys, would have had to use an American accent to be convincing.'

Perez shrugged. He thought any accent that wasn't Shetland would have seemed strange to Magnus. And if the mysterious dark-haired woman had come here, she'd have charmed him. Magnus had remained single all his life, but he'd always had an eye for a pretty woman. 'Anyone who watches TV from the US would probably have done well enough to fool Magnus.'

Perez moved on round the room. Willow seemed to realize this was more than a routine investigation, that Perez had a personal connection with the place, because she stood quite still and let him continue the search unhindered.

Under the sink was a galvanized bucket, a scrubbing brush, washing powder and pegs. On the other side of the room stood a large Victorian sideboard. Dark wood, engraved with florid flowers and leaves, lush vegetation that would never have grown in the islands. A prized family possession. In the drawers were the records of Magnus's life, personal and business. Receipts for lambs sent to the slaughterhouse, the details of sales, in a sprawling hand. A savings book showing a balance of £2,500 with the Orkney and Shetland building society. Cheque books going back decades, neatly folded and fastened with elastic bands. Nothing had been removed. The distant relatives from the south who had come to bury the old man had taken the ferry back to Aberdeen on the evening of the landslide, anxious that they might be trapped in the islands by another act of nature. Shetland must have seemed a very hostile place to them. Perez had spoken to them briefly. They'd said they would come back when the weather was better, to sort out the estate. One was a businessman and one a university lecturer, and the only sense they had of the place where their grandparents had been born came from stories and legends.

In the sideboard there were Christmas cards, saved in a shoebox. Minnie Laurenson had obviously sent one each year. The subject matter was always religious and the message, carefully written in black ink, always the same: *Season's greetings from your very good friend.* Two single people who were neighbours and friends. Perez wondered if there'd ever been a romantic connection, and thought that even if there had been, Magnus's mother would probably have discouraged it. Then he came across a handmade card. The image on the front a child's handprint in green paint, turned by an adult into a fat Christmas tree. Inside the message: *To Magnus, merry Christmas from Cassie and Fran.* Two kisses, sprawling and drawn by the toddler that Cassie must have been then. Perez put the lid back on the shoebox, shoved it back into the ugly sideboard and moved into the other room.

The bedroom seemed even emptier than the kitchen. In the wardrobe a suit, shiny and threadbare, brought out for funerals and weddings. And for being taken into custody. Perez felt in the pockets, but found nothing. In the drawers there were underclothes grey from age and from washing by hand. In the kitchen it seemed that Willow had wanted to check the sideboard for herself. Perez heard the clunk of the cupboard doors and the opening of the drawers. Perhaps she was curious about what had spooked him. He should have shown her the Christmas card from Fran. How hard would that have been? *Look, Cassie must have been very young when she did this.* He'd lacked the courage even to do that.

'Jimmy, there's a letter from Minnie Laurenson's solicitor.'

Of course Willow's search would have been

more thorough. She wouldn't have allowed herself to be distracted by the handwriting of a dead lover. Perez walked slowly back into the kitchen.

She'd put the letter on the kitchen table. It had the Rogerson and Taylor printed letterhead and was dated nine months previously. The wording was formal and rather imperious:

> We understand that you have in your possession the keys to Tain, Gulberswick Road, Ravenswick, now the property of our client Ms Alissandra Sechrest. We would be grateful if you could return the fore-mentioned keys to our office at 6 Commercial Street, Lerwick, at your earliest convenience.

'Would he have taken the keys into the office?' Willow was standing almost directly under the bare bulb, and her face looked shiny and hard like a plastic doll's.

'Oh, I think so. Magnus was a bit scared of anyone in authority. Something like this would have made him nervous. He'd have been on the first bus into town with the keys in his pocket.'

'So the murdered woman pretending to be Alissandra didn't get the keys from here.' Willow moved a little and now it was her hair that caught the light. Perez thought it was like spun sugar, a little burnt, turned into caramel.

'It seems not.' But he was distracted. He read the letter again. 'Doesn't this seem a bit heavy-handed to you? I mean, why not just phone up Magnus and ask him to drop the keys into the office next time he was in town? They'd know he wouldn't do any damage to Tain.'

She shrugged. 'Isn't that lawyers for you?'

'Aye, maybe.'

Willow had moved into the bedroom and was searching there. It irritated Perez that she couldn't trust him to do a good job. But after all, he'd missed the solicitor's letter, so he was in no position to complain. She came back into the kitchen.

'Anything?'

She shook her head. 'It always seems a terrible intrusion, going through a dead person's belongings. Much worse, somehow, than searching when the owner is around.'

'So a wasted trip,' he said. 'I'm sorry to have dragged you up here.'

'What is it the scientists say? That even negative results are significant. And maybe you're right about the solicitor's letter. It's certainly worth following up with them.'

Perez switched off the light and they stood outside. While they'd been in the house the fine rain had stopped and there were patchy breaks in the clouds, the occasional glimpse of a half-moon. 'Do you want to come back to mine for a coffee?'

She paused for a moment. When she spoke he couldn't see her face, but he could hear the smile in her voice. 'Ah, Jimmy. I don't think you're in the mood for company tonight.'

They walked down the hill in silence towards the lights of his house and he wasn't sure whether to be relieved or sorry.

He saw Willow into her car and waved her away. There'd been no phone reception on the hill, but now his mobile started buzzing with texts and emails. The house seemed empty without Cassie's chatter. The breakfast dishes were still dirty on the draining board and he washed them, before looking at his phone. He thought there was nothing now that couldn't wait and he was still reliving the shock of seeing Fran's handwriting in Magnus's Christmas card. He had little written by her. Neither of them had been sentimental. There was no shoebox full of cards in this house. All he had was her last shopping list, attached to the fridge by a puffin magnet, and the letter she'd written him in Fair Isle, half-joking and half-serious, bequeathing him her daughter in the event of her death. That was hidden away in a secret place. He'd been tempted to throw it away, but knew he'd have to show it to Cassie when she was old enough.

He made a cup of tea and looked at his phone. A list of routine messages that he'd answer the following day. Suddenly he felt very tired. And then he saw there was a recent voicemail from Sandy. The man was so excited that Perez had to play it twice before he could properly understand it. It seemed Sandy had seen Tom Rogerson in the Scalloway Hotel with a strange woman. Perez thought there was little suspicious in that. Tom had business meetings all the time. Sandy's last sentence was more interesting: 'They drove off in separate vehicles, boss. And Tom Rogerson's car has a Shetland flag sticker on his bumper.'

Perez couldn't settle. He knew he should go to bed, but he was too wired, and instead he sat by the remains of the fire and played out the events of the evening in his head. The fact that Tom Rogerson had the Shetland flag as a bumper sticker was interesting, but shouldn't be given too much importance — so did half the local population. Perez worked through the search of Magnus's house. He'd been distracted from the moment he'd entered the place, by memories of the old man and of Fran. Willow had been too sensitive to criticize or insist that they go through the house more thoroughly. Perez pulled on his boots, went outside and walked back up the bank towards Hillhead.

It was colder than he'd remembered and even brighter; there was almost constant moonlight, covered at times by brown-edged clouds. He found gloves in his pocket and pulled them on as he walked. He didn't bother with the torch. At the house he forced himself to concentrate on the present, went straight in and switched on the light. He stood in the centre of the room and looked around, forcing himself to consider places they might have missed on the first sweep. Finally he arrived at the Shetland chair. Straight back, low arms, all once made of driftwood pulled from the shore. And beneath the seat a drawer. Croft houses had been small and shared with animals; no space could be wasted. Willow wouldn't have realized.

He stooped and pulled open the drawer. At first he was disappointed. It seemed empty. Then he saw there was a brown envelope lying flat on the base. It was almost the same size as the drawer, so he'd taken it at first as a paper lining. No writing on the front and not stuck down. So thin that he warned himself it was probably empty. Still wearing his gloves, he slid the content onto the table. A glossy coloured photograph. The head and shoulders of a woman. The shoulders bare, so even though there was only the suggestion of the curve of her breasts, it was mildly titillating. The photo was of the murdered woman, though this was a younger version and must have been taken at least ten years earlier.

14

Late Saturday night, and Jane sat in the house waiting. Kevin had gone to bed, tired after a day working with the engineers on the road. Michael was staying at his girlfriend's house in Brae. But Andy was still out, and it was Andy who worried her. She'd sent him a text and tried to phone, but there'd been no reply.

He'd been on the early shift at Mareel. If someone had called in sick or he'd been asked to stay on to work late, he would have been in touch. Jane knew he wasn't the most reliable son in the world, but there was reception in that part of town and even if he hadn't phoned, he would have texted. Before he'd gone away to university they'd been close. During his study leave for Highers he'd come into the kitchen and perch on one of the countertops, long legs swinging, dark eyes full of mischief, and talk about his dreams. He'd be a film-maker or a script editor, or he'd form a company of clowns and tour the world. She'd never known when he was being serious or when he was winding her up, but she'd loved the conversations. He was a member of the Youth Theatre and some days she'd run through the script with him and help him learn his lines.

Her first response when he'd told them he was staying in Shetland and not returning to university had been selfish. She'd been over-joyed. She'd missed him dreadfully, not just as a son but as a companion. Kevin's talk was of lamb prices and family gossip. Like Simon Agnew, Andy had provided a view onto a wider world. She'd been worried, of course, that he was throwing away a great opportunity, but she'd thought he could make a career for himself in the islands. She was using the Internet to sell her produce nationwide; surely he could use his enthusiasm to make a name for himself in whatever field he chose in a similar way. She even dreamed that he might join her business. He could be her marketing manager, develop her website and use his artistic talents in her advertising.

But the Andy who returned from Glasgow had been very different from the lad who went away on the ferry, the family car full of his belongings and books. He was withdrawn and battered. When she tried to talk to him, he turned away. He still had friends in the islands, but they were never invited back to the house. She no longer woke up to find the living-room floor covered with young people of both sexes curled up in sleeping bags, looking like enormous slugs. He'd found work in Mareel easily enough, but still he seemed isolated. He could turn on the charm and the banter for the customers in the bar, but when he came home he seemed exhausted and spent most of his time in his room. She'd asked Simon's advice, wondered if Andy was clinically depressed, but Simon had said just to give it time.

Her phone pinged with a text and she felt a surge of relief. It would be from Andy, telling her that he was spending the night with a friend — maybe that he'd had too much to drink to drive home. And wasn't that a good sign? Even though her secret fear was that he'd inherited her addictive personality and that at university he'd somehow got caught up with drugs. If he was partying with his mates, at least it would mean that he had started to socialize again. But the text was from Rachel, the young woman she was sponsoring at AA: *Are you still awake? OK to chat?*

At first Jane was tempted to ignore the message. She had her own worries, which had nothing to do with Rachel. Then she thought at least talking to the younger woman might distract her from her anxiety about Andy. There was a kind of superstition in thinking he wouldn't arrive while she was still worrying about him. If she was behaving more normally — talking to Rachel, as she often did — he might sail into the house full of apologies and with a rational explanation for not staying in touch.

Rachel answered on the first ring.

'How are things?' Jane tried to keep her voice cheerful and unworried. 'You're up late. Working a late shift?'

'Yes, just got in.' A pause. 'I was feeling a bit low, actually.'

'Anything specific?'

'Not really. I'll feel happier when they catch this killer. You must be petrified; it happened so close to where you live.'

Jane thought they'd all feel happier once the killer was caught. Now there was a general suspicion of anyone who lived in the area. She'd started looking at her neighbours differently. Wondering.

'How's work been?'

Work was Rachel's stress point, but also her comfort zone. She was more comfortable talking about the patients who turned up in A&E than she was discussing her own problems.

'I saw a child who's been self-harming. She's only thirteen and the family seems stable, happy. Who knows what's behind it? That's for the psychs and not for me.' But all the same Rachel seemed to feel the need for an explanation. 'Peer pressure maybe. She seems to be one of those kids who's a little bit desperate, who tries too hard to be part of the gang. The ones destined to be rejected.'

Was that you? Jane wondered — not about Rachel, but about herself. *Were you destined to be rejected? Is that why you acccpted Kevin so readily, when he came along to sweep you off your feet? Because you were grateful to have been picked out?*

She didn't come to a conclusion because she thought she heard the sound of a car on the track. She strained to listen, but everything seemed quiet outside. Certainly Andy hadn't come into the house. It must have been her imagination. Wishful thinking. She continued her conversation with Rachel, reassured by the stories of other people's accidents and traumas. After all, her own life was almost trouble-free.

When she replaced the phone, Rachel seemed happier. It was almost two o'clock and Jane decided to go to bed. Andy wouldn't be coming back now and she didn't want to try phoning again. He was probably asleep. Perhaps he'd hooked up with a girl. Or a boy — since he'd been a young teenager she'd suspected he might be gay, though she'd never quite found the words to ask. Whatever, he wouldn't want to be disturbed. This was Shetland; if any harm had come to him, someone would soon tell her.

She took her coffee mug into the kitchen and saw that Andy's car was in the yard. It must have been him that she'd heard coming down the track when she was speaking to Rachel. But he certainly wasn't in the house. She pulled on her shoes and went out to check if he was still in the vehicle. Perhaps he was asleep there and she'd wake him and bring him into the warm. But the car was empty. The clouds blew away from the moon and there was a sudden wash of pale light over the land that led down towards the sea. Andy was standing close to the wall that separated their land from Tain's. He was staring down towards the wreckage that had once been a house. She was about to call out to him, to ask what the matter was, but something about the way he was standing, so hard and upright, prevented her from disturbing him. She went back into the house and went to bed.

15

The police station was Sunday-quiet, despite the investigation. They met in the ops room, with superior coffee from the machine in Perez's office and chocolate biscuits on a chipped plate. Perez had the photo he'd found in Magnus Tait's house on the table in front of him. Vicki Hewitt was still at Tain, sorting through the debris, but Willow and Sandy were there.

'You went back to the house, Jimmy?' Willow found it hard to understand that. Perez had seemed almost lost in the old man's house. She'd cut the visit short, partly because it seemed like a wild goose chase — why bother looking for the Tain keys if they'd obviously been delivered to the solicitor? But partly because Perez had seemed so uncomfortable in the place.

'I just remembered that I hadn't looked in the small drawer under the chair.' Perez was dark-eyed and dishevelled. It was as if he hadn't slept at all.

Willow thought this was how he'd been the first time they'd met: exhausted and preoccupied. At least now the preoccupation seemed to be with the investigation. 'And at last we have a name,' she said. She wanted to add a few words of congratulations. *Well done, Jimmy!* But she knew him well enough to realize he'd bristle at that and find the tone patronizing.

Perez turned the photo face-down and they all

looked at the signature on the back. It was clear, almost childish. *Alison Teal.*

'Alis.' Willow looked round the table. 'The letter Sandy found in the box in Tain must have been to Alison, not Alissandra. A weird coincidence.'

Perez turned the photo back so that the image stared out at them. 'It looks like one of those publicity shots that marketing departments send out to fans. There's nothing personal about this. Not even something bland like: *To Magnus with very best wishes.* What do we think? Was she a singer? Actor?'

'I kind of recognize her.' Sandy screwed up his face. When he concentrated he looked like a small boy.

'How would Magnus get the photo of a pop star?' Willow knew she'd have nothing to contribute to this discussion. In the commune, popular culture had been despised. She'd tried to get into rock music and soap operas as a form of rebellion, but the indoctrination had been too deep. 'And why?'

'He only got a television about a year ago,' Perez said, 'and this photo is a lot older than that.'

'She was Dolly Jasper.' Sandy was jubilant that the memory had surfaced. 'The maid in that TV drama set in a big house in the country in Victorian times. You know the kind.' He looked round at them. 'It was on a Sunday night. My parents loved it. I was only a kid; it must have been nearly twenty years ago.'

'So perhaps Magnus got to see the TV show.'

146

Perez spoke slowly, but he was fully engaged now. Willow could see the ideas sparking in his head. 'Maybe at Minnie Laurenson's house — Tain, where all this started. Minnie kept in touch with the old man even when the rest of Ravenswick left him to himself. I can imagine a regular invitation: Sunday tea and then an evening in front of the telly. It would have been a treat for Magnus.'

'And you're saying he fancied the actress and sent away for a photo?' Willow was sceptical. She could imagine the lonely old man becoming attracted to a pretty young actress. Obsessed even. People had considered Magnus simple. But she couldn't see him being sufficiently organized to find the address of the TV production company and write to them.

'Maybe. He liked objects that reminded him of people he'd taken to,' Perez said. 'There was no harm in it.'

Willow wasn't sure about that. It didn't seem healthy, a lonely old man drooling over the glossy photo of a pretty young woman.

'She came to Shetland!' It was Sandy again, almost beside himself with excitement. 'It was a big story. Maybe you were away south working then, Jimmy, or you'd surely have remembered it. The actress who played Dolly suddenly disappeared. There was a media campaign to find her. She'd been depressed and there was stuff in the media about drugs. The first thought was that she'd gone back to rehab somewhere, but she'd just run away to Shetland. When they found her she said she'd chosen Shetland after

147

seeing it on a map. It looked so far to the north that it seemed like an escape. No other reason. Just that she was feeling low and wanted to run away. She drove to Aberdeen, left her car there and came up on the ferry.'

Willow thought that sounded a bit like the Agatha Christie disappearance; she did have a taste for popular fiction and had read about Christie vanishing, before turning up in a hotel in Harrogate some time later. 'Was it just a publicity stunt?'

'I don't think so. One of the diners in the Ravenswick Hotel recognized her. Otherwise nobody would have known who she was. She spent all day on her own, out walking.'

'So she'd come to Ravenswick.' Perez was writing on the whiteboard now, frantically making connections before he lost their thread. 'She might have come across Tain on one of her wanders through the countryside. She might even have met Minnie and Magnus.'

'Was this last trip a return visit, do you think?' Willow was following his train of thought. 'For a similar reason. There was another crisis in her life and she saw Shetland as her sanctuary again. It could explain why she travelled under an assumed identity. Even if she's not as famous as she was in the rest of the UK, a Shetlander might recognize her name.'

'And the desperate call to Simon Agnew at Befriending Shetland fits in with her having some form of emotional turmoil or breakdown.'

'We still need to know how she got hold of the keys to Tain.' Willow felt a wave of optimism, now that their victim had an identity. Not only because it meant a shift in gear for the investigation, but because it might give Perez a more reasoned perspective on the case. A minor soap star with psychiatric problems was less entrancing, surely, than a mysterious dark-eyed stranger.

'Someone in Shetland must have known her real identity and must have been protecting her.' Perez was scribbling on the whiteboard again.

'Tom Rogerson?'

'He seems the obvious person. He has the reputation as a lady's man and he had access to the keys.'

'Would he have written the letter to Alis, do you think? The letter that Sandy found?'

There was a moment of complete silence in the room while Perez considered the question. 'I don't know,' he said at last. 'Maybe it's best to keep an open mind.'

'Magnus? Could he have written it before his stroke?'

This time Perez answered more quickly. 'I know Magnus's writing and I don't think it's his. We have the notebooks, though, and we can get them checked.'

Sandy reached out for the last chocolate biscuit. Willow thought he'd been eyeing it up for some time, waiting to see if anyone else wanted it, but now his arm shot out quickly, like the tongue of a fat snake. 'So what are the plans for today?'

Willow got in before Perez. 'We find out what Alison Teal had been doing since she last turned up in Shetland. I want to know everything about her. Work, family life, medical history. And Jimmy and I are going to visit a lawyer.'

★　★　★

It was Sunday, so the solicitors' office in Commercial Street would be shut. Perez and Willow were still in the ops room; Sandy had returned to his office. 'How do you want to play this?' Willow wandered around the big table collecting rubbish and taking it to the bin, piling up cups. She was restless and couldn't keep still. 'You know the man, and I've never met him. Should we phone him first to warn him that we're coming?' She came to a stop and watched Perez.

'I'm not sure,' he said at last. There was a silence while he thought the idea through and then he chose his words. 'Tom's a committee man. A councillor. He has influence in the islands. Best to follow procedure, show some respect.' Another pause. 'Besides, he's kind of slippery. I don't think anyone really understands him, except maybe his family.' Perez looked out of the window, before speaking again. 'I know his daughter. Kathryn. She works at the Ravenswick school. She teaches Cassie.'

Willow thought that was another complication. It was always that way in a Shetland investigation; within the islands there was a web of relationships, personal and professional, blurred. Perez would feel awkward upsetting the Rogersons, because their daughter cared for his beloved Cassie. He wouldn't let that get in the way of his work, but he'd be aware of it, over-compensating at times.

'So you think we should ring first?' Willow was starting to lose patience. She wanted to be away from the confines of the police station; it was time to start asking questions, to dig around in the solicitor's life, to make it less comfortable.

'It would be more polite.'

'And who should do that, Jimmy? You or me? Let's just get on with it, shall we?'

Again he took a moment to consider. 'I'll do it,' he said in the end. 'It would seem too formal coming from you and it might scare him off.' He took his mobile from his jacket pocket and scrolled down the contacts list to find the number. In the corridor outside, somebody walked along whistling.

The phone rang for such a long time that Willow was expecting a recorded voicemail to kick in. But Perez hung on and, when it was answered, it soon became clear to her that it was Rogerson's wife. Perez sat down at the corner of the conference table.

'Hello, Mavis. I'm sorry to catch you at this ungodly hour on a Sunday.'

Willow couldn't hear the response, but Perez gave a little chuckle. 'No, it's not Kathryn I'm after today, so you can let her have her beauty sleep. I was hoping we might have a couple of words with Tom. It's kind of work-related and we'd like to ask his advice about something to do with this dead woman. We wondered if we could come round and disturb you. Relieve you of some of that baking maybe.'

Willow thought Perez was brilliant at this. The woman would be disarmed.

'I see, I see.' Perez pulled a face at Willow. This obviously wasn't going to be as easy as simply bowling up to the Rogerson house and talking to the man. 'And when are you expecting him back?'

A response from Mavis on the other end of the line.

'So maybe the best thing would be to make an appointment to see him at the office on Tuesday morning. Do you have a mobile number for him? Yes, I understand reception can be a bit tricky there, but I might strike lucky, huh?' Perez reached out for a pad left on the table after a previous meeting and scribbled down the number. 'Goodbye, Mavis. And thanks to you and Kathryn for your help with Cassie last week. I appreciate it.'

'Well?' Willow was starting to think Rogerson was the key to the whole case. She was convinced now that he was the man who'd collected Alison Teal from the Co-op in Brae the day before the landslide.

'He's away to Orkney apparently. There's an EU fisheries meeting there tomorrow and he won't be home until the last flight on Monday.'

'Convenient.' Willow knew she sounded like a spoilt child but couldn't help herself. 'Why the need to fly down so early, if the meeting isn't until tomorrow.'

'According to Mavis, he has friends in Kirkwall. He was using the business trip as an excuse to catch up with them. She's given me his business mobile number. She says that's the one he'll answer.'

Willow began to pace up and down the room again, trying to ease away her frustration with the movement.

'Do you want me to phone him and get him back here?' Perez waved the scrap of paper with the scribbled number. 'He should be able to get on a plane today and take an early flight back to Orkney tomorrow morning before the meeting, if it's so important that he's there. Or we could go to Orkney to talk to *him*.'

Willow was tempted by that suggestion. She liked the idea of a dramatic chase down to Sumburgh to get onto a flight, visiting a group of islands unfamiliar to her, but she shook her head. 'We don't want Rogerson to think he's that important to us. He's a lawyer. As you say, slippery. Let's use the extra days to find out a bit more about him, so that when we do meet we have something concrete to put to him.'

She wandered over to the window, then turned back to face the room and Jimmy Perez. 'Let's set up a meeting with his partner. Did you say his name was Taylor?'

Perez nodded. 'Paul Taylor.'

'Wasn't he the person who drew up Minnie Laurenson's will? It would make sense, if he kept the keys to Tain. Besides, it would be good to get his perspective on his colleague before we meet up with Rogerson next week.'

Perez nodded.

Glancing back at the window, Willow saw that

a rainbow was throwing its stained-glass colours across the grey street below.

16

They arrived late morning at Paul Taylor's house and it was clearly a bad time to roll up. The solicitor had three young boys and they were fractious and bored, rolling around on the floor fighting.

'I was just about to take them to the leisure centre.' Taylor's voice was English and tense. 'Let them get rid of some of that energy in the pool. This time of year they seem to be stuck indoors all day.' He looked out of the window as another shower blew against the glass.

His wife was in the kitchen, slamming pans. A dining table was already laid. Tablecloth and glasses, place settings for seven. 'My parents came up for Up Helly Aa and decided to spend a little time in the islands. They're staying in a hotel — for obvious reasons, they find that more civilized — but we've invited them to Sunday lunch . . . ' His voice tailed off again. Perez understood. His first wife, Sarah, had been a great one for family rituals, but always ended up resenting the effort involved.

'We won't take long.' Willow sidestepped a flailing arm from the tangled heap on the floor and sat down on the sofa. This was a modern house in Gulberswick, a village just to the south of Lerwick and a prime commuting location. Large living room and four bedrooms, double garage and utility room. It would have fetched a southern price. 'Just a few questions.'

Taylor nodded, parted the boys with some difficulty and sent them upstairs. 'You can use the computer in the office. Fifteen minutes. Then we'll head out to Clickimin for a bit, before we eat.'

There were whoops of joy as the boys pounded upstairs. Suddenly the room felt unnaturally quiet.

'Your firm administers Tain, the house in Ravenswick that was wrecked in the landslide.' Willow leaned forwards, her elbows on her knees. She looked relaxed, but the words were formal. 'We're wondering why you didn't contact the police service when we asked for information about the owner.'

Taylor had taken an armchair with his back to the window. Perez was still standing.

'I didn't realize we *did* look after the property,' Taylor said. 'That's routine stuff, and the girls in the office manage lettings for us.'

'It formed part of a bequest in a will that you drew up.' Willow was precise and firm. She could have been a lawyer herself. 'The deceased was a Minnie Laurenson.'

'It was *that* property!' He seemed shocked.

Willow persisted. 'You drew up the woman's will. You must have known where she lived.'

'No. We'd just moved to Shetland when Miss Laurenson came into the office to discuss her affairs. Now I'd be able to place the house, but then anywhere outside Lerwick was rather a mystery. The will was very straightforward. The house was to go to a niece in the States. Any

156

remaining cash to a medical charity. I remember it so well because Minnie Laurenson was my first client in Shetland.' He smiled. An attempt to charm Willow. It was a pleasant smile and Perez thought he probably used it often to get his own way.

But Willow refused to be charmed. 'Last year the house was let out rent-free to Craig Henderson.'

'Yes, we spoke to Miss Sechrest on the phone. She called *us*, in fact, and asked our opinion about allowing him to use it. Then she gave instructions for us to let him have the keys.'

'Did you speak to Miss Sechrest personally?'

'No, but I was in the main office when Marie, our admin person, took the call, so I was aware of what was said.'

'You didn't advise her against allowing a stranger to move into her house?'

Taylor shook his head. 'He wasn't quite a stranger. Craig's family is known to us. We act for them in their business dealings. They have upmarket tourist accommodation. I couldn't see that there would be a problem, if Ms Sechrest was happy with the arrangement. The house was fully insured.'

'What happened to the keys when Craig went overseas again?'

'I'm pretty sure he dropped them back into the office before he left, but as I say, one of the girls in the office would have taken them. There's a locked cabinet where the keys to the properties that we administer are kept.'

'So you'd be able to tell us if the Tain keys are still there?'

'You want me to go to the office to check now?' He sounded horrified. Upstairs, interest in the computer game seemed to be waning. There was a squawk of pain after what could have been a karate kick. Then a wail: 'Dad!'

'You could give us your office keys,' Willow said, 'and we could check for ourselves and just drop them through your door later, so we don't disturb the family while you're having lunch.'

Taylor hesitated, but only briefly. He took a bunch of keys from a hook in the entrance hall. 'This is the front door and this one's the door to reception. The cabinet's in there, and this one will open it. The hooks inside are all labelled with the names of the property and the client.'

Perez waited for Taylor to take the individual keys from the ring, but instead he dropped the whole bunch into Willow's waiting hand. She rewarded him with her own huge smile. 'Thank you so much, Mr Taylor. Now we'll leave you and your family in peace.' At the door she hesitated, though. 'Does the name Alison Teal mean anything to you?'

He was distracted by the kids upstairs and took no time to consider. 'No. Should it?' As they left the house he was yelling at the boys to get ready or they wouldn't have time for a swim. Throughout the whole encounter his wife hadn't appeared.

⋆ ⋆ ⋆

The solicitors' office was on Commercial Street and formed a corner with one of the steep lanes leading up to the library. The street was almost empty and few shops were open. A chill breeze blew down it, occasionally scattering clouds for a moment to lighten the sky before the rain continued. One man stood huddled at the ATM at the bank close by, but he took no notice of them as they let themselves into the building. They walked into a narrow corridor and had to step over Saturday's post lying on the laminate floor. To the right an unlocked door led to a seating area. This was presumably where clients waited to see the solicitor of their choice. A sliding glass window opened from there into the receptionists' office: a desk with two computers, a stack of filing cabinets. This office was reached through a door that faced the main entrance. Willow fumbled a few times to find the right key, then she unlocked it and they walked in.

'Why did Taylor give us access to all the offices?' Willow stood in the middle of the small room and looked around. 'Has he got nothing to hide or was it a kind of double bluff? To make us believe he's not worried about what we might find.'

Perez shrugged. 'He seemed genuine enough to me. Not a natural-born father, perhaps, but harassed and he just wanted us out of his house.'

The keys to the properties that the firm administered were in a narrow painted wooden cupboard on the interior wall. Inside there was a row of hooks, just as Taylor had described. The one labelled 'Sechrest,' Ravenswick' held a ring

159

with one Yale and one Chubb. 'No mention of Tain,' Willow said. 'So Taylor might not have connected it with the house destroyed in the slip. He could be telling the truth.'

'The fact that the keys are here doesn't mean Alison Teal didn't use them to get into the house.' Perez thought they'd become fixated on the small details of the case and that he'd lost the bigger picture. He wanted to escape the office with its heavy furniture and bloated pot-plants. He thought they should have chased down Tom Rogerson in Orkney after all. 'If Rogerson was helping the woman, he'd just have to make copies.'

'Of course. But while we're here, it would be crazy not to have a cheeky look into the offices.' Willow held the bunch of keys by one finger and wiggled them until they made a jangling noise that jarred on Perez's nerves. 'Mr Taylor gave these to us, after all. Of his own free will.'

The partners had offices on the first floor. Taylor's looked out at the lane and faced the blank side of a large hotel. Even in summer the room must have been perpetually dark. Now they needed the light on, to see it in any detail. The desk was under the window and held a fierce anglepoise lamp and a photograph of three apparently angelic boys in identical hand-knitted jerseys. A second photo was of a woman who must be his wife. She had sharp, fox-like features and looked rather severe.

'Hard to believe it's the same family.' Willow shot Perez a grin. He knew she'd never had much time for conventional relationships. The commune had affected her more than she was willing to let on. Perez thought it was unfair to make a judgement about people they'd only met briefly on a wet Sunday.

Rogerson's office was at the front of the building and was the grander of the two, with a large desk that looked genuinely old, shelves of impressive textbooks, more shiny pot-plants on the windowsill and framed diplomas on the walls. Also on the wall, a photo of the man shaking Nicola Sturgeon's hand. Another of Rogerson in a grinning group of men standing next to David Cameron. Willow was ranging around the room and nodded towards the pictures.

'Keeping his options open,' she said. 'Is that the sort of man he is?'

Perez thought about that. 'He'd always want to be on the winning side.'

'Ah, that's not criminal.' She paused for a beat. 'Unfortunately.' She landed up in front of a filing cabinet and tried a number of keys until it opened.

'Is that entirely legal?'

'Taylor gave us the keys. He knew we wanted them to pursue our investigation.'

'He wouldn't expect us to pry into his clients' affairs.' Perez wished he didn't sound so pompous.

'You're quite right, Jimmy, but let me just see if there's a file for Alison Teal in here. If Rogerson is the man she met in Brae and in Mareel, he must have come across her at some point in the past, to develop the relationship

161

— whatever that relationship was. I can just about imagine Magnus Tait falling for Alison's charms when she first visited the islands, and being happy with a signed photo, but that doesn't seem credible for Tom Rogerson.' Willow looked up. 'You said Rogerson worked in the south for a while. Would he even have *been* in Shetland when Ms Teal did her disappearing act?'

'Oh yes, he'd have been working here then. He came home when Kathryn was still very young, still a baby.'

Willow looked as if she was going to say something, but turned back to the filing cabinet. 'Nothing on Alison Teal.'

She moved over to join Perez at the desk and started opening the drawers. None of them were locked and they seemed to contain material relating to Rogerson's council work rather than his legal practice: booklets about health and welfare matters, tourist brochures.

Perez was thinking they were wasting their time here. Under the desk he found a bin that still contained scraps of paper. He pulled out a handwritten note that must have been left for Rogerson's assistant. *Please make sure the client signs this as soon as possible.* He flattened it and stepped aside so that Willow could see it properly. 'What do you think?'

'I'd need to see the original again, but this writing looks very similar to the letter Sandy found in Tain.'

'Another connection then,' Perez said. 'And a possible suspect.'

17

Jane Hay was cooking Sunday lunch for the family. She didn't feel like bothering, but she'd made a big deal about it earlier in the week:

'You're not at Mareel on Sunday, are you, Andy? Let's get everyone together. We haven't done a proper Sunday lunch for ages. Bring Gemma along too, Michael.'

So now she was in the kitchen peeling potatoes and parsnips, and the smell of the shoulder of lamb she was slow-roasting in the bottom of the Aga made her feel slightly sick. She told herself she was tired, that was all. It was her own fault, for being so ridiculous about Andy arriving home late last night. She couldn't blame him. He was an adult and was used to having his own life away at university. He could have been up to anything in Glasgow and she'd never have known about it, so why did she expect him to keep her posted about his every move here?

She set down the knife, slipped her feet into the pair of rubber clogs that stood by the door and went out into the nearest polytunnel. She could do with more rosemary for the lamb and some mint for the sauce, but really she just needed a few minutes away from the house. Since the landslide, it had seemed like a different place. It wasn't just that the view was disfigured and that now, looking down towards the coast, she could see the dark scar left by the mud. It was as if the shifting land had loosened the foundations of the family. There was nothing firm left. She couldn't believe anything that either Kevin or the boys told her.

She pulled a couple of twigs of rosemary from the bush, gathered a handful of mint and returned to the kitchen. Andy was standing there. He was wearing tracksuit bottoms and a sleeveless vest that she didn't recognize and he was staring into space.

'I wasn't expecting you up yet.' Her voice sounded tinny and too bright and seemed to echo from the tiles and the shiny worktops. 'You must have been late back. I was up chatting to Rachel on the phone until the early hours.'

He didn't say anything. It seemed to her then that he was utterly miserable. She wanted to go up to him and hug him to her, rest his head on her shoulder and stroke the soft, dark hair away from his eyes. 'Would you like a coffee?' she said.

It took an effort for him to respond. 'Yeah, that would be good.'

She turned her back on him to fill the filter machine with water and pour coffee into the paper, and when she turned back he was more his normal self. 'I hope you weren't worried. I only saw your texts this morning. No battery last night.'

'Ah, I thought it would be something like that.' She couldn't quite lie to him, but she couldn't tell him the truth. *Of course I was worried. I was frantic. Don't ever do that to me again.* Because, in the cold light of morning, she could see that she'd been overreacting, that her panic had been ridiculous. Andy was clearly going through some sort of crisis. Some relationship had broken down. He was home now. Safe. He would tell her why he was so unhappy, when he was ready. She put out of her mind the vision of her son the night before, standing in the darkness, looking down over the ruined croft at Tain. What connection could there be between him and the middle-aged woman who'd died? The idea that he might have some knowledge of her death — played some part in it even — was ludicrous.

She poured out the coffee and Andy sat with her at the table. When he picked up the mug his hand was shaking. She struggled to find a question that wasn't too intrusive or judgemental. *What were you up to last night?* That would surely alienate him. And she didn't want to put him in a position where he would be forced to lie. In the end they sat for a moment in silence and then she began to whisk egg whites in a bowl to make a pavlova. She'd already taken raspberries from the freezer. There would be two puddings, one cold and one hot, because both boys had a sweet tooth. The lunch seemed to be taking on a great significance; it almost made her think of a last supper. She whisked the eggs by hand, because she didn't want the noise of the machine. If the room was quiet, perhaps Andy would talk to her. But neither of them spoke and her arm became sore and strained with the beating, until she slipped the meringue into the bottom oven underneath the lamb.

Kevin was still out working on the road. Jane had been in bed when he left, but she'd been awake and had seen that he was jubilant because Sunday working meant extra money. He'd always valued his own worth according to the money he made for the farm. He'd brought her a cup of tea with two biscuits in the saucer and kissed her forehead before going out. Recently he'd been more thoughtful. It was like the old days when they'd first started dating.

Now she heard the tractor in the yard and he was there with them, in his stockinged feet after leaving his work boots in the porch. He pulled off his waterproofs and overalls. She was making a crumble now and looked up. 'How's it going?'

'It's going splendidly.' He seemed to be bursting with health, his cheeks red, droplets of rain in his hair and his beard. 'I suspect there'll be no more work after tomorrow, and it'll be left then to the council.'

He washed his hands under the tap by the sink. 'Something smells good.' He hadn't picked up any tension in the room, had hardly acknowledged Andy sitting there.

'I'll make some fresh coffee.' She rubbed her hands together to dust the flour from her fingers and waited for him to move away from the sink. 'Are you ready for some more, Andy?'

The younger man shook his head, slid off his chair and wandered away.

'What's wrong with him?' Kevin turned to look at the disappearing back. 'A hangover maybe.'

'Aye, maybe.' But Jane knew that a hangover

166

wasn't always as uncomplicated as Kevin made out and she worried about her son all over again.

★   ★   ★

Michael and Gemma had got the bus from Lerwick and walked down the track from the main road. Michael had been staying with Gemma at her parents' home in Lerwick. He gave his mother nothing to worry about, except that he might turn out to be a bit boring and she might end up with little to say to him. Jane could see his life unspooling ahead of him. He would marry Gemma and they'd build their own little house in Ravenswick. They'd have dull, well-behaved children and in ten years' time she'd still be cooking Sunday lunch for them, pretending to be interested in Gemma's work for the council and in Michael's limited ambitions for the farm.

She was surprised that she could be so spiteful. Why did she think her own life was so interesting? Wouldn't she be glad if Andy had his future mapped out and *he* gave her nothing to worry about?

A shaft of sunlight pierced the cloud and lit up the table. She'd decided that they would eat in the kitchen and was finishing the last-minute preparations for the meal, stirring a little flour into the meat juices to make the gravy. Kevin and Michael were in the living room, watching football on the television with cans of beer. Gemma was with her. She'd offered to help, but when Jane could think of nothing useful for her to do, she'd sat in the chair by the range to chat. Not quite in the way, so Jane couldn't ask her to move, but too close for Jane to be able to cook without the feeling that she was being scrutinized. Gemma was a gossip. Her father worked in the finance department of the council office and sometimes the talk was of island politics, at other times she just rambled about school friends, teachers or relatives. Usually Jane found the one-sided conversations relaxing, even vaguely entertaining, but today she was in the mood to be irritated, and she refused to respond. Gemma continued talking; either she didn't notice Jane's lack of interest or she didn't care. At least she wasn't someone who would take offence.

Jane was draining cabbage into the sink when a phrase from Gemma filtered through the muddle and inconsequence of her conversation.

'Your Andy's a dark horse.'

'What do you mean?' Jane looked up. Green water dribbled between the lid and the pan. She tipped the greens into a serving dish.

'Well . . . ' But before Gemma could say any more, the men came in. The footie was over and they were starving. Kevin gave Gemma a little hug of welcome. Jane wondered if he might have been happier with someone like Gemma. Someone with no imagination, from a safe, respectable family and carrying no baggage.

'I'll just call Andy.' Jane stood in the hall between the kitchen and the stairs. Looking back into the room, where Kevin was cutting the meat and Michael was opening a bottle of wine, she

168

thought anyone suddenly peering through the window would think *they* were a respectable family, with no hidden secrets or anxieties.

Andy appeared at the top of the stairs before she called him. He must have heard the rattle of plates and the voices in the kitchen. He didn't notice her. He looked into the mirror that was hanging in the upstairs corridor and she saw him prepare himself to meet them. She was reminded of his school play days, when he'd been very serious about getting into character. It seemed that had been good practice for what he needed now.

The meal passed without incident. Michael and Gemma always ate with concentration, their eyes on their plates as if they were scared the food would be taken away from them. Jane thought Gemma would grow fat in middle age, but she would be contented, easy-going. She had expected Andy to be quiet and withdrawn, but he became very bright and witty, telling stories about his colleagues at Mareel, holding court and enjoying the audience. Kevin seemed to be filling all their glasses very often and soon fetched another bottle of wine. Jane told herself again that this was all normal behaviour, but she was almost breathless with tension. In other company she might have been tempted to hold out her glass and ask for it to be filled. She looked down at her plate and saw that she'd eaten very little.

Still the meal dragged on. The pavlova was admired. She cut into the meringue and saw that it was perfect, crisp on the outside but just a little chewy in the middle, and felt a brief lift in her spirits. The crumble was eaten. Gemma and Michael took second helpings.

Kevin was on his feet. He seemed to be enjoying himself immensely. He liked to think of himself as a great family man and would certainly, Jane thought, make a perfect grandfather. Again she saw Sunday lunch after Sunday lunch rolling away into the future, the calendar punctuated by bigger but similar events: Christmas, family birthdays, anniversaries.

'You lasses go and sit down in front of the fire.' Kevin was playing with the fancy coffee machine that the boys had given him for his last birthday. 'We'll clear this up, won't we, boys?'

Gemma agreed immediately, although she hadn't played any part in the preparation of the meal, and Jane found herself sitting on the leather sofa in the living room, suddenly very quiet. Even Gemma had stopped talking. It was almost dark outside and the breeze had dropped. Jane got up to draw the curtains. She hoped Gemma had forgotten that she was going to pass on a morsel of gossip about Andy. It would be pleasant to sit here in the quiet. She felt very tired and she didn't want any revelations about her son.

But Gemma, it seemed, had not forgotten, and as soon as Kevin had brought in their coffee and left them alone, the girl continued where she'd left off. Her face was lit by a standard lamp and the rest of the room was in shadow. 'Well . . . ' A pause to make sure she had Jane's attention. 'My Auntie Jennifer saw Andy a couple of weeks ago.'

Jane didn't say anything. Gemma needed no encouragement, though Jane did wonder briefly how the girl's aunt would have recognized her son.

'She was a teacher at the Anderson High before she retired, so she knew Andy at once.' *The explanation.* 'And she said he was a fine boy, and so she couldn't believe what she was seeing.'

'And what was she seeing?' Jane curled her legs underneath her on the sofa, in an attempt to appear relaxed.

'An argument in the street, just outside the Grand Hotel. Andy swearing and shouting at a man old enough to be his father. Everyone staring.'

There was an overwhelming sense of relief. Jane had thought the story might involve the dead woman. She was aware of Gemma staring at her, expecting her to be horrified that Andy had caused a scene. 'Do you have any idea what it was about?' Because Andy was a gentle soul. Even as a child, he'd avoided confrontation.

The girl shook her head. 'I do know the guy Andy was attacking was threatening to call the police.'

'It just sounds like he got into a row with some drunk oilie.' The oilies were convenient scapegoats whenever there was trouble in town.

'It wasn't an oilie! Gemma was enjoying herself now. 'My Auntie Jennifer recognized him.' She'd been holding on to this piece of the story. She might not read much fiction, but she understood the need for dramatic tension. 'It was Tom Rogerson, the councillor.'

18

Sandy sat at his desk in the police station all morning, burrowing into the life of Alison Teal. He thought Jimmy Perez might be happier now that they had a name for her. Sandy had been hoping to meet Louisa for lunch at some point, but she'd decided to head back to Yell straight from the Scalloway Hotel.

'It's not that I don't want to spend a bit more time with you, but my mother will be missing me and, besides, you might be held up at work.'

At one time Sandy might have been offended by that and seen it as a personal rejection. But he understood that Louisa took her responsibility for her mother seriously. And, after the night they'd had in Scalloway, he wasn't in the mood to complain about anything. For the first half-hour at work he'd found it hard to concentrate on Alison Teal. He found himself grinning for no reason at all and wondering when he might ask Louisa to marry him. There was a slight awkwardness about that, because Jimmy Perez had not been engaged long when his woman was murdered. Sandy wouldn't want to do anything to stir up those bad memories for Jimmy, who seemed to have emerged from the worst of the depression; and besides, he felt a strange superstition about it, as if by asking Louisa to marry him, he might put *her* in danger too.

Alison Teal had a website all to herself. It must have been set up when she was playing Dolly, the housemaid in the TV drama, because the photo was the same as the one Jimmy had found in Magnus Tait's house. Nothing had been added to it for years; there was no information about recent roles. The website had the phone number of the actor's agent, but when Sandy phoned it, the call went straight through to an answer machine. It was clearly an office number and the agent wasn't working on a Sunday. Sandy left a message asking the woman to contact him urgently.

They still hadn't found any of Alison's relatives, and Jimmy Perez had told Sandy that was a priority: 'It's not just that they might have important information, but we need to inform them of Alison's death. She might well have parents who are still alive.' Sandy knew Perez had been thinking of the elderly people in the photo that Sandy had found in the box in Tain. It was obviously one of her treasured possessions. Sandy was distracted again now, thinking that he'd like a photograph of Louisa. A proper photograph, not just one taken on his phone to save on the computer. He turned back to the screen and continued his search.

Through Google he found an in-depth interview with Alison Teal in the *Independent on Sunday*. He printed it off, because he could tell it would be useful and Jimmy Perez preferred to have paper copies of anything he thought important. The interview had taken place a few months after Alison had disappeared and then been discovered in the Ravenswick Hotel. They'd fixed a date for the disappearance now: it had happened fifteen years ago. The journalist sounded almost like a psychiatrist, in the piece. Sandy wasn't sure that he'd want such personal information made public and put into a newspaper for folk to read while they were eating breakfast.

There was a lot about the actress's early life. Her parents had been junkies and she'd been brought up by her father's parents, who lived in Cromer, a small town on the Norfolk coast.

'Did you ever see your parents?' the reporter had asked.

The reply had been almost matter-of-fact. 'Not much. They'd turn up occasionally to bum money from Gran and Grandpa. But addicts don't care about much, except getting the next fix, do they? I dreamed about them getting straight and having me back home, but deep down I knew it was never going to happen. And we were happy with Gran and Grandpa. It made us different from the other kids at school, but even then there were lots of single parents around. At least there were two adults in our family. I can't really blame my screw-ups on an unhappy childhood.'

'Did you have any siblings?'

'A younger brother, Jono. Jonathan. He went into the army and we lost touch for a bit. I've seen more of him recently.'

The reporter pressed her on that, but Alison refused to go into more detail about her brother.

Sandy was already scribbling notes. Unless

174

Alison had taken a stage name, she could have inherited the name Teal from her father, and so probably from her paternal grandparents. And now Sandy had the name of the Norfolk town where they'd all lived. Alison had been forty-two when she died, so it was just possible that one of the grandparents was still alive. He could get on the phone to the local force and see if they could trace them. If Jonathan Teal was still in the army, it would be easy enough to get hold of him too. Jimmy Perez would be delighted if they could inform a relative of her death — if they could find a person who'd been close to her and who might grieve for her. Sandy returned to the interview in the newspaper.

'How did you get into acting?' Sandy imagined the reporter as older than Alison, rather cool and sophisticated.

'That was just luck! A friend was a member of a drama club and she dragged me along. I wasn't that keen, to begin with. I couldn't see the point of the warm-up exercises, all that prancing around and improvisation. But once they gave me a script, I was away. It was a chance to be someone else for a bit, I suppose. A kind of escape. My grandparents weren't sure at first. They thought I should get a more secure job. But they could see how much I loved it and, when I got a place in drama school, they were as pleased as punch.'

'Getting the part of Dolly in *Goldsworthy Hall* must have been your big break.'

'Yeah! I mean, I'd done a bit of stage work and a few ads for telly, but I was only a year out of drama school when I got it, and I suppose it changed my life. It was weird walking down the street and having people shouting after me, as if I really was Dolly. I think it turned my head a bit too. All that recognition. Suddenly having money to spend. I got a bit wild and stupid. You'd have thought I'd know drugs were a mistake, after my mum and dad, but I guess it was a confidence thing. I didn't feel I belonged in that life. Not really. And I needed something to help me face it. In the end, it all fell apart. It must have been some kind of breakdown. I found myself dreaming up better and better ways of killing myself. That became almost an addiction of its own. Then I was watching the weather on the telly one night and on the map I saw Shetland. Miles to the north, but still part of the UK. And I thought, *Well, I'm right on the edge. What better place to go?*'

Sandy was imagining himself in the role of the interviewer now. It was almost as if he was questioning Alison as part of the investigation. He would have fixed on the practical details and asked Alison about driving to Aberdeen, getting onto the boat. Perez always said that facts cemented a witness in reality. It stopped people creating stories and turning their lives to fiction. But the journalist skipped all that and had already moved on.

'Were you aware of the response in the English media to your disappearance?'

'Not at all. In my eyes, I hadn't disappeared, had I? I knew exactly where I was. And I didn't see any English papers when I was in Shetland. I never watched the TV news.'

'You didn't think of letting your family know? Or your colleagues on *Goldsworthy Hall?*'

Sandy pictured Alison pausing at this, thinking about the question and how best to answer it. Her response seemed very honest to him.

'Not really, no. I was depressed, you see. And depressed people are very selfish. I could only think about my own feelings. I'd shut everyone else out. It was my way of making myself better.'

Outside the police station Sandy saw a group of women who must be on their way to the chapel further down the street. They were wearing waterproofs and the wind seemed to carry them down the hill, making them run with little footsteps, struggling to stay upright. He turned back to the printed paper on his desk and made another note. It might be worth talking to the woman who'd interviewed Alison. There could have been confidences that had never been printed. Sandy wouldn't want to do that himself; he thought a London journalist would be intimidating, and anyway she would probably respond better to a more senior officer. The woman's name was Camilla White and that seemed to fit in with the classy image Sandy already had for her. Her next question had been about Alison's first stay in Shetland.

'So you arrived into Shetland on the ferry. What were your first impressions of the island?'

'It was winter, so it was dark and rainy and I couldn't see much. I'd only packed a few things into a small bag. There was a taxi outside the ferry terminal and I asked him to take me to the best hotel on the island. He said that would be the Ravenswick, so that was where we went. When they asked me my name at reception, I didn't want to tell them who I was. I didn't want anyone recognizing me. So I called myself Susie Black. That was my mother's name before she was married.'

Sandy made another scribbled note on the paper in front of him. If Alison's mother was still alive, they now had her maiden name as well as her married name. It should be easy to trace her now. He thought how pleased Jimmy Perez would be to have all this information and found himself smiling again.

In the newspaper, Alison was describing her stay in the islands. 'I didn't have a car, so I couldn't explore very much away from the hotel. I walked for miles, though. The day after I arrived, the weather suddenly changed. It was clear and sunny, very cold. I'd wake up to frost in the hotel garden, and the sea was blue and still. I've always loved the sea, since Jono and I moved out to Norfolk. That weather made the island seem like a kind of magic place. All bright and glistening. They sold local knitwear in the hotel, so I bought a jersey to keep warm and just went out walking every day. I met some local people on my wanders. There was one elderly chap called Magnus, who took me into his house and told me stories about the islands. He had a raven in a cage. The stories were about little people who lived underground and played fantastic music. Looking back, it seems like a

178

hallucination. I'm not even sure all that really happened.'

Oh yes, Sandy thought, *it happened.*

'Then you were recognized?' The question took them towards the bottom of the page, so Sandy could tell that the interview was about to come to an end. He read on quickly to find out Alison's response.

'Yeah, I suppose it was going to happen eventually. A local man, a lawyer, came into the hotel for a meal with his wife. I was in the restaurant eating dinner and could see him looking over at me. Then he'd start whispering to his wife. I could tell that would mean the end of my retreat. Because that was what it had been like, a kind of religious retreat. When I saw the man staring, it felt like the world had come back to get me. He came up to my table when he was on his way out and said I was all over the papers in the south and that they were making a great drama of it. They were making out that I was hiding away in rehab, or that I'd taken an overdose. He offered not to tell anyone, if I needed a bit longer to myself, but I realized I'd have to face them all in the end. I phoned my agent that night.'

Sandy thought the lawyer must have been Tom Rogerson. Who else would it be? But if that was the case, how had he not recognized Alison Teal when they'd circulated the drawing of the dead woman's face? She'd certainly aged in the last fifteen years, but she hadn't changed that much. And it would have been Tom Rogerson who had collected her from the Brae Co-op and sat with her in Mareel. He could see how Alison might have kept in touch with him over the years. He'd offered to keep her secret and she'd surely have been grateful for that. Had she asked for his help again? And if they'd got on so well together, what could be his motive for killing her?

Sandy set those questions aside. Willow and Jimmy would be the people to answer them. He put the printed article on Perez's desk, returned to his own office and was about to start making the calls that would help them to trace Alison Teal's relatives. But before he could lift the receiver, the phone rang. On the other end of the line was a woman with a very loud voice. She announced herself as Genevieve Winter. This, it seemed, was Alison Teal's agent, returning his call.

19

They all caught up over tea and sandwiches in the basement kitchen of the guest house where Willow was staying. Rosie set the refreshments on the table, said she was going to put her feet up and left them to their discussions.

Even Vicki Hewitt was there, and Willow turned to her first.

'Anything new from the scene?'

Vicki shook her head. 'I've pretty well finished looking at the debris caught up behind the wall. Nothing's jumped out at me as being significant. I'll send it south as soon as I can, and I'll start inside the house tomorrow.'

'But Sandy, it seems, has had a very productive morning.'

Willow had already read the *Independent* article, but she'd asked Sandy to print out more copies and he passed them round the table.

'So this is an interview Alison Teal gave to the journalist Camilla White a little while after her disappearance fifteen years ago.' He looked serious, like a schoolboy asked to speak in front of the class.

Perez interrupted. 'Is it exactly fifteen years?'

'Aye, almost to the day. She arrived in Shetland on the last day of January.'

'So maybe she saw it as an anniversary trip. Could that be the reason for the champagne?'

'Rather than because she was feeling desperate

again, you mean?' Willow thought either explanation would work. 'Let's not get bogged down with speculation just now. Carry on, Sandy.'

'It's clear from the article that Alison met at least two people while she was here: Magnus Tait and a lawyer who's almost certainly Tom Rogerson. Nobody else is mentioned specifically, but it's possible that she came across other islanders.'

'Yeah, that's certainly suggested.' Willow nodded for him to continue.

'Alison mentions a number of family members too, and talks a bit about her troubled childhood. So now we know she has a brother called Jonathan who went into the army, that her mother's maiden surname was Black and her first name Susie, and that Alison's grandparents lived in Cromer. The article says that Susie and her partner were addicts and handed the children over to Alison's paternal grandparents to be cared for. It seems likely that social services were involved, and they too will have records.'

'Tell us then, Sandy. How many of them have you tracked down?'

This was Vicki, teasing, but Sandy took the question seriously. 'Jonathan Teal was the easiest to find. He left the army five years ago as a corporal with the paratroopers. He's serving time in Wormwood Scrubs for armed robbery. He and a friend held up a family shop in Norwich. Nobody was hurt, but Teal was the person waving a gun around.'

'Which is very interesting and perhaps adds

something to our understanding of the family,' Willow said, 'but it means that he couldn't have been in Shetland strangling his sister.'

'Norfolk Police are trying to trace the grandparents and parents.' Sandy looked at his notes. 'It's probable that at least one of the grandparents has died, but they're checking all that out. The parents both have records for drug-related offences, but they seem to have dropped out of the system not long after Alison's first jaunt to Shetland.'

'So they got clean,' Perez said.

'Or they got clever.' Willow wondered if there was some significance in the timing of all this, but she couldn't work out what it might be.

'And then,' Sandy said, 'I spoke to Alison's agent. A woman called Genevieve Winter.'

'Impressive name.'

'She's a very impressive woman.' Willow jumped in at this point. 'She spoke to Sandy first, but she claimed not to understand him, so I phoned her back later.'

'She got me flustered.' Sandy was turning red. 'I tried knapping, honestly, but she still didn't seem to get what I was saying.'

'Probably because she didn't stop talking long enough to listen.'

'Knapping?' Vicki raised an eyebrow.

'Losing the accent, for the benefit of soothmoothers,' Perez said. 'They expect us to understand Geordie or cockney, but they won't make the effort to understand us.'

'And this was a particularly arrogant woman.' Willow pulled a face. 'But in the end I did shut

183

her up long enough to give her the news that Alison was dead. She had no contact details for a next of kin, but she was able to tell me something about Alison's recent career. Such as it was.'

'How did she respond to the news of Alison's death?' Perez poured more tea from the huge pot.

'Honestly? I don't think she was very bothered. Alison had stopped making her much money years ago. And Ms Winter made it very clear that her business as an agent was all about making money.' Willow paused and then tried to order her thoughts, to sum up the last years of Alison's life. 'Dolly the housemaid — the character Alison played in the costume drama — was killed off very soon after Alison went to Shetland. Alison had got the reputation of being unreliable, and as Ms Winter told me: 'Darling, there's nothing worse for a young actor. Directors hate it.' She got some work immediately after that: a small part in a soap, a panto the following Christmas, some reality show on Channel Five, but about seven years ago the parts dried up altogether. Genevieve still put Alison in for auditions, but recently she'd stopped even doing that.'

'So that could explain her trip to Shetland,' Sandy said. 'If the lack of work had brought on another bout of depression. I haven't managed to get her medical records yet, or speak to social services. Because it's a Sunday, nobody's working.'

'It would be useful to know if she'd been

184

working in any capacity at all recently.' Willow thought it sounded as if Alison's life had stopped completely, several years ago.

'I think she must have been.' Sandy again. Tentative. 'The clothes in the house at Tain all looked pretty classy. She couldn't have bought them if she was on benefit.'

'Good point, Sandy. All the witnesses who've seen her in Shetland describe her as well dressed. And according to Jimmy, she gave Simon Agnew the impression that she was normally confident and in control. That doesn't sound like an unemployed actor. And she'd be unlikely to be splashing her money around on champagne if she was skint. Even if there was a special offer at the Co-op.'

They sat for a moment in silence. The breeze had dropped and outside it was quite still and silent.

'Do we know if Alison had a partner?' Perez said. 'Or even if she'd married?'

'You're hoping she had some romance in her life?' Sometimes, Willow thought, Perez was the soppiest man in the world. 'I did ask Genevieve. She said she couldn't imagine Alison settling down. 'She was always rather a wild child, darling. There was usually some poor bloke in tow. Or, rather, some rich bloke. She went in for sugar daddies. But commitment very definitely wasn't her thing.''

There was a moment of silence.

'So where do we go from here?' Willow looked at them, spread out around the table, surrounded by empty plates and scraps of food.

They were like a family, she thought, with herself and Perez as the parents and Vicki and Sandy as the kids. It felt a responsibility.

'The first priority is to speak to Tom Rogerson,' Perez said. 'He misled us about knowing Alison, he had access to the keys at Tain and his car fits the description of the vehicle that collected her from Brae.'

'What time does his plane get in from Orkney tomorrow?'

'He's booked on the early evening flight.'

'Should we meet that?' Willow thought again that she and Perez were like grown-ups, this time taking decisions that were beyond the responsibility of the kids. 'Or let him get home and visit him there later?'

Perez took a while to consider. He never rushed a decision. 'Maybe it would be safest to meet the flight. I'd hate to lose him. If Taylor tells him we've been to the office, he might be jumpy.'

'Hard to lose a suspect in Shetland.'

'Maybe.' He gave her one of his slow smiles. 'But there are lots of islands. Lots of places to hide. I'd be more worried that he might destroy evidence that we could use later. He could be keeping stuff at home.'

'Where his wife could find it? If we think Tom was having an affair with Alison Teal, would that be likely?'

Another pause. 'Mavis, his wife, strikes me as a woman who would prefer not to know what her husband gets up to. I don't think she'd go sneaking through his things.'

Willow ran through the evidence they had against Rogerson. There was nothing concrete. Nothing at all that they could present to a court. 'I'd love to find a definite connection between him and Alison Teal.'

Perez pulled a plastic evidence bag from his pocket. Inside was the note he'd retrieved from the bin in the solicitor's office. 'I thought we'd get this off to a handwriting expert, along with a page from Magnus Tait's notebook, and see if we can find a match with the letter Sandy found in Tain. Rogerson's writing looks like a match to me.'

'You think Tom was her lover?' Willow couldn't quite see how that played out now. 'But according to the article, Tom recognized Alison in the hotel and the next day she flew back to London. She doesn't talk about seeing him again.'

Perez shrugged. 'People lie. And they make up good stories to cover their tracks.'

Another silence. Sandy and Vicki were listening, but they made no attempt to interrupt. Willow spoke next.

'Do you think it's safe to let Rogerson come back on his own from Orkney? There's nothing to stop him getting a flight south.'

'I don't think he'll run away from Shetland,' Perez said. 'He's got too much to lose here. He likes the power and authority of being a councillor. Rogerson's a classic big fish in a small pool. I think that's why he came home in the first place.'

'So we wait for him at the airport?'

187

'I think so.' Perez had already thought this through. 'His car's there. I checked. So nobody will be coming to collect him. Let's make it informal.'

'And what do you have planned for us for the rest of the day, Inspector?' Sometimes she couldn't help reminding him that she was supposed to be heading up the investigation.

He grinned. 'Well, that would be your decision of course, Ma'am.'

'But?'

'We carry on the great work that Sandy started. We need more information about Alison Teal — her recent work record and details about her mental health. Any problems with addiction.'

Sandy raised a hand, breaking into the conversation, a reminder that the two senior officers weren't alone in the room. 'Could she have been dealing? That might explain the money. She'd have the contacts through her parents.'

'Not very likely, surely.' That was Perez. Willow wondered if he was still wedded to the idea of the woman he'd romanticized, when they knew nothing about her. He didn't want her to be a high-end drugs dealer.

'I'm not sure,' Willow said. 'We certainly can't rule anything out. That's an interesting possibility, Sandy. And you know drugs come into the islands, Jimmy. All those single young men on the rigs and in the floatels. A ready market.'

Perez nodded, but she could tell he still wasn't convinced.

'Anything else urgent for the morning?'

'I'm going to dig out a photo of Rogerson,' he said. '*The Shetland Times* will have dozens. He's on the front page most weeks. Sandy, you can take it up to Brae and show the lad in the Co-op, see if he recognizes him as the man with Alison in Mareel. It's a while ago, but you said he had a good visual memory. It would be something else to face Rogerson with, when we see him tomorrow evening.'

The men left then and Vicki went up to her room to pack. She planned to take the first flight out in the morning. Willow collected together the plates and mugs and stacked them by the dishwasher, then started up the stairs. On the first landing a door was open. It led into a small room looking over the garden. The room was decorated in yellow and white and there was a white cot, with a mobile of the moon and the stars hanging over it.

20

Jane woke the following morning to a clear, cold day. Even from her bed she could sense the change in the weather. There was no noise of wind and rain and the room was cold. She knew it was early. The council workers hadn't started moving the remaining silt from the road above the house, so there was no background rumble of diggers and tractors. Kevin wasn't in bed with her. She was a light sleeper, but she hadn't heard him get up. He must have made a special effort not to wake her or he'd made his way out a long time ago, when she was sleeping most deeply. She had a moment of unease — that sense again that since the landslide everything had changed. It was winter and there was no reason for him to be up before it was light.

She got out of bed, wrapped herself in her dressing gown and looked out of the window. In the moonlight she saw there was a heavy frost. The ruins of the house at Tain had been turned from black to white, so the scene looked like a photographic negative. There was no sign of Kevin in the kitchen; his boots had gone from the rack in the porch, so he must be outside. She put on the kettle to make tea and thought the landslide hadn't only changed things for her, but for her husband too. He'd put on a good show for the boys the day before. There'd been the same weekend rituals: beer and football and too

190

much to eat. But she thought it had been an effort and he was sliding away from her, just as she was growing apart from him.

On impulse she left her tea where it was and went upstairs to get dressed. Michael was stirring, but it was a while yet before he needed to get the bus into school. She pulled on jeans and a heavy sweater, found her boots and coat in the porch and went outside. The cold was shocking. It stung her skin. The light from the kitchen window showed footprints in the frost crossing the grass towards the boundary with the Tain land. What attraction could the place have for Kevin and for Andy? What kept pulling them back there?

She'd been a regular visitor to Tain in Minnie Laurenson's day. The old woman had been fierce and strong almost until the end, but not unfriendly. When Jane and Kevin had first moved into the farm, Minnie had invited Jane in. They'd had tea in a spotless kitchen. Flower-print plates and small crimped cups. Bannocks with orange Orkney cheese and home-made ginger cake. A dog by the hearth, and a cat on the arm of Minnie's chair. 'They're all the company I need,' Minnie had said. 'You'll be welcome to drop by any time you like, but don't feel you have to. I'm not a woman to feel lonely.' Then she'd given a dry chuckle. 'I could have had a man, you know. I've had offers.'

And Jane had dropped in. Those had been her boozing days, but she'd always been sober when she called at Minnie's house. Or almost sober. Minnie might have heard the rumours about

Jane's drinking, but she never mentioned it. The conversation had mostly been about the boys and the farm. 'I see your man has bought up more land. That's a lot for one man to handle. But he was always a good worker, your Kevin, even when he was a peerie lad.'

Minnie had died quite suddenly. If she'd been feeling ill, she hadn't shown it. She'd driven herself into Ravenswick to the kirk on the Sunday morning and Magnus Tait had come to visit as usual in the evening. On the Monday, Jane had seen Minnie hanging washing on the line. It had started to rain in the afternoon, but Minnie hadn't appeared to take in the clothes. Jane had gone down then, intending to bring in the washing herself, thinking that perhaps Minnie had taken an afternoon nap. She'd gone into Tain and seen Minnie, lying back in her usual chair by the fire in the gloom of a late afternoon in winter, the cat purring on her knee. But when Jane had unpegged the clothes and folded them in the laundry basket, Minnie still hadn't stirred. When Jane came back into the house, the cat was by the cupboard where its food was kept and wrapped itself around her legs, almost tripping her up. Jane had gone up to Minnie then, to wake her, and had discovered that she was dead.

That had been horrible of course, but it had been a natural death. Talking to her friends, Jane had said that it was just the way *she* would want to go — in her own home and in her sleep. The murder of the mysterious woman who'd been staying at Tain had been quite different. *She* had been strangled and then her body had been ripped from the house by the tide of moving earth. Everything about that death had been violent and quite unnatural.

Jane had been in recovery before Minnie had died, and she was glad about that. She wouldn't have wanted to be drunk at Minnie's funeral, and by the end of her boozing days she'd almost always been drunk. Alcohol had made her wild and irresponsible and the memories of that time still haunted her; she talked about them occasionally at meetings. About the time she'd picked up a bloke in a Lerwick bar and found herself in the early hours in a strange bed, with a man whose name she couldn't remember. About the time she'd almost fallen into the water after a night out in Scalloway. And on each occasion she'd got a taxi home to Kevin.

She'd been drunk on Andy's first day at school, though nobody would have realized. She'd been hiding bottles by then, in places Kevin would never look: in her car, in the utility room behind boxes of washing powder. Had he noticed? Perhaps he hadn't wanted to. Andy's first day at the Ravenswick school, she'd woken up with a hangover and knew she shouldn't drive, but had felt too rough to walk. Kevin had been away south, buying kit for the farm, so she'd piled both boys into the car. She'd been late already and had taken the track too fast, almost landing them in the ditch. Perhaps that had sent her along to her first AA meeting. The realization that she could have killed both of her sons because she'd been over the limit before nine in the morning. A sudden body-blow of guilt and shame.

She remembered that meeting: pushing open the door to the hall, where she still went each week. There'd been the same smell of propane gas and the shock of seeing some people she recognized. Respectable people from the town, also admitting that they were alcoholic. She'd broken down that first night, as she tried to explain what she was doing there, and there'd been more love and understanding in the room than she'd ever experienced before.

★ ★ ★

It was starting to get light. It wasn't fully dawn yet, but the sky just above the horizon was silver and she could see a silhouette, a darker shadow against the lightening sky ahead of her. It must be Kevin, but he wasn't looking out at Tain. He'd walked all the way to the coast and was standing at the edge of a low cliff, looking down at a rocky beach. Sometimes sheep got down there to forage on the seaweed and struggled to get back when the tide came in, because the paths were so steep. Perhaps that had happened and he planned to go down himself to shove a ewe in the right direction. It was a beach where seals hauled up to pup in the summer. Jane sometimes went there if the weather was very good, to sit in the sun and read.

She looked at her watch. Nearly eight o'clock. Michael would need to be out on the road to get the school bus in half an hour. Perhaps she should go back to the house and make sure he was up. Even though the boys were grown up, she always made them breakfast and checked they had clean clothes to put on. Reparation, maybe, for the time when she was rackety and unreliable, when nappies went unchanged and clothes unwashed. But Michael was a sensible boy and was old enough to get himself ready. She texted him: *Out with Dad. You OK to get yourself to the bus?* Immediately her phone pinged: *Sure. See you tonight.* He had no imagination. He wouldn't be anxious that the kitchen was empty and there was no sign of either parent. He wouldn't start making up scary stories in his head to explain their absence. She thought she should be more like him.

The sky was even lighter now and the silver light in the east was threaded with gold. It would be a beautiful day. She walked on until she'd nearly reached Kevin. He must have heard her boots on the frozen ground, because he turned round.

'Couldn't you sleep?' She smiled at him.

'I'm sorry. I didn't mean to wake you,' Kevin said.

'You must be frozen, standing there.' She put her arm around his shoulder and pulled him in to her. She thought she should be more grateful. He'd stuck by her, when other men would have left.

'We will be alright, won't we?'

'Of course we will.' Because reassurance was the least she owed him. 'Is something the matter, Kevin? Is there something you want to tell me?

You've been kind of weird since they found that dead woman at Tain.' Jane turned his face so that she could see it properly. His eyes were wet, but she couldn't tell if he was crying or if it was just the cold. She couldn't remember ever seeing him cry.

He hesitated. By now the beach below them was flooded with the low sunshine. The water slid onto the shingle, so calm that it was like oil.

'Did you have something to do with her death?'

'No,' he cried. 'Nothing like that. Of course not.'

The strange orange light made his face quite unfamiliar and she couldn't tell whether she believed him or not. She was about to press him, to demand to know why he'd been brooding in the dark here, when her attention was caught by something washed up on the rocks below them. She thought it must have been thrown up by the storm of previous days. 'What's that?'

'I don't know.' It was as if he was too wrapped up in his own troubles even to bother looking. 'An old oilskin, maybe. Something thrown overboard from a ship.'

'No.' She was already scrambling down one of the sheep tracks that led across the slope of the cliff. It was still greasy with ice in places and she scattered pebbles as she climbed. She heard Kevin on the path above her. He'd taken a different route from her and they landed on the beach at about the same time.

It was the shoes that had persuaded Jane that this was a man, not a pile of disused clothes thrown from a boat. They were wet now, either with rain or with sea water, but she thought they would have been highly polished once. The man was wearing a suit and a white shirt, but no tie. On top of the suit a yellow oilskin that looked unnaturally bright in the low sunlight. He lay awkwardly; his head in a shallow rock pool was lower than his body, and fronds of seaweed covered his matted hair.

'You do know who this is?' Kevin sounded oddly excited

She had been thinking it couldn't be a coincidence that Kevin was staring down at a beach where a man was lying dead. And that Jimmy Perez would come prying into their family affairs. Now the question distracted her for a moment, because of course she knew who this was. It was Councillor Tom Rogerson, the lawyer, and the man who'd been seen in Commercial Street arguing with her son.

21

Perez was on his way to work when his phone went. He'd just dropped Cassie with Maggie, the neighbour who would walk her down to school with her own kids.

'Jimmy.' The speaker was breathless, and that and the fact he was using the hands-free set made her voice unrecognizable.

'Who is this?' He pulled into a lay-by. The gritter had been down the main road, but here the gravel was still covered with frost and there was ice on the puddles.

The speaker had regained her composure and her voice was clearer. It seemed suddenly very loud. 'It's Jane Hay, Jimmy.'

'Have you heard from Simon Agnew? Has he remembered any more about the woman who visited him at his office in Lerwick?' Perez had been thinking he should see Agnew again, in the light of their recent discovery about the dead woman's past.

A pause. It seemed his question had thrown her, or had taken a little while to register. 'No! It's nothing like that. You have to come, Jimmy. Much better that you come here and see for yourself than that I waste time telling you on the phone. I'll meet you by the gate.' And then the phone went dead. There was nothing for him to do but turn the car round and go back to Ravenswick.

Jane was waiting for him where she'd promised. She was a tall, fair woman, looking bulky now in a jersey and padded jacket. She had her hands in her pockets and was stamping her feet to keep warm. She'd already opened the farm gate for him and he parked in the yard as she swung it closed behind him.

'What's this about?' He didn't think she was the kind of woman to make a fuss about nothing and he could sense her panic. Her body was rigid. 'Is it Kevin? One of the boys?' He looked across to the house and saw the older son, Andy, staring down at them from an upstairs window.

She followed his gaze and hesitated for a moment. 'No, the family is all fine. Follow me.'

She walked very fast ahead of him across the sheep-cropped grass. The sun was melting the frost in patches, but the air was still very cold. An oil supply ship seemed to be moving very slowly on the horizon. It looked as if it was made of silver. They came to the edge of a shallow cliff that sloped down to a shingle beach, fringed at each end with rock pools. Fran had brought Perez here one summer afternoon. She'd swum in the water, screaming with laughter at the cold, calling him a coward for not following. Later they'd gone back to her house and made love. She'd have done it on the beach, but he'd been too much of a coward for that too.

There were two figures on the beach below him, one lying supine on the shingle, and for a brief moment he thought that his daydream and reality had collided. That Fran was waiting for him there. But the standing figure turned and

Perez saw that it was Kevin Hay, dressed in his work overalls with a jacket on the top. Jane was already sliding down the slope and Perez followed. He could smell the seaweed and felt the cold of the rocky path when he put out his hand to steady himself. Every sense seemed very sharp and immediate in the chill, thin air.

When he saw the body, Perez's first reaction was one of disbelief. Tom Rogerson was in Orkney, not Shetland. So it was impossible that his body could be lying here in Ravenswick.

'How did you come to find him?'

'Kevin comes out this way most days to check on the sheep. It was such a fine day I decided to come with him.' Jane stood close to her husband and held his hand. Perez didn't have the impression that she was seeking comfort, though. It was more that she was comforting the man.

'Could he have slipped, do you think?' Kevin asked. 'If he'd knocked himself out on the rocks, the temperature was so low last night that the cold would have killed him.'

'It'll take a post-mortem to decide cause of death.' But Perez thought an accident was unlikely. There was a blow to the side of the head, visible even when Rogerson was lying where he'd fallen. Perez thought he'd been hit from the front by one of the round, smooth rocks that lay on the beach above the tideline. They'd check of course, but if the killer had any sense, the rock would have been thrown into the sea immediately after the attack and all trace of blood would have been scoured by the salt water.

He was thinking that he needed to call James Grieve. At least in this weather the planes would be running to time and the pathologist would get in on the first available flight. He looked at his phone. No signal.

'I need to call my colleagues. Is there reception up the bank?'

'You can use the phone in the house,' Jane said. 'I'll take you back.'

Kevin Hay stood with his back to the body, looking out to sea. He lived closest to the apparent crime scene and had to be considered a possible suspect. Perez couldn't leave the man in charge of the body. And even though Hay had already had the chance to remove any evidence, Perez was the first officer at the scene and it was his duty to keep it secure now.

'Jane, I need your help. Could you go back to the house and phone Sandy Wilson? Tell him I need a uniformed officer here as soon as possible, and ask him to contact James Grieve and book him onto the first possible plane. And to pass on the information to DCI Reeves.' Perez scribbled a number and a couple of names onto a piece of paper and handed it to her. Then he took it back and added another. 'Tell him we need Vicki to come along too.'

'Can Kevin come with me? It's been a shock and he's frozen.'

'I'm fine.' The man was still looking at the sea. 'I'll stay here with the inspector until the reinforcements arrive. A dead man's not much company, eh, Jimmy?'

Perez thought Hay would rather answer *his*

questions than those of his wife.

They stood in silence until Jane climbed away.

'Did you know Tom Rogerson?' Perez asked at last. 'Socially, I mean. Do you have any idea why he'd be wandering around on your land?'

'None at all. And I knew him to say hello to, if we bumped into each other in the bar of the Ravenswick Hotel, but we didn't mix in the same social circles. He was one of the Lerwick mafia, one of the decision-makers, the movers and shakers.' His tone was matter-of-fact. It was hard to tell what he made of all that.

'Was he a regular in the Ravenswick?' That might explain the solicitor's presence here, though the hotel was a couple of miles north along the coast, and even further by road. Besides, the man should have been in Orkney at a fisheries conference.

'He and his wife came for dinner occasionally. I've not seen them lately.'

'Did you ever see his car at Tain? He drove a Volvo. Black.'

'No, Jimmy, but like I explained when you asked about the dead woman, I probably wouldn't have noticed it, even if he was a regular caller. Those sycamores screen Tain from our land. You might see a car from the main road, but not from our house.'

And that was quite true, Perez thought. The sycamores were windblown and stunted, but they'd provided privacy for Tain's resident. 'We've got a name for her,' he said.

'What?'

'We've managed to identify the dead woman.

Her name's Alison Teal.'

Hay showed no reaction.

'Does the name mean anything to you? She was an actress. At one point in her career, at least.'

Hay shook his head as if the information was of no interest to him. Instead he nodded down at Rogerson's body. 'His daughter's the teacher at the school. Someone should tell her, before news gets out. You know what this place is like. Jane won't be on the phone gossiping. She's not like that. But our lad's at home and she might tell him. You know what kids are like with Facebook.'

'You're right,' Perez said. 'I'll go to the school myself as soon as an officer turns up to control things here. And I'll make sure someone gets to his house to tell Rogerson's wife.' He felt trapped here now and wanted to be away, to start asking questions, to think. He strained to hear the sound of a siren in the distance, footsteps on the grass above them. Nothing.

'He led his wife a merry old dance,' Hay said suddenly.

'What do you mean?'

'Everyone knew he had affairs. He didn't even bother to be discreet. There was something kind of arrogant about that.' Hay had turned back to the sea. 'He was an arrogant man altogether, always flashing his money around.'

'You didn't like him?'

Hay shrugged again. 'Like I said, I didn't really know him.'

Now Perez did hear footsteps and the sound of voices. Jane appeared at the top of the bank with a young officer, who'd only recently joined the service. The man slid awkwardly down to join them. Perez gave him brief instructions about securing the site. 'You let nobody on the beach, whoever they are. And you stay here, well away from the body.' Then he scrambled back up the cliff and walked with the Hays back to the house.

Jane offered him coffee, but he asked if he could take a mug into his car to make a few phone calls. 'The school breaks early for lunch. I'll aim to arrive about then, so I don't have to pull Kathryn out of her class and tell her what's happened in front of the bairns. That should give the school a little while to get in some cover, so she can go home to be with her mother.'

In the kitchen Andy, the dark-haired boy with the piercings who worked in the bar at Mareel, was sitting at the table with a mug of tea. Perez nodded to him. 'Did your mother tell you what's happened?' Just at the edge of his line of vision, Jane was hovering, protective.

'Aye.'

'Only we haven't informed the relatives yet, so please keep the incident to yourself.'

The boy nodded but didn't speak.

★   ★   ★

In the car Perez spoke to Sandy Wilson, who'd been on his way to show Rogerson's photo to the assistant in the Brae Co-op. 'Even more reason to do it now,' Perez said.

'You don't need me in Ravenswick?'

'Not yet.' He paused. 'When you've finished in

Brae, go to see Simon Agnew. He's the chap that set up Befriending Shetland, the counselling service in Lerwick. See if Alison Teal means more to him than Sandy Sechrest. It still seems a weird thing for the woman to do — turn up at the project's office and then change her mind and wander away again after only a brief conversation. Maybe Agnew had met Alison before, in a professional capacity; she certainly had a troubled childhood.' Perez remembered Fran's description of Agnew. *He's just* fun, *Jimmy. But he's done such valuable work with families and young people.* For a moment Perez had hated the man he'd barely met. A second of pure jealousy. Because he himself would never be described as fun, and he hadn't been sure that Fran considered his work had any value at all.

At the other end of the phone Sandy coughed, to show he was waiting for further instructions, and Perez continued, 'Can you get Morag to tell Mavis Rogerson that her man's dead? No details. Just unexpected death. And see if Mavis knew that Tom was back from Orkney. We need to check if he ever went, of course.' Another pause. 'Did you tell Willow what was going on?'

'Yes. She said she'd stay in the office. Awaiting instructions.'

Perez could imagine her saying that. She'd have a laugh in her voice, mocking him for taking charge again. 'I'll speak to her now. I think it might be a good plan for her to come here to talk to the Hay family. I'm too close. We're neighbours, and it would be useful to get another perspective on them. Two bodies in Ravenswick, both within a good stone's throw of the Hays' house. I can't see that as just a coincidence.'

He got out of the car to take his mug back to the kitchen and in the porch bumped into Andy, who was stooping to put on a pair of Converse sneakers. The boy was tall and seemed pipe-cleaner-thin in skinny black jeans and black sweater.

'Are you going to work?'

'No, I've got a day off.' The boy paused. 'I was coming out to see you. Mum said I should talk to you. About something that happened with Mr Rogerson.'

'Had you seen him recently? On your land?'

'No.'

Perez looked at his watch. In a quarter of an hour the kids in the Ravenswick school would be queuing up for their lunch in the dining room that doubled as school hall and gym. When the bell went, he wanted to be there to talk to Kathryn. 'It can wait then. Another officer will be here soon to talk to you all. You can explain to her what happened with Rogerson.'

The boy nodded and disappeared back into the kitchen. Perez had a minute of doubt and was about to call him back, but the door closed and the moment was gone.

22

Sandy drove to Brae. It was a fine day to be out of the office and he felt his spirits lift. He parked outside the shop and wondered again what Alison Teal could have been doing here, buying champagne and couscous. Why hadn't she done her shopping in Lerwick, where she'd have more choice? They still hadn't discovered how she'd arrived in Brae. Without a car, it would take two buses and nearly an hour to get here from Ravenswick. They'd shown her photo to all the bus drivers and to regular passengers at Lerwick's bus station, but nobody had recognized her.

'But we might not,' one of the drivers had said. 'The weather we've had over the past few weeks, all you see is a hood dripping with rain and a pair of eyes.'

Peter, the lad with the acne and the perfect visual memory, was still working at the till. Sandy waited until he had served a customer. 'I need a few words.'

'Here?' He was hoping for another unscheduled coffee break.

'Bit public here, isn't it?'

'You'd best talk to the boss, then.' He gave a complicit grin.

The manager moaned about giving Peter time away from the till, but Sandy insisted. They took their coffee outside so that Peter could smoke, and leaned against the building, squinting against the bright sunlight. 'We've got an ID for the dead woman,' Sandy said. 'She was called Alison Teal. An actress. Does that mean anything to you?'

Peter shook his head. Sandy thought he'd have been too young to have seen Teal on television, and costume drama probably wasn't his thing anyway. He'd be into BBC Three toilet jokes and science fiction.

'We're still trying to track down the guy you saw in the Mareel bar with her. If I show you a photo, do you think you'd remember him?'

The lad shrugged. 'I might do.'

Sandy pulled a photo of Tom Rogerson from his inside pocket. Perez had got it from *The Shetland Times* and it showed the solicitor shaking hands with a minor member of the royal family. 'Do you recognize him?'

Peter nodded. 'Sure. That's Tom Rogerson. He's on the council. He's everywhere in Shetland, like a rash. But it's not the guy I saw in Mareel with the dead woman.'

'You're certain?' Sandy didn't know what Perez would make of that. They'd assumed Rogerson was the man who'd collected Alison from the Brae shop and who'd been with her in Mareel.

'Positive.'

'Can you give me a more detailed description of the man you saw?'

Peter took a last drag on his fag and threw it towards a skip. It missed. He closed his eyes against the sun, dragging out his illicit break from the till. 'Like I said, he was respectable, middle-aged, wearing a suit. I guessed he probably worked for the council. You know, the offices are just over the road and you get folk coming in for a drink early evening.'

'But the man himself . . . ' Sandy couldn't blame the lad for taking his time, but Rogerson was dead and the investigation was carrying on without him.

'Middle-aged. A suit. You know.'

Sandy went into the store with Peter and bought a sandwich and a can of Irn-Bru for his lunch. He told the manager how helpful Peter had been and said that he might be back to talk to him again.

★　★　★

He stopped for his lunch at Voe, because he had good phone signal there, and phoned Jimmy Perez. There was no reply. The inspector must still be talking to the young teacher in Ravenswick school. Sandy would have liked to head straight down to Ravenswick to be with the rest of the team, but he'd had his instructions. Simon Agnew worked three afternoons a week out of a small, anonymous office not very far from the police station and Perez had said that this was one of his days. A small plate on the wall next to the door said: *Befriending Shetland: Family Mental Health Services.* Sandy had walked down the street many times, but had never noticed it. Inside there was a waiting room with a box of toys in the corner. A woman sat

209

with a toddler on her knee. The toddler seemed to be half-asleep; certainly she took no notice of the toys or her mother. The woman looked up. 'You have to ring that bell to let them know that you're here.'

The bell was on the wall with a little notice. Sandy pushed it and heard it ring some distance away. Otherwise the building seemed unnaturally quiet. The window looking out onto the street had the sort of glass that you get in bathrooms and can't see through. It filtered the sunlight and made it form odd shadows like bubbles on the floor. A middle-aged woman with grey hair and glasses on a string around her neck appeared.

'Can I help you?' Her accent was Shetland and very broad, which was a surprise because he didn't recognize her. The whole place had a dream-like feel.

'I'd like to see Simon Agnew.' He wasn't sure if that was the right way of asking. Perhaps the man was a doctor.

'Do you have an appointment?'

'No.' He showed the woman his warrant card, trying to be discreet. He didn't want to frighten the mother with the toddler or start rumours about the man's role in a police investigation.

'Just take a seat.' The middle-aged woman nodded towards the row of chairs against the wall. 'Simon has a client with him at the moment, but he should be free very soon. I'll ask if he can fit you in.' No questions about the nature of his visit. She must have had to learn discretion. Then she seemed to vanish, as silently as she'd appeared, and the only sound was the ticking of the clock on the wall. Sandy leaned back in his chair. He found himself lost in a daydream about Louisa. This was a place where it was easy to lose touch with reality.

The grey-haired woman appeared again, but it was to call through the mother and child: 'Maura will see you now.'

Sandy looked at the clock. Only ten minutes had passed since he'd first arrived, though it felt like hours. There was the sound of approaching voices and a whole family came in through the door that led further into the building. They took no notice of Sandy as they walked out into the street. There was a brief flash of sunlight as the outside door was opened. Silence returned. After a few moments so did the grey-haired woman. 'Simon has twenty minutes before his next appointment. He'll see you now.'

Sandy followed her down a corridor, past a number of closed doors. The receptionist tapped on the one at the end and showed him in. The room was bigger than he'd been expecting. He should have realized that it would have to accommodate a whole family. There was a small sofa against one wall and a couple of armchairs around a low coffee table. Simon's desk was pushed against another wall and he sat to the side of it, so the desk didn't come between him and his clients. The curtains were yellow, and though the same bubble glass kept out the direct sunlight, the room seemed very bright. Sandy felt himself blinking. Again there was a box of toys in a corner. On the wall there was a blown-up photo of a man halfway up a snowy

211

mountain. Sandy wondered if it might be of Agnew himself, but he was wearing climbing gear and a helmet and it was hard to tell.

'Sergeant. How can I help you?' The man was already on his feet, hand outstretched. Sandy caught the flash of white hair and white teeth, before he sat down again.

'We have the identification now for the woman who died, the one who came to see you here. Her name was Alison Teal. Does that mean anything to you?'

The psychologist shook his head. 'I'm afraid it doesn't.'

'She was an actress.' Sandy thought this interview was a waste of time. He could have been out at Ravenswick with his colleagues. He put a copy of the photo of the younger Alison on the desk in front of him. 'Was this the woman who came here to see you?'

It took the man a while to answer. Sandy could tell that he was at least taking the matter seriously. 'She was obviously a lot younger then.'

'But it was the same woman?'

'Yes, that was definitely the same woman.'

'Did you know Tom Rogerson?' Sandy supposed he could pass on the news of the man's death. If Agnew hadn't heard about it already, he soon would.

'The councillor? Of course I know him. He was a great support when we founded this place. He was one of the very few people who seemed to *get* what we're about. He's one of our trustees.'

'He's dead.' Sandy wasn't sure how to say this

212

tactfully. 'I thought you might have heard. His body was found on the beach below Tain this morning.' He paused. 'We're treating the death as suspicious.'

'No, I hadn't heard.' Agnew turned away, so Sandy couldn't tell what he was thinking. 'I was in Fair Isle for the weekend. The minister there asked me to speak about the Befriending Shetland project to his congregation on Sunday, and it was a chance to visit the island. I went out on Saturday and I only got back this morning. I've come here straight from the airstrip at Tingwall.' He looked back at Sandy. 'I'm not sure this place will keep running, without Tom to fight our corner with the council.'

23

Jimmy Perez parked by the gate of the Ravenswick school. It looked very similar to the school he'd attended in Fair Isle: a single-storey building with whitewashed walls, surrounded by a playground with a climbing frame and hopscotch squares painted on the concrete. It was quiet. The children were still working. His tension grew. He hated this — telling relatives of an unexpected death. He knew how the news would change their lives, shift their perspective and make everything seem different.

A bell rang and there was a clamour of children's voices. They'd be leaving their classes and moving to the dining hall for lunch. He got out of the car.

He found Kathryn in her classroom. She taught the older primary children and she was collecting exercise books from the tables. The sun streamed in through the long windows. Perez tapped on the door and let himself in.

'Jimmy.' She seemed pleased to see him.

'Will we be disturbed here?' He didn't want a child to burst in and see that she was upset. Or to be interrupted by a staff member with a frivolous question.

'No, everyone else is at their lunch. I've brought a salad. I'd be the size of a horse, if I ate Mary's dinners every day.' She sat on one of the small tables. 'What is it, Jimmy? You look very serious. Do you want to talk about Cassie? Has she been having those nightmares again?'

He perched on a table next to her. 'I need to talk to you,' he said, 'about your father.'

'He's in Orkney. Some council business.' She looked up, curious about his interest, but with no premonition of bad news.

'He's dead, Kathryn.' There was no gentle way of saying this, of making it easier for her. 'His body was found on that shingle beach close to Tain. Kevin Hay found him, when he was out checking his ewes this morning.'

He saw that she couldn't take it in. 'No, I've told you, Jimmy, he's in Orkney.' Her voice was implacable. Hanging onto that fact like hope.

'Your father had a flight booked, right enough.' He realized that he was talking to her as he did to Cassie, when she woke in the night screaming for her mother. 'But he never got onto the plane. We've spoken to Flybe. I've seen him, Kathryn. It was his body on the beach this morning.'

'I don't believe it!' Now she was shouting like a confused child responding to her fears with a tantrum. He could imagine her drumming her heels on the floor and lashing out at him. 'You have to show me, Jimmy. I have to see him.'

He didn't reply immediately, but gave her a few moments to collect herself. 'I can't take you to see him yet. Not on the beach. A little while and he'll be in Annie Goudie's funeral parlour in Lerwick. You and Mavis will see him then.' A pause. Some of the children had already finished their meal and were running into the playground. 'You have to trust me about this, Kathryn. Now, we'll need to talk to your colleagues and ask them to cover your class for this afternoon and I'll take you home.'

Perhaps it was talk of her work, but suddenly she seemed to grow up, to become herself again. Confused still and full of questions, but not an angry child any more. 'They'll be in the staffroom. We can talk to them there.' At the door she stopped. 'He wasn't a perfect man. But he was such a good dad. Fun, you know. He could turn even the boring things into an adventure.' Only then did she ask the question that he'd been expecting since he'd walked into the classroom. 'How did he die?'

'We can't know for sure,' Perez said. 'But I don't think it was an accident.'

Again she looked at him as if she didn't understand the words, so he spoke again.

'I think it was murder.'

★　★　★

Morag was waiting with Mavis Rogerson in the big, gloomy house in Lerwick. The sunshine was muted by the stained glass in the front door, so the hall seemed so dark after the police officer had let them in that it took some time for Perez's eyes to get used to it. They sat in the kitchen and Morag made tea. Mavis hadn't moved from the table and seemed hardly to notice their presence until Kathryn went up to her and put her arms around her.

216

'Are you up to answering some questions?' The kitchen was at the back of the house and in shadow. Perez wished they could go outside to talk, but there was no question of moving them.

The women looked up.

'What do you need to know?' It was Mavis. Her face was puffy and the colour of putty, but she wasn't crying.

'I need to understand why Tom didn't get on that flight to Orkney. Was there a last-minute change of plan?'

'I thought he was there,' Mavis said. 'It was all arranged. He gets on very well with my brother. He still lives in Kirkwall, and they were going to meet up on Sunday night.'

'Did your brother contact you? To say that Tom hadn't turned up?'

She shook her head.

'Could we have his contact details? So we can check what happened. Or would you like to phone him?'

'Oh no!' The answer was immediate. 'I can't talk to anybody.' A pause. 'I don't have the strength.' It was an odd phrase, but Perez thought that was just how he'd felt after Fran's death. He'd been too weak with grief to carry out even the simplest of tasks.

Mavis got her phone and found her brother's number. Perez scribbled it into his notebook and passed it to Morag. The police officer slipped out of the room. While the three of them sipped tea, they could hear her muffled voice from the hall. At least she'd managed to get through first time. Morag came back into the room and they all stared at her. It was as if she was an actor appearing onstage and the attention seemed to make her a little flustered.

'Tom phoned your brother on Sunday to cancel.' Morag directed her words to Mavis. 'Tom told him that something unexpected had turned up and that he'd be delayed. He wasn't sure he'd be able to make the Orkney conference. He gave the impression that it was council business.'

'Ah.' Mavis sounded sad rather than angry. 'That was always the excuse he used.'

'Excuse me?' Perez could guess what she meant, but he needed her to explain.

'Tom had other women, Inspector. It was hardly a secret.'

Perez shot a look at Kathryn, but he couldn't tell if this was news to her or whether she'd known about the affairs. She sat now, unmoving. Perhaps that was what she'd meant when she'd said her father wasn't perfect. The room seemed very stuffy. It was as if everyone was in a slow-motion film, and Perez found that it was taking him a long time to put together his questions. He leaned across the table towards Mavis.

'Did you have any suspicion that he wasn't going to Orkney as planned this time?'

She lifted her head. 'None at all. He liked visiting my family. He liked the conferences. He was a very sociable man. I always loved that about him.' She paused for a moment. 'We were happy, Jimmy. I knew what he was like when we married. Tom needed to be admired. It was a kind of addiction — the sex. It was clear very soon that I couldn't meet all his needs. But I wanted to be with him. I could live with the fact that he strayed. I wish he'd been faithful, but he loved his family and the home we had here. I was his rock. He always said that. He wouldn't have been the man he was, without me.'

The room was suddenly so quiet that Perez could hear the purring of the cat that was lying on the windowsill. He turned to Kathryn. 'Did you know that your father had affairs?'

'Of course. At first it all seemed just a bit of fun. My dad was a ladies' man. He flirted at parties and weddings. He was a little bit mischievous, but everyone said there was no harm in him. As he got older and the women he chased got younger, it became embarrassing. He gained a reputation as a bit of a pest. I'm not sure there *had* been other women recently. Or only in his dreams. Single women would know they could do better — and that he would never leave his wife — and there aren't that many women in Shetland willing to cheat on their partners. My father had become a bit of a laughing stock. You wouldn't want to be seen out with him. It was all a bit sad.'

'He was still an attractive man!' Mavis cried. 'You can't talk about him like that.'

There was another silence. Perez thought it strange that the woman would prefer to think of her husband as a sexual predator than an embarrassment. It was an odd kind of loyalty.

'Was Tom seeing anyone just now?' He was thinking of the woman who'd been with

219

Rogerson in the Scalloway Hotel. Sandy had thought that might be a business meeting, but he might not have been reading the situation accurately.

'As I've just said, Jimmy, I don't think he'd been seeing anyone for a while.' Kathryn's tea must have been cold by now, but she sipped from the mug.

'There was some business deal that was taking up a lot of his time,' Mavis said. 'He was out some evenings, but he wasn't with a woman. I could always tell when he'd been with a woman: he'd come back to me and he'd be kind of tender.'

'Was it legal business?' Perez asked. 'Or something to do with the council?'

'Maybe something to do with the oilies.' Mavis was wearing a big hand-knitted cardigan, but despite the heat in the room she still seemed to feel cold. She pulled the garment around her. 'Tom said he couldn't tell me about it just yet, but it would make us money.'

'Was money important to Tom?'

'Not for its own sake,' Kathryn said. 'He couldn't save. But he liked the things it could buy.'

Power? Perez thought. *Influence. Women.* But he wondered if the deals Tom bragged about were real or if they were fantasies, as were, according to his daughter, his relationships with young and beautiful women.

'When did you last see Tom?'

'Early Sunday,' Mavis said. 'Then he drove down to Sumburgh to get the morning plane.'

And he had done that. His car had been found in the airport car park. So what had happened between arriving in Sumburgh and checking in for his flight?

'Who knew that he'd be going to Orkney?'

'Everyone who reads *The Shetland Times*.' Kathryn allowed herself a little smile. 'There was a big article about the fisheries conference and about how Dad was going to fight for Shetland's fishermen.'

'But they wouldn't know that he was leaving on Sunday morning.'

'No. Just that he'd be in Orkney for the meeting on Monday morning.'

Perez thought Rogerson must have intended to go to the conference. Otherwise he wouldn't have driven to Sumburgh and he wouldn't have encouraged all that publicity. They'd need to question the check-in staff and other passengers. Perhaps there'd been a chance meeting in the airport that had made him change his mind. Or had someone been waiting for him there?

He turned his attention back to the women. 'What were you up to over the weekend?' He tried to keep his voice chatty and light.

Mavis stiffened and her voice was suddenly bitter. 'Do you think I killed him, Jimmy? Because he'd been making a fool of me with other women? I'd have done that years ago, if I'd wanted him dead.'

'I have to ask, Mavis. You must understand that.'

The women looked at each other. For a moment Perez suspected they were preparing to lie, but perhaps they just wanted to check the accuracy of the details they were about to give.

'We had breakfast,' Kathryn said, 'and then we went to church.'

'Here in Lerwick?'

'No, in Ravenswick,' Kathryn said. 'We like the minister there.'

So they were in Ravenswick on the Sunday. Perez couldn't work out the significance of that.

'And after the service?'

'We treated ourselves to Sunday lunch in the Ravenswick Hotel.' Now Kathryn sounded almost defiant. She must understand the implication of Perez's questions, even if Mavis didn't. 'Then later the weather cleared a little and we went for a walk in the hotel gardens. But we didn't go anywhere near Tain, Jimmy, and we didn't go to the beach.'

He nodded and waited for her to continue.

'On Sunday night we were here. Together. I had marking to do, and my mother was watching television in the same room. I arrived at school at about eight this morning. It was icy and I'd allowed time in case there was a tailback from the traffic lights by the landslide. I didn't see my father. Not over the weekend or this morning. As far as I knew, he was in Orkney.'

Perez stood up. They were back to where they'd started when he'd first met Kathryn in the school, and he didn't want to be in this overheated room any longer. He left Morag with the women, shut the kitchen door behind him and stepped out into the sunshine.

24

Willow found the Hays' farm easily. Perez had pointed it out when they'd driven from the airport and she'd remembered the polytunnels and the solid stone house that seemed a little grand. There was still the ghost of the croft house it had once been, but it had grown over the years and become a comfortable family home, with rooms in the roof and an extension at the front. The attached outbuildings, which had once contained animals or a dairy, were now part of the living space.

There were three people in the kitchen, along with a uniformed officer. It was early afternoon by now, but they looked as if they'd been sitting there since Perez had left. There was a smell of home-made soup, but the bowls must have been cleared away because there was no sign now that they'd eaten lunch. The officer must have recognized her, because he jumped to his feet when she tapped at the door and let herself in. The family turned and stared. Perhaps she didn't look much like their idea of a police officer. She saw the young man who'd served her and Perez at Mareel and gave him a little smile. 'Andy, isn't it? We've met.'

He nodded. It looked as if the movement had taken a lot of effort. Willow reached out her hand to his parents. 'Chief Inspector Willow Reeves. I'm afraid I'll have to ask you some more questions. But we'll get it over with as soon as possible and let you get on with your lives.' Because she found it hard to think of these respectable, ordinary individuals in their comfortable house as possible killers. They had too much to lose.

'Is there a room I could use to chat to you? We'll do it one at a time, so you're not all inconvenienced at once.' She could see that none of them were taken in by that, but she was here for more than a cosy chat around the kitchen table and it wasn't a bad thing for them to know that this was serious.

'There's the office.' Jane Hay got to her feet. She looked as if she hadn't slept for a few nights. Willow wondered if the shock of finding a dead man on your land would do that to you or if something else was worrying her. 'I'll show you.'

It was a small room that might once have housed animals and led off from a long corridor that stretched the length of the building. Far enough away from the kitchen that no one would be able to eavesdrop. There was a desk with a computer, shelves with reports and gardening books, a chair to go with the desk and another in the corner.

'Perfect.'

'Would you like some coffee?' Jane hovered in the doorway.

'Fabulous.' Coffee was Willow's drug of choice. Her parents had lived caffeine-free lives and it still felt like a guilty pleasure. 'Do you mind asking Andy to bring it through? I'd like to chat to him first.'

Jane nodded as if that was what she'd been expecting. She was about to say more, to give some excuse or explanation for her son's behaviour, but seemed to think better of it and walked away.

The boy carried a tray and the smell of the coffee came before him. There was a mug and a little jug of milk and a sugar bowl. A plate of home-made biscuits. All very fancy, but Willow was used to witnesses trying to impress. And this would be the parents' doing, not his.

'Are you not having any?' She reached out for a biscuit and pushed the plate towards him.

He shook his head. 'We've been drinking coffee all morning.'

'Jimmy Perez said you had something to tell me about Tom Rogerson.'

He looked up sharply. 'My mother said I should say something, but really it wasn't a big deal.' A pause. 'Nothing for her to make such a fuss about.'

'All the same, your mother's right. We hear about stuff anyway, so it's best if it comes from you.'

Andy paused. 'We had a row in the street. I'd had too much to drink. Rogerson was an arrogant bastard.'

'According to Inspector Perez, your father said much the same thing. Was this a family problem, then? Is there some reason why you and your dad had taken against the man?'

There was no reply.

'Only Rogerson had a reputation, I understand. If he'd been hassling your mother, I can see that you might both be angry . . . ' She let the implication drift into the air. The possible explanation for the tension within the family had only just come to her, but she thought now it made sense of Jane's anxiety and Kevin's resentment. It might also provide a motive for murder. Perhaps the respectable family was less comfortable than it seemed on the surface.

The boy looked up with a start. His surprise seemed genuine. Perhaps he was reflecting any young person's horror that their parents might be sexual beings. Or perhaps he was a good actor.

'No,' he said at last, 'there was nothing of that sort. Of course not.' A pause. 'Though it was just the sort of man Rogerson was. I mean I could see him doing that, being a nuisance with a woman. But my mother's not like that. She wouldn't be taken in by a man like him.'

'Perhaps she wasn't taken in. Perhaps he wouldn't take no for an answer.'

But Andy only shook his head. 'I don't even think they knew each other.'

'How did *you* know him? Was he a regular in Mareel?' Willow was feeling her way here. She thought it would take very little to make the boy clam up altogether.

'He came in sometimes.'

'But he was older than your dad. I'm trying to understand what you might have been fighting about. We don't have arguments with people we scarcely know.'

'It wasn't important. I'd had too much to drink and Rogerson was in my way. He was rude and shoved me aside, and I lost it. There was nothing personal. I was just being stupid.' He was getting impatient with the questions. Willow could see that he was struggling to hold on to his temper. So, all the more reason to push him.

'Was anyone else there, to see what was going on?'

'I wasn't with anyone,' Andy said. 'There were people in the street, but not close enough to see exactly what was going on.'

'Why did you leave uni?'

The sudden shift in questioning threw him. He looked even more twitchy. 'I don't know. I didn't like the course much. I might go back. Try something a bit different.'

'I grew up on an island,' Willow said. 'North Uist. Much smaller than Shetland mainland. No facilities. Nothing like you have here. I couldn't wait to get out.' She paused. 'But I found it tricky to settle away from the place. No boundaries, you see. No limits to my territory. All that space stretching out around me. It made me kind of loopy for a while. And no boundaries in the emotional sense. I could do what I liked, and there was nobody I knew to stop me. Not like the island, full of gossiping busybodies. I'd guess that even though this is bigger, it's hard to get away with stuff here too.'

'Oh, you'd be surprised.' The words hard and bitter.

She gave him a moment to explain, but she could tell that he was already regretting the outburst. 'What do you mean?'

He shrugged and took a while to answer.

'People think there are no secrets in Shetland, but they're wrong. We all have secrets. It's the only way we can keep sane.'

'What secrets do you have, Andy?' She kept her voice soft, a little ironic. She didn't want to sound intense and frighten him off.

He looked up at her, with a sharp, jagged grin. 'If I told you, they wouldn't be secrets.'

She could tell that she would get nothing more from him and she let him go.

★ ★ ★

Willow saw Kevin Hay next. She thought the woman had more to tell her and it wouldn't do any harm to let her stew. The man was big and bluff. Not stupid by any means, but with a limited outlook. He would read *The Shetland Times* but news away from the islands would hold no interest for him.

'This woman who was staying at Tain . . . ' She smiled at him, but didn't complete the sentence. There was an awkward silence.

'What about her?'

'I find it hard to believe that you didn't know she was there. I can just about believe that your wife hadn't realized that the place was lived in. But you? You were out on your land. You must have walked past most days. You'd have seen a light in the house. A car on the track.'

'I saw no cars. I told Jimmy Perez the day that he found the body.'

'You were aware of the tenant before that.

Craig. You saw *his* car.'

'I've known Craig and his family for my whole life. Of course I knew he was taking over the place for a peerie while. I helped him out with a few repairs before he moved in. When he went off to the Middle East he didn't say anything about a new tenant.'

'The tenant's name was Alison Teal. Does that mean anything to you?'

His face gave nothing away. She thought he'd be a good poker player and wondered what it must be like to live with a man who was so impassive. But perhaps he was different with his wife. Perhaps he revealed himself to her.

He shook his head.

'She was an actress,' Willow said. 'Quite a long time ago. She's been to the islands before, caused a bit of a stir. She'd gone missing and turned up in the Ravenswick Hotel. Just down the road. You were living here at the time?'

That was barely a question, because she already knew the answer and again it seemed he thought it wasn't worth speaking, because there was just a brief nod of the head.

'You don't remember the fuss?' She leaned towards him. She'd arranged the chairs so that she wasn't sitting across the desk from him, and her face was very close to his.

'When was it?' Still not a real answer.

'Fifteen years ago.'

'My wife wasn't very well back then. She had mental-health issues. All my time was taken up looking after the family. Looking out for her. There could have been another landslide and I'd scarcely have noticed.' He turned his face so that he was looking out of the narrow window and not at her. 'I certainly wouldn't have paid any attention to gossip about an actress.'

'Rogerson.' The name hung between them.

Again he waited for the question to come.

'It seems a bit of a coincidence,' she said, 'to have two bodies within walking distance of your house.'

Still there was no comment and Willow came out with the question at last. 'Did you like the man?'

'I scarcely knew him. We didn't mix in the same circles.' For the first time Hay showed some emotion. A little sneer.

'You must be about the same age. Did you go to school with him?'

'He was a couple of years older. That was too much of a gap for us to be pals.'

'Jimmy Perez had the impression that you didn't like him.'

'I didn't know him personally.' Hay paused for a moment. 'I knew the sort of man he was.'

'And what sort was that?'

'One of those charmers who take folk in. A user and a taker.'

Willow leaned back in her chair. 'You know, Mr Hay, that does sound very *personal* to me.'

In the silence that followed, sounds from outside came into the room. A flock of whooper swans calling from the sky. A dog barking. Still mid-afternoon, but the shadows were lengthening and soon the light would be gone. Willow let the silence grow, before speaking.

'And your wife? Did she know Tom Rogerson *personally?*'

There was no response for a few seconds. Kevin Hay stared back at her. No expression at all on his face. Then he got to his feet and walked out. For such a big man, his feet made no sound at all on the stone floor.

25

Jane wasn't sure what to make of the female detective who turned up on their doorstep. Jane had just cleared the lunch things and was wondering if they'd have to spend all day indoors. Odd inappropriate thoughts had flown in and out of her head all morning: *The first nice day for weeks and we're not allowed out of the house.* Then: *What will I make for tea tonight, if I can't get to the shop? Maybe I could invite Simon along. He'll put all this into perspective and cheer us up.* And then, a little guiltily, because she should have thought of it earlier: *Should I phone Michael and let him know that there's a dead man on the beach?* Interspersed with the random thoughts, pictures forced their way into her head. She saw Tom Rogerson, lying on the shingle, only half his head left intact. *Like the hill after the landslide. Recognizable, but not at all the same.* And Kevin, standing on the edge of the cliff as the first light came.

She'd asked the young officer about phoning Michael. 'I don't want my son picking up rumours at school. You know how news spreads here. If he hears there's a body, he might imagine it's one of us.'

'I think perhaps you should ask your son to come home,' the policeman had said. 'The boss might want to talk to him.'

'But Jimmy's gone.'

'Not Jimmy Perez.' The man had seemed a little confused. 'The boss from Inverness who's in charge of the case.'

And then the woman from Inverness had floated in like a kind of weird Mary Poppins. Only she'd looked more like one of the hikers that turned up on the NorthLink ferry, with their big boots and heavy rucksacks. She was wearing a long jersey and jeans and her hair was wild.

'Mrs Hay was wondering if she should contact her youngest son.' The police officer seemed a little out of his depth and anxious for advice. 'I thought maybe you'd like to talk to him, so we should get him back.'

'How old is he?' The detective turned to Jane and smiled.

'Sixteen.'

'Perhaps it would be a good plan to get him home then. No need to wait for the school bus. Sandy Wilson will be driving down from Lerwick. He can give him a lift.' Then she asked Jane if there was a room they could use, and called Andy in to speak to her, so for Jane the waiting continued.

★   ★   ★

When Andy emerged from the office, it was impossible to be sure what mood he was in. He just waved at them as he walked past the open kitchen door to his bedroom. Jane thought there could be something manic about the wave, the glittery eyes, the jerky walk, but she was hyper-sensitive at the moment. Perhaps her

233

eldest son wasn't anxious or excited at all, just bored and wanting some time to himself.

The detective shoved her head round the kitchen door and Jane prepared herself for the interview to come, but the woman turned to Kevin.

'If you're ready, Mr Hay, I'll see you now.' As if they were patients in a dentist's waiting room. Then Jane was in the kitchen alone, watching the shadow of the house lengthen until it reached the polytunnels, while the young policeman sat nervously in a corner, picking at his fingernails until she wanted to scream at him to be still. She offered him tea and he accepted — grateful, she thought, to have something to relieve the boredom.

Suddenly there was a flurry of activity. Kevin burst in from the hall, his face red and his fists clenched by his sides. He was furious and she was anxious about what might have triggered the change in mood. He didn't lose his temper often, but when he did he was terrifying. He simmered and then exploded. She was on her feet to hold him, to try to calm him before the rage overtook him, and at the same time Michael arrived with Sandy Wilson, the young detective from Whalsay. After its previous silence, the room seemed full of people, all talking and asking questions. And then Willow Reeves appeared at the door. She ignored the tension and the raised voices, smiled a greeting to Michael, nodded to Sandy Wilson and asked Jane to follow her. Jane put her hand on Kevin's arm, a gesture of understanding, a message for him to be calm, and she left the room.

In the office the detective was already seated. 'You make truly fab coffee.' A wide smile. 'Jimmy will be sorry he had to rush off.'

Jane knew this was a tactic — the woman would make her feel at ease and then start to ask the difficult questions. Waiting in the kitchen, Jane had been preparing her answers, but now she wasn't sure how convincing they would be. She took her seat and waited.

'How well did you know Tom Rogerson?' Another bright smile.

This close, Jane could see that the detective had freckles along the line of her cheekbones. Lines around her eyes too, so she must be approaching middle age, but somehow the freckles gave her the look of a schoolgirl.

'I knew of him,' Jane said. 'He was one of those Shetlanders who seem to be on every committee going. And I met him occasionally at social occasions. Charity dos, parties.'

'But you didn't know him *personally?*' Willow Reeves put great emphasis on the last word. 'You would never have invited him and his wife to supper, for instance, or gone out for a meal with them?'

Jane shook her head. 'We were never on those terms.'

'Only your husband seems to have taken a dislike to him, and I can't work out why that could be. If he didn't really know him.'

'Kevin's a very black-and-white sort of person. He'll make up his mind about someone without knowing them at all. Politicians, folk he reads about in the paper . . . ' Jane stopped herself from rambling further.

The detective nodded as if she, too, knew people like that.

'This morning,' she went on, 'you said Kevin got up to check on the ewes, but it was very early when you found Mr Rogerson's body. Wouldn't it still have been dark when he set off? And I wonder why you went after him. I'd be tempted to stay in the warm, a morning like today.'

This was one of the difficult questions Jane had been planning for, but now her practised response seemed incredible. She paused before answering. 'It was a beautiful morning. After all that rain, it was good to be outside. We wanted to see the sun come up together. You get fantastic sunrises on the east side.'

'Very romantic.' The detective sounded sincere, even a little envious, but she continued, 'If you and your husband spend so much time out on your land, even at this time of year, I do find it very strange that you didn't realize there was anyone staying at Tain.'

'I did see someone inside,' Jane said. 'I told Jimmy Perez.'

'You didn't mention that to Kevin? Because he didn't seem to know the place was occupied at all when the landslide took place.'

'I can't have done.' She paused. 'We're both very busy.'

'Of course.' Another wide smile, to put Jane at her ease. 'Tell me about your mental-health problems.'

'I'm sorry?'

'The woman who died at Tain was called Alison Teal. She was an actress, famous for disappearing while she was playing a role in a popular television drama. She was discovered in Shetland, in the Ravenswick Hotel, which is just down the coast from here on the south side of the landslip. Kevin told me he couldn't remember the publicity surrounding the story because you were very ill at the time.'

Jane wondered if that conversation had made Kevin angry. Perhaps it was being taken back to the past that had caused the clenched fists and the simmering rage. He'd always said that he forgave her for the betrayals and the thoughtlessness of her drinking days. One of the steps of her recovery had been to be honest with him. 'You were ill,' he'd told her. 'Not yourself. Of course we can start again.'

But she'd never been entirely convinced by his reassurance. She knew he needed her; he'd never been much good on his own. Whether he forgave her was another matter altogether.

Now she looked up at the detective. 'I'm an alcoholic,' she said. 'In recovery now, but then my life was completely chaotic. We had two small children and Kevin had to hold things together at the same time as he was expanding the farm. He was magnificent. I'm not surprised he couldn't remember a news story about an actress from the south.'

'Do you remember anything about the woman's disappearance?'

Jane shook her head. 'It was a bad time.' She caught a sudden glimpse of her past: the panic attacks, the craving and the crippling hangovers and the overwhelming self-pity. She shook her head again to clear the memories from her mind.

'What did you do last night?' Willow Reeves was satisfied, it seemed, by Jane's answer and had moved on.

'Not much. We had a big Sunday lunch. The family all together and Michael's girlfriend was here too. After that I only felt like sagging out in front of the television.' She paused, expecting another question. None came and she felt compelled to fill the silence. 'I went to bed early. I hadn't slept well the night before.'

'Why not?'

'Oh, my son was late home. You know what it's like. Even when they're grown-up, you never stop worrying about them.' Though Jane thought the detective probably had no idea what it was like to be a parent. It was impossible to imagine the woman with the responsibilities of a baby.

'Which son?' The detective had been scribbling notes, but now looked up and gave Jane her full attention.

'Andy. The big one. He dropped out of uni and has a bar job at Mareel. Sometimes they ask him to stay on for an extra shift.'

'And that's what happened on Saturday night?' Willow Reeves's voice was deceptively calm, but Jane wasn't taken in. This was important to the woman. And she would check anything Jane told her, so it was important not to lie.

'I'm not sure. I assumed that was why he was late. Maybe he just went on to catch up with

238

some friends in town.' A pause. 'Why are you interested? Tom Rogerson died on Sunday night.'

'Did he?' Willow stared at her.

'I don't know!' Jane felt herself start to panic. 'Surely someone would have seen the body, if it had been on the beach for a whole day. Can't you tell when someone died?'

'Not with any accuracy. You shouldn't believe what you see in television dramas. Tom was last seen on Sunday morning, though. We don't have any anxieties about Saturday night. We're asking everyone involved to account for their movements yesterday.'

'But we're not involved!' Jane's voice rose almost to a shriek.

Willow smiled. 'But you are, aren't you? Even if it's only a matter of geography. Two people have died very close to where you live. There are no other houses nearby. I'm not suggesting that any of you are killers, but I do think you can help us.'

In the silence that followed they heard the sound of a vehicle on the track outside. Headlights lit up the polytunnels as the car swung into the yard.

'Are you expecting anyone?' Willow asked.

Jane shook her head. She couldn't think who might be visiting, unless Simon Agnew had heard of the death and had arrived to offer comfort and support. That would be his style. But the silhouette that they saw at the door into the house was shorter than Simon's would have been, and the voice he called in was Shetland.

239

'Kev! Are you alright, man? I've just heard about Tom Rogerson. Is there anything we can do?'

Willow looked at Jane.

'That's Craig Henderson.' Jane was thinking that if anyone could calm Kevin down, it would be Craig, and in this situation he'd probably be more useful than Simon, who always seemed to delight in a drama. 'He's an old friend of my husband's.'

'And he used to be a close neighbour.' It wasn't a question. The detective seemed almost to be talking at herself. 'He used to live next door in Tain. We've already talked to him about the dead woman. And I'm sure he knew the dead man too.' She turned to Jane and smiled. 'That's the way of islands, isn't it? So many connections.'

It seemed then that the interview was over, because the detective got to her feet. Jane stood for a moment at the office door.

'I hope you find the killer. This is too close to home. We all want things back to normal.'

The detective nodded as if she understood.

Standing outside in the corridor, Jane paused for a moment to compose herself. Perhaps the interview hadn't gone too badly after all. There was still a lot of noise coming from the kitchen. Loud men's voices, a sudden burst of laughter. It sounded almost like a party. Almost certainly Kevin would have offered Craig a beer or a dram. She couldn't face it and instead took the stairs to her room.

26

They met up again in Jimmy Perez's house in Ravenswick. Nothing was said about the decision to meet there, but everyone knew he liked to be home for Cassie in the evenings. Sandy had become more comfortable in these informal discussions, felt almost as if he belonged with the others now. Willow had gone back to Lerwick to shower and change and had turned up with foil cartons of Chinese food that were keeping warm in Jimmy's oven. Sandy was the last one to arrive. The fire was burning and Jimmy had lit candles. Sandy wondered what that was all about. This was work, not some kind of dinner party. His mind jumped for a moment to Louisa, who'd said she wanted to invite some of her friends to supper to meet him. He imagined they'd all be very clever people and he was already feeling anxious about it.

As soon as Sandy came in, Jimmy jumped up and started setting plates and cutlery on the table. Whatever conversation he'd been having with Willow in the candlelight seemed to be over. Willow ate her food with the chopsticks they'd sent from the Great Wall, not showing off, but as if that was the most natural thing in the world. Sandy couldn't help staring at the deft way she caught up the food and got it into her mouth. Once or twice he caught Jimmy staring too.

'Did you get a chance to talk to Michael Hay

241

when you gave him a lift from school?' Perez had finished eating.

'I told him a body had been found on the beach below Tain.'

'What did he make of that?'

Sandy thought for a moment. He pictured himself back in the car, driving south from Lerwick, the low sun very bright, slanting across the road. The boy had been sitting beside him in the passenger seat, his school rucksack by his feet. He'd seemed like one of those boys who turn into a man at a very young age, with square shoulders, big feet and an already grown-up face.

'What's all this about?' Michael had turned to Sandy. There was something aggressive in the voice, which could have been the result of nervousness. Or just because he was a teenager and that was his way of speaking to everyone.

'There was another dead body found close to your house.'

'Whose?' The question immediate, demanding a swift response.

'A guy called Tom Rogerson. Do you know him?'

'I know of him.'

'A friend of your parents?'

Michael had shrugged. 'Not as far as I know. I've never seen him in the house.'

'Where were you last night?'

'At home. I stayed at Gemma's, my girlfriend's place, on Saturday night and she came to ours for lunch yesterday. We usually spend the weekends together.'

'Did Gemma stay over last night?'

'Nah, she works, and it's a bit of a trek from Ravenswick to town on a Monday morning. Besides, I had stuff to do for school. I'd be happy enough to leave and start work with my dad, but my mum has a thing about sitting Highers.' He'd pulled a face and given Sandy a look that suggested he realized the man hadn't cared much for school work, either.

'Did you notice anything unusual?'

Michael had shaken his head. 'I didn't leave the house much yesterday. It was dreadful weather. More a day for being indoors.'

'What about when you came down from Lerwick with your girlfriend on Sunday morning? Did you see any cars you didn't recognize?'

'I didn't notice.' And Michael had stared out of the car window, closing down any further conversation.

Now, in Jimmy Perez's house, Sandy tried to answer the question. 'When I told Michael there was a dead man on the beach, he wanted to know who that was. Once I told him, he didn't seem much bothered.'

'He'd have worried that it might have been his father.' Willow pushed away her plate. 'So close to their house, he'd have assumed it'd be someone he knew.'

'Maybe.' Sandy paused. 'He didn't seem to me to have much imagination. More one for action than dreaming, I'd say.'

'Has any of the family come to the attention of the police?' Willow had swivelled round in her chair so that her feet were facing the fire. When the light went, the temperature had dropped.

There'd be another sharp frost.

Perez looked up. 'No. I did check, but there was nothing. They've always seemed like a close and loving family. I didn't think there'd been any trouble.'

'Did you know that Jane's a recovering alcoholic?'

'I'd heard she was a bit wild in her youth. When Kevin brought her back to the islands, after they were married. You could say the same about lots of young people at the time. The oil was pouring money into the place. Some weekends the whole of Lerwick was like one big party.'

'She still goes to AA.'

'Do you think that's relevant?' Perez seemed defensive now.

'Ah, Jimmy, you know enough about murder investigations to realize that everything's relevant. Until we decide that it's not.'

There was an awkward silence. Jimmy got to his feet to make coffee.

'Do you think one of the Hays could be a killer?' Sandy felt the need to speak. Really he didn't know what he thought about the family.

'Both bodies were found right on their doorstep,' Willow said. 'It's an odd coincidence.'

'Is it at all possible that someone might be trying to implicate them?' Jimmy brought a coffee pot and mugs to the table.

'That seems a bit elaborate.' Willow pulled a mug towards her. 'I just think there's more going on in the family than they're admitting. Someone's keeping secrets.'

'The whole case seems elaborate,' Perez said. 'Why would Alison take a false identity, for example? It's not as if she's a household name any more. And there are strange coincidences and connections. These are victims linked by a chance meeting years ago: an actress who was hiding away and the man who recognized her. If the letter we found at Tain was from Rogerson, they must have kept in touch.'

'What did Rogerson's wife say?' Willow looked up from her coffee. 'If there was a relationship between Alison and Rogerson, then Mavis Rogerson has the strongest possible motive.'

'Jealousy, you mean? If Mavis was going to kill Rogerson and the women he'd slept with, James Grieve's mortuary would be full.'

'Maybe it was different with Alison Teal,' Willow said. 'Perhaps he brought her here and set her up in the cottage at Tain. Perhaps he intended to leave his wife for her. What do you think?'

'I wish I knew what had brought on the crisis that took Alison Teal to the Befriending Shetland offices. If we understood that, we might understand why she was killed.' Perez paused for a moment. 'Have we tracked down her medical records yet? It would be useful to know whether she still suffered from depression or anxiety.'

'Perhaps the crisis had nothing to do with her mental health.' Willow was speaking almost to herself now. 'If there was a relationship with Tom Rogerson and it had lasted since they first met in the islands all those years ago, any problem between them might have provoked some kind of meltdown.'

'She'd changed her mind, you think? Decided she didn't want to stay here after all? And perhaps Rogerson threatened her, scared her?' Perez seemed suddenly to come to life. 'I can see that he might have been controlling.'

'You think Rogerson killed Alison?' Sandy had been watching the exchange between the senior officers with growing confusion. All this speculation gave him a kind of dizzy feeling. The fire had made the small room very warm. He wanted to take off his jersey, but he wasn't sure what sort of state his T-shirt was in.

Willow and Perez stared at him. Perhaps they'd even forgotten he was in the room. Sandy was used to being overlooked.

'I suppose it's a possibility.' Willow spoke slowly. 'Alison was dressed to impress, wasn't she, when she was killed. We'd always assumed that she was entertaining some man. Perhaps there was an argument that got out of hand. There'd have been no danger of the body being discovered before Craig Henderson moved into Tain, and Rogerson knew about the arrangement with Sandy Sechrest. He'd have realized he'd have time to dispose of her body when it was convenient for him. Easy enough to carry it to the cliff and tip it into the sea at high tide. Even if it had been washed up again, I doubt enough of her would have been left to make an identification. It was only the landslide that got in the way of his plans.'

'Then who killed Tom Rogerson?' Sandy realized his voice might be a bit loud, because Perez looked at the door into the bedroom where

246

Cassie was sleeping. But he couldn't believe this scenario: two different killers in the south end of Shetland.

Willow gave one of her lovely smiles. 'What do you think, Sandy?'

'I think this is all nonsense. I can't see that we could have two killers.'

'We're telling stories here, Sandy. Dreaming things up, just to see if we can make some sense of the situation. So if Tom Rogerson killed Alison, who might have killed him?'

This felt like a kind of test to Sandy. 'I don't know,' he said at last. 'I just don't see it.' Sandy felt as he had when he'd been put on the spot at school: that any intelligent idea had seeped out of his brain, like water leaching from a rock pool at low water. It didn't help that all day he'd been distracted by thoughts of Louisa. 'Perhaps she had another man — someone who murdered Rogerson in revenge for her death.'

'Maybe.'

Perez leaned back in his chair. 'This is all fantasy,' he said. 'Like you said, it's storytelling. We have no real evidence that Alison was having any relationship. Never mind that there were two men scrapping over her.'

'Well, we know she had contact with two men.' Sandy forgot his reserve for a moment. 'The guy who picked her up from the Brae Co-op. He was most likely Rogerson, because of the Shetland-flag bumper sticker. And the different man in Mareel. And she must have been buying the champagne to drink with one of them.'

'We can dream up as many theories as we like,'

247

Perez said. 'But at the moment it's all fairy tales. And the one person who might have given us hard information is dead.'

He gathered together the mugs and carried them to the sink. Sandy took that as a sign that Perez was ready for them to leave, but Willow didn't move. 'So what are the plans for tomorrow?'

Perez turned back from the sink to face her. 'We need to find out where Tom Rogerson went, after leaving his car at the airport. Sandy, you go back to Brae and show your pal Peter some photos of our possible suspects. Let's see if we can identify the man who was drinking with Alison in Mareel. And I'd like to get a handle on what she'd been up to recently. Who'd been paying for the smart clothes and the executive cabin on the NorthLink, if her agent says she hadn't been working. Can we see if there have been any unexpected payments from Rogerson's bank account?' He turned to Willow. 'Anything else, Ma'am?'

She grinned at him. 'I think you've got it covered, Inspector.'

Now Sandy did get up. He had his own car outside and he was starting to feel that he was in the way. The sense that he'd been intruding into a private conversation, when he'd arrived at the house, had returned. But as he made his way out, Willow joined him. And when they left together to walk down the bank to the road, there was no physical contact between her and Jimmy Perez. She just gave a friendly wave before he shut the door on them both.

27

Willow parked in the street at the top of the lane. A group of English men spilled out of the Chinese restaurant opposite the library and walked away towards the pier, shouting and laughing. Willow supposed they were heading for one of the floatels moored in the harbour. The barges looked like prisons and she thought it must be an odd, unnatural life, cooped up with the people you also worked with. She took the narrow path that led down to her B&B. There was a thin slice of moon and the lane was already icy. The house was separated from the path by a stone wall, with an arched wooden gate that led into a garden sufficiently sheltered to allow sycamores to grow. The bare branches of the trees were covered in hoar frost.

There was a light in the basement kitchen and she saw the couple who ran the place inside. The woman was sitting by the Aga with her feet on a low stool, her hands on her swollen belly. The man was ironing. There seemed to be a snatch of conversation between them, because the man laughed. Willow shouted down to them, so that they would know she was in, and then made her way up the stairs to her room. She couldn't face sitting with her hosts, even though she would have liked a cup of tea and knew that they'd be great company.

There was a window in the roof that sloped

almost to the floor on the longest side of her bedroom. She pulled up the blind and saw the lights of Lerwick below her, and the late ferry on its way back from Bressay. She supposed she should be thinking about the investigation, worrying over the details of alibis and motivation. But she was too distracted. Before Sandy had burst into Perez's house, there'd been a strange moment of intimacy between her and Jimmy. It had started with a domestic crisis. She'd arrived earlier than he'd expected and she'd caught him pulling damp washing out of the machine.

'Sorry, I'm not really ready for you.' He'd grinned. 'The tumble dryer's bust. I'll have to stick this stuff on a clothes horse by the fire. Not exactly attractive, with guests in the house, but Cassie'll have nothing to wear for school . . . '

'Sandy and I aren't real guests!'

'All the same . . . '

'Turn off the big light and stick some candles on the table,' she'd said. 'Then we'll not notice.' He'd done as she'd suggested. 'There you are,' she'd said, 'we could be having a romantic dinner now.'

There'd been a long silence before he'd spoken. 'Perhaps we should do that one day.'

It had seemed so out of character that she hadn't been sure she'd heard properly at first. But he'd been staring at her: all the intensity that was usually focused on work directed at her. She'd moved towards him, so she was close enough to smell the washing powder on his hands as well as the peat on the fire. 'I'd like

250

that,' she'd said. 'I'd really like that.'

'Maybe when Cassie's at her father's. I'll make sure there's no washing in the room.'

She'd been about to say that she wouldn't care at all about that, when they'd heard Sandy stomping up the path outside and the door had opened.

Now, she wondered if she'd misinterpreted the situation. Perhaps Jimmy Perez had been joking and when she'd taken him up on his offer, he was just being kind, to go along with it. She'd never met a man who could do kind as well as him. While she was undressing and cleaning her teeth, and when she was lying in the soft bed, she dreamed of the dark-haired man, haunted by him.

★   ★   ★

Willow woke the next morning full of energy and oddly content. The space in the loft bedroom seemed perfect for yoga and she allowed her mind to calm while she stretched and held the poses. Perez intruded only occasionally. It was too early to wake the rest of the house, but there was Wi-Fi in the room and she started in motion the bureaucracy that would enable her to access Tom Rogerson's bank accounts. When she heard someone moving around in the room below, she went downstairs for breakfast. The man was there, and already there was the smell of coffee.

'Only me this morning.' John was setting cereals and fruit on the long scrubbed table. 'Rosie had a bad night.'

251

'Is she OK?'

'Fine. It's just a bit uncomfortable, now she's so big, so I said she should have a lie-in. I can manage scrambled eggs, if you'd like some. My signature dish when I was a student.'

'When's the baby due?'

'Not for a week. And first babies are always late, aren't they? That's what everyone says.'

Willow found herself hoping that the child would arrive while she was still staying with the family. She was curious to see a newborn; thought she might take a vicarious pleasure in the warmth and the strange routines. At the breakfast table, she pondered the rest of her day and decided she didn't want to go straight to the police station. Perez might feel a bit awkward to see her, after his invitation of the previous evening. She poured herself more coffee and sent him a text:

I'm going to talk to Simon Agnew in the manse at Ravenswick. Not sure Sandy asked all the right questions. If Agnew is Jane's friend, he might be able to throw some light on what's going on with the Hay family.

There was an answering text almost immediately:

Sounds like a good plan. I'll send Sandy up to Brae to chat to his contact in the Co-op. Good luck with Agnew!

She read the message several times and found

herself grinning like some sort of lovesick schoolgirl. It didn't sound as if Jimmy was offended; indeed, the tone was almost cheery. She ate the landlord's perfectly adequate (though rather dry) scrambled eggs and left the house.

★   ★   ★

Willow drove south into sunlight. The ice on the roads was melting where the gritting lorry had passed through, but it was still very cold outside. The hire car she was using had a temperamental heating system and she shivered all the way to Ravenswick. As she passed Perez's house she could tell that he'd already left for Lerwick; there was no vehicle parked outside. The old manse where Agnew lived formed part of the scattered settlement of Ravenswick that spread out towards the southern headland that circled the bay. It was a square grey building tucked into the bank, close to a small loch. The kirk where Mavis and Kathryn had come to morning service stood next to it. Its nearest neighbour was Gilsetter, where the Hays farmed.

Willow hadn't phoned in advance; the decision to visit had been made on impulse and she hoped it was still sufficiently early for Agnew to be at home. There was a garage by the side of the house, but a red VW was parked on the flat grass by the front door. Willow stopped beside it, stepped out of the car and rang the bell.

The door was opened almost immediately. Willow was taller than most men, but she had to look up at Simon Agnew.

'Can I help you?' Easy, confident. Her father had been like that before the commune had disintegrated in acrimony and his dreams of saving the world had faded.

Willow introduced herself.

'Another representative of Police Scotland. I'm honoured.' Not sarcastic, but playful. 'Come in. I've just made some coffee.'

'I know you've spoken to my colleagues, but I'm afraid I have more questions.

'Of course, these dreadful murders.'

He led her inside. From the outside it looked like a traditional Scottish manse, but he'd knocked through two rooms, so the kitchen was lit by three sash windows facing the loch. There was a lot of light wood and sunshine. He must have sensed her admiration. 'I got a local guy to build the units for me.' He poured coffee and they sat at the table.

'Looks like a good room for a party.'

'Well, there've been quite a few of those.'

'Did Tom Rogerson come along to any of them?'

He paused for a moment. 'Once or twice. He was here just after Christmas with his family.' He looked up. 'You know his daughter's the teacher here.'

Willow nodded.

'Kathryn's a lovely young woman.'

'I wanted to ask you about Jane and Kevin Hay. Both victims were found close to their land.'

'Close to my land too, if it comes to that.' He

254

got up and poured himself more coffee. She thought he'd be a person who found it hard to be still. 'I'm sorry, Inspector, but Kevin and Jane are good friends. Generally I love to gossip, but I get a bit squeamish when it comes to chatting about my friends' problems to the police.'

'Do they have problems?'

He hesitated for a moment and she thought he might be tempted to confide in her after all. Then he thought better of it and laughed. 'We all have problems, Inspector. What's important is how we deal with them.' That could have been her father too. He'd always been full of words of wisdom that sounded deep, but were actually trite and banal.

'What problem do *you* have, Mr Agnew?'

'Oh, I'm terrified of boredom. Always have been. When I'm bored I get up to mischief.'

'What brought you to Shetland then? It's not the most exciting place in the world.' Willow thought this was an odd conversation to be having with a witness, but under the lightness and banter she suspected he had something useful to say.

'I've always loved it. I came here as a boy, before the oil, and I always promised myself that I'd retire here.' He looked out of the nearest long window to the loch. 'And it is dramatic, even if it's not exciting. I've been here for ten years now, made friends and put down roots. I know I'll never leave.' A grin. 'But I'm always on the lookout for new projects, new adventures.'

'Was that why you started Befriending Shetland?'

'Maybe. But there is a need, you know. When I first got here I thought I'd find an ideal community. Close. A place where people would support each other in times of crisis. Of course that's largely true. But shame's a big factor in a place like this. It can be a very destructive emotion. Sometimes it's hard to admit that one isn't surviving so well and it's easier to talk to a stranger. I had the skills and training to meet that need.'

'Have you had any further thoughts on what might have led Alison Teal to contact you?'

'I have been thinking about it.' Agnew closed his eyes for a moment. 'I had the impression it was very much an impulsive call. Perhaps she was in the town and saw our office. Or saw our advertisement in *The Shetland Times*. And when she met me, she thought I wasn't a person who could help her.' He gave a little shrug. 'Sometimes it happens.'

'So tell me a bit more about the Hays,' Willow said. 'Jimmy Perez thinks they're a perfect family.'

'Ah well, Jimmy idealizes the family, don't you think? He's always looking for perfect examples. I'm not sure that Fran could have met his standards, if she'd lived. It's easy to turn a dead person into a saint.'

'You knew Fran?'

A brief grin. 'She was a guest at some of my parties too.'

Willow wanted to ask for details, but stopped herself in time. Jimmy would never forgive her if he found out she'd been prying.

'And the Hays?'

'Well, Jane doesn't drink of course. You'll have picked up that piece of gossip by now. But she comes along and she still has a good time.' He paused. 'She's a very special woman. I admire her.'

'What about Kevin?'

'There's more to Kevin than most people think. It can't be easy to be the partner of an alcoholic. Very few relationships survive.' Again she thought he might elaborate, but he turned away again.

'Do you know the boys?'

'I knew them better when they were younger. Kevin was busy on the farm when they were growing up, and I love kids, so they were always welcome here. Just to hang out, to give Kevin and Jane a bit of time to themselves. I enjoy wild swimming and I persuaded them along a few times. Once I took them down to Edinburgh for the festival. I'm not sure what Michael made of it, but Andy had a ball.' He pulled a clown's sad face. 'I never had children. My one big regret.'

'Did you know them when Jane was still drinking?'

'No, she'd stopped by the time I moved up.' He looked at her over the coffee cup. 'I didn't take her up as a good cause, if that's what you're thinking, or because I thought the kids needed protecting. I've never had any problems separating work from my private life. I enjoy her company. She's fun to be with.'

'Any idea why Andy left university?'

Agnew shook his head. 'We stopped being so

close a while ago. Jane talks about them, of course. Children must always be a worry, even when they're old enough to be independent.'

'What do they do now to make Jane worry?'

He opened his mouth to speak at once and Willow thought that at last she might get something useful from the conversation.

But Agnew only smiled. 'I think that's something you'll have to ask Jane, Inspector, don't you?'

28

Perez sat in his office. He'd been relieved when he'd received the text from Willow. He hadn't known quite how he'd respond to her this morning. The night before, she'd caught him in an unguarded moment, and now his invitation to cook her a romantic meal seemed embarrassing and inappropriate. She was his boss.

Sandy had gone north to Brae first thing with a sheaf of photos he'd collected of the men involved — even in a remote way — in the investigation, to show the shop assistant in the Co-op. Perez had stayed at home until it was time to take Cassie to school and was surprised to see Kathryn Rogerson come to the school door, when it was time to let the children in.

'I thought you'd be taking some time off.' He'd waited until the children were in the classroom before speaking to her.

'I'd prefer to be here.' She'd looked grey and drawn, as if she hadn't slept. 'My mother's sister arrived from Orkney on the last plane yesterday. They're very close. She doesn't need me at home.'

'You should take care of yourself.'

Then she'd given him a brief, thin smile. 'You mustn't worry about me, Jimmy. I'm the tough one in the family.' She'd reached out and put her hand on his arm. 'Thank you, though. I'm glad it's you looking for my father's killer. It would be dreadful if it was someone who didn't know us.' And she'd turned and walked with a straight back into the school.

He was sitting in his office and running the scene in his head, wondering what it was about Kathryn Rogerson's composure that he found so disturbing, when his phone rang. He answered it, still slightly distracted. It was Sandy and he forgot the teacher to give the man his full attention.

'I showed the photos to Peter in the Co-op.' Sandy's voice was a little too loud. He sounded like an excited child.

'And?'

'You'll never guess who he picked out.'

'Just tell me, Sandy. We're not playing games here.'

'Paul Taylor!'

For a moment Perez struggled to place the name and then he remembered. Taylor was a solicitor, Tom Rogerson's partner. He'd given them the keys to Rogerson's office on a wet Sunday morning while his wife was cooking lunch.

'And that's not all!' Sandy hadn't waited for a response from Perez. 'Taylor was the man chatting to Alison Teal in the bar, but Kevin Hay was in Mareel that night too. Peter picked him out from the photos I'd spread out over the table.'

⋆ ⋆ ⋆

Perez waited until Sandy returned, before interviewing Paul Taylor in the office that he'd

260

shared with Tom Rogerson. He thought Sandy was owed the right to accompany him; he'd cultivated the shop assistant until he'd come up with the information they needed. They walked to the solicitors' office along Commercial Street. Everywhere people were talking about the weather and turning their faces towards the sun.

In the office a receptionist greeted them. 'I'm afraid Mr Taylor's very busy. You'll have heard that Mr Rogerson died suddenly at the weekend. We're all very shocked and there's such a lot to do.'

Perez didn't recognize her. She was English and he thought she was probably new to the islands. Perhaps she'd moved with her family in the hope of finding an idyllic community where nothing bad happened, only to be confronted with the murder of her employer. He introduced himself and Sandy and she became flushed with panic and a kind of voyeuristic excitement. 'I'll see if Mr Taylor is free.'

Paul Taylor came down the stairs to meet them himself. He led them not into his own poky office, but into the space that had once been Tom Rogerson's.

'I'd been half-expecting you, Inspector. I'm sure you'll have questions about Tom's clients. I'll be happy to help in any way I can.'

'What plans do you have for the business now?' Perez thought Taylor seemed very comfortable behind the large desk that had once belonged to his partner.

'It's too early to say yet.' The man who had been so fraught and out of control with his small

261

sons was entirely relaxed here. 'I might see if I can go it alone, or take on another solicitor. Of course there will be financial implications and I'll need to have discussions with Tom's widow, but it wouldn't be appropriate to consider that yet.'

'We're not here to talk about Tom Rogerson,' Perez said. 'Not yet. We've identified the woman who was killed at Tain. Her name was Alison Teal. She'd stolen the identity of Ms Sechrest, who inherited the property Minnie Laurenson left. Alison was an actress who grew up in Norfolk. Do you know anything about the identity theft? You managed the property, after all. Does her name mean anything to you?'

'Didn't your colleague mention it, when you collected the keys on Sunday? Apart from that I've never heard of the woman.'

'Yet you were seen having a drink with her about ten days ago in the Mareel bar.' Perez took some delight in the panic on the man's face.

'I'm sorry, but I have no idea what you're talking about.' The voice had become rather haughty.

'A reliable witness identified you as the man seen drinking with Alison Teal in Mareel.'

'Then they must be mistaken.'

Perez took a copy of the drawing of Alison from his briefcase and set it on the desk in front of Taylor. 'Perhaps this will jog your memory.'

For a moment Taylor stared at it without speaking. 'Ah, I do remember that woman,' he said at last. 'But I don't know her.'

'Yet you were having a drink with her. The

witness says you were on obviously intimate terms.'

There was another silence and Taylor seemed to be choosing his words with considerable care. 'I'd had a bad day at work. Nothing dramatic had gone wrong, but it was one of those days full of minor irritations. I'm sure you have those too, Inspector.' He looked up, as if he was hoping to get Perez on his side. Perez didn't answer and the solicitor continued. 'Usually at the end of work I drive straight home, so I can help my wife get the boys ready for bed. They're not at an easy age and they're a nightmare to get to sleep. But that night I wanted some time to myself, before facing the mayhem that is bathtime in the Taylor household. I went to Mareel for a glass of wine. One small glass. I was driving, and a lawyer can't afford to be charged with drink-driving. It was relatively quiet when I got there — perhaps it was too early for the film to start — but I took my drink upstairs. I wanted some time to myself. A woman came in. In contrast to me, she seemed to be looking for company. She asked if she could join me. I suppose I was flattered. She was attractive, with dark hair and dark eyes. We chatted for a little while. Inconsequential stuff. I suppose I was flirting with her. Or we were flirting with each other. She was good company and time passed very quickly. I bought coffee for us both and by then the bar was filling up. Then my wife phoned, wanting to know where I was. I said goodbye and left. She told me her name was Alice. I assumed it was spelled in the traditional way. I don't know anything else about her.'

Yet you wanted to, Perez thought. *If your wife hadn't phoned, would you have gone with her to the little house in Ravenswick?* He wondered what *he* would have done, if he'd been there. Perhaps *he'd* have been seduced by her too.

'We've been asking for information about her,' he said. 'Haven't you seen the news reports?'

Taylor shook his head, but he wasn't quite convincing. Perez couldn't tell whether it was the police he'd been frightened of or his wife.

'It's quite a coincidence, you see,' he said. 'Now we know you had a connection to both murder victims.'

'I'd never seen the woman before in my life.' Taylor looked up, shocked. 'I swear.'

'How did she seem?' Perez asked. 'What sort of mood was she in?'

'Lonely.' Taylor didn't need time to answer that. 'A little bit desperate.'

'Did she tell you anything about her private life? Her family? Did she tell you what she was doing in Shetland?'

'She said she was here for work.' Taylor shuffled in his seat. 'I assumed she was something to do with the oil or gas.'

'Did she mention where she was staying?'

'She said she was renting somewhere for the duration of her contract.'

'And you never connected her with the Alissandra Sechrest who owned Tain?'

'Of course not! The Alice I spent those couple of hours with was English, not American.'

Perez tried to work out if Taylor was telling the truth. Perhaps the meeting in Mareel had been coincidental, a chance encounter between a man overwhelmed by domestic responsibilities and a lonely woman. Perhaps.

'Did you talk to her about your work? Did you give her your name, for instance?' Because Alison might have recognized the name of the solicitor she'd defrauded of the American publisher's keys.

Taylor looked uncomfortable. 'I told her my name was Paul, but I didn't give her my surname and we didn't talk about my work. She assumed I worked for the council.'

If the flirtation turned into something more serious, you didn't want her to be able to trace you.

'What did she do when you left her to go and see your wife? Did she come out with you?'

Taylor shook his head. 'When I left her, she was still sitting in Mareel, drinking the last of her coffee.'

'Do you know a man called Kevin Hay? He farms most of the land around Ravenswick.'

Taylor shook his head. 'Is it important?'

Perez wasn't sure how to answer that. He'd lost all perspective on what might or might not be important. He got to his feet and thought that the Alison Teal described by Taylor was rather closer to the Alison who'd called into the Befriending Shetland office to ask for help than any of the impressions they'd had before. Lonely and a little bit desperate.

Out on the street the sun was still shining and the shoppers were still talking about the fact that spring had come early this year. Sandy was obviously full of questions about what Perez had learned from the interview, but he knew better than to ask them. He bounced along beside the inspector as they walked back to the police station, waiting for his boss to speak.

Perez took no notice because he had nothing to say yet. He was thinking about Alison Teal and deciding it might be easy to get to a position where you were so lonely that you couldn't stand your own company for a minute more and wandered into a bar just to find someone to talk to. Willow came into his mind. Perhaps it would be good to spend some time with her and talk about anything other than work. The idea made him smile.

29

Willow took her time driving back to Lerwick. She was pondering her conversation with Simon Agnew and found the omissions — the reluctance to talk about Kevin and the boys, for example — more interesting than the information she'd been given. She was approaching the turning to Gilsetter and had seen the light bouncing off the huge polytunnels, when Sandy phoned to say that the email with Rogerson's bank statements had come through and that she might want to see them.

'Can't you give me the gist, Sandy?'

But that made him anxious. 'I might just be reading them wrong. Much better that you see them for yourself.'

When she got into the office, Perez was on his way to a meeting with the new Procurator Fiscal. He waved as they passed in the corridor and called after her to suggest that they might catch up later. 'Maybe over a late lunch? I probably won't be finished until gone two.'

He'd disappeared before she could answer. She found Sandy in the operations room with the printed emails on the big table in front of him. When she came into the room he gave her a smile that made him look as if he was still in primary school. 'It's great to see you. I didn't want to show these to Jimmy just yet. Not while he's off to see the Fiscal. Not until I've checked that I'm reading them right.'

'What's the problem?' She made herself coffee, then stood behind him, looking down at the sheets of paper.

'You know we thought Rogerson might be paying Alison Teal?' Sandy twisted in his seat so that he was looking up at her. 'We thought that might explain the fancy clothes and the fact that we couldn't find any evidence of her working while she was living at Tain, or even for some time before that.'

'Yes, but she might have set up an account in another name. We know she doesn't mind stealing other people's identities. We need to be aware of that when we're checking Rogerson's records.'

'But according to the statements, he wasn't paying anyone.' Sandy turned back to the table. 'Not from his business or his personal accounts. I mean, there were direct debits for his electricity and phone from his home account, and his wage bill and rent for the business premises in Commercial Street, but otherwise no unusual payments at all.'

'Could he have added Alison as a fictitious employee and paid her along with the other staff?'

'No, I've checked. There are National Insurance numbers for all the workers and they match the staff names.' Sandy frowned.

'Seems as if you've covered everything then.'

'But that's not the strange thing!' He pulled one of the detailed statements towards him and pointed to a list of entries, which he'd highlighted with a yellow pen. 'These are a list of payments made *to* one of his business accounts.'

'Surely they'll be from clients. Nothing unusual in lawyers getting paid!'

'But I've been onto his office manager to check. She doesn't recognize any of the names I've highlighted. She has no record of the firm ever having done any work for them. And although this is classed as a business account, it's separate from the one she has access to. It seems to be something Tom Rogerson has set up by himself.'

Willow tried to make sense of this. 'So Rogerson had a secret account?'

'That's what it seems like.' Now Sandy sounded excited rather than anxious. 'Look at the list!'

Willow ran her eyes down the statement. She didn't recognize the first names on the list and there was nothing obvious to connect them. The amounts paid into Rogerson's account varied from a couple of hundred to several thousand pounds. There were often multiple payments from the same person. Some of the payers had Shetland-sounding names. There was a Tommy Jeromeson and a William Eunson, for example. Others were more obviously English, and a few sounded as if the people were from mainland Europe or the Middle East. 'Have you got the account-holders addresses?'

'Not yet. Apparently that'll take extra authorization.'

'I'll try to sort it out.'

'But look at these!' Now Sandy was almost beside himself. He pointed a stubby finger at two of the names at the bottom of the list. One was Stuart Henderson. 'That's Craig Henderson's father. You remember Craig. He was the guy who rented Tain from Sandy Sechrest.'

'But we already knew that Rogerson worked for the Henderson holiday business. He's the one with the fancy lodges, right?' Willow didn't want to discourage Sandy, but she thought his imagination was running away from him now. She'd always been dismissive of weird conspiracy theories. 'It's not surprising that he should be paying legal fees.'

'This money comes from Stuart Henderson's personal account, not the business. I've checked. And according to Rogerson's office manager, none of these sums tally with any of the business invoices she's ever sent out.'

Willow took a seat for the first time. She'd been hovering behind Sandy for long enough. 'So what are you thinking here, Sandy? Bribery and corruption?'

'A lot of people wondered how the Hendersons got planning permission for that tourist accommodation, and Rogerson was on the council.' Sandy looked at her. He was begging her not to tell him he was a fool with an overactive imagination.

'Well, it wouldn't be the first time a politician's been slipped a sweetener to clear the path of a development.' Now Willow's mind was racing. This opened up another strand to the investigation. A different set of motives and more suspects. 'But there are more than a dozen names on this list. They can't all have been involved in complex planning issues.'

'I was wondering about blackmail,' Sandy said. 'Rogerson was known as a sociable kind of a guy. He'd hear gossip. Some of it related to council business, some to the development at Sullom Voe. Some personal. Maybe he didn't get the sweetener from Henderson, but he knew the person who did, or at least guessed that something dodgy had been going on.'

Willow nodded. She could see how that might make sense. 'It seems risky, though. According to Jimmy, Rogerson enjoyed being Mr Popular on Shetland Islands Council. Why would he put all that in danger?'

'He needed the cash,' Sandy said. 'If you look at both his other accounts, he went right up to the overdraft limit each month. It was only transfers from the secret account that kept him solvent.'

'I wonder if his wife knew.' Willow thought that a woman who could tolerate a string of embarrassing infidelities probably wouldn't ask too many questions about regular payments into her husband's current account. 'You've done some brilliant work here, Sandy.'

'But Stuart Henderson's not the only man linked to Alison Teal and Tom Rogerson to be on the list.' Sandy was flushed with pleasure. He leaned across her and pointed to the last highlighted entry. 'Have you seen this?' He moved his finger so that she could read the name. 'Kevin Hay.'

* * *

271

Willow wanted to consult Perez before she decided how they should play an interview with Kevin Hay. She wondered if Simon Agnew had been discreetly pointing her in his direction. But she wanted some action. She couldn't spend the rest of the morning talking to bank managers and studying spreadsheets while she waited for Perez to come out of his meeting. She asked Sandy for the way to the Rogerson house and walked out into the sunshine.

The house was solid and grey with an enclosed garden in the front. A neatly trimmed hedge and shrubs with orange berries. Strangely suburban for Shetland. She knocked at the door and a small, bustling woman opened it. 'Mrs Rogerson?'

The woman narrowed her eyes. 'Who wants to know?'

'Willow Reeves. Police Scotland.'

The woman looked sceptical. Willow supposed she wasn't most people's idea of a police officer. She pulled out her warrant card.

'Only you can't be too careful.' The woman's voice was sing-song Orkney. 'That Reg Gilbert from *The Shetland Times* was here earlier, weaselling for an interview with Mavis.'

'You're not Mrs Rogerson?'

'I'm her sister. Joan.'

'Could I speak to her?' Willow inched towards the open door. They were still on the step.

'She's not here. It's her day for the Red Cross shop and she insisted on going. I told her nobody would expect it, but she said she'd rather be there. She was a bit hysterical when I tried to

272

stop her, and I thought it was best to let her go for a couple of hours, if it made her feel better. Maybe the routine would be good for her.' Joan stepped away from the door so that she could look back at the town-hall clock. 'She'll be finished in five minutes, if you want to wait. It'll not take her long to walk up from the street.'

But Willow thanked her and headed away. She was in no mood for waiting.

★ ★ ★

She arrived at the charity shop just as Mavis Rogerson was leaving. The woman was like a more square and solid version of her sister. Despite the sun, she was wearing a heavy overcoat and sheepskin boots. Willow waited outside until Rogerson's widow was on the street.

'Mavis, my name's Willow Reeves. I'm a detective from Inverness and I'm part of the investigation team working on your husband's death. I wonder if I could ask you some questions.'

'Do you want to come back to the house?'

'We could do that if you like, or we could just have some coffee and chat.' Willow wanted to keep this informal. 'I don't expect you've eaten much today. I hear the Peerie Shop Cafe does very good cake.'

Mavis gave a little smile. 'Tom and I went there every Saturday morning when he was free. A little treat.'

'We all need a little treat.'

The lunchtime rush at the cafe was over. A few people sat smoking on the chairs outside, but there was nobody upstairs. Willow sat Mavis there and went down to the counter to order. The woman was docile when Willow helped her out of her coat, as if she was grateful that someone else was taking charge. Willow ordered cappuccinos and lemon-drizzle cake for two. It had been a long time since the scrambled eggs in the guest house. She wondered fleetingly if there was any news of a baby.

'I need to talk to you about Tom.'

Mavis nodded, but she hardly seemed to hear what Willow was saying.

'We're looking for reasons why someone should want to kill him.' The detective fell silent while a young waitress brought their order; then she continued. 'We've been checking his bank accounts. It's something we'd do routinely in a case like this. You do understand?'

Mavis nodded again. She seemed incapable of speech, but had cut through the lemon cake and put a large piece into her mouth. Willow understood that. Shock made her hungry too.

'Did Tom ever talk to you about money?'

'He was never good with his finances.' The cake seemed to have brought Mavis to life. 'He was a good earner, but there was never any cash to spare.' She paused and then felt the need to explain. 'He always needed to be liked. It was a kind of compulsion with him. It didn't always come naturally, though, and sometimes he had to buy his friendships. With gifts. Loans that were never repaid. If ever we went out for a meal with another couple, Tom insisted on picking up the bill. In the end folk came to expect it.'

This time Willow nodded to show that she understood. Mavis took another bite of cake.

'There are some unexplained payments *into* your husband's account,' Willow said. 'Can you think what they might be? Perhaps they came from people paying back earlier loans.'

Mavis considered. 'I don't think that's likely. Like I said, Tom was always the one who coughed up. Nobody felt the need to pay back.'

'Could Tom have been doing some legal work that wasn't going through the company's books?'

Mavis shook her head. 'Paul Taylor was a junior partner,' she said. 'Tom liked him. He wouldn't have tried to defraud him.'

'That wasn't what I meant. I'm trying to explain these payments.'

But Mavis seemed to have lost concentration again. Willow hadn't touched her cake and Mavis was staring hungrily at it.

Willow swapped plates, so the cake was in front of Mavis. 'You'll be doing me a favour. I'm supposed to be going out for a late lunch. It'll only spoil my appetite.'

30

The meeting with the Fiscal took longer than Perez had thought and he expected Willow to have gone for lunch without him. But when he hurried into the ops room, she was still waiting for him.

'I have a lot of news. Mostly down to Sandy's persistence and hard work.' She'd swept her wild hair to one side so that he could see the bare skin of her neck on the other.

Perez looked away. 'Have you eaten?'

She shook her head. 'I ordered lemon cake in the Peerie Shop Cafe, but I sacrificed it to a greater good. I'm starving.'

He tried to think of a good place to take her to eat, but in the end they bought fish and chips and ate them out of the wind in the shelter of the Garrison, hidden from view in a corner between two grey walls. He put his jacket down so they could sit on the grass and felt suddenly that he was in one of the dens that he'd built when he was a bairn. There was the same sense of being hidden away from the rest of the world. 'Shall I start?'

'Why not, Inspector?' She was licking the grease from her fingers, rolled the paper into a ball and carefully put it into her pocket.

'Did Sandy tell you his contact recognized two men who were in Mareel the night Alison was there?'

Willow shook her head. 'He was too distracted by the information that came in later.'

'Alison was having a drink with Rogerson's partner, Paul Taylor, but Kevin Hay was in the building too. Sandy and I chatted to Taylor in his office.'

'And?' A gust of wind blew a strand of Willow's hair across her face.

'Taylor claims it was a chance meeting with Alison in Mareel. He was there because he'd had a bad day at the office, and she was lonely and looking for a sympathetic ear.'

'Sounds like a weird coincidence,' Willow said. 'Do you believe him?'

Perez thought about that while he watched the herring gulls in the clear sky above them. 'I think I do.'

He listened while Willow described her conversation with Simon Agnew in Ravenswick. 'He wasn't giving away much about the Hays, but I had the impression he thought the relationship wasn't as perfect as they liked to make out.'

'So it could be relevant that Kevin Hay was in Mareel at the same time as Alison?'

'You think he might have been following her?' Willow said. 'Stalking even?'

'I don't think we have enough information even to make a guess.'

'Could Alison have had a relationship with Kevin when she ran away to Shetland fifteen years ago? We've assumed that the letter in Tain was written by Rogerson, but we haven't had confirmation back on the handwriting yet.'

Perez considered. 'The Hays were living in Gilsetter then. Two small bairns, and Jane was still drinking. It wouldn't have been an easy time. You can see how he might have fallen for an attractive stranger staying in the hotel.'

'Why don't you talk to him, Jimmy?' Willow leaned forward and again he could see the skin on her neck. There was a light scattering of freckles. 'He might open up more to a man.'

'Cassie's father's back in Shetland today.' Duncan Hunter was Cassie's natural father and he'd been away from the islands for some weeks. 'She was going to stay with him tonight anyway. I'll call down to the Hays this evening and see if I can talk to Kevin on his own.'

'Find out why he was paying money into Tom Rogerson's secret bank account!'

'He was what?'

'I got authorization to get information on Rogerson's accounts. Sandy had all the statements when I got back from Ravenswick this morning.' Willow explained in detail what they'd discovered. 'I chatted to Mavis Rogerson, but she claims to know nothing about the payments. Any idea what might have been going on? Sandy's theory is council corruption, but I'm not quite sure what Hay might have to gain from that.'

'It sounds more like blackmail.' Perez thought this shifted the whole perspective on the case. Money was a motive he could understand. 'If Rogerson had found out that Hay and Alison were lovers, and threatened to tell Jane.' He imagined how that would have been for Kevin.

The woman living just across the field from him in Tain — had he become obsessed by her, only to find out she was part of some sort of extortion scam with Rogerson?

'It's another reason for chatting to Kevin Hay.' Willow stood up and shook a few scraps of food from her clothes. She reached down and gave a hand to Perez to help him up. 'Shall I come along to your place later, Jimmy? I'd be interested in finding out what Hay says.'

He hesitated for a moment. Willow knew Cassie wouldn't be in the house. 'Would you like me cook for you? Nothing grand, though. A late supper.'

There was a moment of silence that made the question seem more significant than he'd intended.

'Don't go to any trouble, Jimmy,' she said at last. 'You know me, I'm a simple girl. 'Some bread and cheese will suit me fine.'

★ ★ ★

Duncan Hunter turned up at Perez's home in the early evening with a tanned face and an armful of gifts for his daughter. 'Leave these here and open them later,' he said to Cassie. 'There are plenty more at our house.' His house was the Haa, the crumbling heap he shared with his older woman, Celia. Sometimes. The relationship was tempestuous and Fran had bequeathed her daughter to Perez, not to Duncan. A kind of gift from the grave.

Cassie went off happily enough, though, and

Perez was pleased to have the house to himself. On impulse he changed the sheets on his bed and cleaned the sink in the bathroom. Then he made himself tea and beans on toast, washed all the dishes and wiped down the draining board. He'd got in good bread and a variety of cheese, a stalk of grapes and some watercress. He laid the fire, so it would be ready to light when he got in.

Just as he got to the turn-off to the Hays' place, a car pulled out onto the main road and drove off towards Lerwick. It was quite dark by now and he couldn't tell whether the vehicle was driven by Jane or Kevin. Perez went on down to the house. There was a light in two of the upstairs windows. He supposed at least one of the boys must be at home. He got out of the car. Kevin must have heard the engine noise, because the door opened and he was standing there silhouetted. 'Jimmy. This is kind of late for an official call.'

'If it was official, I'd be calling you into the station.' Perez kept his voice light and easy. He didn't want the words to sound like a threat. 'This is just a chat.' Kevin stood aside to let him in. 'Are you on your own?'

'Jane's at a meeting in town and Andy's working in Mareel. Michael's upstairs, but he won't disturb us. Once he's plugged into his computer he's in a different universe.' Kevin was wearing thick knitted socks and he padded ahead of Perez into the kitchen. There was a lingering smell of cooked food, but everything was tidy. 'Will you take some coffee, Jimmy? Or a beer, if this is unofficial?'

'Coffee would be great.' Perez smiled to recognize that Kevin had almost cracked a joke.

Kevin Hay switched on the kettle and spooned instant into mugs. It seemed Perez didn't deserve the effort of the good stuff. 'What's this about?' He was quite serious now.

'A couple of things. I'm sure you'll clear them up in no time.' Perez waited until Kevin was sitting at the table with him. 'You paid some money into Tom Rogerson's business account. Could you tell me what that was for?'

The man didn't respond immediately. Perhaps he'd been expecting a question of the sort, because although it made him uncomfortable he wasn't completely surprised. But he wasn't a habitual liar and his answer was tentative and unconvincing. 'Rogerson was my lawyer,' he said at last. 'We did business from time to time.'

'Could you show me the invoices from Rogerson and Taylor?'

'Not now, Jimmy. It would take me some time to find them, and anyway Jane looks after the admin side of things.' He turned away and wouldn't meet Perez's eyes.

'Only we can't find a record of any business dealings with the firm and that seems a bit odd.' Perez almost felt sorry for the man. He'd started to blush. 'This would be confidential, Kevin, unless it had some bearing on Tom's death. You're not the only man to be paying sums into this secret account.'

There was a long silence. Kevin didn't speak and he didn't move.

'Perhaps we're talking blackmail here,' Perez

281

said. 'That's how it's looking just now. If it was blackmail, you'd be a victim. An anonymous victim. But someone has to tell us what's been going on. You do see that, don't you, Kevin?'

'It wasn't blackmail.' Now his voice was firm. 'I've told you, there must be some mistake. An accounting error. There's nothing sinister here. Nothing that can be related in any way to Rogerson's death.' Upstairs a door banged shut and Kevin's voice grew more urgent. 'That'll be Michael. He'll be coming down to fix himself a drink and a snack. I don't want him worried. These sudden deaths have caused enough disturbance to our lives. It's time for you to go, Jimmy. If you need to talk to me again, call me into the station. Like you said, that's the proper way to have a conversation, if it's official business.' He was on his feet and almost shooed Perez towards the outside door as if he was a troublesome cat. That image made Perez think of another question.

'Have you lost one of your cats?' He was already in the yard. Kevin stood in the doorway.

'I don't think so. The farm cat had kittens and we've given all those away. Why?'

'There was a dead cat found in Tain when they cleared through the rubble. I thought it must be one of yours, wandered in just before the landslide.'

Kevin seemed about to say something, but he shut the door without speaking. Perez sat in the car for a moment before driving away.

★ ★ ★

It was still only just gone seven and Willow wouldn't be at his house until nine. Perez couldn't think what he'd do at home for the next two hours except fret and get anxious, so he headed out again towards the complex of holiday lodges owned by the Henderson family. Willow had said that Stuart Henderson was on the list of people who paid money into Rogerson's secret account. Perhaps he'd be more forthcoming than Kevin Hay. The chalets were grouped around a landscaped area, which in the brochure was described as a traditional Shetland hay meadow. The grass was brown and scorched by wind and salt now, but perhaps in the summer there would be wildflowers. Perez was sceptical. The scene was lit by wrought-iron street lights that would have been more in keeping in an English village square. The whole effect was of a bizarre film set, but two of the chalets had lights at the windows, so tourists must be attracted even in winter.

Stuart's giant 4x4 wasn't parked at the big bungalow and when Perez rang the doorbell, it was Craig Henderson who answered.

'I was hoping to speak to your parents.'

'They're out,' Craig said. 'Country-and-Western night in the Marlix in town. That's their thing.' He flashed a quick grin. 'At least it gives me an evening a week to myself. No nagging.'

'Could I have a word with you?'

'Aye, why not?' He'd been eating supper from a tray, which had been set on the floor beside his chair. Perez supposed Angie would clear it up for him when she got in. A huge television screen was showing a European football match. Craig turned the sound down. 'How can I help you, Jimmy?'

'We're following up information about Tom Rogerson. He seems to have been receiving rather mysterious payments. I wondered if you could shed any light on them.' After all, he couldn't accuse the man's father of bribery and corruption or of paying blackmail to the dead man.

He'd expected a flat denial and for the television to go back on, but Craig's attention was on Perez now.

'There have been rumours,' he said.

'What kind of rumours?' Perez thought it was odd that a man who only spent part of every year in Shetland should know the gossip about the place. But he could see that Angie would be one for spreading any news.

'I didn't hear it from here.'

That was even more tantalizing, but Perez didn't want Craig to think the information was important, so he said nothing.

'But oilies talk, you know.'

There was a goal on the television that caught Craig's attention for a moment. Perez started to lose patience. 'And what do the oilies say?'

'They're here on their own. All the men locked up in the floatels, away from their wives and girlfriends for weeks at a time. Those that have wives and girlfriends . . . ' He paused and grinned. 'You can see that might provide a business opportunity for some enterprising person.'

Perez was starting to see where this was going.

Willow had noticed that all the names on Rogerson's list were men, but she'd assumed that was because most councillors and business people were male. 'Spell it out for me, Craig. What was going on here?'

'Rumour has it that Rogerson could get you a girl, if you wanted one.' He looked up and grinned again. 'A selection of girls.'

31

Willow sat in the car below Perez's house in Ravenswick. There was a moon, and shreds of cirrus cloud floated in front of it, so the light was milky and opaque. She knew that he was back from talking to Kevin Hay because his car was there and there was a glow behind the curtained window, but she was a little early and didn't want to disturb him before he was ready for her. Eventually she walked up the bank and tapped at the door.

The fire had been lit, but there were no candles this time. She wasn't sure whether she was pleased or disappointed. Perez was sitting at the table writing notes under an angle-poise lamp. There were still shadows in the corners of the room.

'What have you got for us, Jimmy?' She wanted him to know that she had no expectations of this meeting, that she could be entirely professional.

'Kevin Hay would tell me nothing.' Perez hesitated and then stood up. 'I was thinking it was time for some supper and I might open a bottle of wine. Will you join me in a glass?'

'Why not?' One glass over a whole evening wouldn't cloud her judgement.

He didn't ask what she would prefer, but pulled the cork from a bottle of red. He had cheese arranged already on a plate on the counter, bread on a board, ready to cut. He set the food with plates and two glasses on a low table in front of the fire.

'So how did Kevin explain the payments to Rogerson?'

Perez poured wine. 'Rogerson was his solicitor and they undertook business for him from time to time.'

'But what sort of business?' The wine was light and sharp.

'I rather think that I've got to the bottom of that too.' He reached out and offered her the cheese. She thought how easy it would be to reach to take his hand. *Confide in me, Jimmy. Let me rescue you from your dreams and your ghosts.*

'And?'

He smiled. 'First of all, let me tell you a story. Several years ago, just when it was decided to bring natural gas ashore in Shetland because the oil supplies were dwindling, there was an advert in *The Shetland Times*. A woman from Aberdeen, who ran an escort agency in the city, was thinking of setting up a branch in Lerwick. I can't remember the name now. Something flowery and fancy, but it was a name that made it quite clear what the business was about. There was a mobile number, and interested parties should contact her. She intimated that contractors and men working in the oil and gas industries would be especially welcome. There was an outcry and the *Times* was berated for running the ad. The council made it clear that such a venture would definitely not be allowed in Shetland.'

Willow sipped her wine. 'You think Tom Rogerson stole the idea?'

'I think it would explain the random payments from islanders and from incomers. I checked into the background of some of the islanders on the list. Many of them are lonely single men.'

'Do you have any evidence for the theory?' She was thinking this would be hard to prove. Tom Rogerson's clients would be too embarrassed to talk, especially the men like Kevin Hay who were married, and the working girls would have their own reasons for keeping quiet. She imagined many of them would be Eastern European. Perhaps they'd come to Shetland to work as chambermaids or in the fish-processing factory and Rogerson had recruited them with the promise of easy cash.

'None at all. And it wasn't even my theory. I went to see Craig Henderson and he told me there were rumours among the contractors that Rogerson could put them in touch with the women.'

'But Rogerson can't have paid the women,' she said, 'because there's no trace of regular sums leaving his account. He must have charged an introduction or arrangement fee, and the women would have been paid direct. So there was no evidential link between him and the girls. He was very careful.' She was thinking through the details. 'That was a lot of cash to pay just for an introduction.'

'The islanders would have had no idea of the going rate,' Perez said, 'and the incomers wouldn't have been short of cash. Besides, perhaps Rogerson didn't just make the introduction and sort out the logistics. Perhaps he provided somewhere discreet for the parties to meet.'

'The house at Tain?'

Perez nodded. 'Over the winter at least. Before that, who knows?'

'How did Alison Teal fit into the scheme?' Willow thought Alison must have been a part of the business. It would make sense of the unexplained affluence and the expensive clothes. Her presence in Tain. 'There was no record that Rogerson shared his profit with her. Was she just another of his working girls? A high-class whore imported from the south to serve Rogerson's more discerning customers.'

Perez didn't answer directly. 'I've been sitting here going over and over the possibilities.' He looked up and smiled. 'It's been driving me a little bit mad.'

'Well, we're all a bit mad.'

'Maybe I've been madder than most, brooding about the past. I've not been great to be with, over the past couple of years.'

'I can understand that,' Willow said. She expected some response, but none came. Perhaps it was too soon for him after all, too raw. Perhaps he just didn't fancy her. 'Look, would you rather be on your own? Would you like me to go?' She was already on her feet.

'No,' Perez said. He didn't move from his seat and his face was in shadow, so it was still hard to tell what he was thinking.

She'd already pulled on her coat and had her bag over her shoulder.

'Please stay. Have another glass of wine, something else to eat. I'd like to talk to you. Just for the pleasure of your company. If you don't mind.'

She let her bag drop down her arm. Now he got to his feet and he helped her out of her jacket. He stroked her hair away from her face and pulled her to him.

32

It hadn't been the best fellowship meeting. Rachel had turned up drunk and Jane had sat with her while the others spoke, and afterwards Jane had checked that Rachel wasn't driving and had seen her home. She knew better than to think of the woman's lapse as her own failure, but she was sad for her. More selfishly, she knew there would be more late-night phone calls, more self-pity and floods of remorse. Jane's sponsor had seen her through her own recovery, but there was so much stress at home now that she wasn't sure she could stand more disruption within the family. When she got into the house she turned her phone to silent. Rachel would probably sleep tonight anyway.

Kevin was waiting for her. 'You're late. I was starting to get worried.'

'I had to give someone a lift home.' She switched on the kettle. 'Would you like tea? Coffee?' She hated these brittle conversations when nothing was really said.

'Jimmy Perez was here earlier.'

'What did he want?' She hovered with her hand reaching for her mug. Frozen with a kind of fear. She knew Kevin was involved in some way with the dead woman. The certainty came almost as a relief. She wasn't making things up or going mad. But even if Kevin was a killer, she didn't want him caught. She wanted the whole affair to be over and for Jimmy Perez to leave them on their own to work out their marriage.

'Just some questions about Tom Rogerson. They'd found a couple of payments I'd made to him. I've been through the files. They must have been when he bought that piece of land out towards the school for us.'

She felt a moment of relief. Kevin was always buying parcels of land. Andy sometimes joked that he wouldn't stop until he'd bought up the whole of Shetland mainland. It was the woman from Tain, the actress from London, who most risked their stability, even now she was dead; not business deals with Tom Rogerson. It occurred to her suddenly that she would have killed the woman herself to save Kevin and the boys.

'Jimmy told me it was nothing official,' Kevin said. 'He was just tying up loose ends.' But he didn't look at her and she wasn't reassured by the words.

She put a camomile teabag into a mug and poured on the water. The last thing she needed tonight was caffeine. 'How are the boys?'

'Michael's up in his room. He came down a while ago for something to eat. He's doing school work, he says. More likely sitting in front of that computer of his and watching rubbish.'

'He spends too long in front of the screen. I wonder what he's looking at. You hear such dreadful stories. Maybe we should keep a closer eye.' It was a conversation they'd had before. Kevin thought she was fussing about nothing.

Michael was almost a man. Settled and almost married. What did it matter what he accessed on the computer? Occasionally Jane had wandered into the office and Kevin had quickly switched off the screen, so she wondered if her husband was watching the same sort of material. Now he didn't bother answering.

'What about Andy?' She'd seen his car in the yard and had thought with relief that he must be home. One less thing to worry about. *The last few days all I've done is worry.*

'He hasn't been here all day. I thought he must still be at work.'

'His shift finished at five and his car's here.' The worm of anxiety, so familiar, was already burrowing into her brain. 'Did you see him come back?'

Kevin shrugged as if he had more important things to worry about. 'Maybe he didn't take the car this morning. If he was meeting up with friends for a couple of pints after work, perhaps he decided to go up on the bus.'

She thought Kevin was right. She couldn't remember if the car had been in the yard all day or not. It wasn't late yet and Andy was probably in town. She phoned him all the same, though she wasn't surprised when there was no reply. When she went to bed he still wasn't home, but it was as if she'd lost her capacity to continue worrying. There'd been so much anxiety that her brain couldn't take any more. She fell immediately into a deep sleep.

* ★ ★ ★

293

She woke suddenly when it was still quite dark. There was no moonlight and she knew immediately that the weather had changed again. It was as if a switch had been flicked and they were back in winter. Wind rattled through the house, battering at the windows and howling down the chimneys. No rain yet, but she could tell by the sound that the gale was north-westerly, and she knew that it would soon come. Kevin was lying beside her, still fast asleep. She looked at the radio by her bed. Nearly six o'clock. Not too early to get up and make tea.

This was a solid and well-built house, but the wind must have found its way through small cracks because she could feel the draught eddying around her ankles as she made her way downstairs. She refused to wonder if Andy was home. Much better to believe that he was still in Lerwick, having crashed at a friend's flat. That way she wouldn't be disappointed. Much better to make a cup of tea, sit in the warmth of the Aga and plan the small routines of the day. That way she could keep the panic at bay.

When she reached the ground floor there was a chill and the breeze was even fiercer. Sometimes a north-westerly wind blew out the Aga and she thought that must have happened again. It would be a nuisance to relight it and she thought she could do without the bother. Then she realized that the door to the yard was open. They never locked it, but the catch was strong and it had never blown open before. She shut it firmly and went into the kitchen. Andy was sitting at the table. His arms were crossed in front of him and his head was resting on them. She couldn't tell if he was dead or just sleeping and for a moment she couldn't move. Then he lifted his head and with unfocused eyes stared towards her.

'I'm sorry,' he said. 'I'm so sorry.'

33

When Sandy got to the police station Willow and Perez were already there. He checked his watch when he saw them, just to make sure he wasn't late. Most days Jimmy tried to drop Cassie at school, so usually Sandy was at work first. They all sat in the ops room for what Willow called morning prayers, but what he knew as a briefing. She and Jimmy seemed kind of dazed. Perhaps it was because they'd been bombarded the evening before with new revelations and revised theories; Sandy soon had a sense that the direction of the case had changed completely.

'Had you heard any of these rumours, Sandy? About Tom Rogerson arranging girls for the men in the floatels. And for anyone else who'll pay him.'

Sandy shook his head. 'But folk are careful what they say in front of me. You know what it's like, Jimmy.' Then he thought Perez might *not* know what it was like to have conversations in bars suddenly stop as he was approaching. Forced laughter. Over-elaborate descriptions of the stories that were being told before he'd walked in. Perez had never been very social, even before Fran's death. Recently he scarcely left the house in the evening unless it was for work.

'What do you think about the Shetlanders on the list? Are they likely candidates, do you think, for Rogerson's services?'

'Maybe.' Sandy thought if he hadn't met Louisa, he might have been one of the lonely men on the list in ten years' time. 'I'm surprised by Kevin Hay, though. I always thought he was very happy with his wife.'

'Perhaps the happy-family thing just wasn't enough for him,' Willow said. 'Perhaps that was what Agnew was trying to tell me.'

Jimmy Perez shot her a look, but he didn't reply directly. 'We need to get one of these men to talk. Any idea who'd be willing to speak to us, Sandy?'

'I can't see even the single guys who come from the islands wanting to admit that they've been using a prostitute.' He felt himself blushing just at the thought of it. He wouldn't want to interview any of them. 'Maybe you're best targeting the oilies.'

'I've checked,' Willow said. 'They don't all stay in the floatels in Scalloway or Lerwick. A good number give their local address as the new hotel near Sullom.'

'That might explain what Alison Teal was doing in Brae just before she died.' Perez seemed to have woken up a bit. He leaned forward across the table. 'She was there for work.' He paused and it was if Sandy could see his brain working. 'Either on her own account, to interview potential clients, or to recruit more girls for the business.'

Sandy remembered visiting the hotel and passing round an image of the dead woman the day after her death. He'd sensed some of the staff had recognized her. Perhaps she'd paid them to let her work there and to keep quiet about it. 'So we definitely think she was working for Tom Rogerson?'

'Well, they were certainly connected in some way. We're pretty sure that Tom collected her from the Co-op that day, aren't we? He must have known what she was up to.'

There was a moment of silence broken by the wind outside. There was a sudden sharp shower and the rain was blown like gravel on the window, so hard that Sandy thought the glass might smash.

'They must have kept in touch.' Willow's voice was as hard and sharp as the rain. 'Rogerson and Alison. From that first meeting years ago, when Alison went missing and turned up in the Ravenswick Hotel. It's the only explanation. And I can't believe there's no evidence of that. Even if she didn't come back to see Rogerson, he must have gone south to meet her. There'll be hotel receipts, plane, boat and train tickets. She'll have talked to her family and friends about him.' She looked round the table. 'I've been onto the prison where Jono, her brother, is being held. Alison's visited a few times. They lost touch for a while when he first went into the army, but there's obviously been contact since then. Let's get him on the phone and find out what he knows.' She paused for breath. 'I'll get on to that.'

Perez seemed about to speak, but she was still issuing her instructions. There seemed to be something different about her today too, but Sandy couldn't quite work out what it was.

298

Maybe she was slightly more distant with Perez. Perhaps they'd fallen out. 'Jimmy and Sandy, you go north and visit the Sullom Hotel. Get a couple of guys on Rogerson's list to talk to you. We know the oil and gas companies have a 'one strike and you're out' policy here in Shetland, so assure them that we'll be discreet, as long as they come clean with us. If they tell us what was really going on, they won't lose their jobs.' She looked around the table. 'Any questions?'

Perez shook his head and Sandy followed.

'Then head up to Sullom and bring back some evidence that Alison Teal and Tom Rogerson were working together. That'll be a start. Without that, this whole theory crumbles to pieces.'

★　★　★

Perez drove north towards Brae, with Sandy in the passenger seat beside him. Sandy had been looking forward to the time they'd have on their own together. It would be like old times, just the two of them, with Jimmy Perez talking through his ideas about the case and Sandy occasionally throwing in some notions of his own. But today Perez drove in silence. The rain and the wind made driving tricky, but even so, Perez still seemed in a world of his own. Sandy thought again that perhaps he and Willow had been arguing about the investigation before he'd arrived at the station that morning.

Perez showed his warrant card at reception and asked to speak to the first man on the list. He was called Stephen Barnes, he was a civil engineer and his home address was in Carlisle.

'I'm sorry, but he checked out this morning.' The receptionist was bland and unmoved. His English was perfect, but there was a slight accent. 'Most of the men on your list checked out on Monday, but he was delayed. A problem at work, I believe.'

Sandy wondered if it was a coincidence that most of the men who were possible clients of Alison Teal had left the islands, once news of her death had been released. Jimmy Perez always said that he didn't believe in coincidence.

Now Jimmy was replying to the receptionist. He was just as polite, but there was a steely tone to his voice.

'There are no flights from Scatsta this morning,' Perez said. Most of the oil- and gas-related flights left from the airfield at Scatsta, very close to the terminals. 'Not in this dreadful weather. I assume that Mr Barnes is still in the hotel.'

The receptionist stared at the inspector for a moment. Perhaps he was considering the possibility of lying, but at the last moment he seemed to think better of it.

'You're quite right, sir. Mr Barnes has vacated his room, but he's waiting with his colleagues in the lounge for news of his flight. The weather is forecast to clear briefly early this afternoon and there's also the possibility of a coach to Sumburgh. Would you like me to fetch him for you?'

'I'd like that very much.' Perez gave a sudden smile. 'And I'd like you to find a room for us to

300

talk in private, and to arrange for a tray of coffee to be brought for us.'

The receptionist remained impassive, but he gave a brief nod of his head.

The room they used was a conference space with a huge oval table and twelve matching chairs. Perez sat at the end with a notebook in front of him, as if he was chairing a grand meeting. Even Sandy felt intimidated and he knew it was just a tactic, because Jimmy seldom took notes when he was interviewing; he relied on Sandy to do that.

'Mr Barnes. Thank you for giving us your time.' Perez had already offered coffee, which had been curtly declined.

It seemed that Mr Barnes was a senior professional who wasn't used to being summoned by the police. He was already put out because of the delay to his flight. 'It's our wedding anniversary,' he'd said when he'd arrived in the room. An explanation perhaps for his bad temper. An excuse. 'I'd planned something rather special for my wife.'

'We're very grateful for the delay, although I do see that it's inconvenient for you. You might prove to be a very useful witness.' Perez could have been a senior manager himself. Sandy was deeply impressed. 'We're investigating two murders. I'm sure you've seen the news.'

Barnes muttered something about being too busy to watch television.

'Your name appears, along with colleagues, on a list. You made a number of payments to a solicitor called Thomas Rogerson. We have

301

evidence to suggest that Mr Rogerson could be charged with living off immoral earnings, were he still alive. You have committed no offence to date, although if you withhold information in such a serious investigation, you would of course be charged.' Perez paused just long enough for Barnes to take in the implication of the words and then explained them anyway. 'Your company operates a policy that states that an employee found guilty of any offence will be removed from the islands immediately and dismissed. You signed that contract.' Another pause, after which the tone was more conciliatory. 'Of course if you can help us with our enquiries, your company need know nothing about this line of investigation.'

Perez drank coffee, reached out for a mass-produced biscuit and waited.

Barnes was an intelligent man. It didn't take him long to decide that it was in his interest to cooperate. 'Tom Rogerson was a lying bastard,' he said. 'He told me that there would be no record.'

'Why don't we start at the beginning?' Perez leaned forward. At the other end of the table Sandy turned the page of his notebook so that there was a clean sheet of paper in front of him and marvelled at Perez's skill.

It seemed that Stephen Barnes had met Tom Rogerson at a social function to celebrate the completion of one stage of the new terminal's construction. They'd met at the town hall. There'd been speeches, warm fizzy wine and oatcakes with smoked salmon. Barnes had thought Tom was a good chap and when the solicitor had suggested they go back to his house for a 'proper' drink, he'd agreed.

At this point in the story, Perez interrupted. 'Was anyone else in the house? Tom's wife, for example?'

'Not his wife, no. I think his daughter was there when we arrived. A pretty young thing. But she soon said she had work to do and left us to it.'

Perez nodded for Barnes to continue.

'We'd had quite a lot to drink by then, and he brought out a selection of good malts. We were talking about our families, and Tom said he'd worked away in the past and how difficult that was and how wives didn't always understand. He had this way of persuading you to confide in him.' For the first time Barnes seemed embarrassed rather than simply resentful. 'By the end of the evening I'd given him a cheque.'

'Can you be more specific, please? For the notes.' Perez nodded briefly towards Sandy. 'The cheque was payment for what service?'

'It was an introduction fee. Tom Rogerson had promised to set me up with a woman.' Barnes paused briefly. 'The next day I told myself I'd simply been ripped off and nothing would come of it.'

'But it did?' There was curiosity in Perez's voice, but no judgement.

'Exactly a day later I received an email in my personal account, giving a time and a place for the meeting.'

'When was this?'

'About three months ago.'

Sandy looked up at Perez and knew exactly what he was thinking. Alison Teal hadn't been in Shetland three months ago, unless she'd made a trip for which they had no record. But Tain had been empty then and available for Rogerson's use.

'The name of the woman you were to meet, please?'

'Elena.'

'And the place?'

'A small house in Ravenswick.'

Sandy knew exactly what that meant. Barnes might not have known the name of the house, but they did. Tain. Once the home of an elderly spinster called Minnie Laurenson, left to an American publisher called Sandy Sechrest, and occasional residence of Craig Henderson and Alison Teal.

'Did you keep the appointment with Elena?' Perez asked.

There was a pause. 'I did.' Barnes seemed about to justify or excuse his decision but thought better of it.

'And was the encounter satisfactory?'

Another pause. 'It was.'

'Could you describe Elena to me, please?'

'She was tall and slender with very long and very straight fair hair. Small features. Is that enough?' Barnes was starting to become resentful again and to bluster, but the description was enough for Sandy, who recognized the woman he'd seen with Tom Rogerson in the

304

Scalloway Hotel on the evening of his Valentine's treat with Louisa.

Perez continued to ask Barnes questions, but the civil engineer had little other useful information. He was quite clear that he'd never met Alison Teal or anyone of her description. In the end they let him go. His colleagues were already boarding a coach to Sumburgh, where, it seemed, the storm was less ferocious.

34

Willow didn't waste time thinking about what had happened at Jimmy Perez's house the evening before. There would be opportunities for that later and, besides, perhaps nothing of any importance at all had happened. She might feel dizzy with hope — giddy, as she felt when she was at the top of a cliff looking down at the waves breaking below. But she knew it would be wise to limit her expectations. Perez had promised nothing. Today she had to focus on getting the information they needed from Alison Teal's brother. Nothing else could be decided until the case was over.

A local police officer had informed the man of his sister's death. He'd gone along to the prison where Jono Teal was being held, with the probation officer who'd known Jono for some years. Willow talked to the probation officer first. Her name was Hazel Sharpe and she was middle-aged and tough, more cynical than most police officers Willow knew. Hazel gave the impression that nothing at all would shock her.

'Tell me what you know about the family,' Willow said.

Much of the information Hazel passed on they'd gleaned previously, from interviews Alison had given at the height of her popularity. It seemed the actress hadn't exaggerated the tough childhood; the feckless parents and the informal adoption by the grandparents on the Norfolk coast still formed a part of the story.

'I have the impression that Alison was the golden girl,' the probation officer said. 'Perhaps she was an actress even then, becoming what was needed to survive, the sweet little girl that her grandparents doted on. Jono was trickier to handle. Not so bright and he hated school. I think they were all relieved when he left home and joined the army as soon as he could. I think he did OK in the forces. The discipline suited him and he made good friends. He only started getting into trouble when he left.'

'Did he keep in touch with Alison?'

'I think they saw each other when he was on leave. Jono was scarcely literate and I can't imagine the woman I met as a great writer, so I doubt they kept in touch by letter. It was a long time ago, before everyone used Skype or Facebook. They seemed fond enough of each other, but when Jono was still in the army they were leading very different lives.'

'So you met Alison?' Willow thought this was an unexpected bonus.

'Only once, and that was a bit later, soon after Jono left the army, when I was preparing his first pre-sentence report. He'd been picked up that first time for shoplifting and he'd said he was homeless. The court wanted an address before they'd give him bail. Alison took him in. She'd already been written out of the TV drama then, but she still saw herself as a minor celebrity. She was living a very different life from her brother. There was a flat in a swanky bit of North

London. A kitchen full of gadgets, but no food in the fridge. What my Nan would call 'fur coat and no knickers' style.'

'What did you make of her?'

There was a pause. 'It's a long time ago and I did so many of those home visits, so it's hard to remember details. She sticks in my mind because I'd liked that drama on the telly and I was a bit star-struck. That flat wasn't the usual sort of place I visited through work. The first thing I noticed was that she was beautiful. Model-beautiful. More stunning than she looked on the screen. I visited in the morning and she'd just got up. No make-up and still in her dressing gown, but gorgeous all the same. And perhaps because of that I could see she might be a spoilt brat. But she'd put Jono up, hadn't she? She didn't have to do that. I thought she was alright.'

'How long did Jono stay with her?'

'I don't know,' Hazel said. 'That time he was let off with a fine, which I presume his sister paid, and I didn't have any involvement until his next court appearance. By then he'd shacked up with a woman in Bermondsey, and Alison was out of the picture.' The probation officer paused. After that his route through the criminal justice system was pretty predictable. The woman left him and he drifted into stealing again. He met up with some thugs inside and they started giving him driving jobs when he came out. That was the closest he could get to the friendships he'd found in the army, I suppose. Now he's serving a stretch for armed robbery. It's bloody sad.'

Willow was using Perez's office to make the call and looked out of the window. The sea was churning and spray was blowing almost into the town. It was a long way from criminal London. 'What's Jono Teal like? As a man.'

Hazel paused again. 'A bit pathetic, by the time I knew him. Likeable enough and desperate to please, but he's never really grown up. He just seems weak these days. It's hard to think now that he was once a soldier and fit enough for active service.'

'I was hoping to talk to him,' Willow said. 'I don't know if he's told you, but his sister was killed. Here in Shetland. We could use some up-to-date background. Only it's a long way for me to do a visit.'

'I'm sure he'd cooperate. He's always been a model prisoner. It's the outside, when he has to make his own decisions and take responsibility for himself, that he finds hard to cope with. Besides, he's due a parole board soon.' The woman seemed to be thinking how much effort she was willing to put into helping Willow. 'We could see if the prison would let you use the video-link they have for court appearances.'

'That would be wonderful. Time's short, though. I'd like to get it set up for today.'

The probation officer barked a short laugh. 'Are you joking? Do you know how long anything takes these days? You need forms signed in triplicate to get a visit authorized.' A pause. 'But I'll see if I can work a little miracle. Leave it with me, yeah? I know the assistant governor.'

And so, two hours later, Willow was sitting in

the ops room, staring at a computer, and the shaky image of Alison Teal's only surviving relative appeared on the screen.

Jono was, as the probation officer had explained, likeable. Charming even, in a smarmy, desperate-to-please sort of way. He knew what was expected and first of all had to tell Willow how sad he was. 'Alis was the only relative I had left. And now that's been taken away from me too. Do you know when the funeral will be? Only they've said I might get a day-release to come along.'

It was hard to believe he'd once been a soldier. He looked very skinny and grey in his prison denims and striped shirt. A middle-aged man's face on a child's body.

Willow said they didn't know when his sister's body would be released, but he'd be kept informed. 'When did you last see Alison?'

'She came to see me sometimes. Not regular, like, but when she could. I'd always get a visiting order to her, just in case.'

'So when did you last see her?' Willow thought time must pass differently inside. Each day would be much the same as the last. She allowed him time to work things out in his head.

But the answer came more quickly than she expected. 'It was two months ago, to the day. I remember because they gave me the date for my parole hearing.' The grief at his sister's death left him for a moment. 'They say I've got a good chance of getting it. And I'm not going to screw things up this time.' He paused for a moment. 'I'm her only relative, so everything will come to me, won't it? She owned that flat, bought it when she was still on the telly, and it must be worth a fortune, the way prices are in London.'

'I guess it depends whether or not she made a will.' Willow thought this wasn't something they'd explored. Had Rogerson been Alison's lawyer, as well as her business partner? She rather hoped this thin man *would* inherit. Perhaps the security of a little money would help him turn his life around. She looked at him smiling out at her from the screen. *And perhaps pigs might fly.* 'How did Alison seem when you last saw her?'

'She was really well.' The response seemed genuine. 'Better than she's been for ages. Optimistic, you know. She said she was going away. She'd been given a business opportunity. It meant she had a chance to catch up with a few old friends and make some cash at the same time. She might not be able to visit for a while. But if it all worked out as she hoped, she'd be able to help me sort myself out. When I was released, like.'

'Did she say where she was going?'

'No.' But Willow thought Jono was so self-absorbed that he might not have remembered. And he seemed to her completely institutionalized. His life was the routine of prison. He would find it difficult to imagine life outside.

'Was Alison working?' This was the big question, but she asked it lightly. 'I mean, when she came to visit, before her big trip. I presume she must have chatted about her work.'

311

'She had her own business,' Jono said. 'She always told me that was the way to go. I should be my own boss. She'd never liked having people telling her what to do. I didn't have her drive, though. Alis was always the one with ambition.'

'What kind of business had your sister set up?' Willow was almost glad that they were separated by hundreds of miles and a dodgy video-link. She didn't want him to see how important this was for her.

For the first time he seemed wary. 'She was a very attractive woman. No harm in making the most of what you've got.'

'Absolutely.'

'She ran a legitimate company. Once the acting dried up, she still had to make a living.' He paused and seemed deep in contemplation. 'And it was a kind of acting, wasn't it? Making men feel good about themselves. Everyone likes to be seen with a beautiful woman.'

'So she worked as an escort. Is that what you're saying, Jono?' Willow wondered what Perez would make of that. The positive confirmation that the woman with the dark eyes and dark hair, who seemed to have haunted him since he'd found her body, had sold herself to men.

'Only to decent blokes. Classy, you know — wanting some company. A bit of arm-candy at works social dos.' He seemed very earnest in his sister's defence. Willow wondered if he was convincing himself as well as her.

'And she was doing well, was she, at the business she was running? She made enough to keep the wolf from the door?'

'Eh?'

'She earned enough to keep herself in nice clothes?'

'She was always well turned out when she came to see me.'

Willow thought Jono had gained credibility inside, by having a visitor as glamorous as Alison. Had he told the other men she was his sister or allowed them to think she was his girlfriend?

Jono was still talking. 'I think she might have had a bit of bother lately. Stepped on some important toes. It's a competitive business and people have carved out their own territory.'

So perhaps that was why Alison had been seduced to Shetland, Willow thought. She'd upset some big players in London and had been told to move out for a while. Then she smiled to herself. What did she know about that sort of thing? Only what she'd seen in gangster films. Her police experience was limited to Scotland, and mostly the Highlands and Islands. There were few gangsters in Inverness or Kirkwall. 'So Alison decided to leave the city to let things settle down?'

'Yeah. Something like that. But that wasn't the only reason she moved away. She had high hopes of the new venture. It had great potential. 'If everything works out as I expect, you'll be able to come and work for me, Jono. How do you fancy that? We'll move you out of London and away from all those scrotes you've been mixing with.' I was looking forward to it. I thought it would be a fresh start for both of us.' Now he seemed genuinely sad. 'That's not going to happen now, though, is it? No change of scene for me.'

'Did Alison say exactly where she'd be moving, for her business?' Willow thought it didn't matter now. She had enough information to confirm her theory that Alison had been in partnership with Rogerson.

Jono considered for a moment. The image on the screen flickered and died and then he appeared again.

'She told me I should pack my thermals.' He gave a little laugh. 'But she said it was beautiful. 'It was my place of sanctuary, Jono. I always knew I'd go back.''

That was enough for Willow. Alison had disappeared to Shetland when she'd been depressed and anxious as a young actor, and she'd decided to return to the same place recently, when things were getting uncomfortable for her in London.

Jono was looking off-camera, as if the prison officer operating the system had told him it was time to return to his cell.

'Just one last question.' Willow spoke quickly before the line was disconnected. 'Did Alison mention a man called Tom to you? Tom Rogerson. Was that the person she was going to work with, when she left London?' She knew it was a leading question, but she wasn't a lawyer and she didn't have much time.

'I've got to go,' Jono said. 'I'm missing my dinner. They don't save you any food, if you miss it.'

'Please.' Willow smiled. 'I'd be very grateful.'

He thought for a moment. The need to be liked overcame his desire for his lunch. 'She was a bit mysterious,' he said at last. 'I asked her for details: 'Where will we live, Sis? What sort of place is it?' But she said she couldn't trust me to keep my mouth shut. It had to stay secret.'

Suddenly the screen went dark. Willow couldn't tell if Jono had finished speaking or if the prison officer had run out of patience and wanted his lunch too.

35

On the way back from Brae there was suddenly phone reception and their mobiles started to ping. Perez was driving, so Sandy relayed the messages.

'The boss has just texted that she's setting up a video-link to talk to Alison Teal's brother in the nick.'

The boss, Perez thought. *If we had any sort of relationship, is that what she'd always be?* He wondered how that would make him feel and if it would matter to him or not. He couldn't come to a decision.

'Willow wants to know if you want to sit in on the interview,' Sandy said.

Perez didn't answer. The visibility was so poor now that he could hardly work out whereabouts on the road they were, and he felt as if they were in a grey bubble of water and wind. Thoughts of Willow were swirling around his head, as strange as the furious rain outside. He heard Fran's voice teasing him in his head. He couldn't remember if she'd ever actually spoken these words but, surrounded by the dense cloud, he could hear them as clearly as if she was sitting beside him in the passenger seat: *You're so romantic, Jimmy Perez. A soppy git. One day a wicked woman will come along and take advantage of you. How will you manage without me to look after you then?*

Suddenly he realized that they were at the junction to Voe, and he knew where he was and felt grounded in the real world again.

'Jimmy?' Sandy was pressing him for an answer. 'What should I tell Willow about the video interview?'

'Tell her I'll discuss it with her later. She'll have it recorded, so we can see what the man says when we get back. I'm going to Ravenswick to see Tom Rogerson's daughter. I should be able to catch her just as she finishes school.'

'Do you want me to come with you?' They were approaching Tingwall airstrip now. The cloud had lifted a little, but it was still raining.

'No,' Perez said. 'I'll drop you in Lerwick. I want you to go to school too. Call into the Anderson High and make some enquiries about the Hay lads. Willow seems to think we're missing something with that family. Maybe one of the form teachers will have more information about them. Andy only left last year, so there should be someone who remembers him.'

'Shall we meet up again later?' Sandy sounded a little anxious. It seemed that Perez's refusal to join Willow in the Teal interview had worried him. He wanted their small group to be working together again. He'd sensed the tension.

'Sure,' Perez said. 'Tea and buns in the ops room at about five o'clock. You get the buns. Why not?'

He'd pulled up outside the High School and watched Sandy run across the exposed playground, his hood pulled over his forehead, his coat held tight around him against the almost horizontal rain. The strength of the wind triggered a memory; it was something Willow had said, something he needed to check. But the thought disappeared before he could properly pin it down.

On the road south to Ravenswick, Perez passed Duncan Hunter in his flash new Range Rover. He was driving in the opposite direction and Cassie sat on her booster in the front seat beside him. She'd be staying with her father in the Haa again this evening, something Perez hadn't mentioned to Willow. Cassie caught sight of Perez as the car flashed past and gave him a little wave. Gracious, like a queen. Perez smiled. He was just grateful that Duncan had remembered to collect her from school on time. It didn't always happen.

Kathryn was in her classroom with a pile of exercise books on the desk in front of her. Now he was here, Perez wasn't quite sure what to say to her. He realized now that the trip back to Ravenswick was partly an excuse to put off seeing Willow. He heard Fran's mocking voice in his head again: *Scaredy cat!* Then he remembered his fiancée's grey headstone being tipped over by the landslide, had a fleeting thought that perhaps the shock had released her spirit. But he didn't believe in ghosts.

Kathryn looked up. 'Jimmy! Is there any news?'

'Just a few more questions, I'm afraid. I don't want to bother your mother again, unless I can help it.' He wasn't sure where to sit. Perching on her teacher's desk seemed too close and intimate

318

and the children's chairs were tiny. In the end he sat on one of the children's octagonal tables.

'Mum said that the detective from Inverness came to chat to her yesterday at the Red Cross shop. Bought her coffee and cake. That was kind. I don't think Mum's eaten properly since Dad died. Now she can't stop.' Kathryn set down her pen and gave him her full attention. 'Mum said the detective was asking questions about money.'

'Your father had a bank account,' Perez said. 'Separate from his business or personal account. Over the last six months considerable sums have been paid into it and we were struggling to find an explanation for them.'

She stared at him, her eyes hard and fierce. 'Do you have to do this? Do you have to pry into every part of our lives? My father was a victim, but you're making him sound like a criminal.'

'I'm afraid we do have to ask uncomfortable questions.' Perez had never imagined she could be so angry. 'A lot of people get hurt in a murder investigation. It's not only the victims. Do you have any idea where the money might have come from?'

Kathryn didn't answer directly. 'I miss him so much,' she said and she was more herself again: the gentle young teacher who'd comforted Cassie when she'd tumbled in the playground, or who made the kids laugh when she read them silly stories. She looked up. 'Dad was dreadful with money. He made plenty, but he always spent more. He was forever coming up with schemes that were going to make him rich. At one time he was going to invest in Stuart

319

Henderson's holiday lodges along the coast. I'm not sure what happened with that. Perhaps the money you're talking about came from some of those investments.'

'I don't think so.'

'Why don't you come out with it, Jimmy? Was it something shameful? Shameful enough to make someone want to kill him?' The outburst was the last spark of anger. She began to cry very quietly, took a handkerchief from her pocket and dried her tears.

Perez gave her a moment to compose herself and had to force himself to continue the interview. His instinct was to comfort her. 'We think he might have been running an escort service. For contractors and islanders.' He thought that was the kindest way of putting it and hoped she would understand what he meant.

It seemed she did. 'You're saying my dad was a pimp?' The words shocked him, but they were flat and empty. He couldn't tell if she was astonished by the idea or if she'd known all along.

'We have evidence to suggest that he was organizing women in prostitution. Was there anything about his behaviour that might have made you guess what was going on?' Perez thought he should have asked Willow to talk to the teacher. It didn't seem right for a man to be asking these questions of her.

'My father was a flirt. I've already told you that. He liked pretty women and I don't think he would have seen anything immoral in prostitution. But I never guessed that he'd have set up a business supplying working girls. It wasn't something we discussed over the dinner table, along with his council affairs and the price of fish at Shetland Catch.' She looked straight into his eyes. 'Will this have to become public? It would kill my mother if her neighbours and the people she goes to church with find out.'

Perez paused before answering. 'If we have enough evidence when we find his killer, they'll be advised by their lawyer to plead guilty. Then none of this will have to come before a court.'

'I hope you find him quickly,' she said. 'This digging around in other people's business is an act of violence in itself. It's disgusting. There are things that should remain private.' She stood up. 'Please don't ask my mother these questions, Jimmy. Dad wouldn't have talked to her about this and she would never have guessed what he was up to, even if the evidence was staring her in the face.' She looked out across the school yard. It was too dark to see the fields beyond and the lighthouse on Raven's Head was already flashing.

'Did *you* guess?' He stood up too now. He was looking straight down into Kathryn's face, but he couldn't read her.

'I knew he was excited about something. Some new venture or woman, to make him feel alive and young again. He was ambitious, Jimmy, and he was terrified of getting old. But I never guessed the details.' Her words turned bitter. 'Sex and an opportunity to make money, all rolled into one. He wouldn't have been able to resist that. He'd have seen it as a project made in heaven.'

'I'm sorry,' he said. 'You shouldn't have had to know.' He could imagine how he'd feel, if Cassie was ever ashamed of something he'd done.

'My dad was a flawed man. He did stuff that embarrassed me and made me angry, but nothing you tell me will make me love him any less.' A pause. 'Now I need to get back to my mother.' She put the exercise books into a canvas bag and pulled her waterproof from a hook on the door.

They were standing in the school porch and she was locking the door behind them.

'I'm sorry, Jimmy. I shouldn't have had a go at you. You were only doing your job. I'm over-protective about my father and always have been. If there's anything else I can do to help find his killer, do ask.'

'Do you know the Hay family?' He wasn't sure where the question had come from.

'Sure, they're great supporters of the school. We took the kids into the polytunnels to see all the plants grow. Part of a biology project. Why?'

'One of the boys, Andy, was seen having an argument with your father a couple of days before he died. Any idea what that was about?'

'None at all. But Dad always liked a good argument. It was one of the reasons he enjoyed being on the council. His idea of sport. It probably didn't mean anything. I knew Andy a bit at school. He was a gentle soul. He wouldn't start a fight with anyone. Sounds like a rumour that's come out of nothing.' She touched his arm, a final gesture of reconciliation, and ran towards her car.

On the way back to Lerwick, Perez switched on the radio. Radio Scotland had an item about the weather. There was to be no break in the wind and the rain. Shetland got its own mention. There were fears, the newsreader said, about another landslide.

36

Sandy stood outside the office at the Anderson High School, waiting for the secretary to finish answering the phone. He'd never been one for school. He'd made good friends here, but he couldn't remember much of what he'd been taught. Enough of it had stuck just long enough to enable him to join the police service, but he didn't think he'd made use of any of the facts he'd forced into his head. He couldn't see the point of all those years of boredom.

It was coming to the end of the school day. Behind the closed classroom doors there was muffled conversation. Occasionally a teacher would shout for order, but there was no power behind the voice and Sandy could tell that everyone was just waiting for the session to be over. The secretary replaced the phone and came to the desk. She must be nearing retirement, a small bird-like figure with short white hair and big glasses. Sandy thought she hadn't changed much since he was a pupil.

'Don't I know you?' She looked at him over her glasses.

'Sandy Wilson.' He was fourteen again, late for some class. Sheepish and defiant, all at the same time.

'Of course, one of the wild Whalsay boys!' She smiled, much as she had done then. 'And what can I do for you, Sandy Wilson? I hear you're respectable now. Keeping law and order in our beautiful islands. Who'd have thought it, eh?'

Sandy wasn't sure how to respond to that and in the end he just gave her a quick smile. 'I'd like to talk to someone about the Hay brothers. Andy and Michael.'

'Well, Andy's left now of course, but most of his teachers are still around. You're probably best talking to Sally Martin. She taught him English and he was always one of her stars. Michael's home teacher is Phil Jamieson. I know he's in the staffroom now. Why don't you chat to him first and I'll ask Sally to come in when she's finished teaching?'

Standing outside the staffroom, he still felt like an impostor, but he'd been here before as an adult. That time there'd been another murder in Ravenswick. It had been winter and Fran Hunter had found the body of a young schoolgirl lying in the snow. Sandy had come to the Anderson High to talk to her friends. After the interview he'd been taken into the staffroom and there'd been the same feeling of unease, of wandering into enemy territory. He tapped at the door. A male voice shouted for him to come in. There was a smell of old coffee and old building.

A middle-aged man was seated in a corner reading a newspaper. Otherwise the room was empty.

'Mr Jamieson?'

'Who wants to know?' He might have been from Shetland originally, but his voice had been weathered by other places and the trace of accent had almost disappeared.

Sandy introduced himself.

'And how can I help?'

'I'm part of the team investigating the murders out at Tain. We're making routine enquiries about all the people who live close to the crime scene. The Hays' farm is one of the properties nearby.'

'So you want to know all about Michael?'

Sandy nodded.

'I can offer you a dreadful cup of coffee before the hordes arrive.' Jamieson nodded towards a filter machine. 'I warn you, it's probably been standing there since break time.'

'No, thanks.'

'Wise choice.' He nodded for Sandy to take a seat next to him. 'I don't know what to tell you about Michael. He's one of those kids who never stand out. Well enough behaved so that he doesn't irritate. Not particularly bright, but not so stupid that he needs extra help. Steady. Stable. Maybe a little bit boring, but in a school like this there are so many divas that *that's* quite refreshing. His future is mapped out for him. He wants to join his father on the farm. His mother would like him to go away to Agricultural College first, to widen his horizons a bit, but Michael doesn't see the point and neither does his father. He's got a stubborn streak, so I think he'll probably get his own way.'

'He's got a girlfriend,' Sandy said.

'Gemma.' The teacher smiled. 'Cast in the same mould. But a little bit more chatty. She did get her way, and left before Highers.'

'So there were never any concerns about

326

Michael? No sudden outbursts of temper?'

'Nothing at all like that. What you see is what you get. I suppose the only time I ever saw him lose it was with Andy.' He looked at Sandy to check the name meant something.

Sandy nodded. 'The older brother.'

'Hard to imagine two siblings so unalike. Andy was bright and so full of charm that you couldn't help like him, even when he was back-chatting big-style.'

'He must have been a hard act to follow.'

'Maybe. But Michael never tried to. If anything, I think he found Andy embarrassing. A bit of a show-off. I never felt that Michael wanted to be like him.'

Sandy was startled by the electric bell that shrieked from the corner of the room and marked the end of the school day. He asked his next question quickly. Soon all the other teachers would arrive and he might lose the chance. 'So what happened when Michael lost his rag with Andy?'

'I'm not entirely sure what provoked it. Apparently Andy had been goading Michael all day. Something about Gemma and about how they were old and settled before their time. *Why don't you just get married and have done with it?* And finally Michael hit back, said at least he *had* a girlfriend. Andy was all talk and no action. All he did was dream about it. His love life was one big fantasy. And suddenly they were scrapping in the yard like twelve-year-olds, everyone gathered round, watching and cheering them on. You know what it's like.'

Sandy nodded. He knew. The girls with their high-pitched screaming and the boys yelling, 'Fight! Fight!' until a teacher came along to pull the brawlers apart.

'That's it, really. Nothing very major, in the scheme of things.' Jamieson folded his newspaper.

There were footsteps in the corridor. Outside crowds of children ran through the rain towards the gate. Some of them didn't have coats. Sandy remembered that. How somehow it was uncool to come to school with a big coat.

The staffroom door opened and a group of teachers walked in, chatting and laughing. A young woman in a tiny skirt, thick black tights and long boots approached him, arm outstretched. 'You must be Sandy. Maggie said you wanted to chat about Andy.'

Sally Martin made him fresh coffee and, once the machine had started to work, the room was nearly empty again. The teachers who had any sort of commute home wanted to be on their way. Sandy could hear them talking about the possibility of another landslide as they left.

'What about you?' Sandy took the mug of coffee from her. She looked so young that she could have been a student herself. 'Do you need to get off?'

'Oh, I've got a flat in Lerwick. I can walk home. Not much fun in this weather, but I'm so new to it that I still enjoy the drama of being out in the storm.' Her voice was English, quite deep and classy.

'Is this your first job?' Sandy thought it must

328

be. It wasn't just that she looked so young; it was something about the starry-eyed enthusiasm.

'Yeah. My parents are island freaks and brought me and my brother here when we were children. I'd just finished my postgrad teacher training and saw the post advertised. I didn't think I had a chance of getting it, but here I am, already in my third year and loving it.' She looked up at him. 'Maggie said you were investigating the murders out at Ravenswick.' She paused and gave a little frown. Something about it made Sandy think she was like an actress, always conscious of her audience. Perhaps because she was so bonny that she was used to people staring at her. 'I'm sure Andy wouldn't be involved in anything like that.'

'It's just routine enquiries,' Sandy said. 'We're checking all the people who live close to the crime scene. I'm sure you understand.'

'Of course.'

'And Maggie said you were the best person to talk to about Andy Hay.'

'He was the first student I met when I arrived here,' Sally said. 'The head got him to show me around. He'd just started the sixth form and had that swagger that kids get because they suddenly feel grown-up. And Andy was funny. He described the other teachers as we walked past their classrooms, summing them up in a couple of lines. The comments weren't always complimentary, and I knew I shouldn't be encouraging him, but I couldn't help laughing.'

'You taught him?' Sandy wondered why he'd never had a teacher like Sally Martin.

'English and theatre studies. He was really very good at both. He had the confidence to be creative, to take risks, if you know what I mean.'

Sandy didn't, but he nodded his head. He was thinking too that the young man he'd seen at the Hays' farm hadn't seemed very confident to him. He wondered what had changed between Andy leaving school and arriving back in Shetland after dropping out of university. Perhaps when he was with other bright kids, he'd realized he wasn't quite so brainy and that had come as a shock. Sandy had known friends go south and come back happier to be a big fish in a small pool than to flounder in an anonymous city without any support.

'Did Andy have a girlfriend?'

'I don't think so.' Sally had finished her coffee. She crossed her legs. Sandy tried not to be distracted. 'He was part of the arty gang that hung out in Mareel and were members of the Youth Theatre there, but I don't think there was anyone special.'

'A boyfriend perhaps?'

She paused for a moment. 'You think he might be gay? I don't think so. And it wouldn't have been a big deal, not in the crowd he mixed with. Not in this school at all, really.'

'Mr Jamieson said there was a fight with his brother and that was something about a girl.' Sandy wanted to have something to take back to Willow and Jimmy Perez.

'I heard there was a fight. I didn't know what it was about. I'm guessing that Michael provoked it. Andy really wasn't the fighting kind.' She flashed him a smile, but Sandy could tell she was starting to lose interest. Perhaps she wanted to be home, out of the storm, to start her evening. He wondered if she lived on her own in the flat in Lerwick.

'Andy had a very public argument with one of the victims,' he said. 'Tom Rogerson.'

'Well, I can guess what that would have been about. Most of the guys in the Youth Theatre would have had a go at Rogerson, given the chance. He was the councillor leading the campaign to cut arts funding by seventy per cent. I don't see it as a credible motive for murder, though.' She turned to face him. Her dark hair was cut in a bob and it caught the light as she moved.

'No.' Besides, Sandy thought, that wouldn't explain Alison Teal's death. It seemed that her acting days were long behind her, and she wouldn't have had any dealings with island politics.

The teacher's phone buzzed. She looked at the text, smiled and her fingers moved swiftly over the keypad to send a reply. 'Oh, lovely! My boyfriend's finished work early, so he can give me a lift home.'

It seemed the drama of the storm had lost its magic. Sandy had pictured himself walking into town with her, them battling together against the weather, and felt oddly resentful. As if she'd led him on, though he could see that was ridiculous.

'He's waiting outside.' Sally was already on her feet, pulling on her coat. 'Have you finished? I really don't think there's anything else I can help you with.'

'Yes, I'm sure that's all for now.' He thought of asking if he could have a lift, but decided against it. He imagined how awkward it would be, crammed in the back while she and her man chatted about their days. Suddenly he wanted to be in Louisa's house in Yell, in the quiet room where her mother sat in her chair by the window. Standing at the main door into the school and watching the teacher run across the yard to a waiting car, he thought that Sally Martin was a woman who could really screw up a young man's mind. He wondered if Andy Hay had some sort romantic crush on her, what she might have done to encourage it, and if that was why he'd ended up back in Shetland.

★ ★ ★

By the time Sandy got back to the police station his trousers were soaking and the rain had run down the neck of his coat. But he'd remembered the buns and, when he opened the door to the ops room, Jimmy and Willow were there talking as if they were friends again. They gave a little cheer when they saw him, laughed when he hung his coat over the radiator and it started to steam. Willow made a pot of tea and put the cakes onto a plate. Sandy thought that between them they'd soon bring the case to a conclusion. It seemed that all was well with the world.

37

When he arrived back at the police station after speaking to Kathryn Rogerson, Perez found Willow watching the recording of her interview with Jonathan Teal. She was hunched over the desk in a small room, her hair falling over her shoulders. He remembered stroking her neck the evening before, rubbing the tension from it. Without a word he pulled up a chair so that he was sitting beside her. She pressed a button to replay it and her voice filled the space.

All the way back to Lerwick he'd wondered if he should speak to her about the night they'd spent in the house in Ravenswick. Apologize maybe, though she'd not been a passive partner. *I'm sorry, that's not usually the way I behave when I invite a woman into my home.* Then he'd thought perhaps it might be the way she *did* behave, if the opportunity arose. Sex without strings. Nothing wrong with that after all, between consenting adults. Perhaps there was no need for either of them to speak about it and she'd think he was making a fuss about nothing, if he did. He heard Fran's voice in his head again: *Jimmy Perez, you're probably the nicest guy in the world, but you do worry far too much.*

However, and this was the big deal, the cruncher: he wanted the strings. Not some work fling or one-night stand. He'd never seen the attraction in those — he was so arrogant that he felt he deserved better. Or he was too naively romantic. Now he knew that he wanted Willow as part of his life. If he'd been free and without responsibility, he'd have found a way to make it work. He'd sorted out that much, on the drive back from Ravenswick. And what did that say about his commitment to care for Cassie? How could he possibly consider bringing another woman into her life when his stepdaughter was still so young? Fran had entrusted the girl to him. It would seem like the worst kind of betrayal.

He still wasn't sure how to play it, when he went into the office and found Willow watching Jono Teal again on the screen. She turned and smiled at him.

'Jimmy Perez, I thought you were avoiding me.'

'Maybe I have been.'

Suddenly she pressed the button again and Teal was frozen on the screen, his face turned to the camera, his mouth still open. 'I want you to know that I don't go to bed with all my colleagues. No pressure, but I just wanted to tell you that I don't take that sort of thing lightly.'

He looked at Willow carefully, thinking for a moment that she was still teasing him, but she was just waiting for his response. 'Nor do I,' he said.

She threw back her head and laughed. 'Jimmy Perez, don't you think I don't know that? You've never done anything lightly. You're the most serious man I've ever met.'

'It's complicated,' he said.

'I know. Guilt and responsibility, and all those grown-up emotions that I probably don't understand. You need time to sort yourself out.' Suddenly she was serious herself. 'I can wait, Jimmy. For a little while at least.' Then she switched on the screen again, so he could watch the interview from the beginning.

★　★　★

Soon afterwards they moved to the ops room. Sandy came in from the High School, drenched and miserable, but with a bag of cakes bought from the shop in the street. The cakes were almost dry, because he'd been holding them under his coat, and they gave a little cheer when they saw he had not forgotten them.

'Oh God, I'm so sorry, Sandy,' Perez said. 'I should have phoned to arrange to pick you up on my way back from Ravenswick. I just had other stuff on my mind.'

Willow caught his eye and started to giggle. Sandy was hanging his coat on the radiator, so he didn't notice.

'Where do we go from here?' Willow took charge, focused again on the case. 'From what Alison's brother told us, it's clear that we were right: she and Rogerson were organizing sex workers in the islands. I'm guessing they were mostly targeting the guys in the floatels and in the hotel at Sullom, but islanders seem to have signed up as clients too.'

'Does that mean we're looking at a killer who

wanted to shut down the whole operation?' Sandy was eating a chocolate brownie and the words were muffled.

'Did your mother never tell you not to speak with your mouth full?' But Perez thought the man had a point. 'So who are we looking at? Some religious nut who hates the idea of prostitution? An aggrieved partner of one of the men using the service?'

'It seems we have one of those conveniently close to both crime scenes,' Willow said.

'Jane Hay?'

Willow nodded. 'We know that Kevin paid Rogerson. Alison Teal was living practically on his doorstep and there must have been some activity in the place, but he claimed not even to know that Tain was occupied. That suggests to me that he was covering up something. I'd bet he was one of the clients. If Jane found out, that would give her motive for both murders, and there's nobody with a better opportunity.'

'I'm not sure.' Perez thought of the Jane Hay he knew. She'd been a friend of Fran's. Not a close friend, but Fran would call into the farmhouse for coffee, if she was painting out that way. She'd been Simon Agnew's friend too, and Perez wondered what Fran would have made of her neighbours' involvement in the case. Fran had described Jane as calm: *You get the sense that she could survive anything with equanimity.* That didn't sound like the sort of woman who would kill two people, however badly her husband had behaved.

Then he remembered what Kathryn had said

of her father. 'Was it something shameful, Jimmy? So shameful that someone would want to kill him?' Shame worked in all sorts of ways, and maybe there were things in Jane's past that Rogerson or Teal had discovered. Something she'd kill to keep hidden. Then he thought he was straying into Agnew territory and this was a question for a psychologist, not a cop.

'What did you get from the High School, Sandy?' Willow asked. 'Did any of the teachers mention the boys' mother?'

'No, only to say that she has ambitions for Michael to go away to college, but he wants to stay and work on the farm.' Sandy looked guilty. 'But I didn't think to ask about the parents. I was talking to them about the sons. Sorry.'

'Anything interesting?'

'Not really. Andy was the bright one. Sparky, arty, a bit cheeky, but with the charm to get away with it. I wondered if he might have fancied his English teacher. She was one of those women who like to be admired. Maybe she only went into teaching because she had a captive audience. You could see she wouldn't discourage the attention, even from one of her students.' Sandy paused to slurp his tea.

'And Michael?' Perez couldn't really see where this was going, except to provide a bit more background to the Hay family, but he was even more convinced that the four individuals at the farm should be at the centre of the investigation.

Sandy shrugged. 'The teacher I spoke to didn't have much to say about him, except that he was one of those kids who don't stand out.

Not terribly bright, but not needing special help.'
He looked up and grinned. 'A bit like I was at
school, maybe. I don't get the sense that the
brothers were very close. They had one scrap in
the playground, in Andy's last year. Nobody
could work out exactly what triggered it, but it
seems to have been teasing about a woman that
got out of hand.' He paused. 'And Sally Martin,
Andy's teacher, shed a bit of light on what that
argument in the street could have been about.
Apparently Rogerson was leading calls in the
council to cut arts funding. All the kids in the
Youth Theatre were protesting about it.'

'No.' Willow leaned forward. 'If it had been
about that, Andy would have said so. It would be
another opportunity to make a political point.
That row in the street was more personal.'

'Could he have found out that Kevin was
seeing Rogerson's women?' Perez thought there
was a link here about children standing up for
their irresponsible parents: Kathryn and Tom,
Andy and Kevin. 'It might explain why Andy's
seemed so twitchy. He might think his father is a
killer.'

'Or he might be a killer himself,' Willow said.
'He sounds like a young man given to
melodrama. Could he have seen murder as
revenge for corrupting his father and betraying
his mother?'

'Isn't that a bit far-fetched?' It sounded like
one of the gothic films Fran had sometimes
enjoyed, late on dark winter nights. Besides,
Perez wasn't sure if the young had that kind of
concept of sexual morality.

'Yeah, I know. It's clutching at straws. We have so much information now, but I haven't any sort of feel about who's responsible.' Willow looked at Perez. 'What about you, Jimmy? You know this place. What's the next move?'

'There's still some basic policing. Routine stuff. We haven't found anyone yet who saw Tom Rogerson after he left his car at the airport. He can't just have vanished into thin air.' He paused. 'Apart from that, I think we have to wait.'

'For the murderer to make a mistake?'

'Or to attempt to kill again. We know that the Hays have secrets. Even if one of the family isn't responsible for the deaths, it's possible that they know who is. Or have their suspicions. So we wait and we watch them.'

Willow nodded to show that made sense to her. 'Sandy, you have another go at the airport. Local folk will talk to you. How do you see the watching, Jimmy? It'd be hard to hide any surveillance in a place with so few people and so little cover.'

'I can see their place from my house.'

'Ah, so it's just an excuse for staying home and drinking tea all day?'

He held up his hands in mock surrender. 'Just give me one day,' he said. 'Sometimes waiting is the hardest thing.'

She caught his eye. A flash of understanding. 'One day. If you're sure that's all you need.'

He walked her back to the sheriff's house. The rain had eased a little. From the bar at the bottom of the lane, fiddle music suddenly spilled out through an open door. Wednesday night, when locals came together to share their music. In the summer it would be packed with visitors, but tonight and this early in the evening the musicians would be playing mostly to themselves.

'Will you come in for a coffee, Jimmy? I'm sure they'd like to see you.'

He looked at his watch. He still had an hour before he had to be home for Duncan to drop off Cassie. 'Aye, why not?' He knew he had a decision to make about their future, but he felt very easy in her company. Whatever he decided, they would still manage to work together.

She unlocked the door and walked into a warm house. There were voices in the basement kitchen. They hadn't been able to see in from outside because the heavy curtains had been drawn.

'Hi there, I've brought Jimmy in. I hope that's OK.' Willow walked ahead of him down the stairs.

Rosie was sitting in the chair by the Aga and her husband was making tea. The place smelled different. Milky.

'Come in!' the man said. 'Come in and meet my son.'

Then Perez saw that the dozing Rosie had a baby in her arms.

'He was born last night,' John said. 'You weren't here, Willow. We left you a note and some stuff for your breakfast. We've only just got back from the hospital.'

'No,' Willow said. 'I didn't get back.

340

Something came up.' Perez looked at her to see if that was a private joke, but he could tell that she only had eyes for the child, who was pink and wrinkled and wrapped in a yellow blanket. 'What will you call him?'

'We don't know yet.' Rosie smiled. 'We thought we'd wait and see what suited.'

'But as we can't call him Prune, which is what he most looks like,' the man went on, 'we'd better come up with something else.' He poured water into a teapot. 'Will you both have a mug? And a dram to wet the baby's head?'

'Don't you want to be on your own?' Willow was still looking at the baby. 'Your first night as a family.'

'Oh, we'll have years and years of that.' Rosie lifted herself onto her feet and handed the child to Willow. 'Here, have a cuddle while I take myself off for a pee. I might be some time.' She was wearing baggy pyjamas and huge slippers and shuffled away to the stairs. 'I can't do anything at speed.'

'You should have seen her,' John said. 'She was so brave.'

Willow took a seat at the table and sat, with the baby on her knee, while the tea was poured into mugs and the whisky into small glasses.

38

Jane woke to rain on the window and a sense of dislocation. Perhaps she'd been somewhere else in a dream. There was a moment of panic when she imagined she'd been drinking again; there was a taste in her mouth that reminded her of the self-disgust and failure that had always followed a bender. Then Kevin turned in his sleep and she knew where she was, and that she was still strong and sober. Sober at least. But despite that, there was little relief in the reality and she went back to sleep.

When she woke again, Kevin was out of bed and the light was on. He'd been in the shower and stood with a towel around his waist, his hair wet. He was looking down at her in a way that was almost fatherly. She thought how grateful she should be that he'd stood by her. Other men would have ditched her years before.

'I was thinking we should get away,' he said. 'Have a bit of a holiday, just the two of us. The boys are old enough to leave alone and there's not much work at this time of year.' He sat on the bed beside her and she tried to push from her mind the thought that the wet towel would make the sheet damp. 'Would you like that?'

'Of course! Where would we go?'

'Somewhere hot,' he said. 'Morocco, maybe. We should have a bit of adventure in our lives.'

She imagined hot sand and a market full of

brightly coloured spices. 'I'd love Morocco. And you're right — we could use some time on our own.' Then immediately she wondered how she could consider leaving the boys, if the killer hadn't been found. If the situation was still unresolved.

'I'll go online to see if I can find a last-minute deal.' He bent and kissed her lightly on the lips. 'And perhaps when we get back they'll have found the killer and all this will be over.' He stood up and pulled on his clothes. She watched him and thought he'd worn better than she had. He still had the body of a young man, could easily be an older brother to her sons. But although she'd been thinking of the murders too, she wished he hadn't mentioned the killer. It was as if he'd carried a distasteful smell into the bedroom with him.

When she got downstairs she could hear Kevin in the office, tapping away on the computer keyboard, looking for a dream holiday that somehow she couldn't believe would ever happen. She made a pot of coffee and shouted up the stairs to ask the boys if they'd like breakfast. She'd already decided that she'd do a fry-up as a treat for Kevin, taken bacon out of the fridge and started grilling it in the pan. Michael appeared, dressed for school, apart from his socks. 'Has Andy already left then? I was hoping he'd give me a lift.'

'He's still in bed, I expect.' But already she felt the familiar sickness in the pit of her stomach. At one time she'd thought she'd known what her eldest son was thinking. They were kindred spirits, weren't they? Now he drifted between home and Lerwick and she didn't have a clue what he was up to.

'I've checked. He's not there.'

She looked out at the yard. It was still dark, but the table lamp in the office shone like a spotlight onto the parked vehicles. 'His car's still there. He must be around somewhere.' She didn't know what else to say, but she knew she wasn't convincing either of them. Andy had disappeared the two nights ago and turned up wet and wan in the morning, refusing to speak to her, shutting himself in his room.

'I'm not sure he slept in his bed last night.'

'When did you last see him?' She knew it wasn't Michael's fault, but she couldn't keep the accusation out of her voice. She needed someone to blame.

'Last night. When you were out at your meeting.'

She caught the trace of accusation in his voice too and wondered, not for the first time, how much he and Andy had resented the meetings — the fact that she'd had to juggle her recovery with their needs as they'd been growing up.

'How did Andy seem then?'

Michael shrugged. He fished in the laundry basket for a pair of clean socks before answering. 'Moody. The way he's been since he came home from uni.'

'Did he tell you where he was going?'

'He's never told me anything important. *You're* the person he talks to.' There was more resentment and something else in his tone.

344

Jealousy. 'Didn't he leave you a note? He said he was going to. But I thought he'd be back late last night.' Michael nodded towards the fridge, where recipes, photos and scraps of paper were fixed with magnets.

You might have told me last night! But Jane held her tongue. She knew Michael was right. Andy had always been . . . not exactly her favourite, because she'd known from the start that it would be wrong to have a favourite, but the son she felt closest to. 'Oh, that's OK then.' She refused to rush over to the fridge to see what the note might say. She turned the bacon under the grill. 'Would you like a bacon sandwich? I can give you a lift to school, if you like. It'd save you waiting for the bus in this weather and that'd give you a bit of extra time.'

'That would be great.' He didn't sound enthusiastic exactly, but more conciliatory.

She waited until the men had finished breakfast and Michael had gone upstairs to fetch his school bag before she went to look for the note. She recognized Andy's writing as she approached. It was wild and big and spidery:

*I'm not great company at the moment, so
I'm taking myself off for a while to sort
myself out. Don't worry about me and
don't try to phone because I won't answer.
I'm being well taken care of and I'll be back
when I'm more fun to live with.*

She couldn't help smiling, because this sounded almost like the old Andy. She took the note from the fridge and folded it up in her handbag, hiding it, just as she'd hidden love letters from Kevin from her parents when she was young. Michael was standing at the kitchen door in his outdoor clothes, ready to be off.

'Where's Andy gone then?'

'Just to stay with a friend for a day or two.'

'Why didn't he take his car?'

Jane had to think about that. 'I don't know. Maybe he'd had a drink and didn't want to drive. He must have got a lift. Did you hear a car last night?' She picked up her keys and put on her jacket.

'Nah.' But Michael wasn't really interested now. He was on his phone texting to one of his friends.

★　★　★

Jane dropped him right at the gate of the Anderson High. He met up with a mate and swaggered inside, not even bothering to wave goodbye. She thought that Andy would never have been so graceless, then told herself that Michael wouldn't have run away, leaving only a short note behind. Driving home, she saw there was a light on in the old manse, so on impulse she pulled off the road and drove down the track out onto the headland. When she tried the door it was locked, so she knocked again and at last Simon came to answer.

'I don't usually lock up at night,' he said. 'I suppose we've all got a bit scared about what's out there in the dark.'

Jane felt suddenly chilled. She'd never imagined Simon would be frightened of anything. His fear made the danger more real than seeing Tom Rogerson's body on the beach.

There was a biro stuck behind his ear and when he led her into the kitchen, Jane saw a notebook on the arm of the chair.

'Oh, I'm sorry,' she said. 'I'm disturbing you.'

'Not at all. It's just an article I'm pitching, and I was going to stop for coffee anyway. I'm doing a shift in Befriending Shetland soon, though. I can't be very long.'

So Jane found herself in a chair by the stove trying to explain why she was so worried about Andy. She took his note from her bag, smoothed it out on the table by her side and slid it across to Simon.

'What does Kevin say?'

'That I'm worrying about nothing.'

'He could be right.' A gust of wind rattled rain against the window so that she could hardly hear what he was saying. 'Has Andy talked to you at all about what might be worrying him?'

'No.' Jane sipped the coffee. 'In fact I think that's why he keeps disappearing. He doesn't want to talk to me.'

'Have you got any idea where he might have gone?'

'To a friend's, I suppose.' Jane paused. 'This is Shetland. I could probably track him down if I wanted to. But he doesn't want me to and I should probably re-spect that, don't you think?'

'Probably. It depends how desperate you think he is.'

'I don't know.' Again the rain was blown against the window, sharp and hard. 'He's been different since he came back from university. He doesn't talk to me any more.'

Simon stood up to put his mug in the sink. 'That detective was here yesterday. The woman from Inverness. She was asking about your boys.'

'What did you tell her?'

'Nothing. I had nothing to tell.' He was still standing, his back to the bench. 'Look, there's probably nothing sinister at all in Andy taking himself off for a while. It will have been a blow to his pride, giving up on university and coming home. And then there were two murders so close to your land — all the tension and suspicion at home. He's bound to feel troubled and confused.'

'Do you think he knows something about the murders?' Jane looked up at her friend. She wasn't sure she wanted to hear the answer.

Simon stared back. 'You can't think Andy's a killer.'

'No!' the answer came immediately and Jane knew that at least she was certain about that. Her son was gentle and he might have a temper, but he would never take a life. 'But he might suspect someone else.'

'Who are you thinking about?' The words were soft and apologetic. 'Who do you think Andy might be protecting, Jane?'

'I don't know! All these theories and suspicions — I hate it.' She paused. 'He was out for most of Tuesday night. I have no idea where he went, but he was in a terrible state when he got in.'

'He needs to talk to someone,' Simon said. 'Send him a text and say I'll be at Befriending Shetland all afternoon. Perhaps he doesn't feel he can talk to you because it's too close to home.'

'What are you saying?' Suddenly she thought he wasn't being entirely honest. Not lying, because Simon had always been too brave for that. But not telling the whole truth, either.

'I think you should give him a day. To talk to the friend who's putting him up or to talk to me.' There was a pause. 'And if he doesn't turn up, then perhaps you should tell Jimmy Perez.'

'I'm not sure I could do that.' Jane thought it sounded as if Simon was telling her to shop her son to the police, although she was certain he'd done nothing wrong.

'Andy could be in danger.' Simon's voice was firmer now. 'Two people have died already. His safety is more important just now than his relationship with you.' Another pause. 'You really don't have any idea who might have taken him in?'

Jane shook her head. 'I presume it would be one of his old school mates.'

'I wondered if he might go to Kathryn Rogerson,' Simon went on. 'Weren't they in the Youth Theatre together when he was a young lad, before she went south to university? I always thought he might have a bit of a crush on her. The older woman.'

But Jane didn't want to think there might be another connection with the Rogersons. 'If he comes to see you in Lerwick,' she said, 'will you

349

ask him to get in touch with me? Just a text to tell me he's safe.'

'Of course.'

'Now I'd better let you get on with your article.'

Simon walked with her to the door. It was still raining and the tip of Raven's Head was shrouded in mist.

On her way home, Jane saw that Jimmy's car was still outside his house and she was tempted for a moment to stop there and ask for his help immediately. If Andy could be in danger, why should she wait to start looking for him? But she drove on past. Andy had left her a note to tell her he was safe. He'd be with a friend somewhere, nursing a hangover or tucking into a late breakfast. She'd texted him to ask him to talk to Simon in Lerwick, and Simon would let her know if the boy got in touch. There was nothing for her to worry about. Nothing more that she could do.

39

Sandy Wilson pulled into the Sumburgh Airport car park. The traffic had been heavy all the way from Lerwick and there were still lights controlling the single-lane stretch close to the landslide. It was ten o'clock, but the low cloud meant it was barely light. In the terminal building disgruntled passengers were waiting for the weather to lift and for the delayed flights to take off. Sandy felt as if this was a wild goose chase, as if he'd been sent to go through the motions while the exciting part of the investigation was happening elsewhere.

He went into the shop to buy coffee and a bacon sandwich. He'd overslept and left without time for breakfast. He recognized the woman behind the food counter, but struggled to remember her name. She was big-boned and red-faced, and he thought she'd once worked in the chip shop in Lerwick. A few years ago, before he'd met Louisa and had tried to get in better shape, he'd been a regular customer.

'Hi there!' She'd recognized him too, greeted him like an old friend. 'Where are you off to?'

He shook his head. 'I'm here on work, not away on holiday.'

An announcement over the PA system called passengers for the Glasgow flight through to security. There was a similar call for people for Aberdeen and the shop emptied, as if by magic.

'Ah,' she said. 'Those murders . . . ' An excitement in her voice, hoping for details that wouldn't be known to the general public. He remembered that she'd been a terrible gossip.

'I don't suppose you saw Tom Rogerson on Sunday? He was supposed to be flying off to Orkney, parked his car here, but never arrived. You did know Tom Rogerson?'

'Oh aye. And Mavis, his wife. He led her a merry dance, you ken.'

The woman's name came back to him. Susan. He'd never known her surname.

'Were you working on Sunday?'

'Aye, it was another day just like this. Flights cancelled and delayed. Lots of passengers around, just waiting for the visibility to improve. I was rushed off my feet.' Susan hauled herself onto a stool behind the counter to make her point. She had short, stubby legs and calves shaped like upturned bottles.

'Did you see Tom Rogerson? He was a sociable kind of guy, wasn't he? He'd be buying coffee for anyone he knew, sitting at one of the tables there, chatting. I doubt if you'd miss him.' Sandy took a bite of the bacon sandwich. He'd already paid for it and there was no point in letting it get cold.

'I did see him, but he wasn't here for long. Maybe he thought it wasn't worth hanging around, because the flights were obviously delayed, and he'd come back later. I saw him chatting to one of the lasses at check-in. He probably wanted to get the latest news on the planes.'

'Did he come into the shop at all?' Sandy wasn't sure why he asked that, except that he was trying to picture Rogerson's movements.

Susan paused for a moment before answering. 'Yes, he did come in. The newspapers had arrived in with the first flight and he bought one of the fat London ones. You know what they're like at weekends. A pile of magazines and adverts tucked inside them.'

'Did he come into the shop before he spoke to the people at check-in or after?'

She pondered again. Sandy thought it was helpful for him that Susan took such a great interest in people. *He* would have taken no notice at all in the random movements of the passengers, and he'd be a terrible witness.

'After,' she said. 'He went to check-in almost as soon as he came into the terminal. Then he made his phone call and then he came into the shop. I was on the till at the door then, not doing the cafe. We had a very busy patch soon after that, and I didn't see what happened to him after he'd paid for the newspaper.'

Sandy was thinking about the phone call. He assumed Perez would have put in a request to Rogerson's service provider to get a list of his calls, but it might be more urgent to see the details now. There had been no phone on Rogerson's body, and no mention had been made of one at his house or office, but Mavis would have his personal and business numbers. It should be easy enough to track down the call history.

'Did you hear anything of his phone conversation?' Because he knew Susan would be interested. She already had Rogerson marked down as a philandering bastard and she'd be looking out for more evidence.

She shook her head sadly. 'He was out there in the lounge and I was in here behind the till. I saw him make the call, but there was no way I could have heard a word.'

Sandy had a sudden thought. 'Are you sure he made the call out? He wasn't answering one? You might not have heard it ringing, if the airport was crowded and noisy.'

She considered the idea. 'You're right. I just assumed that he was calling out, but I don't think I saw him press the buttons. It could have been either.'

★　★　★

Sandy waited in line to speak to the officials on check-in. He didn't want any aggro by pushing to the front of the queue, and anyway it wasn't too long; planes were arriving in from the south now and turning round very quickly. The woman he spoke to was English, young and bright. He showed her his warrant card and he could tell she was impressed. If he'd come across her in the past, he would already be chatting her up with a view to asking her out. Now he concentrated on Tom Rogerson.

'He was booked onto a flight to Orkney on Sunday morning,' he said, 'but he never took it.'

She pressed a few keys on her computer, muttered under her breath because the system was so slow.

'Were you working on Sunday?' he asked while she waited to retrieve Rogerson's booking.

'Yes. On the early shift. I finished at two.'

'Maybe you remember talking to him then? He had a kind of flirty way of speaking to the ladies.'

She raised her eyebrows. 'Late middle age? Had hand-luggage only. A small rucksack. Talked like something from that cop show set in the Seventies. *Life on Mars*.' Dismissive.

'Aye, that sounds about right.' Sandy gave her a smile. He thought that since Louisa, he'd changed his style; he felt good about that, a bit superior.

She looked at the screen in front of her. 'Rogerson, Thomas. Booked on the ten-thirty flight to Kirkwall. He checked in on time and was told that the flight would be delayed and he should listen out for announcements. Then he came back and said that because of the severe delay, he'd miss his meeting and he might as well cancel. Because he only had hand-luggage there was no problem, but he lost nearly two hundred quid, because the return flight was automatically cancelled too.'

Sandy tried to think that through. Missing the meeting was obviously a bollocks excuse, because the fishery conference wasn't going to start until the Monday morning. So what had happened between checking in for his flight and coming to the desk to cancel? Tom Rogerson had spoken to someone on the phone. If they could find out who the caller was, they might know the identity of the killer. Sandy thanked the young woman and moved away from the counter.

He was about to phone the police station in Lerwick to tell Jimmy Perez what he'd discovered when he remembered that his boss was working at home all day, looking out for comings and goings at the Hays' farm. He thought it would be just as easy to call in on Jimmy on his way back to town, and that his boss might even provide a spot of lunch.

But when he arrived at the house in Ravenswick, Perez seemed preoccupied. He was sitting at the window with a pair of binoculars on the sill, staring down towards the valley where the Hays lived. In the distance there was the scar in the hill left behind by the landslide. The ruin of Tain was just out of sight.

'Get back to the station and chase up those phone calls,' Perez said. 'You're right. We need to know who Tom spoke to in the airport that morning. We know he phoned his brother-in-law in Orkney, but that would have been after he changed his plans.'

'Anything happening here?' Sandy still had hopes of lunch.

'Jane Hay drove north with a passenger. The youngest lad, I think. She could have been taking him to school. Then she turned down towards the headland and I lost sight of her. She wasn't away long and she's home again now.' Perez looked at Sandy. 'This feels like a serious waste of time.'

'Just give it a day.' Sandy didn't know how else to respond. 'Isn't that what Willow said?'

'Aye.' Perez lifted his binoculars and stared out

once more. 'That's what she said.'

Sandy was reminded for a moment of the Jimmy Perez who'd lost Fran in a stabbing on Fair Isle. The Jimmy who brooded and snapped and refused to tell anyone what he was thinking. Sandy said goodbye, but he didn't get any response, so he let himself out of the house and drove back to Lerwick.

40

Jimmy Perez sat in the house that he still thought of as Fran's and saw Sandy drive away. It had been his idea to watch Kevin Hay's farm for unusual movements, but now he found the lack of activity frustrating. That wasn't the only reason for his feeling out of sorts. He knew he'd set himself an unreasonable deadline. Willow would be expecting some sort of answer from him at the end of the day and he knew he would have nothing coherent to tell her. He should be giving all his energy and attention to finding a double killer, not becoming angst-ridden about a relationship with a senior colleague.

The post van stopped outside his house and Davy Sutherland ran up the path with his mail. Perez stooped for the post, glad of the distraction. Three bills and a letter from the council, which he nearly threw into the bin unopened. When he looked more closely he saw it was labelled *Confidential* and when he opened it, he realized the letter was about the Ravenswick cemetery:

> You will be aware that the recent landslide caused considerable damage. We want to assure everyone that while headstones were overturned and in some cases washed away, your loved ones should not have been disturbed. We need to make a decision about

358

the cemetery's future and, in view of the possibility of further extreme climate events, the council is considering turning it into a green burial site. If that was the decided option, headstones would not be replaced, but a suitable environmentally friendly way of marking your loved ones' graves would be explored. We would welcome your comments.

Perez found himself smiling. Fran would have loved the idea of a green burial site in Ravenswick. She'd be one of the first to volunteer to plant wild-flowers and small native trees. He thought he should talk about the idea to Cassie, and again it came to him that this wasn't the right time to bring a new woman into their lives. Cassie already had enough to deal with. He returned to the letter and saw that Tom Rogerson's name was at the bottom of it. He must have been one of the councillors who'd come up with the idea, immediately after the landslide. There was no signature of course. The letter must have been drafted, approved and then slowly made its way through the council bureaucracy, to be printed without anyone realizing it might not be appropriate for it to carry Rogerson's name.

All the time he'd been keeping half an eye on the valley and the road. The cars were moving steadily, despite the single-lane traffic south of his house. No movement from the Hays. No sign of the eldest son, the one who had given Perez most concern. Was Andy in the house, helping his parents, or had he stayed overnight in Lerwick? Perez ate oatcakes and cheese, still perched at the window, not really hungry.

Cassie would come out of school at three. A neighbour usually collected her and kept her until Perez had finished work. He thought that today he would go himself. He'd still have the Hays in his sight for most of the way and he couldn't bear the idea of being trapped in the house any longer. The rain had stopped and the cloud had lifted a little. There might even be sufficient light for Cassie and him to look down at where the cemetery had once been, and he could talk to her about the green burial site. It would be a way for her to think about her mother's life, her dreams and ideals.

Cassie was first out into the playground and was delighted to see him, though she tried to be super-cool about it. She moaned a little because he didn't have the car and they'd have to walk back. 'You don't know how hard Miss Rogerson makes us work.'

'How does she seem?' Usually Kathryn came out into the playground to see the children off the premises, but today the classroom support teacher was there instead.

'OK.'

He didn't walk with her up the footpath to the main road and home, but down towards the sea. They would skirt Tain that way, but the sycamores would hide most of the devastation and there was a rise in the land where they could look down at the remains of the cemetery. The afternoons were already getting lighter; there was an hour of the day left. Cassie was chatting about her friends and about the costume she'd need for the end-of-term performance. 'But Miss Rogerson says you're not to worry about that. She'll sort it out for us.'

'That's very kind of her.' But now Perez was thinking that Kathryn Rogerson might not be so kind. How could a woman who'd just lost the father she claimed to adore continue working as if nothing at all had happened?

In the distance Perez could see Kevin Hay working on a big machine, a tractor with a bucket on the front. He was digging a trench that might be a new drainage ditch by the side of a field, heaping the damp black soil in piles to one side. From a distance, the ditch looked like a long grave. The rumble of the machine sounded animal, like a monster from one of Cassie's stories, but she seemed not to notice it.

There was a figure standing on the bank, just where Perez had thought he and Cassie would have their conversation about her mother's headstone. He felt a moment of resentment. Usually there was space enough in Shetland not to be disturbed. As they approached he recognized the figure as Jane Hay. She turned as she heard them.

'You got the letter too,' she said.

'You had someone buried there?' He supposed he shouldn't be surprised. Kevin's family had crofted here for generations.

'Kevin's grandfather, though his parents looked after his grave.' She paused. 'I never knew him. I suppose I'm here for Minnie Laurenson.'

'The old woman who used to live at Tain.'

She nodded. 'She didn't have any family locally and she was the closest thing I had in the islands to my own relative.' She qualified the words quickly. 'I mean, Kev's mother and father were always lovely to me, but it's not quite the same.'

Cassie was pulling at his hand, making it clear she wanted to be on her way home. She had no interest in the adult conversation taking place above her head. Perez nodded towards her. 'I wanted to talk to the bairn about the green burial idea.'

'Of course. I'll leave you to it. I'm not sure what Minnie would make of it. She was always a great one for tradition.' A pause. 'When you're done, Jimmy, why don't you bring Cassie into the house? I've been baking. We might find her something to keep her going until tea time.'

He nodded again, thinking that it was good to have an invitation to the Hays' house. Much better than staring out of his kitchen window into the dark.

41

Willow was doing her morning yoga when she heard the baby. It was a strange noise, more like a bleat than a cry. Rosie started singing then, and the combined sounds — the mother singing and the baby calling — moved Willow almost to tears. She thought she could understand those sad, lonely women who snatched children from prams outside shops. In the kitchen John was sitting in his dressing gown drinking tea.

'Oh God,' he said when he saw her. 'Is it that time? What must you think of us? Are you OK with cereal and toast?'

'I'll make it.' She preferred to be in the kitchen on her own. Something about his sleepy, rather smug face made her want to hit him. It was deep and basic playground envy: *You've got something I want, and I hate you.* She knew it was ridiculous, but she couldn't control it.

'Are you sure?' He was already on his feet. 'You know where everything is?'

'Quite sure, and I'll find it.'

After breakfast she walked through the drizzle to the police station: up the lane, emerging opposite the library, and then past the town hall. Lerwick had become familiar to her now and some of the passers-by recognized her, gave her a wave. It was early and the place was quiet. Sandy had planned to head straight to the airport and Perez would be in the house in Ravenswick,

363

staring down the valley towards Gilsetter and Tain. She hoped he wasn't brooding over Fran; she hadn't intended to give him some sort of ultimatum.

She spent the morning attempting to lose herself in the details of the investigation and stuck a mind-map on the wall — a contemporary-art extravaganza of different-coloured marker pens, all circles and connections: Alison Teal's sudden crisis in Simon Agnew's office linked to the crisis that had first brought her to the islands; Tom Rogerson's relationship with Alison, with Kevin Hay and with the developers of the smart cabins north of Ravenswick. The second generation — the Hay boys and Kathryn Rogerson — marked in red; the earlier generation — Magnus Tait and Minnie Laurenson — circled in green. Willow was still staring at the map, feeling that she was starting to see a strange inverted pattern, when Sandy came in. He looked at the map briefly, but seemed to dismiss it as the ravings of a lunatic and started to tell her about his trip to Sumburgh. Willow turned away from the wall to listen and felt her theory dissolve into nothing.

'Rogerson took a phone call while he was waiting for his plane,' Sandy said. 'Or made a call out. My witness couldn't be sure. And suddenly his plans changed and he cancelled his flight.'

'We asked Kathryn for her dad's mobile number.' Despite herself, Willow began to see why Sandy was so excited. 'She didn't get back to us. We know he had two phones — one for business, and I have that number; and a personal one. I don't think we've ever been given those details.'

'You think the killer took Rogerson's mobile?' Sandy was back in bouncy puppy mode. Excitable. He'd let slip that he'd dropped in on Perez, but had given no details.

Willow shrugged. 'If so, I doubt we'll ever find it. Easy enough to chuck it into the tide, if the killer didn't want anyone to know that they'd called.' She stood up and picked up her coat. 'I'm going to talk to Mavis Rogerson. She'll have Tom's number.'

★   ★   ★

She found Mavis in the big house near the park. She was alone. 'I sent my sister back to Kirkwall. I couldn't stand her fussing.' She stood aside to let Willow into the house.

'We could go out,' Willow said. 'Coffee and cake. My treat.'

'Nah.' Mavis gave a little smile. 'People just want to tell me how sorry they are for my loss. They didn't have much good to say about Tom when he was alive. It sticks in my craw now he's dead. Besides, I've been baking.'

They sat in the kitchen and she switched on the kettle. There were scones cooling on a wire tray on the table. 'I can't seem to stop cooking,' she said. 'Since you took me out and bought me cake that day. It's something to do. Kathryn took a batch into school today for the bairns.'

'I wanted to ask you about Tom's phone numbers. It's always something we check. I've got his work number from his office, but they don't have his personal one. And he didn't have his phone with him when we found him.'

'Sure.' Mavis took a mobile from her bag, searched for the number and handed the phone to Willow, who copied the number into her own contact list. She pressed *Call* just in case, but there was no ring tone anywhere in the house.

'Did you phone him on Saturday morning when he was waiting for his flight?'

'No.' A pause. 'I didn't call him much. He didn't always answer, and then I'd start imagining what he might be up to.'

'Why did you stay with him for all that time, when he treated you so badly?' Willow couldn't help asking the question. She couldn't imagine what it must be like to be in a relationship with someone it was impossible to trust.

'I don't know. Maybe I don't think sex is that important?' Another pause. 'And I liked all the things that came with being his wife. This house. Nice holidays. Social events. And his company. He was such good company.' She turned away from Willow to make instant coffee. 'Sometimes I thought the sex was an illness. Like an addiction. That maybe if he got help, he could stop. Then other times I thought it wasn't about the sex at all, but it was the admiration he needed. That there were things he needed that I couldn't give.'

'It was never your fault.' Willow took a mug of coffee and blew across the surface.

'Aye, maybe.' Not really believing it.

They sat for a moment in silence.

366

'Do you know the Hays at Gilsetter?'

'Kevin and Jane?' Mavis split a couple of scones and buttered them, passed a plate to Willow. They were still warm and the butter began to melt. 'I've met them a few times, but we're not pals. I know the boy better.'

'Which boy?' Willow kept her voice even, but in her head she was Sandy, dancing around the room in anticipation.

'Andy, the oldest one. He was at the house a few times when Kathryn was at school and in college.'

'But she'd be older than him.'

'Six or seven years, maybe.' Mavis was eating a scone with intense concentration.

'That's a big gap between friends when you're a teenager.'

'They weren't friends exactly.' Mavis put down the scone and tried to find the words she needed. 'Andy was more like a pet.'

'A pet?'

'Kathryn took up with him when he started at the Youth Theatre. He was the youngest there and she was one of the oldest. Maybe 'pet' is the wrong word. He was more like a mascot. He played up to the big ones, showing off and making them laugh. Tom liked having the young people around.' She paused. 'Maybe it made him feel not quite so old. Or perhaps he just enjoyed staring at the bonnie lasses. Sometimes they held informal rehearsals here; sometimes they just came back for supper afterwards.'

'When did you last see Andy?' Willow thought this was another connection, another colour for the mind-map on the board.

'Just before Christmas. He'd dropped out of uni and wanted to ask Kathryn's advice. He was thinking about applying to drama school and wondered what Kathryn thought of the idea.' Mavis smiled. 'I hadn't seen him since he was about twelve years old and I hardly recognized him. He's got so skinny, and those dreadful piercings on his face.'

'Was Tom here then?'

'I think he was out at a meeting and came in just as the boy was leaving.'

'They had a row in the street, the week before Tom died.' Willow resisted the temptation to take another scone. 'Any idea what that might have been about?'

Mavis shook her head. 'Tom didn't really do confrontation. He wanted everyone to like him. If there was an argument, the boy will have provoked it.'

Willow tried to think through the implication of Andy's friendship with Kathryn Rogerson. Did it really have any significance? In a place like Shetland perhaps there were always going to be unexpected connections. She stood up. 'Thanks for the number. If you come across the phone, just give me a shout.'

'It was good of you to come.' Mavis followed Willow out into the dark hall. 'You seem to understand. Everyone thinks of Tom as a monster. Or a bit of a joke. It's hard to grieve for him when everyone thought so badly of him. There's nobody to talk to.'

'There's always Kathryn,' Willow said. 'She

seems to have loved him.'

There was a moment of silence. 'Ah yes, Kathryn.' There was a pause. 'She's very much her father's daughter.'

42

Jane stood at the kitchen window watching out for Jimmy Perez and Cassie. She was already regretting the impulse that had made her invite them back to the house. What was the point, when she'd already decided it was too soon to tell Jimmy that she was anxious about her son? Beyond the polytunnel she could see the lights on Kevin's tractor. This was his new project: he was digging a drainage ditch to save them from the water that he was convinced would soon sweep down the valley again. He'd been at it all day, but the light was fading and Jane thought he'd surely stop soon. She hoped he'd be in before Perez and Cassie arrived. He had an easy way with children and she would feel less awkward if he was around.

She was thinking again that Kevin would make a brilliant grandfather when there was a tap on the door. It had started raining again, a soft misty drizzle that had been invisible from the house. Perez and the child stood hand-in-hand, hoods up.

'Come in,' she said. 'You'll catch your deaths. We'll give you a lift up the bank when you've had some tea.' Sounding, she thought, almost normal.

Perez took off Cassie's jacket and hung it up, before removing his own. 'You're on your own today?'

'Kevin will be in soon,' she said, 'and Michael's staying in Lerwick with his girlfriend tonight.'

'What about Andy?'

She gave a little laugh that she knew was unconvincing. 'Ah, we never know where Andy is these days.' She switched on the kettle. 'Would you rather tea or coffee, Jimmy? And I have orange juice, if Cassie would like it.'

She didn't hear his answer first time round, because she was suddenly lost in her own thoughts. 'I'm sorry, Jimmy, what did you say?' Feeling foolish — the socially incompetent woman with the dirt ingrained into her fingers.

'Are you OK, Jane?'

She'd found Cassie a box of toys that had belonged to the boys when they were little. The girl was on the floor building a Lego monster. Perez was sitting opposite Jane at the table, very still, very serious; more like a priest, she thought, than a detective. 'We're all under stress,' she said at last. 'How can we relax when there's a killer out there?' She nodded towards the darkness. 'When will it all be over?'

He hesitated too. 'Soon,' he said. 'Very soon.'

She wondered if that meant the police were close to an arrest. If so, why was Jimmy Perez sitting at her table, drinking tea? She pushed away the idea that they must somehow be implicated. Her head was full of questions, but she knew he'd tell her nothing further. The silence was broken only by the click of Cassie's bricks as she created her own brand of villain.

'How has Andy settled home?' Perez asked. 'It

must be hard coming back once you've made the break. Well, I know how hard it is. I did it too — came back to the islands after working in Aberdeen.'

She shrugged. Andy was the last person she wanted to talk about. 'It's not so unusual these days. Kids go south for adventure, only to find that it's pretty tough out there in the big, wide world. We have it easy in Shetland in lots of ways.'

'I understand Andy was pals with Kathryn Rogerson. Have they hooked up since he came back?'

Jane felt a moment of panic. How could the police know the trivial details of a weird friendship that had happened when Andy was still a boy? It occurred to her that they were probably digging around in *her* past too. She felt herself blushing as she wondered what they might come up with. Tales of her exhibitionism in the more rowdy bars in town. Her one-night stands.

'I don't know. That was a long time ago. I doubt they have much in common now.'

'Apparently he went to see her before Christmas. Asking for career advice, according to her mother.'

'Why ask the question then, Jimmy? If you already know the answer.' She was angry but didn't raise her voice. She didn't want to upset the child and she'd never enjoyed a scene. Not sober.

Suddenly he smiled. 'Sorry. Sometimes it's hard to get out of cop-mode. We turn every conversation into an interrogation. Forgive me.' He finished his coffee. 'Now we should go.'

'No!' The last thing she wanted was to be alone in the house, listening to the rain running down the gutters. 'Kevin won't be long. Wait until he gets in and he'll give you a lift. I shouldn't be so sensitive. You have your job to do.'

'It just seems an unusual relationship.' Despite his earlier apology, it seemed he couldn't let the subject go. 'A young lad and an older girl. What could she get out of it?'

'Admiration,' Jane said. What harm was there in discussing it, after all? 'Andy was devoted to her.'

'Did she ever come here?'

'A few times, one summer. Not so much to spend time with Andy, but to talk to the old folk in Ravenswick. Minnie Laurenson and Kevin's parents. She was doing a history project at the start of her Highers. Something about local agriculture and the changes there'd been. I think Andy might just have been a way in. She lived in town and didn't have much access to the crofting communities.'

'So she was using Andy; his friendship was just an excuse for her to get her project finished?'

'Maybe that's a bit harsh.' Jane remembered the girl's visits. Andy hadn't hidden his excitement on the days she'd been expected. There'd been nothing cool about his approach to the girl. He'd run up the track to be at the stop long before the bus from Lerwick was due and then they'd walked together back to Gilsetter.

They'd made an odd pair: the lanky, hyperactive boy and the girl who'd been confident even then. Kathryn had looked strangely old-fashioned. Long hair in plaits, wearing a hand-knitted gansey before they'd come back into fashion. She might only have been sixteen, but there'd been nothing shy or awkward in the way she'd talked to the old people. Jane had sat in on a couple of the chats and had seen that Kevin's parents had felt totally at ease with her. Looking back, it had been one of those golden Shetland summers, fog-free and mild. She saw that Perez was waiting for her to continue. 'Kathryn helped Andy too.'

'With his acting?'

She nodded. 'We always said she'd be a teacher, because she was so good with the young ones.'

'It was a bit of a coincidence that she ended up teaching here in Ravenswick.'

'Maybe, but it was always her plan to come home as soon as she could find a job here. She loves Shetland.' Jane found herself lost in thought again. Kathryn and Andy. She'd thought the relationship had ended when the girl had gone south to university; now she thought they must have kept in touch. She felt strangely hurt that Andy had kept the friendship a secret. She stood up and began to put home-made biscuits in a tin for Jimmy Perez to take away. There was the sound of the tractor in the yard, and then of Kevin stamping his boots on the concrete to get off the worst of the mud. She opened the door into the hall to catch her husband before he took off his waterproofs.

'Jimmy and Cassie are here. They walked up from the school. Would you be able to give them a lift home?'

He raised his eyebrows: a silent question to ask if there'd been more to the visit than she could say in the detective's hearing. She shook her head.

'Sure,' he said. His voice was loud enough for the pair in the kitchen to hear him and there was something of a performance in it. 'They certainly wouldn't want to be out in the dark on a night like this. Such dreadful weather!' Cassie stuck her head round the door. 'Now, young lady, are you going to sit beside me in the Land Rover?'

There was a flurry of activity while Jimmy and Cassie hurried to put on their outdoor clothes and then the house was quiet again, except for the sound of water running down the drain in the yard. Jane gathered up the mugs and coffee cups and felt a little lost. Aimless. It had been good to have a child in the house again. Caring for children gave you some sort of purpose. She'd made a shepherd's pie for tea and it was ready to go into the oven, so there was nothing more to do in the house. She was thinking that it might be worth talking to Kathryn. It would be right to pass on her condolences, and the teacher might have some idea what was troubling her son.

Her mobile was lying on the table. She stared at it, planning in her head what she might say to the teacher, when it rang. The noise seemed very loud and startled her. She picked up the phone.

'Mum.' The voice was strained and sounded very young. 'Mum, it's me. Andy. I need to talk to you.'

43

Back in the police station, Willow was on the phone to Rogerson's mobile service provider. 'I need a call record list for this number. The past month. Immediately.' The knowledge that she'd cocked up, by not asking them to check it sooner, was making her aggressive.

At the end of the line there was a young man who managed to be patronizing and unhelpful at the same time.

'OK,' she said. 'Any calls made into or out of that number last Sunday. You should be able to give me that now.'

'I'm really sorry.' Not sounding sorry at all. 'It won't be possible. Certainly not immediately.'

At that point Willow lost her temper, demanded to speak to his manager and was eventually promised the information she needed by email within the hour. She was seldom angry and hated the lack of control; she ended the encounter shaking and it took a moment before she was ready to speak to Perez. It was already mid-afternoon and she had the sense of time slipping away. He answered his phone straight away, but the line was crackly. 'Anything?'

'I've just walked down to collect Cassie from school. Getting stir-crazy in the house.'

'It seems Kathryn Rogerson and Andy Hay were close at one time.' Willow tried to explain the relationship between the young people, as

Mavis had described it to her.

He didn't answer immediately and she thought his phone might have lost reception altogether. In the end, when he did speak, it was just one word. 'Interesting.' Then the connection was lost and the line was dead.

Sandy seemed to have picked up Willow's restlessness, because he couldn't settle, either. He kept sticking his head round her door to see if they'd heard from Rogerson's mobile provider. He was still triumphant after finding the witness in the airport, and he had a stake in the information. In the end she sent him to make tea, though she was awash with the stuff. All the time she was looking at her watch or staring at the white plastic clock on the office wall. She could hear the minutes tick. Despite the yoga and the mindfulness, she'd never been much good at waiting. She was just about to call the phone company again and was building herself up for another confrontation, when the email came through. Sandy came in with the two mugs of tea and she swivelled the screen so that he could read it at the same time as her.

'What do you think?'

She thought Sandy must have spent too long in Perez's company, because he gave the same one-word answer as his boss had done half an hour before. 'Interesting.'

Willow was on her feet, staring at the mind-map, which was still on the whiteboard. The pattern that had seemed fuzzy and inexplicable now made perfect sense.

'I need to talk to Alison Teal's brother in

378

prison. Can you phone them, Sandy? See if you can sort it out?' Because words and ideas were tumbling through her head and she needed to concentrate to make sense of them. She didn't need distractions. Besides, Sandy would be good at a task like that. Persistent but polite. She was so wired that she worried she might end up shouting again. 'I don't need a video-link this time. Just a phone call will do.'

He nodded and left the room, bewildered, but knowing better than to ask for more details.

He bounded back a quarter of an hour later, grinning. 'All sorted. If you ring this number in ten minutes, Teal will be in the governor's office ready to talk to you.'

'Sandy Wilson, you're a bloody miracle-worker!' She could feel the case moving forward now. It was physical, like a rumble beneath her feet, like the soil sliding down the hill during the landslip. Unstoppable.

'No problem.' But Sandy was blushing, as delighted as she was. It seemed the assistant governor was a birdwatcher. Obsessed. A regular visitor to Shetland. He'd been happy to help in any way he could, glad of another, informal link to the islands. 'I've promised to take him out for a beer next time he's up.'

'I'll tape the conversation,' Willow said, 'so I can play it back to you as soon as we're done, but I don't want an audience when I'm talking to him, Sandy. Is that OK? I need to be able to focus.' She paused. 'My performance has to be just for Teal.'

Sandy left the room without comment. If he

was disappointed, Willow didn't notice. She was making notes on a scrap of paper on the desk in front of her.

She looked at her watch again, took a deep breath, made the call. The man who answered had an educated southern accent. Warm, interested. He sounded more like an old-fashioned schoolmaster than someone who worked with offenders. Willow created a back-story for him in her head as he introduced himself: he'd be someone who'd been brought up to take responsibility for people less fortunate than himself. His father was a priest, maybe. Or a socialist intellectual. She wondered what his colleagues made of him and hoped he wouldn't become hardened and cynical. She forced herself to listen to his words.

'I wish I were in the islands with you.' His voice was wistful. 'It's my favourite place in the world.' Then he dragged himself back to the present. 'I have Jonathan with me. I'll put him on the line.'

Teal sounded even younger than he had on the video-link. Perhaps he had no idea why he'd been dragged to the governor's office and was scared. Willow took the interview slowly, felt the rhythm of it like a poem and pulled him with her, so eventually he felt the need to answer as he would join in the chorus of a song.

'I'd like to talk about the time your sister disappeared, Jono. Could you cast your mind back to then?' A pause. 'It was a while ago, I know, but let's go through the details again.'

A mumbled response.

380

'Anything — however trivial — might help us find Alison's killer. You do want to do that?'

'Of course.'

'It was 2002: you in the army, Britney Spears at the top of the charts. Alison at the height of her fame in that drama on TV.'

'I remember like it was yesterday. Good times.'

'Brilliant, Jono!' Willow felt as if she'd caught him now. In his mind he was fifteen years younger, still with a purpose and a famous sister. Contacts and parties when he was home on leave. 'What might have happened, do you think, to make Alison run away and give it all up?'

'She was pretty messed up.'

'Man trouble?'

'Oh, she could never keep a decent man. Always wanted more than they could give. And she never took to the good ones. It was always the losers, the druggies and the wasters. The older ones who reminded her of Dad. Or the exciting ones who promised her the world.'

Willow was about to ask another question when Jono spoke again, and she could tell that he was back with his sister, sharing the glamour and the heartache. The stories spilled out. Details he'd probably forgotten for years. Names and places and the parties they'd been to, the meals they'd eaten. No need for Willow to ask leading questions, to tease out the facts. The recorded conversation might be used in a future court case, so she had to be careful. All the same, she felt in total control of the exchange.

Twenty minutes later Sandy knocked quietly and looked in, but seeing that she was still talking, he went away again. At last, when she could think of nothing else to ask and the man at the end of the line had fallen silent, she thanked Teal and told him they were done. The assistant governor came onto the line again.

'I hope that was useful.'

She assumed he'd been in the room all the time, listening in. 'Terrifically. All confidential at this stage, of course.'

'Oh, absolutely. You can trust me.'

'I'm sure that I can.'

There was a pause. Willow was impatient to end the call so that she could consider the implications of the conversation with Teal, but the man spoke again.

'Perhaps we could meet up next time I'm in Shetland.' He sounded nervous, almost as if he was inviting her out on a date. Perhaps he was. She imagined it would be hard to meet many women in his profession, and birdwatching seemed to be a predominantly male activity.

'Ah,' she said. 'I probably won't be here when you next visit. I don't actually belong here.' Replacing the receiver, she thought that was true. Whatever Jimmy Perez decided, she would never truly belong in Shetland.

She found Sandy in the ops room, staring out of the window down at the street below. The traffic was heavy; it was just after five and this was the nearest Lerwick got to a rush hour. The rain made everything look slick and shiny in the headlights. He turned back to face her. 'Well?'

'Listen to the call yourself. I want to know what you think.' She paused and came to a sudden decision. 'I'm going out. I've just tried to get Jimmy on the phone, but there's no reply: no reception on his mobile and he's not answering the landline in his house. He was picking up Cassie from school, but he should be home by now.'

'So you're going south?'

'Yes,' she said, already almost out of the room. 'I'm going south.'

44

Kevin Hay dropped Perez and Cassie right outside their door. He'd talked Cassie through the vehicle's controls and let her switch on the indicators on the drive back from Gilsetter. She was squeezed between the two men on the front bench seat and Perez didn't speak at all. There was no mention of the murders until the Land Rover had stopped and Kevin had let Cassie out of the driver's door to run inside. Then the two men were alone, standing in the drizzle on either side of the van.

'I wasn't very civil last time we met, Jimmy. I'm sorry.'

'No problem. It's a stressful time for everyone.' Perez was in a hurry to join Cassie; he didn't like her being alone even for a few minutes, and this was no place for a useful conversation. 'Thanks for the lift.' He turned away to walk to the house.

'Jimmy!' Perez looked back and Kevin Hay continued, 'These killings have nothing to do with my family. We all make mistakes, but we're good people.'

Perez wasn't sure how to answer that, so he just raised his hand in farewell. Inside, he saw there were missed calls from Willow on his mobile and his landline, but when he tried to call her there was no reply. He felt a moment of relief. He still wasn't sure what he would tell her.

Perhaps they could work out a compromise, a way of staying close without disrupting Cassie's life. But he thought Willow wasn't a woman who would be comfortable with compromise. Besides, he wanted more than that.

He made scrambled eggs for Cassie's supper and then realized he was hungry and made more for himself. The dark outside was dense now, the remaining daylight had long gone and there was no moon. But still he stared out of the window down the valley towards Tain and Gilsetter. Partly because it was what he'd been doing all day and had become a habit, partly out of a kind of superstition. If he stopped looking, something dreadful might happen. The cluster of lights must come from Gilsetter, from the polytunnels and the house itself. They were familiar, a part of the night-time landscape. He wondered what was happening there, pictured Jane and Kevin at the kitchen table, discussing the case. Making plans. Inventing excuses for themselves or their sons.

He dragged his attention back to the child, bathed her and prepared her for bed. Cassie seemed to pick up on his mood and was quiet and a little subdued, making no protest when he said it was time for her to go to sleep. He went back to his seat by the window and noticed that it was still raining. He could hear that the ditch running past the house where Magnus Tait had once lived was full. It crossed his mind that perhaps he and Cassie should move away for a while and stay with friends in Lerwick, in case the hill was still unstable and likely to slide again. But he couldn't bear the thought of the disruption to both their routines.

When he was sure Cassie was asleep he went outside to put rubbish in the bin by the track. The lights in Gilsetter remained, but now there was another light a little way to the south. At first Perez thought it might come from a stationary car on the main road, but it wasn't a usual place for a vehicle to park. The light taunted him. He couldn't ignore it and kept staring, trying to fix it in his mental map. It didn't shift. He went back inside and phoned Willow again and still there was no response. On impulse he picked up the phone once more and called Maggie, the friend who usually cared for Cassie after school.

'Sorry to be a pain, but is there any chance you could babysit? It's a work thing. I shouldn't be long, and Cassie's in bed.'

'No bother, Jimmy, and be as long as you like. I'll be there in ten minutes.' Her voice was comforting and normal and made him believe he was overreacting.

By the time Maggie had arrived, though, he'd convinced himself that the light was in Tain. Where else could it be? There were no other houses in that part of Ravenswick. The only other building was the manse, and that was east of Gilsetter. The school was further north. When his neighbour tapped at the door, he had his boots and waterproofs on and his car keys in his hand. Outside, he changed his mind about driving. It was only quarter of an hour's walk down the hill and he didn't want to warn whoever was in the ruined croft of his presence.

It was muggy and unseasonably mild. The low cloud seemed to hold in the smoke from the settlement's open fires and the smell of peat mixed with the compost scent of damp vegetation. He almost ran down the bank to the road, crossed it and looked over the valley towards the coast. His eyes had adjusted to the murk. Occasionally cars passed behind him. The Gilsetter lights were clear from here and spilled outside onto the sycamores that surrounded Tain. The trees were bare now and Perez could see quite clearly that there *was* a light inside the ruins. Not the same constant brightness of the glow in Gilsetter, but uneven, flickering. A candle or a torch.

He walked more slowly. There was no vehicle parked at the end of the short track. Whoever was inside Tain had walked, like him. The light was in the space that had once been the bedroom and was still relatively intact. Perez slid closer, then moved round to the side of the house that faced the sea, treading carefully because there was still debris underfoot, shattered crockery and smashed furniture. There was no glass in the window here and he could hear at once that there were two people inside. This was a conversation between a man and a woman.

'You haven't been staying here?' Jane Hay's voice was strained and tense, but she was reining in her emotions and trying to keep calm. 'What's been going on?'

Perez shifted position so that he could see inside. The mother and son were standing, uplit by a candle which had been stuck onto a saucer and placed on a plain wooden chair. Jane had a torch in her hand, but that had been switched off.

'No,' Andy said. 'I haven't been staying here.' He seemed lost inside a big parka, and in the candlelight looked even thinner than Perez remembered. Skeletal. Perez could see the bones in the boy's face and in the long fingers that never seemed to rest. The piercings near his eyebrow glittered. 'I told you. I was staying with a friend.'

'Why didn't you come and see me at home tonight?' She was trying not to sound accusing, but the words came out as a cry. 'Why all this drama and mystery?'

There was a moment of silence. *Because he's a young man,* Perez thought. *And because he's always been attracted to melodrama.*

'I couldn't face Dad.' Andy looked directly at her. 'I needed to talk to you first.'

'Your father isn't even at home.' She was growing impatient now. 'He took Jimmy Perez and his daughter home and then went straight to the Henderson house to watch the footie. There's a Scotland game.'

The ordinary, banal words seemed almost to offend Andy. Perez thought again that he preferred the tension and the high drama.

'So why don't we just go back to Gilsetter?' Jane went on. 'You can explain everything to me in the warm.'

'I used to come here.'

'I know you used to come here. You came with

me to see Minnie Laurenson. She had a tin of toffees and home-made fudge and she told you stories.' Perez saw that Jane was smiling. It was probably easier for her to think of Andy as a small boy, eager to please. She didn't know what to make of the angry young man.

'No!' He sounded frustrated now. 'I mean I came to Tain recently. While Alis was living here.'

'Alis?'

'Alison,' he said. 'Alison Teal.'

Of course. Perez should have known all along. Kevin Hay hadn't been Alison's client. The regular visitor to Tain, paying Tom Rogerson with his father's stolen debit card, had been Andy. Not Kevin. Andy, the boy teased for his lack of sexual experience and his attraction to older women, would have been easy prey. Hay must have guessed why the payment had been made in his name and was protecting his son. Perhaps he believed that Andy had killed the woman. And perhaps, Perez thought as the idea chased around his head, perhaps that made sense.

Jane seemed to be following the same logic. 'Did you kill the woman?'

'No!' The boy was screaming. 'I loved her.'

Again there was a moment of silence.

'She was a prostitute,' Jane said. 'You do know that?'

And how did you know? A wild guess? Been listening to the same rumours as Craig Henderson? Or did Kevin tell you?

'Of course I knew. She wouldn't have had sex with someone like me if I hadn't paid her. But it didn't matter. She made me happy.' He looked round the filthy room. 'She made this place seem special. And she did *like* me.' A pause. 'I brought her a kitten from the farm to keep her company. She was going to cook me a meal on Valentine's Day.'

'Did your father know what you were up to?' The woman's voice was even now.

'Not at the time.' The boy's bony fingers continued to move. Perez couldn't stop staring at them, flexing and twisting as if they had a life of their own. 'I think he followed me down one night, but he couldn't see what was going on. He worked it out later, when the police started asking about the money.'

'So *after* they were both dead?'

'Of course after they were dead!' Andy was howling now. 'You can't think Dad would commit murder?'

'Of course not.' But Perez could tell that the woman had considered the possibility. 'Where have you been staying, Andy?' Her voice was quiet. 'Where have you been running away to, the nights you didn't come home?'

For a moment Perez thought the boy would refuse to answer, that like a petulant child he would stand in the flickering candlelight with his mouth clamped shut. But Andy shrugged and began to speak. The answer wasn't unexpected, but it triggered a shift in perception for Perez, an entirely new way of looking at the investigation. He remembered why the bad weather on the day of Rogerson's disappearance was so important. He moved away from his hiding place and through the hole in the wall where once the back door had been.

Jane and Andy stared at him in horror, as if he was an apparition, and then they both began to speak at once. At the same time he must have chanced upon a patch of mobile reception, because his phone started to go wild with electronic sound.

45

Willow drove south out of Lerwick. The roads were quieter now and she scarcely passed any traffic. There was a light in Jimmy Perez's house and she was tempted to stop, but after a moment's hesitation she continued on her way. He might have personal reasons for not answering her calls, and she had too much pride to turn up unannounced on his doorstep. She slowed down to avoid a jogger in a high-vis jacket running north. Willow wondered at the dedication that drove people to exercise in weather like this and at this time of night. She checked the clock on the hire-car dashboard. It was only seven. Not so late after all, although it had been dark for hours.

The building appeared before she was quite expecting it. Her headlights swept across it and it appeared as a solid black shadow. She had decided against a clandestine approach. She wouldn't be able to hide the car and, besides, she was only here to ask questions. There was no need to make a big issue of the visit. The building was unlit, as far as she could see. Perhaps she'd misjudged her timing and had made her dramatic chase south for nothing. She could have called ahead and saved herself a wasted journey. All the same, she got out of the car and knocked at the door. Silence. She turned the handle and it opened. That struck her as odd. Shetlanders might not usually lock the doors even of their work places, but there had been two murders within a few miles of this place.

'Hello! Anyone at home?'

She walked further inside. It had the air of a place that had been left recently. There was a kettle, warm to the touch. In the office a file left open on the desk, and the PC on standby. The occupier could be home any minute, but Willow thought she would have some warning. There hadn't been a car parked outside and she'd see the headlights coming down the track, hear the engine noise. The office faced out towards the road. Willow would have time to move back to the other room and pretend that she was just waiting out of the weather. She'd left on the hall light and could see well enough just from that. A light in the office would show that she'd been snooping.

She opened the desk drawers one by one, not entirely sure what she was searching for. In the top drawer there was the same self-help book that they'd found among Alison's possessions; she recognized the title and the publisher's name. Sandy Sechrest, the owner of Tain, worked as an editor for the company in New York City. Willow was pondering the significance of this — excited, because in a small way it confirmed her theory — when she was aware of a change in the atmosphere. A slight draught. Somewhere a door had been opened. She turned quickly, preparing to leave, but she was too late. There was already someone else in the room, blocking the exit. Willow was about to smile apologetically and mumble an excuse; she felt embarrassed, but not in any danger. Then there was a brief moment of bewilderment and everything went black.

★　★　★

When Willow woke, she was outside. Her face felt wet: blood from the wound on her temple mixed with a gentle drizzle, and the damp was soaking through the back of her jeans. She was wearing the waterproof jacket she'd had on when she'd been hit, and that was keeping the top of her body dry. She shifted slightly and the pain in her head was so severe that she wanted to scream. She didn't scream. That pride again, but also an instinct for survival because somewhere close by there was the sound of footsteps. Willow heard the suction of boots lifted out of mud and the splash of surface water. She knew she was in no state to take on her attacker, so she lay still.

Strong arms grabbed her under her shoulders and began to drag her along the ground. Willow tried to distract herself from the pain. She could do this. It was why she got up before work every morning and practised the discipline of yoga. She could keep her breathing even, control her muscles and force herself to relax. Her attacker had to believe that she was still unconscious, that she posed no danger. Willow imagined coming to the scene as the first officer present. Her heels would be making tracks in the mud, and any competent detective or CSI would work out what had happened here. The killer was panicking and getting careless. The movement stopped and Willow's upper body was dropped on the ground. This time there was no need for pretence. The pain was so intolerable that she slipped back into unconsciousness.

When she woke once more she was lying on her back again. The rain on her face was heavier, sharper. It was still and dark. Thick black. Usually her eyes adjusted to the island dark and after a while she'd make out shades of grey, a house light in the distance, the beam of a lighthouse sweeping the horizon. Now there was nothing and it came to her that she must still be unconscious, dreaming or dead. But her other senses were working. She felt cold and wet, and a heaviness on her lower limbs and her torso, as if something or someone was lying on top of her. There was a smell of damp earth. And a sound. Rhythmic, repetitive and oddly familiar.

At once Willow was a child again, at home in the commune in North Uist. It was the heyday of the establishment; three families and assorted hangers-on were living in the big laird's house and the surrounding farm buildings. She was outside on a blowy spring day. Golden light broken up by cloud shadows that raced across the headland. Her father was turning the sandy soil in the vegetable garden so it would be ready for planting. That was the sound she could hear now. A spade slicing into the earth and then the thud of soil landing in the previously dug trench. Except that now the soil was being tipped onto her. It wasn't rain on her face, but the wet earth that had already covered her body, trapping her legs and arms and making movement impossible.

She tried to scream, but as she opened her mouth, it was filled with mud. She spat it out and began to yell for help. The cry seemed to disappear into the dark, and all the time above her she heard the sound of the spade cutting and lifting and felt the soil as it rained down on her body and her face.

46

Jane walked with Perez and Andy back towards Gilsetter. Perez's appearance had shocked her, but she was pleased that he was there. It was easier than being on her own with Andy, who was trailing behind them like a recalcitrant toddler. Perez had lost phone reception again once they'd left Tain and she could tell that he was preoccupied. There'd been a message that had disturbed him and he'd said he would walk with her back to the house, so that he could use their landline. She knew he'd have questions for Andy too, though. He'd have questions for them all. She still wasn't sure where it would all end.

The Lerwick bus drove along the main road, lighting their path so that for a moment there was no need for her torch. It stopped to let off a passenger, and briefly the land around Gilsetter could be seen clearly in its headlights. Glancing up, Jane caught sight of a figure in the field beyond the house, a silhouette. And a reflected gleam. Then the bus drove on towards town and everything was dark again.

'What's your father doing out at this time of night?' Because she'd seen that the figure had been standing next to Kevin's new drainage ditch. It was her husband's pride and joy, and who else would be standing in the rain inspecting his handiwork? He'd said he'd line the ditch with concrete, so there'd be no chance of floodwater seeping into the ground and drowning the polytunnels. 'He told me he was taking the evening off.'

Andy gave a non-committal grunt, but Perez had already started to run, with a speed and lack of concern for his own safety and comfort that seemed like panic. Or desperation. The evening flights must just have come into Sumburgh, because now there was a steady stream of cars and taxis heading north, their headlights passing over the scene and then disappearing, so that the activity in the field had the jerky, flashlit appearance of an early cartoon. Every couple of seconds she caught sight of Perez. First he was vaulting over a wall, then sprinting across the open field towards the figure by the ditch.

There was no sound. He was too far away already for them to hear his laboured breathing or pounding feet. This was a silent movie. The person standing next to the ditch seemed oblivious to his approach. If it hadn't been for Perez's desperation, the scene would have been ridiculous. Then Jane thought she *could* hear something. The thin cry of an injured animal. She peered through the darkness, but the traffic had disappeared; other cars coming from the airport had probably been held by the traffic lights controlling the one-way system further south. Everything was quiet and dark once more.

47

All that Perez could think, as he started to run towards the ditch, was that he couldn't let this happen again. He couldn't see in detail what was happening on the hill, but he'd recognized the person standing there and he'd picked up Willow's message explaining that she intended to visit. As he moved, time seemed to be working differently; it warped and stretched. In reality it must only have taken minutes to reach the field where the ditch had been dug, but in his head it took hours. In his head he wasn't even in the present. He was back in Fair Isle, running to the loch where Fran — his love, the woman he would marry — was dying of a stab wound. He'd seen the knife that killed her as a flash of blue lightning at the same time as he'd caught the glint of a murderer's spade reflected in a bus's headlights. He was a crazy Time Lord trying to turn back the clock, to save this woman when he'd failed to save the other. As he forced himself to maintain the pace and his heart thudded with the effort, the same phrase pounded to the rhythm of his footsteps. *Oh, please God, not again.*

The digger, dressed in dark clothes, was almost invisible, even when headlights swept across the field. The spade gave no reflection, its surface dulled now by the earth. Perez crouched behind a drystone dyke to catch his breath. Just for a moment, because time was flying on, unreliable. In another minute Willow could be dead. He hadn't been seen, but was close enough to hear the shovel as it sliced through the earth, and the soil landing in the trench below. There was a Maglite torch in his pocket and he held it in his hand, balanced and comforting. He switched it on at the moment that he leapt down from the wall, and the killer was caught in the full beam. Perez had anticipated an attempt to run away, for in the last two days there'd been an increased desperation in the killer's responses. No matter that there was nowhere to run to — no boats or planes this late in the evening — Perez still expected flight. Instead there was silence and stillness. Simon Agnew threw down his spade and held his hands out wide. A gesture of surrender or resignation, almost that of a charismatic believer giving themselves up to God. Perez was reminded for a second of the *third* woman in his life, his ex-wife Sarah, who'd been a member of a happy-clappy church. Again time seemed to collide. He knelt on the edge of the ditch.

There were two eyes, blinking as if the torchlight was painful, and a face so muddy that at first he couldn't tell it was still uncovered. He pushed the torch into the mud at the top of the trench, then slid in beside Willow and pushed the soil away from her neck and body with his hands — careful, like someone moulding a sculpture out of sand, scared that he would hurt her if he used the spade. He glanced back up at Agnew. He hadn't moved. When Willow's body was free, Perez put his arm around her neck and lifted her into a sitting position. He found he was murmuring reassurances, the same words he used to Cassie when she had nightmares. He forced himself to stop. Willow wasn't a child and she'd hate being treated like one. Now at last Agnew dropped his hands to his side, but still he stood motionless.

The next half-hour passed in a blur. Looking back, Perez saw the action as a series of unrelated scenes. Jane Hay taking charge of Simon, despite Perez's protestations, and pushing him towards Gilsetter. Furious, and showing a courage that would surely keep her family together. Andy at her side, proud and protective. Jane calling back across the ditch, 'We'll look after him there, Jimmy, until Sandy arrives.' So Perez realized he must have phoned Sandy. Or Jane had. Willow fierce and more angry than he'd ever known her, when he suggested calling an ambulance. 'All I need is a bath and a very large drink.' A pause. 'Now!' Willow stumbling away into the dark, so he'd followed her and wrapped her in his coat and started walking with her up the bank towards his house. Sometimes he was almost carrying her. All the way he was offering a prayer of thanks to a God he'd never quite believed in, even as a child.

He'd worried that he wouldn't have the strength to get her there, when Kevin Hay arrived in his Land Rover.

'You need to go back to Gilsetter,' Perez yelled above the sound of the engine. 'Jane's there with the killer.'

'Don't worry, Jimmy. The boys are there too,

and they've locked him into the tractor shed.' Kevin jumped down from the vehicle and between them the two men lifted Willow inside. 'You just look after your friend. We'll deal with all the rest.'

In the house Perez sat Willow in the bath and rinsed away the mud with the hand-held shower. Tender. Grateful that she wasn't pushing him away. He washed the soil and blood from her hair, using Cassie's shampoo, then filled the tub with clean water.

'Shall I leave you to soak?' He thought she might want to be on her own. He'd prop the door open, so he could hear that she was still conscious.

'Nah, but bring in the bottle and a couple of glasses.' A pause and a thin grin that took some effort. 'I always think it's wrong to drink on my own.'

Later they sat in front of the fire. She wore his dressing gown and a pair of his thick socks. Her hair was wrapped up in a towel. He could tell she still felt cold. He wanted to hold her tight to him, but since she'd emerged from the bathroom something about her body language, frozen and tight, made him think it wouldn't be the right thing to do.

'Shouldn't you be at the station interviewing Agnew?' she said. 'I could stay here, if you'd trust me with Cassie.'

He almost said that she needed someone to be with *her*, but stopped himself just in time. 'Nah. It's about time we gave Sandy some responsibility and they're sending some of your colleagues in on the first flight from Inverness tomorrow. Besides . . . ' he lifted his empty glass, ' . . . I'm not fit to drive.' He paused. 'But you're a witness. I could talk to you and make a few notes, if you feel up to it. Nothing that would stand up in court of course, but it might help us to jot down a few things while it's still clear in our memories.'

Willow took a moment to speak and he thought he'd played that all wrong. She wouldn't want to relive the nightmare so soon and would think he was an insensitive oaf.

'When did you know it was Simon Agnew?' she said at last.

'Not for certain until I saw him standing by the ditch, with the spade in his hand. But I remembered you'd said that Agnew had told Sandy he was speaking in Fair Isle over the weekend. I checked with the *Fair Isle Times* and he was certainly booked to be there. But he couldn't have made it. The weather was so bad on Friday and Saturday that neither the plane nor the *Good Shepherd* would have gone, and there are no planes on Sunday. That was why your phone message made me so anxious. And when Andy Hay told his mother he'd been staying at the manse, it just seemed bizarre that Agnew hadn't told Jane he'd seen him. She visited this morning. Agnew must have realized that Jane would be worried stupid. Surely he'd have encouraged Andy to go home and talk to his parents, or at least told Jane that the boy was safe. When she went to see Agnew, his door was locked. She thought it was because he was scared, but it was to give him time to hide Andy, if a visitor arrived.'

'Why did he take the boy in?'

'I think he supported Andy and encouraged him to confide in him, because it was a way of keeping in touch with the investigation. And Andy needed someone away from the family to talk to. He saw Simon Agnew as a man of the world. Someone who'd understand.' Perez threw another peat onto the fire. It was as hot as a sauna in the small room already. 'Agnew pointed us in the direction of the Hay boys, of course. He couldn't appear too interested in the case himself, and I think it amused him to throw us off-track. He had that sort of arrogance.' Perez looked at her. 'But you got to the killer way before I did.'

'Naturally.' Willow tried to sound flippant, but didn't quite manage it. 'Really I can't take any credit. Sandy did the legwork. He just has a way of persuading people to talk. He found a witness at the airport who remembered seeing Tom Rogerson take a call just before he cancelled his flight to Orkney. When we checked with the phone company, we found out that the caller was Agnew.' She held out her glass for more whisky. Perez had stopped drinking, but he tipped a little into her glass. She was suddenly serious. 'It's hard to believe all that only happened this afternoon.'

Perez saw that time had gone crazy for Willow too. It must have seemed like hours while she was lying in the drainage ditch, helpless.

She stirred in her chair. 'Would he have done

it? Would he really have buried me alive?'

He waited for a moment before answering. 'I think he was pleased when I turned up to stop him.'

There was silence. Perez realized that the rain had stopped. He went to the window and saw a thin moon, covered immediately by cloud. When he turned back to the room, Willow was checking her phone. He'd rescued it from her mud-encrusted jacket. She looked up with a smile and began to talk.

'When I found out that Simon Agnew had been in touch with Rogerson, I went back over the details of the earlier investigation. He was the only person who'd described Alison Teal as depressed and desperate. Every other witness had said the woman was cheerful in the days before her death. She'd bought a bottle of champagne. Whatever we might think of Alison's business venture with Rogerson, it was doing well. She was making plans for the future. But why would Simon Agnew lie about Alison's visit to the Befriending Shetland centre in Lerwick? The only reason I could think of was that he was the killer.'

'That's a big step to make.'

'Which is why I wanted to talk to him. I couldn't believe it. Even when I spoke to Jono and he described Agnew as one of Alison's rich junkie boyfriends. They ended up in rehab together; Agnew got clean. He already had a first degree in psychology and went on to do a PhD in addiction studies. That's why he could understand Jane Hay so well. It seemed an odd sort of friendship because they're from such different backgrounds, but he knew what she needed.'

'You should have told us what you were doing.'

She paused before answering. 'I tried to phone you, Jimmy. I thought you might be avoiding my calls.'

The silence lengthened while he struggled to find the right words to apologize or explain. In the end she rescued him and went on with her own explanation.

'We knew that Alison's parents were addicts and that she'd had her own problems. One of the articles we read about her disappearance talked about the possibility that she'd gone *back* into rehab. That suggested she'd tried rehab before. That was when she was knocking around with Simon Agnew. He was much older than her, but rather glamorous then. From a smart family, famous for his exploration and his partying. And maybe she was looking for a father figure. When we were thinking about the murders, we talked a bit about shame as a motivating factor. It occurred to me that Agnew might have a past that he was ashamed of. He was happy to admit to a rackety past as an adventurer. But not as a heroin addict, who'd turned his back on his children and stolen from his wife to feed his habit.' Willow looked at Perez. 'Those last details only came through to my phone a few minutes ago. He'd become a psychologist, helping other people with their problems, settled and happy in Shetland. A pillar of the community. He'd be the last person who'd want that past to come back to haunt him.'

'Did he know that Alison came to Shetland to escape her problems?'

'I think that was a coincidence. They'd lost touch by the time she ran away from her life as an actress in a popular drama. She must have been a very young woman when he first knew her. And very lovely, of course.' Willow hesitated. 'I found the same self-help book in his office as the one we found in Teal's room. It was probably standard issue at the clinic they both attended.'

Willow was thawing out a little now, engrossed in her story. 'So Simon becomes respectable and invents a past for himself. An ex-wife who couldn't cope with his energy and his passions. No kids. He *did* work as a psychologist in a teaching hospital and briefly as an academic, but he exaggerated his success in those fields. He loved Shetland. People admired him. But then Alison turned up, almost on his doorstep, wanting to take advantage of all the single men in the floatels and the workers' hotels.'

'Setting up in business with her old pal Tom Rogerson.' Perez supposed he should be taking notes, but this was never going to be a formal interview. There would be time for that later.

'Then Alison and Agnew met up somehow. By chance. Or perhaps Andy Hay mentioned one to the other. Agnew had always got on with the boy.'

'And Alison saw another business opportunity.' Perez saw now how neat this was, how it all hung together perfectly.

'You think she was blackmailing Agnew?' Willow had finished her whisky, but set her glass on the floor without asking for more.

'Don't you?'

'I think it might have been more subtle than that. More complicated. Alison wanted friendship, some kind of recognition. They'd been lovers, remember. Perhaps Simon Agnew was determined to put his old life behind him. In his mind, the bad stuff never happened. Or at least wasn't his fault.'

Perez supposed he could understand that. 'Then Alison turned up at the Befriending Shetland office. An attempt to renew the relationship. Or demand money from him.' He still believed blackmail was a more plausible motive.

'And later Simon went to Tain and killed her. Perhaps he'd convinced her that they had a future together. She dressed up for him and cooked him a meal. He was worried that someone had seen Alison coming into his office in Lerwick, so he had to make up an excuse for her being there. Alison was still calling herself Alissandra Sechrest, so Agnew used that name when he described the distraught woman coming in out of the rain.'

'What about Tom Rogerson?'

'Simon believed that Alison had talked to Tom about him,' Willow said. 'Tom had been in contact with Alison since they'd first met at the Ravenswick Hotel. The note we found in her house was cementing the business partnership and *he* suggested that she used Sandy Sechrest's identity to get to the island. Alison Teal's discovery here, fifteen years ago, was a big deal and Tom worried that the name might be recognized.'

'So Tom had to die?' Perez thought Agnew had always been reckless and a risk-taker. He'd gambled that no connection would be found between him and the two victims.

'Simon had served with Tom on island committees and knew Rogerson would delight in making mischief. Simon phoned him and arranged to meet him. He probably said that he knew something about Alison's death. That would have intrigued Tom. Worried him. He wouldn't have wanted his relationship with Alison being general knowledge in the islands. Agnew picked him up at the airport and drove him to the manse, took him for a walk so that they could talk things through. He's always been one for exercise. He used to swim from the beach where Rogerson's body was found.'

'But it wasn't so healthy for Tom.' It was Perez's attempt at flippancy, but he was thinking that Fran had swum from that beach too. He was wondering if she'd ever been there with Agnew.

'That's one way of putting it. Agnew left the body there, perhaps hoping that a high tide or a strong gale would take it away. But the weather calmed and Kevin Hay found it.'

'Agnew would have got away with double murder, if you weren't such a good detective.'

'Like I said, that was all down to Sandy working his magic with the witness at the airport.' Willow unwound the towel around her head and shook her hair loose. 'I saw Agnew, you know, this evening. He was jogging along the road. I thought he'd be in his car and that I'd have some warning of his return. And of course he left his door unlocked — *he* wasn't scared of a killer in the dark. If I hadn't been so stupid, he would never have caught me.'

'Would you like coffee?' Perez wanted Willow to change the subject, not to think beyond the point when Agnew had found her in the office at the manse.

'I want sleep,' she said.

'Use my bed. I'll stay here on the sofa.'

'Nah, come in with me.' A grin that made him see she was stronger than he'd ever be. 'I won't make unreasonable demands, Jimmy. I'm not up to that tonight. And no strings. But I could use the company.'

He lay beside her and slept fitfully. She hardly stirred. The next morning he made sure he was up and dressed before Cassie was awake, and he had an excuse prepared for Willow being in his bed.

48

Willow decided she'd go south on the ferry. The weather was calm and still again, and she needed a slow trip. Time to get her head round all that had happened, to prepare for life away from Shetland and Jimmy Perez. The day had been spent waiting. In the Gilbert Bain hospital, for the required check-up before her bosses would allow her to travel. In the police station, while Sandy and her colleagues from Inverness finished interviewing the man who'd almost killed her.

'He's confessed to everything.' Sandy had been flushed with triumph. 'He says Alison's death wasn't planned, that he walked to Tain, just to persuade her to leave the islands. Found her all dressed up and ready to entertain him. *It's been too long, Simon. There's champagne on ice and I've cooked your favourite food.*'

'He ate with her before he killed her?'

'Apparently. 'She was a bloody good cook. I wasn't going to let a meal like that go to waste.' That's what he said.'

'Sounds premeditated to me.' Willow had thought Agnew's need to show off would mean that no jury would believe any manslaughter plea.

'He even went to bed with her,' Sandy said. 'Afterwards, when she was lying there, he got the belt round Alison's neck and twisted it. He's still

411

a strong man for his age.'

Agnew was being flown south. Another reason for Willow's decision to take the ferry.

Jimmy Perez insisted on carrying her bag onto the ship and seeing her settled in her cabin. He stood awkwardly and seemed to take up the whole space between the two narrow beds.

'We never had that talk,' he said.

'Ah well, other things got in the way.' The last thing she wanted was for him to go all soulful on her. She wanted to leave with some dignity.

'We *will* stay in touch?'

'Of course, Jimmy.' Now she just wanted him to go, so that she could lie on the cold, clean sheets on the bunk. She was suddenly very tired again.

'Look out for Fair Isle as you go south,' he said. His face lit up and she remembered why he'd haunted her. 'You should see the lights from this side of the boat.'

'You promised to take me there one day.'

'And so I shall.'

She leaned forward and kissed him lightly on the lips. 'Off you go, Jimmy Perez, or you'll be carried away with me. And what would Shetland do without you?'

'But you'll come back to see me?'

She smiled. 'Just try to stop me.'

We do hope that you have enjoyed reading this large print book.

Did you know that all of our titles are available for purchase?

We publish a wide range of high quality large print books including:
Romances, Mysteries, Classics
General Fiction
Non Fiction and Westerns

Special interest titles available in large print are:
The Little Oxford Dictionary
Music Book
Song Book
Hymn Book
Service Book

Also available from us courtesy of Oxford University Press:
Young Readers' Dictionary
(large print edition)
Young Readers' Thesaurus
(large print edition)

For further information or a free brochure, please contact us at:
Ulverscroft Large Print Books Ltd.,
The Green, Bradgate Road, Anstey,
Leicester, LE7 7FU, England.
Tel: (00 44) 0116 236 4325
Fax: (00 44) 0116 234 0205

THIN AIR

Ann Cleeves

A group of old university friends leaves the bright lights of London and travels to Unst, Shetland's most northerly island, to celebrate the marriage of a friend. But late on the night of the wedding party, one of them, Eleanor, disappears — apparently into thin air. Soon her body is discovered, lying in a small loch close to the cliff edge, and Detectives Jimmy Perez and Willow Reeves are dispatched to investigate. Before she went missing, Eleanor claimed to have seen the ghost of a local child who drowned in the 1920s. Jimmy and Willow are convinced that there's more to Eleanor's death than they first thought. Is there a secret that lies behind the myth — one so shocking that someone would kill many years later to protect it?

WILD FIRE

Ann Cleeves

Drawn in by the reputation of the islands, a new English family moves to the area, eager to give their autistic son a better life. But when a young nanny's body is found hanging in the barn of their home, rumours of her affair with the husband begin to spread like wild fire. With suspicion raining down on the family, DI Jimmy Perez is called in to investigate, knowing that it will mean the return to the islands of his on-off lover and boss Willow Reeves, who will run the case. Perez is already facing the most disturbing investigation of his career, when Willow drops a bombshell that will change his life forever. Is he ready for what is to come?

THE MOTH CATCHER

Ann Cleeves

Life seems perfect in Valley Farm, a quiet community in Northumberland. Then a shocking discovery shatters the silence. The owners of a big country house have employed a house-sitter, a young ecologist named Patrick, to look after the place while they're away. But Patrick is found dead by the side of the lane into the valley — a beautiful, lonely place to die. DI Vera Stanhope arrives on the scene with her colleagues, and when they search the attic of the house, where Patrick has a flat, she finds a second body. All the two victims have in common is a fascination with moths. As Vera is drawn into the claustrophobic world of this increasingly strange community, she realises that there may be deadly secrets trapped here . . .